Praise for the
Gracelin O'Malley trilogy

Leaving Ireland

"Gripping. . . . The relentless drama of Grace's fight to survive, as well as the rich contextual details, make Moore's sophomore effort as absorbing and accomplished as her first."   —*Publishers Weekly*

"Moore blends romance and adventure with memorable accounts of the brutal occupation of Ireland, the harsh reality of New York tenement life, and the comfort of family. Strong and likable characters and a well-paced story will make readers look forward to Gracelin's next appearance."   —*Booklist*

"A deep, action-packed historical novel that leaves the audience with a full five-senses feeling for the 1840s."   —*Midwest Book Review*

"Engaging characters . . . a nicely paced tale . . . This . . . researched saga p   ells . . . satisf   , WA)

"Exce   ish immigra   rogue and s   -*Kliatt*

ed . . .

Writ   rican
Libr   eart,
from   The
Con   the
indiv   topics to

Visit

Gracelin O'Malley

"If you love the lilt of Irish laughter and understand the river of tears that runs beneath it, you'll take Gracelin O'Malley to your heart and keep her there."
　　　　　　　　　—*New York Times* bestselling author Cathy Cash Spellman

"Will lift your heart with its stirring tale of love—for the land, and for the unforgettable Grace, torn between two worlds. . . . Immerse yourself in a grand story."
　　　　　　　　　—*New York Times* bestselling author Eileen Goudge

"Vivid historical detail . . . sensitively drawn."　　　　—*Kirkus Reviews*

"[A] finely wrought tale . . . lyrical, pitch-perfect prose. . . . Historical fiction at its finest."　　　　　　　　　　　　　　—*Publishers Weekly*

"Truly great fiction . . . a grand historical novel . . . full of triumph, full of tragedy, full of hope and strength of spirit."
　　　　　　　　　　　　　　　　—*The Historical Novels Review*

"Beautiful descriptions of the countryside, the lilting Irish brogue, and the colorfully drawn characters bring to life rural Ireland of the 1840s . . . suspenseful . . . passionate."　　　　　　　　—*Kliatt*

ANN MOORE

'Til Morning Light

CONVERSATION GUIDE
NAL
ACCENT
INCLUDED

FICTION FOR THE WAY WE LIVE

NAL Accent
Published by New American Library, a division of
Penguin Group (USA) Inc., 375 Hudson Street,
New York, New York 10014, USA
Penguin Group (Canada), 10 Alcorn Avenue, Toronto,
Ontario M4V 3B2, Canada (a division of Pearson Penguin Canada Inc.)
Penguin Books Ltd., 80 Strand, London WC2R 0RL, England
Penguin Ireland, 25 St. Stephen's Green, Dublin 2,
Ireland (a division of Penguin Books Ltd.)
Penguin Group (Australia), 250 Camberwell Road, Camberwell, Victoria 3124,
Australia (a division of Pearson Australia Group Pty. Ltd.)
Penguin Books India Pvt. Ltd., 11 Community Centre, Panchsheel Park,
New Delhi - 110 017, India
Penguin Group (NZ), cnr Airborne and Rosedale Roads, Albany,
Auckland 1310, New Zealand (a division of Pearson New Zealand Ltd.)
Penguin Books (South Africa) (Pty.) Ltd., 24 Sturdee Avenue,
Rosebank, Johannesburg 2196, South Africa

Penguin Books Ltd, Registered Offices:
80 Strand, London WC2R 0RL, England

First published by NAL Accent, an imprint of New American Library,
a division of Penguin Group (USA) Inc.

First Printing, February 2005
10 9 8 7 6 5 4 3 2 1

FICTION FOR THE WAY WE LIVE

REGISTERED TRADEMARK—MARCA REGISTRADA

LIBRARY OF CONGRESS CATALOGING-IN-PUBLICATION DATA

Moore, Ann, 1959–
'Til morning light/Ann Moore.
p. cm.
ISBN 0-451-21404-8 (trade pbk.)
1. Widows—Fiction. 2. Ship captains—Fiction. 3. Single mothers—Fiction. 4. Women
immigrants—Fiction. 5. Irish-American women—Fiction. 6. San Francisco (Calif.)—Fiction. I. Title.

PS3563.O5695T55 2005
813'.6—dc22   2004021113

Set in Adobe Garamond
Designed by Ginger Legato

Printed in the United States of America

PUBLISHER'S NOTE
This is a work of fiction. Names, characters, places, and incidents either are the product of the author's imagination or are used fictitiously, and any resemblance to actual persons, living or dead, business establishments, events, or locales is entirely coincidental.

For Rick, Nigel, and Grace—
my family

ACKNOWLEDGMENTS

I am thankful for the inspiration of so many people and their work in this world and, to that end, wish to give special mention to the public library system, for providing readers and writers alike access to worlds they might not have otherwise discovered; to the historians who so painstakingly—and often with little glory—preserve those worlds for us; to Bono and U2, for their stewardship, for using the spotlight of fame to illuminate issues of human dignity; to my children, Nigel and Gracelin, who realize the importance of understanding the past in order to make a difference in the future, and who are already such fine citizens; to my parents, David and Elizabeth Schweinler, for their presence in our lives; to old friends, for their encouragement, and to those in all the lively book groups I have visited; to Teri Smith, who loves life and works tirelessly to better the lives of others; and finally, there is no better man than a family man, so I thank my husband for the love and support he provided while I followed my heart in writing these books.

I tell you the truth, if you have faith as small as a mustard seed,
you can say to this mountain, "Move from here to there"
and it will move.
Nothing will be impossible for you.

—MATTHEW 17:20

One

Hundreds of square-rigged vessels listed aimlessly in San Francisco Bay, eerie for the mist that swirled up and over their neglected decks, through the gaping holes punched port and starboard by lumber scavengers who took what they wanted, then deserted the ships a second time, leaving them half-submerged in murky waters. These ruined schooners, clippers, and whalers were not the only ships in the littered harbor—plenty more were battened down and well tended, safe at anchor—but it was the appearance of hasty, reckless abandonment that gave Gracelin O'Malley pause as her eyes scoured the bay for the proud masts of the *Eliza J.*

It was the earliest of morning, barely dawn, and Grace told herself that the ship was in, the ship was there, only shrouded by fog, and that was why she could not see it from her place on the wharf. Even if she'd found it, she reminded herself, she had no boat with which to row out. And surely Peter and Liam would not be sleeping aboard anyway; they would be at home, in the house they shared with Peter's partner, Lars Darmstadt, and Darmstadt's wife, Detra, somewhere in the city on the hill that rose up behind her. She turned her back on the harbor now and considered the city, its streets unfamiliar and difficult to follow in the hazy light. It had been dark when she arrived last night; it was dark still, but she had written instructions, which she pulled out of her pocket and consulted.

Tightening her grip on her young son's hand, she towed the sleepy four-year-old away from the Jackson Street Wharf, up block after block, until she came to the opera house on Montgomery; from there she turned south on Montgomery until she found California Street, and then she began to search out the houses on a plaza surrounded by banks, warehouses, shipping offices, and import merchants. Slowly, she walked up the street, each structure emerging from the fog as if it were the only one in the world. Some had numbers, some had signs, others had nothing, but finally she arrived at the one she wanted—of course, it faced the waterfront—and then she stopped abruptly, her eyes traveling the walkway, the entry, the first floor, the second, the third; it was bigger than she had imagined. Even though Grace realized that it housed Peter and Liam, Lars and Detra, and their servants, the address had given no clue as to the grandeur of the place itself. Swallowing hard, she looked down at Jack, straightened his cap and then her own bonnet, then determinedly pushed open the heavy iron gate.

"Does the captain live *here,* Mam?" It was Jack's turn to lift his eyes from the long dark windows on the first floor to the smaller windows on the second, and then to the tiny casements on the third.

"I think so." She led the way up the gravel path to the entrance, the crunch of their boot steps loud in her ears. "Watch yourself, now, son." She supported him under the arms so that he could take the tall steps required to reach the front door.

"Big." He yawned when they'd gotten to the top.

"Aye." She smiled down at him and pointed to the bell. "Go on, now; have a pull."

They listened as it rang inside the house; when the echo faded, it was again deathly still, and they looked at one another, Jack shrugging his little shoulders. He had reached out to pull again when Grace put a hand on his arm; somewhere inside the house a door opened and closed, and then another, the slow tip-tap of footsteps growing louder. After what seemed an eternity, the front door was opened by a man holding a lamp that merely served to shed light on the fact that he'd been roused from his bed and forced to dress hastily. His frown deepened as he looked Grace up and down and saw the state of her own clothing—the muddy, stained cloak and battered hat, the dirty leather moccasins, her peeling sunburned face, the equally weather-beaten and bedraggled boy by her side—and then his eyes narrowed with intense disapproval as he realized that she was wearing what appeared to be men's trousers.

"Servants and tradesmen around back," he directed scornfully and started to close the door.

"I'm no servant," Grace told him quickly before it was shut in her face. Mustering her confidence, she announced, "Missus Donnelly to see Captain Reinders, please."

The butler hesitated, clearly suspicious, lifting the lamp to better see her face as he weighed her credibility. Finally, much to Grace's relief, he saw fit to answer.

"Captain Reinders is at sea, madam."

Grace blinked. *At sea. Of course he was at sea. Of course.* "Will he . . . ?" Her mind was racing. "When do you expect his return?"

"Not for some time. Good day." Again the butler began to close the door.

"Wait!" Grace stuck out her foot, planting it firmly on the threshold. "I must get a letter to him."

Certainly, it wasn't the first time an unknown woman had come knocking for the captain, the butler reminded himself, but usually they were not so bold; he glanced pointedly at the foot he wished removed from the territory he was charged to protect.

"Impossible, madam."

Instead of withdrawing, Gracelin took another step forward, pushing her shoulders back and standing as tall as she could. The butler leaned back, nostrils flared as if suddenly assailed by a most unpleasant odor; he was also slightly fearful—a woman in trousers was an unpredictable creature, most certainly, but he would not allow her to bully her way in here. He opened his mouth to shoo her away, but she spoke before he could.

"Look, you—Captain Reinders is my close friend. And"—sensing the butler's uneasiness, she leaned even closer—"his ward, Liam, is my son." *Adopted son,* she mentally corrected, though no need to explain that to this dullard.

"Master Kelley?" The butler's eyebrows rose ever so slightly as he considered this new information, but he did not open the door any wider.

"Aye." Grace's gaze did not waver. "Now call Mister Darmstadt here to me, or his wife."

"They, too, madam, are away."

Grace studied the butler's impassive face but could not discern whether this was the truth or not.

"Where *is* Captain Reinders?" she asked, determined to maintain her outer composure though her heart and head were pounding.

"Panama City, madam."

Panama City? Where in Heaven's name was Panama City?

"I do not expect him for some weeks. Perhaps longer."

Grace bit her lip, her stomach now in a knot. "I'll leave a message for him, then," she decided. "Bring me paper and pen, please."

Since the woman had not resumed her proper place on the other side of the door, the butler reluctantly left it ajar and fetched the required items from the drawer of the writing desk in the foyer. The realization that this "Missus Donnelly" could not write where she stood and that she would only make more fuss if he tried to make her do so perturbed him, so, grudgingly, he motioned her in.

With Jack at her side, stealing sidelong glances at the formidable butler, Grace bent over the desk, dipped her pen, and began to write.

> *Dear Peter,*
> *'Tis unexpected, but I've come now with the children. Mary*
> *Kate is ill, but not with the cholera, thank God, and is at hos-*
> *pital with the Sisters of Mercy. We'll stay in the city 'til your re-*
> *turn—I'll let your man know where we're lodging. Please come*
> *to us as soon as you can.*

She quickly reread her note before signing her name, hoping it did not sound as desperate as she felt. She'd not planned on arriving like this, not dirty and tired and sick; instead, she'd envisioned herself strong and self-sufficient on a small farm up the coast in Oregon, the determined widow woman of a sea captain who loved her and wanted to marry her one day. *But did he still?* she asked herself. A wave of dizziness brought on by fatigue and anxiety washed over her then, and she leaned against the desk, closing her eyes and pressing the palm of her hand to her forehead.

"Madam?"

There was a note of concern in the butler's voice, but Grace supposed it was more for the mess he might have to clean up should she vomit in his foyer. She pulled herself together, folded the note, slipped it into an envelope, and handed it to him.

"See that Captain Reinders gets this the moment he returns," she ordered, looking him square in the eye though it hurt her head to do so.

"Of course." The butler held open the door until she and Jack were back on the other side, then closed it firmly behind them.

Jack was frowning. "Don't like him."

"Nor I, but I suppose we gave him a start, looking as we do. Not exactly proper callers, are we? Come on, then." She took his hand. "Let's get ourselves back to Mary Kate, and I'll give you a roll to eat on the way. What do you say, my Jack?"

"How big?" He looked up, his silver spectacles askew, and a wave of tenderness for him clutched her heart as it always did.

"Biggest I can find," she promised, straightening the specs.

He laid his forehead against her for a moment, and Grace was surprised; before leaving Kansas, Jack had not been a child to show affection, and she'd often had to resist the impulse to sweep him into her arms and cover him with kisses. Though she'd worked mindfully to make him her own again, he still sometimes kept her at arm's length. Julia Martin had been the first woman he'd ever called "Mam," and though he'd been transferred ever so carefully to his true mother over a period of months, Grace knew that Julia's eventual departure had confused and saddened him; she only hoped that as he got older and was better able to understand the extraordinary circumstances of his birth, his heart would heal. She was encouraged by the fact that he adored his sister but knew that even Mary Kathleen did not receive many embraces from the stalwart little fellow. Grace's step quickened at the thought of her daughter, and her hand tightened around Jack's. Even though the doctor had seen Mary Kate upon their arrival last night, and Sister Joseph was with her this morning, Grace was anxious to return to her daughter's side.

The mist still clung stubbornly in glistening droplets to overhangs and rail posts, but it was just beginning to evaporate now that the sun was coming up; Grace could feel the first tentative rays of warmth pushing through her cloak. Despite her fatigue, her feet did not fail to move, and this brought a wry smile to her lips, for these feet had just carried her across two thousand miles in the past four months. Even in her dreams, her feet traveled, one foot in front of the other, walking endlessly across sage-covered prairies and hot salt deserts that tormented even the hardiest pioneers, through deep, slippery mud and the high grass of lush valleys, over mountain passes so narrow and high she had wondered whether it was even possible to cross. She and the children had walked and walked and walked, some days getting only two miles farther on, other days making twenty good miles. She knew now in her heart that should she die on the spot, her feet would continue to twitch and turn, as if she were walking all the way to Heaven.

As she and Jack left Peter's house to return to the hospital, they could appreciate the view he had of the waterfront and its activity, as well as the city to the south up to its highest point, Alta Loma, which Sister Joseph had told her was called Telegraph Hill, as from the semaphore station on top, house flags were flown, identifying the various ships coming into port. The sister had told her that there was never so much commotion as when the Pacific Mail steamers arrived every two weeks with their precious cargo, and that had brought Grace to mind of the letters she must write now that she was here.

From Peter's descriptions, Grace knew that San Francisco never really went to bed at night, that its evenings were loud and raucous, its mornings the quietest time of the day. As early as it was even now, however, the place was coming more fully awake and Grace could see that there was much to learn about it. When Mary Kate was well again, she decided, they would explore the city at length, for this would be their home now; she had promised the children on the steamship from Oregon that they would never have to leave another home, and she intended to keep that promise, no matter what it took.

She and Jack retraced their route back down Montgomery, stopping on Clay Street to stare at the *Niantic,* one of the ships abandoned at the start of the gold rush.

"Did it sail right up on land?" Jack asked, baffled.

"The captain wrote about this," she told him. "This land we're standing on now used to be the waterfront, but as the hills are behind, they started filling in between those long wharves to make more space for building." She considered what she was saying. " 'Tis amazing to think about, really. Filling in the bay. Anyway, you saw all the deserted ships in the harbor this morning—the *Niantic* was abandoned when her crew and captain left off to find gold."

"Is there still gold?" Jack asked, hopefully. "Will we get some?"

"Not lying about the rivers like it used to be. But still out there, and plenty of people still looking to get rich quick by it. We're not going to be miners, though, if that's what you're asking me."

"Oh." His face fell.

"Oh," she repeated in his exact tone of voice, then winked. "We'd best hurry now, and find your breakfast."

Grace followed carts loaded with chicken crates and produce into a large plaza, around which sat hotels, restaurants, theaters, casinos, saloons, and a host of other shops. Jack stopped abruptly and stared as a Chinaman hurried past in a long blue tunic over cotton pants; on his head he wore a wide straw hat that tied neatly under the chin, a long black queue falling down his back. Across his shoulders he carried a long pole with a basket attached to each end. On his feet were black slippers on wooden patens; he kept his eyes lowered. Grace had seen China people in New York City, but never this close; Jack, she knew, had never seen anyone like this at all.

"A Chinaman," she explained quietly. "From the other side of the world. They call them Celestials out here. Do you see his long braid, then?"

Jack nodded.

"If he cuts it off, he can never return to China."

"But hair grows back," Jack pointed out.

"Aye. Takes years, though, maybe never gets long again." She paused and sniffed the air. "Is that fresh bread I'm smelling?"

Jack sniffed, too, then nodded enthusiastically.

"I think it's coming from over there."

Grace led him around the side of the plaza to a street lined with market stalls. She stopped at a stall piled high with hot, fresh breads and bought a roll from the man for Jack, who tore into it ravenously, causing her to turn back immediately and buy three more, though the price was astonishingly high. Bread in hand, they continued moving along from stall to stall, making additional purchases of fresh yellow cheese and a piece of hard salami on a string. From the back of a farm wagon, she bought a handful of small tomatoes, a dozen reddish apples, and a woven basket in which to carry her marketing. Her money pouch, though considerably lighter, was still full enough to keep them for a short while, depending on what she owed at the hospital. Soon, however, with prices like these, she would need to find work as well as lodging. Having experienced firsthand the unpredictability of a sea voyage, she knew it could be months instead of weeks before Peter actually returned.

"Will we get anything else, Mam?" Jack spewed bread crumbs as he spoke.

"Not today, love. Time to go."

Jack did not put up a fuss, had not put up a fuss for some time now, and by this, Grace knew how worried he was about his sister. When Mary Kate had started to fall ill on the trail, he'd watched her carefully, helping her with chores and trying to give up bits of his food to her. By the time they'd reached the settlement in Willamette, Mary Kate had barely been able to lift her head for the pain of it, and she'd no longer eaten much or drank. There'd been no reliable doctors in the settlement and, with the steamer about to depart for San Francisco, Grace had not hesitated in her decision to ensure passage for them all, counting upon the readily available medical care Peter had described in his letters— from true doctors as opposed to the hundreds who simply hung out a shingle offering to purge, blister, cup, or cauterize. Jack had been obedient and helpful on the voyage south, had helped her get Mary Kate and their single trunk to the hospital, had slept uncomplaining on the floor by her side last night as she waited first to see whether Mary Kate would survive, and then for dawn and the chance to see Peter.

"You've been a good boy, Jack," Grace praised him as they left the plaza. "A big help to your mam. Now, which way did we come in?"

"Over there." He pulled at her hand. "I'll show you."

Jack led Grace across the enormous plaza, which dazzled them with its huge stone buildings and columns, lavish storefronts, parade of Peruvians, Chileans, and Mexicans in colorful dress, local Indians in beads and blankets, black men in formal dress and mining clothes both, Chinamen in tunics or silks, their long queues topped by wide-brimmed straw hats or small embroidered caps, Bohemians and Gypsies with their flamboyant shirts and vests, broad-chested Kanakas from Hawaii; all of their accents combined with those of the French, Germans, Italians, Turks, Russians—the flood of emigrants still hoping to find nuggets of gold awaiting them in the California desert rivers, though ready to turn their hand to any job that appeared lucrative. The smart ones, it occurred to Grace, had taken up the building trade. She followed Jack through the maze of humanity, picking her way around the droppings of horses, oxen, mules, dogs, as well as those left by the more exotic pets of the city—the bears, foxes, goats, and deer on leads, the parrots and falcons on shoulders, the snakes around necks. Eccentric dress, eccentric pets, flashy silver and gold accessories, and weapons of every sort—it seemed to Grace that San Francisco was one enormous circus.

Once through the plaza, they navigated a series of smaller streets and finally arrived at the hospital doorstep. Relieved, Grace patted Jack on the head and pushed open the doors, then hurried through the small lobby, into the ward, and straight to the cot upon which Mary Kate lay, eyes closed, a cold compress across her forehead. Sister Joseph, the stout Irish nun from County Cork, was bending over the girl, humming a familiar tune; she straightened up when she saw Grace and offered her a wide smile of reassurance.

"Sleeping well, she is," the nun whispered. "No worries here. And were you able to see your friend?"

Grace shook her head. "He's at sea." Much to her embarrassment, tears welled up.

"There now, child; sit down. Sit down." Sister Joseph helped her onto a stool and took the marketing basket from her. "And when will he be coming home, then, the captain?"

"I don't know." Grace pressed a handkerchief to her eyes, then saw that Jack's had gone wide with concern. "Never mind, son." She reached out and pulled him close. "I'm only tired, is all."

"Aye, worn out and why shouldn't you be?" Sister Joseph patted Grace's shoulder, then whispered in her ear. "Do you have any money a'tall?"

Grace nodded and the nun looked relieved.

"Opened her eyes a bit ago, she did," Sister Joseph reported loudly enough for Jack to hear. "Doctor Wakefield come by again. 'Twas a tick, he thinks, seeing as how you and the boy aren't afflicted."

Grace's eyes burned again and she closed them. *God forgive me for*

dragging this child across Ireland, across an ocean, across all of America.
Oh, Father, what am I doing here?

Sister Joseph put a hand beneath Grace's chin and tipped it up so that the young woman opened her eyes and looked into those of the older one.

"Faith, daughter," she reminded gently. "Worry saves not a single hour, you know."

"I can't lose her," Grace whispered.

"And you won't," Sister Joseph resolved. "Not this time." She stood and smoothed her long white apron. "Rest a bit now. Let the boy come with me, why not? I need someone big and strong to water the horses out back—think you can do that, young Jack?"

"Oh, aye!" Jack looked up at his mother expectantly. "May I, Mam? Feed the horses?"

"Go on with you, then, but mind what she says." Grace smiled at him, then added gratefully, "Thank you, Sister."

"You need a bit of peace to sort it all out, I'm thinking. See you in a bit." The nun took Jack's hand in hers and led him down the aisle to the back door that opened onto an alley stable.

Grace moved her stool closer to Mary Kate and smoothed the thick, flyaway hair that had come out of its braid. This child had lived two, maybe three lifetimes in her nine years on earth; Grace could barely remember a life before her. Together they had survived the darkest days of famine and illness, had left the baby behind for safekeeping and escaped to Liverpool, then boarded a ship for the long and difficult voyage to America, where Mary Kate had witnessed even more suffering. In Manhattan, in their rooms above Dugan Ogue's saloon, the little girl had settled in and begun to bloom, a steadfast companion to her mother and to Liam, the boy they'd taken in after his own people died aboard the *Eliza J*. But they'd been forced to pull up roots again after fire burned them out, and from there they'd moved to Boston to live with Lily Free and her family. Boston had been hard living, and Mary Kate had known prejudice both in school and on the street; the only good thing had been the reunion with Jack, though no longer an infant at nearly two years old. Mary Kate had rejoiced in her brother, had taken the boy to her heart without hesitation, and, like a second little mother, had cared for him in every way.

Grace often thought that despite the hard going in Boston, had she known how grueling the overland journey would be, she would have stayed on until she'd earned enough for her family to sail to San Francisco instead. And yet, she had to admit, if she'd done that, she would have arrived in the middle of the cholera epidemic and perhaps lost both her children. Peter's letter had come to her in Lawrence, Kansas, where she'd stopped with the Frees—they to buy a farm and she to rest up before joining another wagon train west. He was adamant that she stay there until the epidemic had passed—they were dying like flies in San Francisco, and he and Liam were heading up to the Pacific Northwest. Grace had ended up spending two years in Kansas, living in a small cabin on the edge of a busy town, working as cook in the only hotel and making a passable living, though it was unbearably hot in the summer and bitterly cold throughout the long, long winter.

There had been good things in Kansas: Grace had become an excellent cook and was able to put away money; after a rough start, Mary Kate's schoolhouse had come under the direction of a worthy and enthusiastic teacher, and Mary Kate had inhaled knowledge with every breath she'd taken. Jack, too, had thrived in this frontier environment, though not in the way Grace might have chosen—no longer quiet and watchful, he had become outgoing to the point of unruliness, the beloved pet of every cowhand and gunfighter passing through town, who took delight in showing the charismatic little boy how to ride a pony and shoot a pistol. She cringed, remembering the day he'd fired it off in the hotel, attempting to rid the dining room of flies.

But Kansas itself had become more and more unruly as the battle heated up between those who wanted it declared a Free State and those who wanted to claim it for slavers. Violence had escalated as the two groups fought for control of burgeoning cities and towns; hangings and midnight attacks became common occurrences, and no one had felt safe anymore, especially the Negroes. When Lily, newly reunited with her husband—a runaway slave and wary of every white face that appeared on his land—had decided to move the family to Oregon, where land was still being given away by the hundred acres to homesteaders, Grace had realized that she, too, longed for a more peaceful existence and wanted her children out of the way of gunfire. Not only were the whites fighting one another, but the Indians—heretofore peaceful—

were increasingly aggressive and, though Grace understood their anger at being pushed off their land, she had become afraid of them, as well. Toward the end of her time in Kansas, the Indians had often rode hunting parties close to town; Jack had loved them, had loved the whoops and hollers, the paint, the fierce expressions of the young braves, but Grace had read the stories of attack, of scalping and torture, of vicious slaughter. Sensational though they may well have been, she'd no longer slept through the night.

Along with hundreds of frontiersmen, including escaped slaves for whom Kansas was not nearly north nor west enough, Grace read eagerly of Oregon Territory's rich, black soil and temperate climate, of fertile valleys, abundant wildlife, sweet mountain streams, and plentiful lumber for building. She'd thought that at the Willamette settlement, she'd be closer to Peter and to Liam; they would only have to sail up the coast, then upriver in order to see her. And so she'd sold up what little she'd accumulated, bought a wagon and oxen and supplies for months on the trail, and left with the Frees for Oregon.

Jack had complained bitterly about leaving Kansas, though he'd quickly become enamored of life on the trail; it must have seemed one long picnic to him, Grace often thought, with campfires, sleeping under the stars, being out in all weather day after day. She'd tried to keep him with her as much as possible, sometimes banishing him to the back of the wagon, where he huffed and pouted; more than one child had been crushed beneath a heavy wagon wheel or trampled by oxen; more than one had been burned by fire, gone missing off the trail, fallen into the river and drowned. Grace had needed to focus on driving the team each day, and keeping track of Jack was difficult; the chore had fallen to Mary Kate, who assumed it—as she did all things—with dutiful graciousness, at times tethering Jack to a long rope, the other end of which she belted around her waist. Jack had survived that overland trek because of Mary Kate's constant attention to him. Grace picked up her daughter's limp hand and pressed it to her cheek. *If only you'll be well, I'll make it up to you,* Grace prayed. *If only you'll be well, I'll never move you again.*

"That's a mighty anxious face you're wearing, Missus Donnelly."

Grace looked up at Doctor Wakefield. "I can't help it." She bit her lip, determined that no more tears would come today. "What would we do without this one?"

"You'd carry on, ma'am, as so many have before you." Wakefield's cadence had the slow, steady swing of a South Carolinian. "But you needn't bother yourself with that this time around. For as I can tell, your daughter is on her way to recovery, though it may be some time before she's back to her little girl ways."

Grace nodded, unable to speak.

"You know, Missus Donnelly, we don't usually permit family to sleep on the floor beside our patients." The doctor eyed her trunk. "But Sister Joseph has said you are somewhat stranded at the moment, so I'll make an exception until proper arrangements can be made. You'll have to keep the little boy quiet, however."

"Oh, aye, Doctor." Grace stood up, mindful of her trousers, wishing she looked a bit more presentable. "We'll stay well out of your way, and thank you. Thank you very much."

Wakefield was startled by the warmth of her gratitude, by the keen light that shone in her eyes despite her very obvious fatigue.

"Well, it's my pleasure, Missus Donnelly, I'm sure. And now, if you'll excuse me, I must see to my other patients."

He left her, and Grace sank again onto the stool. She'd been afraid that his news would not be good, afraid that he wouldn't let her stay with Mary Kate, or that she'd be allowed, but not Jack, and then what would they've done? Her thoughts were interrupted by the shrill whinny and thud of an excited horse kicking hard against its stall. *Oh, Jack, please behave.* She was not very good at disciplining the boy, though she knew it was necessary if he were ever to become self-disciplined; her admonishments were too little, too late, and she feared she would fail him. Her inability to be firm with him lay, she knew, in the fact that he was, in fact, a miracle—the infant she'd been forced to abandon, the baby she'd thought dead, only to hear that he was alive and safe in Ireland, and that her friend Julia Martin would bring him to America, to Grace, his true mother.

During the months that Julia had stayed with them in Boston, Grace had never questioned her about keeping Jack. So much had been lost during the great hunger and the struggle for a free Ireland; women, perhaps, had suffered the most. And Julia had loved Jack's father, had loved him more than anyone would ever know—anyone but Grace, to whom she'd confessed as much in Liverpool before Grace and Mary Kate set sail. Grace alone knew all that Julia had lost, and so she would not listen to Julia's desperate apology, stilling her instead, then thanking her for keeping the boy alive through the worst of it. If not for Julia— Grace had pointed out—Jack could not have survived; at the very least he would have been blind. It was Julia who'd taken him to London, to Nigel Wilkes, the only surgeon willing to try his hand on so young a patient. After Jack had recovered and been fitted with the little spectacles that gave him such a misleading air of scholarship, Nigel and Julia had married. *The Lord does His work in ways mysterious,* Grace acknowledged. With her husband's gentle encouragement, Julia had determined to right the situation and had set about locating Grace, after which she and Nigel sailed to America with the little boy they loved as a son.

While Nigel had worked with physicians in New York City, Julia had remained in Boston, slowly distancing herself from Jack, spending more and more time in New York, until—the following spring—she and Nigel had gone back to London. Soon after that, Grace had made her decision to remove the family from Boston, in part so that Jack's old life might fade as if a dream.

And, always, there had been the hope that Grace might gain news of her brother, Sean, who by all accounts had joined up with the Mormon wagon train heading to Utah Territory. She had yearned to find him, hoped that he might be persuaded to join them again. A pitiful hope, she thought now, shaking her head and thinking of her brother, a charming man of serious convictions and fanatical commitments. He'd be married to Marcy Osgoode by now, she reasoned; perhaps he even had children. She looked down at Mary Kate, at the freckled face that was so dear to her; if Sean could not be with them, then she hoped he was married and happy and raising a child of his own.

There was a bang as the back door to the ward slapped open and Jack bolted in, cheeks flushed, eyes sparkling, entire body aquiver.

"Mam!" the boy called, and Grace stood immediately, finger to her lips as a warning to be quiet.

"Sorry, Mam," he whispered loudly when he'd reached her side. "The horse was grand, Mam! Really grand! Sister Joseph says I can feed him after I rest." He frowned. "Do I have to rest, Mam?"

"Oh, aye." That was a very good idea. "Doctor Wakefield says we can stay by Mary Kate, but we're to be still and good, and close our own eyes twice a day."

Jack nodded soberly and Grace was impressed; clearly, the boy wanted to remain with his sister, no matter the cost of a nap. They fashioned a rough nest out of their cloaks, then sat down, leaning against the battered trunk. Grace peeled first one apple and then another; Jack yawned, and slowly his eyes began to close.

"Shall we stretch out a bit, then, son?" Grace was becoming drowsy, too, in the warm pool of sunlight that fell upon them from the high windows.

"Aye." Jack took off his spectacles and handed them to her. "Will you tell a story, Mam?"

"Sure, I will." She smoothed the hair off his forehead, looking down into the dear face. "Which one'll it be, then?"

"You know." The little boy pulled off his boots and lay on his back, hands under his head, ankles crossed. "Go on, now," he urged softly, his eyes closed. " 'Long ago in Ireland . . .' "

Grace's throat closed immediately, and she wondered if she were destined to spend the rest of her days fighting tears. She tipped her head back against the trunk, then closed her own eyes and—without even trying to conjure him up—saw him there, the young man she'd loved, so real she could almost feel him. He grinned, then threw his head back and laughed in that way he had that always lightened her heart; she listened to the echo of his laughter and felt it strengthen her now, felt her spirit rally in the face of the courage he'd shown his entire life. She took a moment longer to remember him, to love him, and then she cleared her throat.

"Long ago in Ireland . . . there was the bravest warrior that ever lived. He was a hero to his people, and they sing of him in every lane. His name was Morgan McDonagh . . ."—Grace paused, a hand atop the head of her son—"and he was your father."

Two

McDonagh plunged his bloody hands into the icy creek, glad for the shock of it, for the blinding brilliance of morning light reflected full force in his eyes, for the smell of the damp earth on which he knelt, his hands on fire in the freezing water. Since leaving Ireland, he'd had many days when he'd felt more dead than alive, but this was not one—this morning saw him profoundly grateful for his life, for all their lives, after the long and terrible night.

Fingers numb, he scrubbed the blood off his forearm, then probed the slashes that lay beneath, relieved to see that they would not require stitching. More serious, he knew, were the puncture wounds in his shoulder, and for these he would need the help of the boy. Stiffness was setting in, causing him to wince as he reached again into the river, gasping as it rinsed away the fog of exhaustion as well as sweat and blood. He tipped his face into his good shoulder, drying cheek and brow on the shirt, and saw that Nacoute now knelt beside him at the water's edge, staring into it, seemingly numb, though no water had touched his young hands. Moving slowly, knowing the boy to be wary of a man's touch and especially jumpy in the aftermath of last night's violence, Morgan took Nacoute's chin in his hand and turned the boy's face toward him. The gash on Nacoute's left cheek needed stitching, but perhaps it was too late; the blood had caked and dried next to a nose, bloodied and swollen, beneath an eye, blackened and oozing. There was a host of evidence of the beating he'd received, from the imprint of knuckles and belt welts to the knife slashes along his arm. In Morgan's urgency to save the boy's mother, whose wounds were far worse, there had been no time to deal with these injuries, though they must have been painful. He raised his eyes to the boy's again and met Nacoute's unblinking intensity, hiding nothing; if there was any truth to any question to be had in that gaze, let the boy find it, he thought, for God knew he'd no answers himself.

"Come on, boy." Morgan rose wearily from his haunches. "We've work still to do."

He picked up the two wooden buckets at his feet, filled them with river water, then started back toward the small cabin, trusting the boy to follow as he always did.

Nacoute rose gracefully, lean and handsome like his mother, and, glancing back over his good shoulder, Morgan caught a glimpse of the man, the warrior, he would become. At fourteen, Nacoute was easily as tall as Morgan though his build was still slight; what softness of youth had yesterday existed was gone now, erased completely by an act of brutal killing—self-defense or no—that left a sharpness honed by the weight of an act that could never be undone. Nor did Nacoute wish it to be undone; Morgan could see it in his eyes—the watchful eyes of one who cannot speak but does not miss a word of those who can—the boy was not sorry, just unsure. The world was a different place to Nacoute this morning. Morgan understood; he, too, had killed men.

" 'Twill be all right," he said when the boy touched his arm. "We'll make a plan."

Again he wished he had more than just a few words of Mi'kmaq, or even French, which he knew the boy understood from living with the trapper. He thought of Remy Martine—dragged off and buried in the woods, no sign left of him but a large, sticky stain on the cabin floor. He glanced at the sun, now higher in the sky.

"Someone'll be along soon. We'd best clean up." Morgan spoke as he always did, as if the boy understood.

Nacoute nodded and walked a little faster.

They hesitated only a moment outside the cabin door, Morgan glancing along the footpath that led to other cabins in the settlement, including his own, Nacoute's eyes following the trail where they'd carried the big man into the bushes, then deeper into the woods. There was a scuffled path through the dirt to the edge of the clearing and a pronounced demarcation where they'd dropped the body; Nacoute put down his pail, picked up a large fir bough, and quickly swept the area free of tracks. Morgan nodded his approval, then pushed open the door, securing it so that they had light enough to scrub the floor. He carried the buckets in and was looking for the scrub brush when the woman moaned and became restless. Morgan hurried immediately to her side, soothing her, so that she would not break the stitches.

"Shhh, Aquash. Hush now." He pushed the hair off her face, tried to smile reassuringly.

Her eyes searched his wildly as she struggled to sit up.

"Nacoute!" she called. "Nacoute!"

"Come here to me, boy." Morgan motioned him over. "See there, woman; he's fine. A bit worse for wear, but he'll live."

Nacoute took his mother's hand and listened carefully as she spoke to him, responding with a series of gestures, subtle facial expressions, twitches, and nods—their own special way of communicating: she in Mi'kmaq, he with the physical language of the mute. When she put her hands to her breast, Morgan knew what she was asking and went immediately to the wooden cradle near the hearth, put there for warmth though the fire had died down hours ago. The infant girl lay awake, eyes calmly open and still. He picked her up gently and carried her to her mother, watching as Aquash swiftly undid the swaddling clothes, then checked the infant's arms and legs, her tiny back and shoulders. Near her mother, the baby was reminded of food and began to mewl. Aquash opened her tunic and put her daughter to breast.

"Henri?" Aquash looked up at Morgan, fear in her eyes. "Remy?"

"Remy is dead," Morgan told her. "Buried. *Fini.*"

She looked up at her son, who nodded, and then she spoke to him at length, pausing to let him confirm or deny. Morgan watched Nacoute's hands and guessed they were reviewing the events that led up to Remy's death. Aquash repeated the name "Henri" several times, and Morgan understood that they were worried about being discovered. Henri DuBois was Remy's right-hand man in camp, though even Remy himself did not trust the man much. Morgan had his own reasons for loathing DuBois—DuBois and Martine both, if truth be told.

Aquash was growing more agitated now, and Morgan shushed her again, though he knew she had every reason to worry. It would make no difference that Nacoute had been defending himself, his mother, and his baby sister—Remy Martine was admired and feared in this quarter: he'd been here the longest, had the greatest wealth and the most knowledge, was the trapper most sought out by rich European buyers. He'd also married and brought back to camp a beautiful woman, a Mi'kmaq for whom he'd traded with her family a year's worth of supplies, even agreeing to take on her young, mute son because they were so close and he would be a comfort to her during the months Martine trapped.

As settlement lore stood, Remy was a generous man who indulged his beautiful wife by letting her keep her son too long at home; he'd been repaid with a stubborn, sullen boy who ate his food and lived in his cabin but refused to work by his side. Martine had dragged the boy off repeatedly, as the story went, but Nacoute always ran away at the first opportunity and returned to his mother, whom he refused to leave alone in the camp even though it meant a severe beating when his stepfather returned. Martine had finally given up, and there was no love lost between boy and man; Remy beat him regularly, but Nacoute stubbornly refused to leave his mother. It made no difference that he hunted in the surrounding forest and fished the river, putting more food on the table than Martine ever did himself, or that he kept the cabin in good repair and made himself scarce when Remy was home, living in the forest or—later—on the floor of Morgan's cabin. He had earned the contempt of Remy Martine, which made him fair game for any of the other trappers or their sons who wanted a bit of sport.

What Martine did not know was that Nacoute stayed in camp to protect his mother; Morgan had witnessed the boy interrupting that kind of sport more than once, and it did not endear him to those who wanted a taste of the beautiful Aquash. He had not understood why Aquash kept quiet about the assaults until he heard the story of Martine's first wife—raped by men in the camp, she was no longer good enough for Remy and one day turned up dead on the riverbank. Leaving Nacoute on his own in this world of strangers was probably Aquash's worst nightmare, Morgan figured, so she simply endured, and as the boy grew up and realized what was happening, he became his mother's silent defender.

Morgan had unwittingly stepped into this quagmire when he befriended the boy; he had lost even more friends when he came to Nacoute's aid and then to Aquash's. No one had stepped up to help him when the tree had fallen on his supply wagon, and he would've died out there had it not been for Nacoute, Aquash, and May. May's husband, Louis, was a decent enough fellow—kind to his wife and loving to his children—but he was a man who avoided trouble at all costs; he wanted to make a good living, raise his children, and someday move back out to Nova Scotia, where his people still lived. He would make noises about a fair hearing should Nacoute be accused of killing Martine, but he would not put himself or his family at risk should the others decide to string the boy up—or worse. No one would come to Nacoute's aid, and Morgan would be unable to save him. The sureness of this drove him to his knees, and he began scrubbing furiously at the dark stain on the cabin floorboards. Some of the blood had seeped down between the cracks or been soaked up by the dirt he'd sprinkled over it, then swept away and buried, but a stain still remained, large and dark enough to raise suspicion.

Nacoute had laid a small fire in the hearth to heat food and water for his mother, and Morgan had nearly finished scrubbing when a shadow blocked the light from the door. Morgan looked up, then got to his feet.

"What do you want, DuBois?"

"What are you doing here, Irish?" Henri asked in his heavily accented English, though he did not seem particularly surprised to see Morgan in Martine's house. "And where is my friend Remy, eh?"

Nacoute had frozen at the sound of Henri's voice but now resumed stirring the pot, though he did not look up. Aquash quietly covered the baby's head, keeping her eyes lowered, as well.

"Who knows?" Morgan shrugged. "Wore himself out tearing the place up last night. Probably passed out under a tree somewhere."

"He was not so drunk," Henri countered. "I know." He looked over Morgan's shoulder toward the hearth, taking in Nacoute's battered face. "Is the boy's doing, no?"

"No." Morgan moved to block his view of Nacoute. "He was mad with drink, Martine was—attacked them all, even the baby."

Henri snorted. "But you break in and save the little family, eh, Irish? And now the little family . . . she be yours, eh, *mon ami*?"

"I didn't break in. The boy come for me, beat my door . . ."

Nacoute banged the spoon against the pot and stood up, anger flushing his cheeks. He shook his head at Morgan, then pointed at the Frenchman.

Henri strode across the room and shoved the boy, speaking rapidly in French, menacing him. Nacoute stood his ground, shaking his head.

"Get off him," Morgan warned. "Or answer to me."

The Frenchman, no stranger to McDonagh's fists, let go of the boy and stepped away, cursing under his breath.

"No one wants you here, DuBois. Get out."

"This is not your house," Henri spat, and then he paused, eyes widening. "Or maybe it is? Have you killed Remy, Irish? Is that what you have done?"

"He deserves a good beating, true enough," Morgan replied. "And I did my best. 'Twas him give it up in the end, though, smashing his way out the door, and good riddance to him."

The Frenchman crossed his arms. "I think . . . no, I think I go into the forest and find Remy. If not today, then another day—when the animals, they have dug him up." He jerked his head toward the stain on the floor. "There is blood. Remy's blood."

"No."

"*Oui*," he insisted. "It is the end of you now, Irish. No one will believe what you say, only what they see—with Remy gone, Aquash is yours, and her *bastard*. And, of course, the money." He nodded, smiling now. "But you did not count on Henri DuBois. I am looking at a dead man. A dead boy, too." He laughed. "You see how it all works out?"

Morgan stared, his mind racing; how *did* it all work out? He registered the smug look on Henri's face, but also the beads of sweat along the man's grimy hairline, the narrowed eyes that darted glances around the room, taking stock. The mother, the baby. The baby.

"I do see it now," Morgan said evenly. " 'Tis *your* child Aquash bore."

Henri spat on the floor in disgust, but Aquash had raised her eyes to Morgan's and he saw that he was right.

"I should've known." Morgan took a step toward the Frenchman, hands balling into fists. "I should've killed you the first time I caught you trying to force her."

Henri laughed. "But you did not. And now it is too late for you. The whole camp says you are the father of this child."

Morgan studied the man in front of him, took in the set of his jaw, the tremor that ran along his chin. "You were first with a bottle when Remy came home last night," he surmised evenly. "Got him all fired up, then made a few comments about the size of the baby—big for having come early and all. Let him know folks were talking. Isn't that right, you slimy son of a bitch?"

Henri scoffed and returned the curse in French.

"And it doesn't look a thing like him, once you point it out. Wrong coloring altogether, wouldn't you say?" He narrowed his eyes. "So he started to beat her, of course, and threatened to kill the baby, and that's when you ran to my place, knowing I'd think 'twas the boy needed help." He stepped a little closer. "You knew he was drunk out of his mind, and well armed in the bargain. You knew I'd have to kill him. And then I'd hang. And the boy. Aquash would be *yours*; the cabin would be *yours*. And the money, and everything that was Martine's. You set him up, you bastard. I almost feel sorry for him."

Henri took a step back. "What you say is a lie, Irish. No one will believe you. You killed Remy, and for that you will pay."

"Not me." Morgan shook his head. "The blood on that floor's Martine's—you're right about that: Remy's and mine and the boy's. 'Twas a hell of a fight. But somewhere out there, the big man is sleeping it off, and when he comes back, I'll be waiting to tell him whose child that really is and how it got here. He'll know you set him up, DuBois. And then we'll see who pays."

"Hah!" Henri barked, but there was doubt in his eyes and, behind that, fear. "Go on, Irish, and maybe we will not hunt you down. Take the boy. No one wants him here. But leave now, if you wish to live."

"I'm not going anywhere." Morgan crossed his arms calmly. "You'd like me out of the way; the boy, too—tired of him watching over his mother, getting in your way. But him and me, we're tired of you, DuBois. Tired of the way you treat the Indian women round here, tired of your drunken, lazy, dog face. This was *your* plan—your stupid, stupid plan—and I'm not answering for it. Not to Martine, not to anyone. You hear me, now?" He reached behind his back and pulled a long knife from a sheath stuck in the belt of his trousers. "Start running, Frenchie. Before I cut your scheming throat."

Henri's eyes widened with surprise, then narrowed with rage. "It is your throat that will be cut," he threatened as he backed out the door. "Don't think you have won today." And then he turned and ran.

Nacoute quickly closed and bolted the door, then leaned against it. Aquash held her baby close, and all three eyed one another helplessly. Aquash spoke to her son in their language, and he answered, then went to the hearth, brushed away the smoking embers, and pulled up a stone with the metal bar from which they suspended their cooking pot. After pushing the stone aside, Nacoute reached far down into the hole and pulled out a leather sack tied securely. This he brought to Morgan, lifting the man's hand and putting the sack into it, folding Morgan's fingers around it.

Money. Silver and gold. Morgan shook his head. " 'Tisn't mine and I'll not be taking it," he said firmly, trying to hand it back.

Nacoute went to the door and opened it, motioning for Morgan to leave.

"No." Morgan shook his head again. "I'll not leave you here to face them alone." He appealed to Aquash. "They'll hang him," he told her and made as if to wrap a rope around his neck, pointing at the boy. "And you'll spend the rest of your days bearing babies for DuBois and any other man he chooses to give you to." He sighed, frustrated again by his inability to communicate.

He had no plan. He had no way to protect himself or the boy, or the woman and her baby. These trappers were a rough bunch, and if they decided to hang him, they would, and there'd be little in the way of discussion. He sat down at the table, head in his hands, trying to think of a way out of this. Should he steal a wagon and take them all back up north to the immigrant settlement where he'd first landed? It had been a year since he'd been there, a year spent recovering from legs so shattered he'd been sure he'd die right here, sure that at the very least he'd lose them both and never be able to make it to America, never be able to find his wife. After he'd come so far and lived through so much, the thought of dying alone in the Canadian wilderness nearly unhinged him, but Aquash had arranged to have him carried back to his cabin, had lit a fire and begun her silent, steady care of him.

Morgan could only think it was because he had made a friend of her son, Nacoute, the wary boy who always seemed to be in a fight. He'd looked out for the boy every time he'd come down from the settlement

with supplies, liking him instantly, recognizing in him the same fire
that shone from the eyes of Sean O'Malley. Morgan had rescued the
boy from more than one beating, which made him less appreciated by
the trappers and their sons but secured the devotion of Aquash. She
and her friend, the other Indian woman, called May, repaired Morgan's
shattered legs, applied poultices when he burned with fever, brought
him food every day, and washed and changed him like a baby. He owed
these women his life, and he would not abandon Aquash and her family now.

But they'd never reach the northern settlement on foot—not with
Aquash in her condition and with a baby—and a cart would be too
slow, too visible. And, though he was loath to admit it, it meant going
in the wrong direction. He needed to go south; he dreamed of traveling south. It had been five years since he left Ireland, five years that had
slipped away so quickly and yet whose every passing day had been
agony. But where else was there to go? Silently, he prayed to the God
who had sustained him thus far, and was so fervently beseeching that
he did not hear the soft rap on the door. It was the murmur of voices
that caught his attention.

"May! What are you doing here?" He rose as Nacoute closed the
door behind her.

"You must go." May's English was better than his French, though
she was easily flustered. "Men coming soon."

Then she spoke to Aquash, who began to climb painfully from her
bed.

"What?" Morgan asked.

"Men come for you, for Nacoute. Put away 'til Remy come home or
find dead." She frowned and shook her head. "Know me?"

"Aye." Morgan nodded grimly. "I'll take the boy with me and go,
but what about Aquash? I can't just leave her."

"Aquash go home. Nacoute go home. You go."

"Home?" Morgan knew that Aquash had lived here with Remy for
nearly ten years. "Does she know how to find it?"

May frowned, confused.

"Where home?" Morgan pointed in different directions.

"Ah! By river. There." She pointed south. "Many day."

"Follow the river, then," Morgan said more to himself than to anyone else. Many days, he thought. How many days? And could she do it in her condition? He looked at her now, and she met his gaze, steady and determined despite her swollen, bruised face and what must be an aching body.

"They go home," May repeated. "They go, you go."

"Right." He nodded. "I know you. Nacoute—get blankets, food, your quiver, the knife."

"I do," May insisted. "Go out Nacoute. Help."

Morgan followed Nacoute out and around the back of the cabin. Leaning against the wall was the sledge they sometimes used to drag wood in from the forest; Nacoute put this on the ground and began reinforcing it with leather strips, small branches, and bark. They would take this with them for land travel, put their belongings on this, Morgan thought, or—if Aquash weakened—it could be modified to carry mother and child. He helped, bringing Nacoute everything the boy indicated.

Then Aquash came around the corner dressed in her warm leggings and boots, the baby in a carrier on her back, fur rugs in her arms. May had put food and water in leather sacks and handed these to Nacoute.

"I've got to go back to my cabin," Morgan said suddenly.

"No time, no time!" May urged.

"No choice." He thought for a moment. "Start for the river and I'll meet you there. May—" He kissed her cheek quickly. "*Wela'lin,* May. *Wela'lin.*"

She nodded soberly, accepting his thanks, then watched with the others as he disappeared down the bank to the creek.

He moved quickly along the creek, crouching to remain hidden by the bank, and suddenly he was back in Ireland, running through the hills with the rest of his ragged band, evading the English soldiers who hunted them for insurrection. He stopped and shook his head—this was Quebec, not Ireland, and if he ever wanted to see his home again or the woman he loved, he needed to stay focused. He moved forward cautiously, listening for the sounds of men; hearing nothing, he slipped up the bank, then around front and into the tiny room. *Quickly, quickly,* he told himself, throwing his only change of clothes into a knapsack and then lifting the mattress off his bed. There was the Bible Gracelin's gran had given him years ago in Macroom, and inside it a sketch of his mother made by his sister Barbara—the only things that had come with him on that frantic, secret trip from Ireland. *Eejit,* he scolded himself; stupid to risk coming back for these things, and yet how could he leave them behind when they were all he had left to remind him of who he'd once been. Not Mac, the Irishman who ran the supply wagon from town to settlement to trapper camp, but Morgan McDonagh, son of a proud poor man and a humble mother—both dead now; brother to eight sisters—dead, as well, for all he knew; best friend of Sean O'Malley—alive, God willing, and still in New York City; husband of Gracelin—alive, please God, please God, please God; and maybe even the father of a child who walked the earth thinking his father was dead. He mustn't let himself become this new man, this Canadian Irishman, and he fought against it daily; he must remember where he came from, what brought him here, who he was. He looked around the cabin one last time for anything he might need. There was nothing. He had not allowed himself to make a life here.

Aquash and the baby were climbing into a canoe at the river's edge when he got to them. Behind it, another canoe waited—May's, most likely—carefully balanced with their supplies and the travois. Nacoute motioned Morgan into this one and handed him the paddle.

"You can?" May asked anxiously.

Morgan had never been in a canoe. "I can," he reassured her, then awkwardly maneuvered his vessel into position behind Nacoute's.

Once in the middle of the river, Morgan relaxed and let his body feel the motion of the water, the roll of the canoe, the rhythm of the paddle. The sun beat down on his head and warmed his aching shoulder through the cloth of his shirt; large black crows landed heavily on low-slung branches, cawing loudly as the boats worked their way upstream. To his right, a flash of silver caught his eye as a salmon jumped, startling the elk who'd come down for a drink, and overhead, an enormous bald eagle soared gracefully, following their progress.

It was beautiful country, with an abundance of wildlife, but also cruel and unpredictable, and Morgan knew that the Indian village they sought might well be long disappeared. Winter could be months away or merely weeks; it was bitterly cold this far north, and there were no marked roads through the wilderness, no signs pointing the way to the nearest town. There were no nearest towns. He was traveling with an injured woman and her newborn babe, with a boy who could not speak, who had killed his stepfather and now ran from those who would make him pay; yesterday morning was a far cry from this one, and never had he dreamed this would be the day he finally moved on.

Where are you taking me now, Father? Morgan asked silently, face tipped up to the sun. The answer didn't matter; he was headed south and the Lord was with him. He did not look back.

Three

Grace leaned back against the wall into the looming shadows cast by lamplight. She listened to the toss and turn of anxious sleepers, experiencing an otherworldliness she had not felt since those long nights aboard the *Eliza J*, the endless voyage from Liverpool to Manhattan. Some nights, in the twilight before wakefulness, she even felt the ship sway, felt the salty winter sea damp against her skin, heard the calls and whistles of sailors, the clang of rigging against the masts. Awakening with a jolt, she would reach out for Mary Kathleen, who lay . . . not beside her in the narrow ship's bunk, but on a cot in a row of cots lined up uniformly across the hospital ward.

Grace checked her daughter—sleeping well, sleeping better every night, thank God, and talking during the day. She and Jack had stayed by Mary Kate's side for nearly a week, and soon the girl would be well enough to leave this place, well enough to go home. Grace let the images of cabins, houses, rooms, inns, wagons, boats, ships, file through her mind—in how many different places had they laid down their heads, and where would they lie down now?

She tightened her grip around Jack, slipping from her lap with the sweaty weight of a four-year-old gone dead-to-the-world asleep. He struggled briefly in protest but did not wake up, and Grace was glad. It was hours until morning, and she needed the rest that came when Jack was down for the night. He twitched occasionally, kicked his heels, and Grace knew that he dreamt of the pony left behind, of cowboys and lawmen, the revolving gamblers and preachers who had peopled his life, gunfights and horse races in the middle of town, cattle drives and

Indian parties passing on the outskirts. Jack—with his dark sweep of hair and glasses, his little swagger and his true fearlessness—stirred something in everyone and anyone he ever met.

He stirred now, and she kissed the top of his sweaty head, closed her eyes, and breathed in the particular smell of him. She loved him almost more than she could bear, especially when he threw back his head and laughed, when she saw in him the essence of his father. Imprisoned for insurrection, Morgan had never seen his son, though he'd known a child was on the way and had managed to get a letter to Grace before he'd died. That letter, and the knowledge that he was lost to her forever, had brought on an early labor. With no hope of a life in Ireland and wanted by the guards, Grace had been forced to leave behind the tiny infant at a convent in Cork with Morgan's sister and Grace's father; she'd hoped her da would come with the baby in the spring, but instead she'd learned that all in the convent had perished of fever. She bit her lip hard, knowing that the breakdown she'd suffered then had been yet another bane for Mary Kate to endure. Thank God for the Ogues; she owed Dugan her life in more ways than one and had been loath to leave him and Tara. The last time she'd seen them had been in Boston when they came to celebrate Jack's arrival. Dugan had taken her aside and asked her to consider Peter Reinders' proposal, for wasn't he a fine man and wouldn't young Jack need a father's hand in the years to come?

Peter *was* a fine man, a good man—she'd known it the day she set sail from Liverpool on his ship; he'd watched out for her, making sure that Liam would disembark as part of her family rather than ending up in the orphans' asylum. He'd proved himself over and over again during the years in New York, and she had very nearly married him. Her excuse for not doing so had been her brother, whom she'd wanted so much to find; her excuse had been the children and the treacherous voyage around the Horn; her excuse had been time—she'd needed more of it—but here she always stopped, because the truth was that she loved the memory of a dead man more than the presence of one who lived and breathed and loved her as no dead man ever could.

"Your mam's a great eejit," she murmured against Jack's damp head. "Only you look more like him every day."

Grace had wed her second husband in secret, in the wee hours of a misty Irish morning, only to watch him disappear moments after. He'd told her to go to America, that he would follow, but instead he'd died and she had come alone. Grace kissed her boy again and accepted that in coming here to San Francisco, in asking Peter for help, she was resuming their courtship; she was agreeing to the consideration of marriage should he still want it. And she did love him, perhaps not with the passion of her youth, but she was twenty-five now, and wiser. With two children to raise, she could not afford to cling to memories; Morgan was dead and Peter was not. There could be no more excuses.

"Ah, Missus Donnelly. Awake and on guard, as usual, I see."

Grace hadn't heard the doctor approach and looked up, startled but pleased. "Are you still here, then?" she whispered over the top of Jack's head.

"Apparently so." Wakefield stifled a yawn. "How's Miss Mary Kate this evening?"

"Sleeping well enough. She took some broth earlier and spoke to us a bit."

"Color's better, too." The doctor felt Mary Kate's forehead. "You can be thankful it wasn't worse," he said soberly. "A year ago, we wouldn't have had a bed available. Four thousand immigrant men arriving each month, and I swear, most of them sick as dogs." He regarded the woman before him. "One person in five dies before their first year here is over—you are quite determined to stay, are you, Missus Donnelly?"

Grace nodded; she'd known far worse odds than that in her lifetime.

"I understand your friend has not yet returned and in fact isn't due back for quite some time." Wakefield tipped his head in the direction of the nurse bent over a patient at the end of the row. "Courtesy of Sister Joseph," he revealed. "She who sees all and knows all."

"He wasn't expecting us, nor had I any way of knowing he'd be away. Where is Panama City, Doctor? Can you tell me?"

"South, madam," Wakefield said wryly. "Plenty of ships are still coming around Cape Horn, but the advent of the steamship has meant an ever-increasing number are dropped at Chagres, on the Gulf side, and they then travel by canoe and mule across the isthmus to Panama City on the Pacific side, in order to hitch a ride up the coast to San Francisco. It's been a lucrative business for ship owners," he continued, "though I hear the steamer trade is cutting them out now. The weather down there is unpredictable this time of year—hence the question of when your friend the captain will actually arrive."

Grace bit her lip, pondering the situation. "Well," she decided at last. "I can take care of my own."

The doctor laughed despite himself. "That goes without saying, Missus Donnelly. Goes without saying."

Wakefield liked this woman; despite the gravity of her situation—quite desperate when she'd arrived with the child—she had maintained her dignity, never succumbing to hysteria, which he admired. Grace Donnelly was more than likely an attractive woman beneath the sun-reddened skin and flyaway hair, the battered hat she never removed, the mud-crusted cloak and—shocking, though he appreciated the practicality—those trousers, but it was the sound of her voice that drew him into conversation time after time; it was like speaking with his mother all over again. Granted, the Sisters of Mercy were all from an Irish order but were also more than a little intimidating with their no-nonsense air of duty and unblinking focus on the will of God. Certainly, they did not remind Wakefield of his witty, flirtatious Irish mother, who had been the epitome of Southern womanhood even though she rode the estate as boldly as any man and jumped her beloved horses at the drop of a hat, much to the mortification of the doctor's father, older brothers, and younger sister.

Missus Donnelly seemed to have the same confident disposition and, like Wakefield's mother, did not back away from lively discourse with a man, no matter how heated it became. When engaged, the young widow had answered his various questions with succinct tutorials on Ireland's fight for freedom and the plight of the reluctant immigrant, the sin of slavery and the brewing warfare in Kansas Territory. Lingering at the end of a day, Wakefield had heard about the overland walk to Oregon, the valley camp, and the illness that brought the Donnellys sailing down the coast to San Francisco, where it appeared the one person they knew was at present in absentia. Wakefield's comfortable life—even the eternal voyage from his family's plantation to the harbor of Yerba Buena with a distraught and, at times, hysterical sister—paled in comparison to the life this woman had led.

"Would you like to sit down, then, Doctor?" Grace broke into his reverie. "Or will you keep on sleeping where you stand?"

Wakefield grinned sheepishly. "Can't let Sister Joseph catch me napping, now, you hear?" He winked. "In point of fact, I was caught up in a reflection of your remarkable travels, and I was thinking how much you remind me of my dear departed mother. She was Irish, you know."

"So you've said," Grace reminded him. "Came away from Dublin with her family as a wee girl, grew up to charm your stodgy old da 'til he would go mad or be wed."

The doctor laughed, delighted with her summary. He crossed his arms and leaned against the post, settling in.

"I'm flattered you remembered. However, my point is that my mother was a truly self-reliant, independent-minded, tough-as-nails kind of woman, but I don't imagine even she could have survived half of what you all did."

"Not on her own, of course," Grace allowed. "But if she'd friends as good as mine, she could've. I'd've never made it this far without Captain Reinders, the Ogues and the Livingstons, my friend Lily, and all her family."

"Ah, yes, the magnificent Free family." Wakefield peered over the top of his spectacles. "Runaways, I believe you said?"

Grace bristled. "I'd never call them that. Running away sounds cowardly, and the Frees are the bravest people I know."

"I've known many Negroes, myself, Missus Donnelly. We have all kinds where I come from—slaves, bonded servants, freemen—and, yes, some can give the appearance of bravery. But no matter what their status, they are not like us. They may pretend to be—and, indeed, the Negro is an expert mimic—but beneath their civilized dress runs the hot blood of the savage, and eventually, like it or not, blood will out."

Grace thought of Lily's husband, January; his silent brooding and rage seemed to come out of nowhere. Lily had been overjoyed at their reunion, but even she had confessed once that Jan was not the man she'd married. The heart had been beaten out of him, she'd said; the beating had cost him his arm and hobbled him, but the worst was the loss of joy that had seeped into the ground with his blood. Solomon, their son, was an angry one, as well, Grace remembered; he was as wary of the white settlers as they of him, and he fought at the drop of a hat.

"Do you not think 'tis slavery itself makes a man savage?" Grace asked then. "Are we not all the less for turning a blind eye to the buying and selling of people?"

"What you're implying, Missus Donnelly—and I grant that it's a debatable point—is that we free the slaves. But you're forgetting that these people are in no way prepared to feed or clothe themselves. And, frankly, if every worker had to be paid, the plantations would fail. Everyone would go under—white man and colored alike. And then where would we all be?"

"Equal," Grace answered without hesitation.

Wakefield shook his head. "Not equal. The white man, with his greater civility and ability to reason, would be able to prosper once again, while the Negro would sink further into vice and degradation."

"Man's character lies in the state of his soul, Doctor, not in the color of his skin."

The doctor frowned. "Believe it or not, Missus Donnelly, most slaves do not *wish* to be free. They are housed, they are clothed and fed, they are given work until they are too old, and then they are cared for until the end of their lives. They have their own families, their own private communities, and most masters are not the ogres portrayed by Northern abolitionists, most of whom have no real interest in the advancement of the Negro, by the way, only political aspirations."

Grace thought of Florence Livingston and her friends, who worked tirelessly in New York to raise money, who lectured and educated the masses about slavery, who had brought hundreds of men, women, and children up from the South and provided the means for them to live a life of freedom and dignity.

"I can't agree with you there, Doctor, though I've no doubt there are slaveholders who are well-meaning people. Only they can do nothing about those who aren't, those who maim and murder, who assault the weak and vulnerable, simply because they have the power to do so."

"You are of the 'power corrupts' school of thought, are you, Missus Donnelly? Let me tell you that power in the hands of good Christian men is exactly what God intended."

"I think the word you're looking for there, Doctor, is compassion. 'Tis the other fellow doles out power, knowing men will become drunk on it and use it to hurt the very people they're meant to look upon as brothers."

Wakefield shook his head. "Assault and murder are not exclusive to the white man, madam. Plenty have suffered at the hands of those we've spent a lifetime caring for, who have betrayed our caring and kindness toward them in the most terrible manner known."

"And so, Doctor"—Grace finished carefully, hearing the personal note of anger in his voice—"have we not come back round to the beginning of our discussion? Slavery brings out the worst in man. Every man."

Wakefield nodded, though his acceptance of what she said was grudging at best. "Well, Missus Donnelly, I know many men—educated, professional men, by the way—who don't argue a point half as well as you do. But I want you to know that I am not an advocate of slavery and do not wish to argue for its continuation. I hope to see in my lifetime a resolve that will not destroy an entire way of life—for the white man and the Negro alike."

"But one has already been destroyed," she said quietly, Solomon's face floating before her. "And now the whites have become slaves themselves—to money. As you've said before, good and decent people own slaves because without them they would lose everything and they cannot bear it, even though it will be their children who pay for it in the end."

Wakefield squinted at the floor as if he'd felt a twinge of pain. "You may be right, madam. Certainly my own family has built its fortune on slave labor and could not survive if forced to pay wages—our plantation is one of the largest in our state." He looked up at her. "I confess it was not a life I could pursue with any kind of heart, and I was grateful to be released from family obligations so that I might come out here to practice medicine."

"I'm grateful, as well. You're a fine doctor, and I don't know what we would've done without you."

"Ah." Wakefield smiled ruefully. "There you have it. I would not be a doctor and could not have traveled here to help build this hospital were it not for the allowance I receive annually. Theoretically, slavery is the price for the life of your daughter. What say you to that?"

Grace put a hand on Mary Kate's arm, her heart suddenly heavy. "This child means everything to me, but if you're saying that all must sacrifice if all are to be free"—she looked up at him—"then so be it."

It was not the answer Wakefield had expected, and his surprise showed on his face. "How can you say that?"

"Because I know where my treasure lies. And I'm no stranger to sacrifice."

"No," the doctor agreed. "That you are not." Fatigued now, as much from the draining conversation as from the long day, Wakefield drew his watch from his vest pocket and checked the time. "Midnight." He showed the face of it to her. "Guess I'd better finish up here and get home to my sister. I'll say good night, Missus Donnelly. As always, it has been stimulating."

"Good night, Doctor," Grace replied. "Thank you for everything you've done. I meant what I said about being grateful."

Wakefield gave her a weary smile, then retreated, moving slowly down the narrow aisles between the cots, pausing to speak to Sister Joseph, who, like him, seemed always to be on the ward.

Grace watched him anxiously, this good-natured man who had been so kind to her and the children. Often during the past long week, he'd stopped for a little visit, talking to Grace and letting Jack play with his pocket watch, complimenting the little boy's inquisitiveness; there weren't many who appreciated that about Jack, she acknowledged. Aye, he'd done a lot for them, and she chided herself for speaking so familiarly to him about his life. She'd not intended their conversation to become personal, and she regretted letting her emotions get the best of her, entering into a heated debate when perhaps she should have been more discreet. She was not good at biting her tongue anyway, and the subject of slavery always made her blood boil. His comment about sacrifice had given her pause, however, and she considered that—for all her talk—she did not really know how much sacrifice she'd truly be able to make in order to free another human being.

Jack was heavy in her arms now, and she eased him onto the floor, where she'd fashioned a kind of nest out of the extra blankets Sister Joseph had loaned her; he stirred and opened his eyes, stared at her for a moment, then closed them again and curled onto his side. Such a handsome boy, she thought again, pulling a blanket up over his shoulders.

Without him on her lap, she was more comfortable and decided to try to sleep herself, though her thoughts still raced. She leaned back in the chair and put her feet up on the edge of Mary Kate's cot, willing herself to let go of worries about past, present, future; fatigue washed through her, but still her mind whirred. Although it felt as if life had

always been these days in the hospital, Mary Kate would eventually be
well enough to leave here, and Grace needed to have a home ready.
She'd spent a part of each day going out with Jack to look for rooms
but had been appalled at what was available. This was immigrant slum
living all over again, unwashed bodies crowded into tiny, dark rooms;
worse, San Francisco was notorious for fire—last year, the entire city
center had nearly burned down twice, with four fires in the year leading up to that. Grace was terrified of the windowless rooms in the back
of these wooden houses, the only ones available for the money she had.
Sister Joseph had pointed her toward better districts, but the price was
much higher and Grace was less likely to find work nearby, necessary as
she was loath to leave Mary Kate and Jack alone for too long a time
during the day. Still, she was determined to find something—there
were many churches in San Francisco, and she would throw herself on
their mercy, imploring a Christian family to rent her decent rooms
until she was properly settled.

Can you hear me, Father? Grace prayed silently. *I'm way over on the
other side of the world now, but it seems I've got the same problems as always and I'm hoping maybe You can—*

"Missus Donnelly?"

Grace opened her eyes, dropped her feet to the floor, and sat up straight.

"Doctor Wakefield." She smiled tentatively, afraid he might be
about to wash his hands of her.

He sat down gingerly on the end of Mary Kate's cot. "Missus Donnelly, our conversation took a rather different turn than I'd intended,
and I had something else entirely that I wished to say to you."

"Ah, Doctor, you must forgive me." Grace shook her head. "I'm always speaking out of turn and I—"

"Please." He stopped her. "Don't apologize. The hour is very late in
a week that has been very long. For both of us. What I had intended to
say to you earlier, is that—contrary to what you might think—I have
enjoyed our conversations very much. It won't be half as interesting
around here after you've left us."

"You've been ever so good to us, Doctor," Grace said earnestly. "You
must pay us a visit, once we're settled in. The children will be happy for
it, especially our Jack, who's so fond of your pocket watch. And bring
your sister, as well, if she's able. She'll be most welcome."

"Thank you." Wakefield nodded, then shook his head. "I mean . . . I wanted— " He stopped, frowning. "Are you saying that you have succeeded in engaging accommodation? I guess I hadn't realized."

"I haven't," Grace clarified. "But I will. Tomorrow, Jack and I will find a place. And, once Mary Kate is home, I'll get work, as well."

"What about the children?" He looked down at Jack's small form sprawled on the floor like a limp puppy. "What will you do with them?"

Grace didn't want to admit that she had no idea. "We'll manage," she said firmly. "If there's piecework to be had, I can take in sewing. Then I'll be at home with them. If not, I'll go out to cook. I was a cook in Kansas, you know, and before that in New York, so I've plenty of experience. 'Tis only 'til Captain Reinders returns."

"I see." Wakefield hesitated. "May I ask a personal question, Missus Donnelly?"

Grace felt her face grow warm. "Of course."

"Are you and the captain . . . I mean—do you have an . . . understanding of some kind?"

"Aye. He's been wanting me to come out for some time now."

Wakefield nodded. "As you may have noticed, this is a town full of men. And, forgive me for saying so, while every man wants a woman, they don't all necessarily want a wife."

"Captain Reinders is the most honorable man I know. He's my dearest friend, and though I'd not planned on making a home in San Francisco just yet, now we're here, I've no doubt he'll be happy to see us."

"Missus Donnelly, I want you to listen to me for a moment." Wakefield leaned forward. "Sister Joseph is my right-hand man around here, and she has come up with a solution, as she so frequently does, that may very well benefit us all."

"I'm not sure I understand you, Doctor."

"You need secure, affordable lodging, and work that allows you to be near your children. And I"—he paused—"I am in dire need of a good cook. Not just any good cook—I've had dozens of those, mostly men, I'll grant you—but a cook of exceptional . . . resilience."

"Are you so very hard to please, then?"

"Not I," Wakefield corrected. "If the food is warm and even remotely palatable, I am most certainly grateful. No." He hesitated. "To be honest, it is my housekeeper, Missus Hopkins, who seems to be the reason I cannot keep a cook. She is a rather demanding woman, and she wields a very sharp tongue."

"Forgive me for asking, Doctor, but why not just replace *her* instead of going to all this trouble?"

Wakefield nodded. "You're quite right, of course, but Abigail is attached to Hopkins and won't hear of dismissal, and, I must admit, Hopkins is very protective of my sister. Abigail's ailment is a nervous condition, you see. Hopkins administers her medication and is better able to manage her than ever I could, though she's a grim woman; there's no denying that. I did try to let her go once, but Abby . . ." He shook his head. "The deterioration was so dramatic, I vowed never to make that mistake again."

"So you need someone who'll get along with your housekeeper," Grace concluded. "What makes you think I'll fare any better than the others?"

"Sister Joseph has vouched for you most highly. She says you are a person not easily intimidated, especially by someone like Hopkins. And, truly, if you cook half as well as you argue a point, Missus Donnelly, then I've no doubt Abigail's constitution can be built up again despite the difficulties." Wakefield leaned forward, his eyes hopeful as he pressed his case. "The cook's living quarters are behind the kitchen, connected by a narrow hall. There is a private entrance and a fireplace—plenty of room for you and the children—and there's a very big yard and a stable, and then a garden, of course. We're at the top of the hill, with a pond, a small wood, and grounds that run down the back. The children could have the run of all that. Miss Mary Kate will need plenty of fresh air and exercise in order to recuperate fully. And, of course"—he paused in order to lend full weight to this final and, he hoped, most persuasive piece—"I'll be on hand should either of your children ever need a doctor again."

Grace looked down at Mary Kate and then at Jack; this last was worth all the others put together, and yet, was it fair to take the position knowing her future was undecided?

"Once Captain Reinders returns," Wakefield continued, guessing her concern, "you are certainly under no obligation to remain in my employ. However, establishing some measure of independence may relieve the pressure of arriving at too hasty a resolve, if I may say so without giving offense."

"No," Grace said slowly. "No, you're right."

She did not want Peter to think she'd come to marry out of desperation, nor did she wish him to feel responsible even if his feelings toward her had changed. And he would; she knew he would—being the kind of man he was, honorable and true, he would insist on marrying her right away, before either one had a decent chance at sorting out the truth of the situation. Grace could not bear the thought of tying him to something he might secretly and stoically regret for the rest of his life.

"If I come, Doctor, will you be expecting my children to work, as well?"

"Absolutely not," he insisted. "Hopkins oversees the inside work, which her daughter, Enid, does. We have an outdoor man for the grounds and stable. Your duties are only those of the kitchen, and how much help your children give is up to you. I intend to pay a very generous wage, Missus Donnelly. Kindly consider my offer as an alternative to damp waterfront lodgings and the drudgery of sewing by candlelight."

Grace wanted to take offense to that but knew he was probably right.

"Your sister," she said, stalling for time. "Her condition is not so bad as to frighten the children?"

"You won't have much contact with Abigail; she used to go out on occasion but is now a total invalid. Rather, it will be Hopkins who might give the children a fright. Enid is better—though she, too, sports a grim countenance."

"You're offering me work in a house full of grim and hysterical women?" Grace asked, shaking her head. "What's the outdoor man like?"

"Grim." Wakefield laughed. "Did I mention the generous wage, Missus Donnelly? With a bonus at Christmastime? Believe me, I know the going rate in this town for a woman who can cook, and I'm well prepared to double that amount."

Grace rapidly weighed her options, which were sadly under scale; looking again at her daughter's pale face and then her son's sleeping form, she made up her mind.

"All right, then, Doctor, you've struck a bargain. You house us and pay me that generous wage, and you'll think it's your very own mother out in the kitchen."

"My mother didn't know a pot from a pan, Missus Donnelly. She had all the sla—" He stopped. "Servants she could ever want. But my grandmother—now, there was a woman always slipping away to the kitchen. She used to make a hot dish of potatoes and cabbage and onions that I can almost taste to this day."

"Colcannon," Grace said at once, pleased. "Not so grand, but we Irish love it. I'll make it up for you the day I start."

"Wonderful." Wakefield stood and rubbed his hands together briskly. "How about Monday morning? I'll have your quarters readied, and you and the boy can bring your things up by wagon—I'll send my man. Mary Kate can follow when she's ready."

"Monday 'tis, then." Grace put out her hand. "Thank you, Doctor. Thank you very much."

"Don't change your mind on me now we've sealed the bargain." Wakefield clasped her hand firmly, then let go. "I'll be dreaming of poached eggs and crisped bacon, pies that don't sink like a stone, savory stews, fluffy biscuits, gravy . . ." His eyes widened in alarm. "You do know how to make gravy, don't you, Missus Donnelly?"

"Oh, aye, Doctor, set your mind at ease." Grace laughed. "Go on home to your dreams, now, and we'll see you in two days. And, Doctor—do you have a milk cow at your place?"

"Well, no, actually, we don't. But I can certainly acquire one," he offered instantly. "You want it for the children, I suppose. For fresh milk?"

"Aye. We had our own in Kansas," Grace told him. "I've seen the price of things in the city, and we'd make up the cost of the cow in cheese and butter and cream alone."

"Music to my ears, Missus Donnelly. A milk cow it is."

The doctor nodded happily, then strode across the ward and through the double doors, whistling softly. As soon as he'd gone, Sister Joseph looked up from the work she'd been pretending to do, then bustled down the aisle toward Grace, her nursing habit floating out behind.

"Well, my dear?" the nun asked breathlessly upon arrival. "What's the news?"

"I'm offered a place as cook," Grace reported dutifully. "With rooms off the kitchen for myself and the children. I know you put in the good word, Sister, and I can't thank you enough. The pay alone is more than I'd ever dreamed of."

Sister Joseph nodded. "Oh, aye, women's skills still fetch a dear price in this town when men pay five dollars for a pan of fresh biscuits. Not to mention, he's paying you to put up with old Hopkins."

Grace bit her lip. "What's that all about, then—the hysterical sister and grim servants?"

The nun laughed. "He told you himself, did he? Well, well, well, good for him. He's not been above painting a prettier picture in order to get himself a decent meal."

"That bad, is it?"

"I don't really know," Sister Joseph admitted. "I've only ever met Hopkins and her daughter the odd time out. They're some sort of fanaticals, you know," she confided in a low voice. "The girl showed a bit of spark, but she's well under her mother's thumb, I'm guessing. I know a bit more about Mister Litton, as he was one of the doctor's first patients. Patched up in a field hospital during the war, but 'twas badly done. Doctor Wakefield set him to rights, though it took a while. Mister Litton was very grateful at the time."

"Then why so grim?"

The ward around them was quiet and dim, warm from the coal stove at the end of the room. Sister Joseph sat down and took a deep breath.

"Well, now," she said, her eyes twinkling. "He was a criminal of sorts in the city of New York until the guards caught up with him and gave him a choice: go to prison or go to war. Lot of them come out that way, you know, though mostly toward the end of the fight. Some never saw a hint of battle, though it don't stop them regaling you with their heroics for the price of a drink." Her smile faded. "You can tell the ones that really fought," she said soberly. "George Litton was one of those. After the war, he wandered out this way but wasn't well. He'd been shot, you know, and the pieces still in him. The doctor took them out and he had less pain. Only instead of finding work, he joined his old B'hoys from the gangs in New York. They ran riot through this town the better part of a year, and no one could do a thing about it. Called themselves the San Francisco Society of Regulators, devoted to protecting us all from foreigners, don't you know, though most of them not more than a generation off the boat themselves. Their slogan was 'Papists, Greasers, Niggers, and John Chinaman—Out,' which was so very poetic, don't you think?" She shook her head in disgust. "Burned Little Chile practically to the ground one night, ran those poor people out of their homes. 'Twas Sam Brannan took a public stand against them. He and his vigilantes finally put the whole lot down. Hung them or drove them out of town."

"But not Mister Litton?"

"I'm coming to that," Sister Joseph scolded good-naturedly. "You know how I warm to a good story. Anyway, Doctor Wakefield himself got caught up in the riot that night—he was trying to stop it, you see— knocked unconscious, he was. Would've been the end of him, what with the fires and all, had not Mister Litton carried him out of there. Later, when the Regulators were being hunted down, the doctor took him in and give him work. Gave Brannan his word that Mister Litton would stay out of trouble and, by all accounts, he has. Bit of a drinker, I hear." She shrugged. "But who isn't, in this town? Especially the soldiers."

Grace recalled the faces of young men she'd known who'd died fighting—mostly Irish, they were, but also men like Henry Adams, an Englishman. And her friend. War and slavery—what a night of conversation she was having.

"What about *Miss* Wakefield?" Grace asked. "Was she always unwell?"

"I'm often here late at night, you know," Sister Joseph said quietly. "People confess things in the midnight hour, even doctors . . . Especially to nuns," she added wryly. "So I know this much to be true—she was thrown over in her engagement to an older man, a judge no less, and the shock of it sent her into decline." She paused and looked around. "What I don't know to be true, but what others say—and you know I've no mind for gossip, but sometimes you hear things you'd rather not—is that she and a young lover were publicly denounced by the judge, or even that she'd married the judge but was then cast out in a most humiliating manner. Perhaps she had a bastard child, stillborn perhaps, or given away to maiden aunts in the country." Her eyes opened wide at the thought of such scandal. "But I can only vouch for what the doctor himself says, which is that her own family wanted her out of good society and would have nothing more to do with her. 'Tis terrible wicked hearsay." She shook her head. "And not worth the repeating. I only tell you now you're going up the hill to live."

"Thank you," Grace said weakly.

" 'Tis my understanding they were hard set on putting her away," Sister Joseph continued. "But the doctor come home from university and convinced them to let him bring her out here. He'd been wanting to come for some time, he told me, but they'd been against it though he was the third son and no reason to stay on the family land. They agreed and he receives an annuity, though to his credit, he keeps Miss Abigail in comfort and spends the rest building hospitals and clinics and the like."

Grace stared, incredulous.

"People do talk." Sister Joseph tipped her head discreetly toward a nurse at the end of the ward. "Though Lord knows I stay well clear of it."

"Aye," Grace agreed dryly. "I can see I'm to get no information out of you."

"Ah, go on with you." Sister Joseph swatted the young woman's knee playfully. "You probably think I'm daft sending you up into all that, but really it's all past and there's nothing for it. Miss Abigail stays to her rooms, Mister Litton stays to the stable, I've no doubt you can handle Hopkins and the girl, and Doctor Wakefield is a fine man, deserving of a little creature comfort for all the good he does." She paused. "And, of course, it doesn't bear thinking—you living on your own in this town; crowded, 'tis, and full of vice. I know plenty of folk struggling hard despite it being the City of Gold, and I'll sleep better at night knowing you and the wee ones are well out of it."

Grace leaned forward and embraced her new friend, holding the woman tightly and kissing her soft wrinkled cheek before letting her go.

"I'll not forget your kindness to us."

"Well, and aren't we both County Cork girls? No sense coming all this way only to scrape and suffer all over again. I'm not so long out of the place I don't know what it was you left behind. I survived it, as well," Sister Joseph added soberly. "There aren't many of us as did."

A lump rose in Grace's throat and she could only nod, not trusting herself to speak. The nun understood and took the young woman's hand, patting it reassuringly.

"You get yourself settled in up there, agra, and welcome to it, grim folk and all. But bring me a wee dish of that colcannon you promised the doctor, will you, now? Oh, I can almost taste it." Sister Joseph cast her eyes toward Heaven with the thought of such pleasure.

"And how would you know about that?" Grace laughed. "I've only just told him!"

"For overseeing the place, I'm second only to God, though I'll deny I ever said such a blasphemous thing." Her eyes twinkled. "Off to bed with you, now, and remember your prayers, for 'tis no city kind to widows and babies, and you've landed on your feet, you have."

Grace looked down at Mary Kate and brushed the hair off the girl's forehead. "Aye," she whispered. "Well I know it."

After drawing the blankets more securely around her children, Grace settled herself on the floor next to Jack, her back against the trunk that held their belongings. She pulled her cloak up over her legs, then rested her head on a folded shawl and closed her eyes.

She must have slept then because, upon awakening, she still clung to the fragments of a dream: She was down on the beach, the wind in her hair, with Jack riding on one hip and Mary Kate walking out front; a ship appeared and drew closer, closer, until a man dove overboard, cutting cleanly into the water. He swam steadily, this man, with sure strokes, until at last he reached the shallow water, whereupon he stood and waded toward shore, seawater streaming from his hair. "Grace!" he called. "Gracelin!" He waved one arm high in the air, and she could have wept because there he was, striding toward her, larger than life itself, and so real she could hear the echo of his voice. She closed her eyes and willed the dream to continue, moved the two people closer together, placed them in the arms of each other, listened to them ask for forgiveness—the one for having died, the other for . . . for what? She opened her eyes. For having married the wrong man in the very beginning—but it had given her Mary Kathleen; for having not gone to Morgan in prison—but she had been heavy with his child; for having left that child behind in Ireland—but the boy was with her now, and he'd been saved from blindness. And yet, her heart cried out to be forgiven—for what, for what?

She gazed at the flickering candlelight, at the shadows dancing on the wall, here on the far side of America. "Ah," she breathed aloud. Because she was going to give her heart to another—one who lived, who was flesh and blood. Because she was about to let go of the dream, the beautiful dream, though she could imagine living alone in a little cabin by the sea, keeping warm with that dream all the rest of her days.

"Forgive me," Grace whispered to the corners of the ceiling. "I've the children to think of—my girl, our boy. Forgive me, love." She tasted the salt of her tears. " 'Tis time we got on with our lives."

Four

Sean O'Malley was nearing the end of his watch. Knowing he'd be unable to sleep, he'd volunteered to take the first half of the night; when it was time to wake up Danny Young for the second half, Sean would be ready to go. He sat against a small boulder in the middle of the desert, pistol in his lap, rifle by his side, guarding his brothers and the gold they were taking back to Utah. Tired, he tipped his head back and peered into the clear black sky, watching the heavens shift above and wondering if he was about to free his soul or damn himself for all eternity.

It was not too late: He could simply go to sleep after his watch, wake up in the morning, and return with the others to Deseret. Marcy would be waiting for him there. But so would Josette. Would he be able to take the girl as his second wife in accordance with the prophet's dictates? Was Celestial Marriage really what God wanted for his people? When Brigham Young had announced that this was God's direct command to his people, Sean, like so many others, had wrestled deeply with it. And even though he knew his mind was made up, he still wrestled, for he had yet to act upon his decision.

He tore his heavy eyes away from the night sky and looked around at the splayed bodies of his slumbering brothers—all married men, like himself, all Saints of the finest and most committed standing. These men were not plagued by doubt; some of them had already been sealed to three and even four women. Brigham Young had led the way, boasting of his many wives in an address to the territorial legislature and predicting that soon the wisdom of Celestial Marriage would be proclaimed by intelligent people the world over. Joseph Smith—the man who recorded God's will in the Doctrine and Covenants—had taken more than thirty wives, though most in secret, believing that the hearts of his followers were not yet ready for such a challenging revelation.

By all accounts given to Sean, Smith had been a strong and charismatic leader who, despite seventeen years of persecution and calamity, had managed to grow his church to over fifteen thousand souls. The city of Nauvoo, Illinois, which Smith had established for his community, was second only to Chicago in size, though it had become a different kind of city by the time Sean arrived under cover of night, wanted for murder in New York and running from the law. Most of the Saints had already begun their trek to the Great Basin, where Brigham Young was building his Kingdom in the Wilderness, and the atmosphere was full of excitement and urgency. Wagonloads of Mormon families daily crossed the Mississippi in order to join the stream of pioneers going west to Utah, to Oregon, to California. The people of the One True Faith would have stayed in Illinois, and gladly, Sean realized, had Smith won his 1844 bid for presidency of the United States; he already had control of the Nauvoo Legion, a well-armed and highly disciplined militia nearly half the size of the entire American army. With his victory, Mormonism might well have become the national religion, though what that would have meant in the end, Sean could only speculate.

Certainly, the Saints were the hardest-working people he'd ever met. Nauvoo, built across a limestone flat and malarial swamp land on the banks of the muddy Mississippi River, was a testament to that. And though the church splintered upon the assassination of Smith—jailed for destruction of property and treason—it did not crumble. News of Smith's death had caused a scramble for control of the church, and those who'd become disillusioned by what were then rumors of plural marriage had their pick of newly emerged leaders. Emma Smith, Joseph's original wife, and their eleven-year-old son, Joseph Smith, Jr., were among the seven hundred who'd become "Strangites," followers of James Jesse Strang. Strang claimed many similarities to Joseph Smith: He, too, had been anointed leader of the church by the angel Moroni and had also discovered a series of pages—though brass, not gold— which he claimed were supplemental to the Book of Mormon. Strang's followers had established a colony on Beaver Island, off the northwest coast of Michigan's lower pennisula, where they could be guided by their prophet. According to the Saints Sean knew, Strang was nothing more than a power-mad charlatan, and they were well rid of him. Those with any sense at all had stayed the course with a steady hand and followed the Lion, Brigham Young, out to Utah Territory.

Those with any sense. Sean sighed and shifted his weight, massaging the leg that always ached, the shoulder and arm that were never completely without pain. He had never known Joseph Smith, who died at the hands of the Illinois militia and became an instant martyr for his people, but he was familiar with the man's history, as was every good Saint. Thanks to past friends at the New York City paper, Sean probably knew more than most about Smith's murky past—his dealings in the occult, the professed divination of buried treasure through crystal-ball gazing and seer stones, his clandestine affairs with young girls, and the arrests for fraud—but this had simply made him more fascinating. Wasn't the Old Testament awash with greatly flawed men whom God still clearly loved and blessed, and couldn't Joseph Smith be a modern-day version of such? At the time, Sean had answered with a resounding "yes"; now he simply did not know.

The occasional flicker of campfire light illuminated the countenances of the men whose faith was far greater than his: Danny Young, Jedidiah Watts, Rulon Frink, Tom LaBaron. These men would return to Utah with their hard-won gold, thereby laying up in Heaven a far greater treasure, would return to wives and take other wives as God decreed through the prophet, never doubting, simply doing as they were directed because they believed what they were told—that they were God's own special people, peculiar unto Him. But Sean was not. Peculiar, perhaps, because of his spiritual blindness, his lack of wisdom and understanding, but certainly not special.

In Nauvoo, Sean had heard the fearsome tales of persecution and massacre that had driven the Saints out of Missouri and into Illinois. Even there, despite their industry, they had been mistrusted and disliked for their clannishness and superior attitude, and—after Joseph's death—the governor had warned that he could no longer offer them protection against mob violence. Fed up with the government at large, Brigham Young had decided to lead his followers into the wilderness, to the seemingly inhospitable desert land of the Great Basin, where they would no longer be subject to the laws of corrupt men. The end of the Mexican-American War had changed all that, when Utah became a territory under the dictates of the United States government. Though Brigham Young was then unable to establish a strictly Mormon country with himself as president and prophet, he continued to thwart any kind of government regulation. Once gold was discovered in California, however, the days of private community were over; nearly every week saw wagon trains passing through on their way to more earthly riches. Sean had watched with grudging admiration as Brigham Young turned a calamity into prosperity by charging exorbitant rates for food and supplies, quickly refilling Deseret's coffers. With new Saints arriving in a steady stream from the East—even from England and France, where converts were made daily—money was needed to build houses, establish farmland, and purchase animals, and this was a way to get it. Kingdom building was hard work, but the Saints had set themselves to the task with signature industry and optimism.

This was the Utah Territory Sean had ridden into after a grueling overland journey by wagon train. Mister Osgoode, his employer in New York and the man for whom Sean had risked life and limb in securing his release from jail, had been given one of the nicer homes in the community; here, Sean and Osgoode's daughter Marcy were quickly ensconced as man and wife. Because the man Sean was accused of killing had been shot during a mob riot that had threatened the lives of Osgoode and several other Mormons, Sean was greeted with warm enthusiasm and treated as a kind of celebrity. The leaders of the community had lost no time in pulling him into their midst in order to make use of his brilliant mind, and Sean had been plunged immediately into the exciting work of laying out and running a colony. His ability to not only grasp a concept but implement it, to organize the accounting and establish a system of order, made him prized by Brigham Young and the upper echelon—the Quorum of Twelve. They could not praise him enough, and he worked his hardest for them, day in and day out, not realizing how quickly time was slipping by.

In those free moments when his thoughts were his own, Sean had convinced himself that his sister Grace either had remained in New York City with the Ogues or was on her way to Utah. He'd written to tell her of his marriage to Marcy and of his meaningful work and to urge her to bring the children out; these letters he'd handed himself to Porter Rockwell, who'd ridden the mail from Utah to Missouri, where they had a mail contract with the U.S. postmaster. The absence of a reply had not worried him; mail notoriously went awry in these days of Indian attacks, bandit robberies, barge sinkings, and warehouse fires; he simply wrote again and trusted that not only would one of his letters get through to her, but one from her would surely find him.

Nearly an entire year had passed before he'd learned the truth from a group of Saints recently quit of New York. Had he not heard of the terrible fires that burned half the city that last summer? they'd asked him after he inquired of them. The Harp and Hound was one of the first to go. Yes, they'd been sure. An Irish saloon, and everyone had perished. Not everyone, a single man had corrected, for he believed the owner and his wife had escaped the flames, but not a serving girl who lived with them nor anyone else. Some in this group were Irish—Sean had known the words were true the moment he'd heard them spoken.

He could remember even now the terrible sinking feeling that had come upon him, could remember stumbling back to the house and collapsing on the stair, head in hands, willing the world to right itself and now. Marcy had tried to console him, then had let him alone. Mister Osgoode, several bishops, many of his friends, had all attempted to relieve his grief; Brigham Young himself had tried to persuade Sean to have Grace and Mary Kate baptized by proxy so that they could enjoy the fruits of their brother's labors in the next life. Sean had simply shaken his head, not wanting to explain that Grace and her daughter had been baptized at their births, as had he, and were most certainly already with their beloved Lord and savior. He did not want to enter into a long discussion of Joseph Smith and the rose-colored glasses, the gold plates that were never seen again, the subsequent and ongoing revelations that appeared to direct a man more clearly than he could ever direct himself. He had not wanted to hear any of it, and Brigham Young had quietly excused himself, leaving Sean alone with his grief. As he stood, looking out the window at his prophet's retreat, Sean had felt a sharp puncture in the bottom of what he thought must surely be his soul, and then the slow, cold trickle of religion slipping away, one tiny grain at a time. Even now, sitting under the dark bountiful heavens, he could trace it to that exact moment.

In the months that had followed, Sean had felt as though he were walking in his sleep. All desire left him, and Marcy—who wanted nothing more than to start their family—was bitterly disappointed when he rolled away from her at night and feigned sleep. It had been during this time that Brigham Young announced God's intention for all men to practice Celestial Marriage; Marcy's father had immediately taken two wives and moved them into another house, with rooms for each wife and for those to come, along with prospective children. Other men quickly followed suit, and Sean felt his dream state fall away, leaving him with brittle clarity. The community he'd loved and worked so hard to build now seemed false and alien to him; to realize he'd left his sister and Mary Kathleen behind for this, had sacrificed them for *this*, was more than he could bear, and he began to contemplate the end of his own life.

Needing to light a fire again in their faithful servant, Brigham Young had informed Sean that God had chosen a second wife for him; she was Josette Beauchamp, the fourteen-year-old daughter of French immigrants who had come to the faith in their own country and then made the arduous journey, first to America, and then to Utah. God had decreed it and her family was honored, the prophet informed him; he must do his duty, for each man needed at least three wives in order to reach eternity. Sean had balked. Josette was a child, he'd argued, and he already had a wife. But Marcy had sided against him—hadn't Sean told her the story of Grace's own arranged marriage at a young age? Girls often married young, and it was a blessing as they were able to help the first wife with chores and could bear babies more easily. Sean had put his hands over his ears, not wanting to hear another word.

Yes, Grace had been fifteen when their father arranged her marriage to Squire Donnelly, sixteen when they actually wed, and for the first time—looking at Josette—Sean realized how very young that had been, how much responsibility Grace had shouldered for her family, and how remarkable a woman she'd become. She would have been aghast at his taking a second wife, let alone one of such tender age. She would have deemed false any religion that sold such precious commodity at will, would have followed him up and down the stairs, in and out of rooms, wagging her finger at him and talking until she was hoarse.

He couldn't help but smile to think of it, could almost hear her scolding, "Are you going to use the mind God so blessed you with, Sean O'Malley, or have you turned that over to the church, as well? Daft eejit," she'd mutter, and he echoed her words now.

"O'Malley," Danny Young whispered from the next bedroll. " 'Tis a sign of sure madness, you know, sitting in the dark, muttering away."

"Maybe I'm praying," Sean whispered back.

"I doubt it." Danny propped himself up on one elbow. "I've not seen you pray the whole time we've been here."

"Have you not?" Sean replied. "For it seems I've been in continual discourse with Himself since the moment we left."

"To what end?" Danny asked.

Sean eyed his old friend carefully. "Do you really want to know?"

Danny looked down and rubbed his fingers in the fine dirt of the desert floor. "Aye," he said quietly.

"I'll not be going back with you in the morning."

Overhead, a nighthawk soared across the face of the moon, letting out its eerie cry. *I said it aloud,* Sean thought. *It's true now.*

Danny pulled himself into a sitting position, arms around his knees. "You've not been yourself, brother." He glanced at the other men to make sure they still slept. "Losing Grace was a blow, but it doesn't mean you have to lose your faith, as well."

"Ah, but I already have," Sean confessed, "though not for lack of trying to hang on." He stopped. "You know, Danny, you're the only one who knew Grace a'tall."

"Aye, she was grand—best there ever was." Danny nodded soberly. "Those were the days, were they not? You and your sister working in Ogue's, meeting you there for a pint before the big rallies, you stirring 'em up for the Cause. Aye, and the dances after, the boxing down in Jersey, racing day and all . . ."

"Not very Saintly activities." Sean laughed quietly.

"I'd be lying to say I don't miss it sometimes," Danny allowed. " 'Twas a grand city and grand times, but killing me it was, every day taking a little more out of me. You remember what it was to be Irish in that town."

"Aye—'Monkey-face,' 'Papist bastards,' and the ever-popular 'Need Not Apply,' " Sean recalled.

Danny nodded. "The Saints have been good to us, Sean, you know they have. They never did care if we were poor or Irish—"

"Or crippled." Sean lifted his arm.

"Aye, or none of that. The Points, for all its rot, was a step up from Limerick for me, but I'd never rise above two rooms rented and full of hungry kids." He paused. "Throwing in with this lot here was the smartest thing I ever did—and you, as well, Sean; you, as well!"

"Can you be sure?"

"Well, just look at us, man! We got our own homes—not just a couple of rooms over someone's saloon, but a real house and farmland, cows and chickens and all. No rent to pay, and help when we need it. And a wife! Who would've ever thought that myself—poor, ragged Danny Young with barely a dollar in his pocket—might live like a lord with acres of land and wives by my side."

"Ah." Sean raised his finger. "There's the rub. Wife, I can accept. Wives, I cannot."

Danny hugged his knees more tightly and leaned forward. "God's commands aren't always easy to follow, my brother, but to my way of thinking, this is one of the better ones! All those Old Testament prophets had plenty of wives—'tis right there in the Bible, plain as the nose on your face!"

"Aye," Sean agreed. "But the model for marriage is in the Garden of Eden, is it not? And I don't see that God created Adam and Eve and Eve's cousin, Evelyn."

Danny frowned, and Sean knew he'd struck a low blow. Danny's two wives were lovely girls, cousins, true enough, and there was no doubt he loved them both. There were babies about the place now, cows and chickens, a solid house, and Danny was respected in the community for his hard work and dedication. It was Danny who'd persuaded the quorum to let Sean accompany the married men on their expedition for gold, Danny who had argued that the change would do Sean good, would clear his head and set him to rights again. Sean had not married Josette before he left, but he'd promised to do so upon his return. He'd made a lot of promises that Danny had adamantly supported, and now his old friend would have to answer for it when he came home without Sean.

"I don't want to quarrel with you, Danny Young," Sean said gently. "You're right—you're better off for having joined up. Here I owe you so much and I'm repaying it by jeopardizing everything you have. Will you be all right?"

"Course I will." Danny shrugged it off. "I'm known for my strong back, but simple mind—when push comes to shove, I'll tell them I was a poor match for your silver tongue. No way to talk you out of the biggest mistake you could ever make."

"Is that what you really think?"

"I think you think too much," Danny said simply. "And it gets in the way of your happiness. I think I also knew you wouldn't be coming back with us in the end."

"Then why in Heaven's name did you argue my case before the council?" Sean asked incredulously. "They absolutely didn't want me to be included in this work party."

"I'm the one brought you into the Saints," Danny stated. "And if 'twas causing your misery, then I had to be the one got you out."

Sean was silent for a moment, studying the man before him. "You're a better friend than I've ever been to you."

"Not true. You and I stood shoulder to shoulder many a time, and haven't we lived through something the rest of the world knows nothing of?" Danny looked Sean in the eye. "We Irish are survivors, and so, my friend, 'tis time you moved on. Don't waste another day mourning what you can't get back. Find a way to live, and then get on with it. Life is too short, and you know that better than most."

"Simple mind, eh?" Sean said wryly, though he was moved. "That was a fine bit of wisdom."

"Aye, so don't let it go to waste—might be my only one." Danny laughed softly.

"Morgan was never a great one for talk, either. So when he had something to say, I listened. You're like that."

"You flatter me, Sean. I'm nothing like the great man himself, but thanks. I know you loved him."

Sean nodded, then looked down. "I left him, though. Got on a ship without him and left him on his own when he needed me most."

"You travel with too many ghosts, my brother. 'Twasn't your fault he died, no more than you're to blame for Grace."

Sean's face grew still. "Truer words were never spoken." He stood and tucked his pistol into his belt, pocketing the extra bullets, then handed over the rifle. " 'Tis your watch now, Danny, but of course I was gone when you woke up—left you all unprotected in the middle of the night."

"Any man knows you, knows you never would," Danny said matter-of-factly. "But if that's the story, I'll tell it. Will you not wait 'til dawn?"

Sean glanced up at the sky, which had softened in the east. "Nearly here, anyway." He put out his hand. "Good-bye, Danny. I hope to see you again someday."

Danny took the hand, then pulled Sean into a brief, hard hug before letting him go.

"Won't be the same without you. Not enough Irish in the place yet to keep the talk lively." His smile faltered. "God go with you, Sean O'Malley, and I hope you find what you're looking for. Where to, then? Back to Sacramento, or all the way to the wicked big city?"

"I don't know yet," Sean replied. "West. I'm only going west." He laughed softly. "Tir na nog, and all that."

"There's always hope in the land of the young. But you better take a horse," Danny added. " 'Tis a long walk into the past."

Sean considered it. "I suppose I'll never make it with this bad leg. I'll take the old mare, 'cause she ain't what she used to be." He winked. "And that makes two of us." He went over to where the horses were tethered, soothing them as they began to nicker.

"I'll give you a hand." Danny picked up a saddle and fit it over the blanket Sean had placed on the mare's back, cinching it firmly beneath her belly. "Best lead her a ways out before you climb on," he whispered, handing the reins to Sean. "And take this, as well." He pulled a leather pouch out of his pocket. "You dug; the money's yours. I'll say you stole it." He grinned.

Sean held the pouch in the cup of his hand, feeling the weight of it. "I don't know."

"Look," Danny insisted. "You're Irish and you're crippled—can't send you out poor, as well. Remember the parable of the talents and do something with this. Write me a letter one day. You know I'll be starving for a good story."

Sean laughed quietly. "Deal," he said and pocketed the gold. "Good-bye, my brother."

Rulon turned over in his sleep, and the other men began to stir.

"Go on with you, now. Hurry, before they wake," Danny whispered urgently.

Sean put his hat on his head and led the mare carefully past the edge of the camp, out of the ring of light, then mounted her. He turned in the saddle to lift his hand to the only man who really knew him anymore, a man he was leaving behind as he'd left so many, and as the sun began to rise, he turned his back on that man, too, and rode off.

Five

"Why?" Jack asked as the cart pulled them slowly up the hill to the Wakefield house.

"Well, because we're going to live there now." Grace put an arm around his stiff shoulders. "For the time being, at any rate."

"Why?"

"Do you remember what I told you this morning?" Grace reminded him patiently. "Doctor Wakefield has given me a job of work in his house. I'm to be the cook and—"

"Like in Kansas?" Jack interrupted.

"Aye. Only I won't be so busy because there's only the doctor and his sister, and we'll live there, as well, you see."

"I miss Kansas," Jack said wistfully, looking away down the hill and out across the sparkling bay.

"I know you do." Grace squeezed his shoulders gently.

"But where will we live?" He turned to her again.

Grace sighed and counted to five. "In the doctor's house. In our own rooms next to the kitchen. Listen, young Jack, 'tis all settled and I don't want you to worry anymore."

"Will I see Sam and them again?" he asked plaintively. "What about our wagon? And where's my gun?" He tugged on her sleeve. "Where's my gun, Mam, that Jimbo give me?"

"In the trunk that Lily has," *and please, God, could he just forget about that?*

Grace hadn't been happy with Jimbo Dread's parting gift to young Jack, but the boy had gone into raptures over it, refusing to get into the wagon until she'd lifted the lid of the trunk to prove it was there. They were well rid of characters like that young gunfighter, she thought, though she couldn't help but feel a fondness for any man who showed her son affection. At least Dread's present was useful—not like the giant buffalo head one of the wranglers had given him, a gift that had to be left behind for lack of space in the wagon.

"You'll see Sam again, once we're settled. Ruth, as well, and Mary. And Sol. Lily will sell the wagon and team for us, then use the money to send down the rest of our things. And we can write them a letter right away, tell them where we're living now."

"So we're not going to make a farm?" Jack's eyes darkened.

"No. We're going to stay in the city. You'll like it here, Jack—the doctor has a nice house with land around it."

"But there aren't any trees," Jack pointed out. "Not any in the whole city!"

" 'Tis a bare place that way," she agreed, looking out at the brown hills. "But the doctor says there's good hunting to the east, and he's got a pond on his place. Dogs and horses, as well," she added the clincher.

Jack brightened considerably. "Horses? And dogs? Why didn't you say, woman?"

Grace heard a snort from Mister Litton, who was driving the team back up the hill, though to his credit, the man did not comment or turn around. She looked her son squarely in the eye and pushed as much warning into her voice as she could muster.

"You listen here, Jack McDonagh—I'm your mam, and if you ever call me 'woman' again, I'll take you down a peg or two, do you hear me, now?"

"Aye, Mam." Jack's head dipped contritely, but in a moment the transgression was forgotten and he perked up again. "Will I ride the horses, Mam?"

"I think they're meant for the wagon and the doctor's carriage. But we'll see," Grace added, not wanting to squash his hope. "Doctor Wakefield's a gracious man and perhaps he'll take you for a ride one day. You mustn't ask him, though, Jack," she warned. "I'm a"—she hesitated, not wanting to use the word "servant"—"a cook in the house; I work for him now, and we must keep to ourselves and not bother him in his own home or we'll find ourselves looking for another place to live."

Jack nodded as if he understood, and Grace was relieved. Keeping him occupied and out from underfoot was going to be her greatest challenge, but she'd already considered ways to keep him busy. If Mister Litton was agreeable, Jack could help in the stable for part of each day, and also in the garden if they had one, as it would need putting to bed come winter.

The street turned into a road and then into a private drive that curved around one side of the house, taking them to the back entrance. It was a wide, solid-looking place, Grace thought; large but manageable; wood and stone, plenty of windows on the first floor, fewer on the second, and a scattering of small dormers on the third. The roof rose to a high pitch, and from the side Grace saw a window high up under the eaves; an attic, then, she hoped—an attic was the best place to dry clothes during the cold and wet months, and she had missed having one in Kansas. The house was situated on the top of a series of gently sloping hills, with a view of the city below and the busy harbor. It was a relief to be out of the confines of the hospital and away from the confusing streets; up here, the air was sweet and salty both, and she could hear birdsong and the rustling of the breeze in the long, dry grass.

Mister Litton pulled the horses up in a circular yard, then got down and lifted out Grace's trunk, which he then carried into the house. Grace got out, holding firmly to Jack's hand, and went the way of Mister Litton, entering a wide back door that opened into a mudroom and then into a large, disordered kitchen. They raised their eyes simultaneously to the ceiling, as from somewhere above voices rose in argument.

There were two voices: the high, sobbing sound of a woman, clearly upset, and the low, soothing murmur of a man. Though Grace could not understand any of what was being said, she suspected that this argument had to do with her new position in the house. *We might not be staying after all,* she said to herself, regretting that she'd gotten Jack's hopes up before all was said and done. When something hit the floor and smashed, she and Jack looked at each other.

"Will we have a look at the garden, then, son?" Grace suggested, taking his hand again.

Jack nodded, eyes blue-black behind the winking glass of his spectacles. Grace led him back out into the sunlight, where they stood for a moment beside the wagon.

"There's the stable, Mam."

He pointed out the building, which was finely kept, as far as Grace could see. In fact, the entire yard was quite orderly and all the out-buildings well maintained. Whatever else Mister Litton might be, Grace thought, he was an excellent groundskeeper.

"Ah, Missus Donnelly, there you are." Doctor Wakefield—a fine springer spaniel at his heel—hurried into the yard, shrugging on his jacket and straightening his vest. "Please forgive me for not greeting you properly when you arrived." His face was flushed and his hair unkempt; the latter he attempted to push into place with his fingers. "I'm, uh . . . I'm afraid my sister is not having one of her better days. Her nerves are especially bad, and she fears a commotion in the house will be more than she can bear."

"I understand," Grace said carefully. "That's a lovely dog you have there, Doctor. Might Jack play with her a bit while we talk?"

Wakefield looked from his dog to the boy. "Why, yes, of course. Of course he may. Her name is Scout," he told Jack. "She's very good on command. She'll fetch sticks if you throw for her. Go easy on her, though," he added. "She's expecting a litter."

Jack nodded happily and picked up the nearest piece of branch, waving it to get the dog's attention. "Here, Scout—c'mon, Scout!"

The dog looked up at her master. "Go on, girl," he commanded affectionately, pointing toward where Jack had run.

They watched Scout fetch a few of Jack's ill-aimed throws, and then the doctor cleared his throat.

"I see Litton's already carried in your trunk. Have you been inside the house yet?"

"Only the kitchen," Grace reported. "We were waiting for you there but then came away to see the gardens."

"Ah." Wakefield squinted and looked down. "Missus Donnelly, I . . ."

Grace shook her head. "You've no need to explain anything to me, Doctor. The running of your house is your own affair. Would you like to reconsider your offer before we get ourselves settled in?"

He looked up, surprised. "Absolutely not. Would you?"

"No," she said firmly.

Relief showed in his eyes. "Well, that's fine, then. Why don't you come with me, Missus Donnelly, and I'll introduce you to Hopkins. She'll show you the rest of the house."

Grace called to Jack, telling him to stay put until she came for him, then went into the kitchen, where she was introduced to a woman much older than herself.

"Welcome to Wakefield Heights." The woman's accent still held a trace of northern England, or Scotland, perhaps, though Grace could not quite tell.

"For want of a name," Wakefield explained sheepishly, then rubbed his hands together briskly. "Well, I leave you in capable hands." He backed out of the room. "Let Hopkins know if there's anything you need in the way of your rooms, Missus Donnelly, and I will have it seen to right away. Oh, by the way!" His face was suddenly boyish. "We have a cow! Litton has made a place for her next to the stable."

Hopkins shook her head and made a little whooshing noise as if to say the whole thing was nonsense, but Wakefield ignored her.

"Whatever you need," he repeated expansively.

"Thank you. Sir," Grace added, though with difficulty.

She'd told herself that it meant nothing to be the servant of another, that it was simply a position and one she was enormously fortunate to have been offered, but now she realized she'd been fooling herself; it did mean something. Grace had grown up in a time of masters and servants, in a class society she'd thought was well behind her; indeed, hadn't she once been mistress of a manor house with servants of her own? Though she had never thought of the Sullivans as servants—not Bridget, who'd helped deliver her twin babies, Mary Kate and Michael Brian, and then had helped her bury the infant boy; and certainly not young Nolan, who'd saved Grace's life on that terrible winter's night, only to lose his own at the hand of the squire. No, not servants—more like family, inexorably woven into the drama of daily living. Is that what she would become here? Grace wondered. She hoped not. She did not want to be subsumed into the life of another family, only to create and sustain a family life that was wholly her own, one that gave her children a sense of who they were in the world.

"Missus Donnelly? Did you hear me?"

Grace returned instantly to the present, realizing that Hopkins had been opening and closing cupboard doors the entire time and explaining their contents.

"Yes. Thank you. It's a good kitchen."

"It should be. I have arranged it myself." Hopkins led Grace through a door that opened into a small passageway. "Here are your quarters, then." She pushed open a second door, revealing a large, sunny room with a smaller area attached. "Furnished, as you can see."

The bed in its simple wooden frame was easily big enough for Grace and Mary Kate; there would be room to put a cot for Jack next to it. In the larger area, there was a cupboard for personal crockery, a table and chairs, plus a bench under the window that afforded a pretty view out the back to the garden. Grace could already see Mary Kate sitting there, wrapped in her shawl, watching the day until she was well enough to be out in it herself. A small hearth would keep them all plenty warm.

"Aye, that'll do." Grace was pleased.

Hopkins sniffed. "I should certainly think so. All this room to yourself and no need to share it with your cow."

Grace bit her tongue. She would strive to put one good meal on the table for the doctor before she put this woman in her place.

"The children and I will be very comfortable," she said evenly.

Hopkins frowned. "Children?"

"My son is just there, playing with the doctor's dog." Grace waved to him out the window. "And my daughter's still in hospital, though she'll be coming any day, now the fever's left her."

"Two children? In this house? And one of them sick?" Hopkins seemed so incredulous that Grace half expected her to put a hand over her heart and go into a swoon. "Is Doctor Wakefield aware of this?"

"Oh, aye. 'Twas all his idea."

Hopkins shook her head. "No, this will never do."

"I know your mistress is unwell, but she won't even know we're here, aside from the fine meals coming her way."

"Miss Abigail requires absolute peace and quiet," Hopkins stated proprietarily. "Not even the doctor knows how she suffers, or he'd never have allowed this. Children are dirty and noisy, and ill-mannered, especially those of . . ." She eyed the old, patched dress and worn boots Grace had put on in place of the trousers and moccasins.

"Those of what?" Grace pulled herself up to her full height so that she stood nose to nose with the housekeeper.

Hopkins took a step back, then glanced again at Jack out in the yard. "Of such a young age," she amended with a tight smile. "Most difficult to keep in hand."

"You leave my children to me," Grace warned quietly. "And I'll keep them well away from your mistress. And from you. Count on that."

"Fine." Hopkins pursed her lips. "Now"—she led the way back into the kitchen—"you'll want to see the rest of the house. Oh, good, Enid, there you are. This is Missus Donnelly, the new cook. Missus Donnelly, my daughter, Enid."

Grace smiled at the young woman, who bobbed her head shyly. Enid looked a great deal like her mother, even to hair and dress, but beneath the stern exterior her manner was more gentle; Grace could see that immediately.

"How do you do, Enid?" Grace put out her hand. "I believe the doctor told me you were maid to his sister?"

Enid blushed. "I help mother with Miss Abigail and see to the rest of the house. As well, I've been doing the cooking."

" 'Tis a big job of work, that. And you've kept the kitchen in fine shape," Grace commended.

"It's yours now, and welcome to it." Enid gave a great sigh of relief. "I've plenty of other work needs catching up."

"Missus Donnelly brings two children into the house with her," Hopkins reported. *"Two."*

"Oh!" Enid's face lit up, but she immediately corrected the show of emotion. "Oh," she repeated, more soberly now. "Does Miss Wakefield know?"

"She may. If not, I'll have to tell her." Hopkins glanced at the timepiece pinned to her shirtwaist. "She'll want her morning drink now, Enid. Go and ask her—tea or coffee."

Enid hesitated, then jumped when a bell began to ring.

"Go on, now," her mother shooed. "Don't make her wait! Not that way," she ordered as Enid started for the door. "The back hall."

Enid turned on her heel and headed toward Grace's new quarters but then made a sharp left in the narrow hallway.

"There's a stair, leads to the chambers above," Hopkins informed

Grace. "She's a flighty girl, Enid, tends to forget these things. Servants are to be invisible, to use the back stair."

"Are you from England, then, Missus Hopkins?" Grace asked. "Were you in service there?"

Hopkins drew herself up proudly. "I was. At a fine country house in the North. Started in the kitchen, but moved up—under maid, then upper. Would've held the keys had I stayed, but I married the Reverend Mister Hopkins and that ended my career."

"Is he living, your husband?"

"He brought us all out here with a mind to ministering to the godless Chinese." Hopkins' eyes darkened briefly, and a muscle at her jawline twitched. "It did him in, in the end."

"I'm sorry. I'm widowed, as well."

"Are you?" Hopkins replied coolly. "Surprising how many come off the boats calling themselves 'Widow This' or 'Missus That'—prostitutes, most of them, but who can tell in a city like this?"

Grace felt her blood begin to boil; she was about to speak when Enid rushed in from the back hall and dashed to the cupboard.

"Tea," the girl announced, lifting down a china pot.

"That is Missus Donnelly's job now," Hopkins directed.

Enid paused, hand midair, and looked from her mother to Grace and back again.

"But she's only just come. Still got her coat on! She don't even know where everything is yet."

"I have shown her." Hopkins removed the pot from her daughter's hand and held it out to Grace while still talking to Enid. "I would like you to finish dusting the doctor's study now he's gone out, and then come back for the tray."

"Yes, Mother." Enid shot Grace a look of apology.

"It'll be ready in a quarter of an hour." Grace smiled at the girl, unruffled. "Thank you, Enid."

Enid blushed and backed out of the room.

"Well, I'll leave you to it. Perhaps this afternoon will be a better time to see the rest of the house, though certainly there's no need as your duties are confined to the kitchen," Hopkins pointed out.

"Don't worry about me," Grace said breezily, taking off her coat and reaching for an apron. "I'll see it on my own whenever I like."

The housekeeper sniffed her disapproval and stood for a moment, then left the kitchen in a decided huff.

Grace was determined to pay her no mind. She checked out the window and saw that Jack was now wrestling around in the grass with the delighted dog, and then she got to work. First, she poured hot water into the pot to take the chill off, swirling it around before emptying it; next, she measured out the tea leaves, then added the boiling water; last, she covered the pot with a quilted cozy to keep it warm. While it steeped, she lay out a tray with linen cloth, cup and saucer, tea strainer, milk pitcher, and sugar bowl, beside which she set a tiny silver spoon.

Rummaging around the food safe and then the cupboard, she came up with a fruited loaf of some kind and a crock of butter that still smelled relatively sweet. She cut two slices off the loaf and buttered them generously, then cut each slice in half and arranged the pieces on a plate. The china was lovely and the silver delicately scrolled—it had been a long time since Grace had handled such fine things, and she remembered the pleasure of it.

Since this was to be a calling card of sorts to Abigail Wakefield, Grace took down a small cut-crystal vase and added it to the tray, then went out to the yard to look for any late flowers. There were a few hardy daisies blooming in a patch by the stable, so she snipped three of them and carried them back to the house. *I guess that sums me up pretty well,* she decided, taking one last look at her handiwork—*tough but friendly.* She was laughing at herself when Enid returned to the kitchen and was rewarded with the girl's wide-eyed expression of surprise and pleasure.

"That's very pretty, Missus Donnelly. Very pretty, indeed!"

"Thank you, but won't you please call me 'Grace'? There aren't so many of us here as to stand on formality, are there?"

"Oh, no, ma'am, I never could." Enid shook her head vigorously. "My mother wouldn't stand for it. No, absolutely not. There is to be no"—she paused, searching for the word—"impropriety," she sounded out slowly. "For it reflects badly on master and servant alike." Pleased that she'd recalled the edict so accurately, Enid smiled.

"Am I to call you Miss Hopkins, then?"

"No, ma'am, as I'm below—Enid'll do." She looked down at the toes of her boots. "Head cook and housekeeper are the same station," she added. "Though I heard the doctor call you Missus Donnelly, while my mother is 'Hopkins' to them above."

"I lived in a manor house once," Grace said, seeing in her mind's eye the grand house of her first husband, the house that would one day be her daughter's to sell or keep, if it still stood.

"Were you cook there, as well, missus?"

"I was a bit of everything there." Grace smiled wryly. "But that was a long time ago. Call me what you like, Enid, but in my book no man or woman is higher than another, all honest work being the same in the eyes of God."

Enid glanced toward the kitchen door. "I wouldn't go sharing that with my mother, Missus Donnelly. You'll not eat a peaceful dinner otherwise. She's set in her ways about things like God and work."

"That's good advice. Though 'tis my table she'll be attending now." Grace grinned. "Best get that up to your mistress before the tea cools."

"Yes, ma'am. Will I meet the bairns later?" Enid asked, a hint of melancholy in her voice.

"Jack's outside there, just there. Mary Kate's still in hospital, but the doctor says she'll soon be well."

"It'll be a nice bit of company with the young ones about the place, though I expect they'll have to keep themselves quiet and out of sight, or we'll be on to looking out another cook in this kitchen. It's always something, you know." Enid lifted the heavy tray. "I'll bring this back down when she's finished with it."

"That'll be fine, Enid; thank you."

Done with the first chore of the new job, Grace went out into the yard and called Jack to her. Together they explored the neatly fenced-in garden, which had already given up its best effort and now harbored mainly gourds of various shapes and sizes—green or yellow squash and orange pumpkin—cabbages, and some root vegetables that would have to be cellared before the first frost. It was a fine garden, Grace thought; Mister Litton was to be commended for coaxing such a thing out of this place.

Taking Jack into the stable was a mistake that took the better part of half an hour to correct, but at last she got him into the kitchen for a meal of the fruited bread and butter and a pared apple from the basket that had appeared mysteriously beside the kitchen door. Promising him another romp with the dog after (if it could be found), she got him to lie down upon the big bed in their new room. Thankfully, miraculously, he fell instantly to sleep. Grace covered him with a blanket and left the door open so he could hear her in the kitchen when he awoke.

Enid had already begun a stew early in the morning, so Grace needed only to ladle this into bowls for those who wanted it. The mistress would have none, she was told, having retreated into sleep, and Mister Litton did not come in, so it was only Enid and her mother who ate a bowl quickly at the table before getting back to their duties. Clearly, Grace had gotten off on the wrong foot with Missus Hopkins, though she sincerely doubted a right one existed; she decided to work on the situation by appealing to the woman's apparent fondness for good food—Missus Hopkins was far more solid in figure than was her willowy daughter, and Grace suspected that a fruit pie here and there, a bit of cream cake now and then, warm puddings, and sweet sauces would make the housekeeper less cantankerous. For the sake of the children and the harmony of the household, Grace was prepared to make an effort.

She sat at the table now, making a list of the provisions she would get at tomorrow's market. There was an account at the butcher's, she'd been told, and Enid knew the best fishmonger stalls. Grace would not need the services of a bakery unless the doctor or his sister requested a particular delicacy, as she had mastered the art of fine baking and could turn out anything once she knew the ingredients. She'd had a look at the stores of flour and sugar, however, and these would need to be replenished. She was looking forward to visiting the market again, as there had been many pieces of produce unfamiliar to her; she assumed these were shipped up from the South fragrant fruits and colorful vegetables, all exorbitantly priced, however—or perhaps they came from the valleys to the east.

Her list completed, Grace set about dinner. From the remains of yesterday's dry chicken and potatoes she fashioned a pot pie to which she added carrots and onions from the garden, covering the lot with a rich gravy sealed beneath her own buttery pastry shell. She would serve that with biscuits and, for after, a bottled fruit compote she'd found on the pantry shelf, though who had bottled it and when, she had no idea, as they'd neglected to label it or leave a note. It would be simple food she prepared tonight, but hearty and nourishing, and after she'd learned more about their eating habits, the meals could be more ambitious. The thought of an abundance of seafood again was enough to spark her memory for recipes she'd not been able to prepare in a very long time.

Thinking of it all made Grace recognize a growing enthusiasm for her new job. Cooking in Kansas had meant beef, beef, and more beef, along with buffalo meat, chickens and eggs, and whatever vegetables she could get from local farmers. She'd missed fresh fish, mussels and clams, grouse and pheasant, venison, crisp apples, juicy pears, wild berries; she hadn't let herself think about it, but now that these things were again available to her, she realized her hunger for them and couldn't wait to reintroduce them to the children.

When Jack arose in the late afternoon, he and Grace carried their carpetbags into the bedroom, then moved the trunk against the wall next to the head of the bed. In her anxiety over Mary Kate, Grace had thrown in only a change of clothing for each of them, medicines, and food for the journey. The one trunk she'd insisted upon bringing, that which she couldn't bear to leave behind, held those things most precious to her, and she resisted the urge to open it right now, to check that everything was still there. She had thought to clean their clothes as soon as she could make time for a wash day, only to be told by Wakefield that she should include her things and the children's with the household wash that went to the laundress every week.

Grace had barely been able to believe her good fortune in that: Wash day in Kansas had meant dragging the two heavy tubs into the yard, building a fire and setting one tub over it to heat the water that was brought up bucket by bucket from the river, filling the other tub with cold water, shaving a bar of lye soap into the hot tub, then adding the clothes in loads—heavy, dark trousers and skirts; blankets and bedding; white undergarments and stockings—to be stirred until they were clean, then rinsed in the cold water, after which they were scrub-rinsed one final time in the river, wrung out, and pegged to dry in the hot sun or freezing air. Backbreaking work, all of it, and that didn't include pressing them with the flatiron. Mary Kate had helped, of course, but Grace had hated to see her little hands burned and reddened by the soap and the boiling water. Now, apparently, Enid would take the household laundry to Wah Lee's Chinese Laundry; Sister Joseph had told Grace that previously the city's laundry had all been sent to the Washerwoman's Lagoon down near Black Point, where it had been pounded and scrubbed by Indian, Mexican, and Chilean laundresses, though now the operations were almost exclusively Chinese. Grace's hands ached just thinking about those women washing clothes day in and day out, and she hoped they were well paid for such arduous work.

She and the children had walked across dusty prairies and through muddy bogs, had waded across dank creeks that smelled like Hell itself, all in the same clothes for weeks on end, but now at last they could settle in, clean themselves down to the skin for once, and dress in things that didn't smell of smoke from the buffalo chips they'd used for fuel, of wood smoke, and of the sweat of beast and owner alike. It would be a relief, Grace had to admit. She hadn't realized how very dirty they all were until Mary Kate was washed in the hospital, the water turning a murky gray as the muck soaked off. Really, she told herself, it was a credit to the doctor that he'd seen their true character beneath the soil and grime, and she renewed her pledge to set his household aright, at least in the manner of its meals.

As evening approached, Grace prepared another tray for Enid to take up to Miss Wakefield, for whom Hopkins had ordered a simple meal of broth. The doctor was not yet returned from hospital, so Grace kept his plate warm while she and Jack sat down at table with Missus Hopkins, Enid, and Mister Litton.

It was an awkward meal at best: Missus Hopkins had little to say, though Grace noticed she ate two servings of the pot pie; Enid was careful around her mother, though she gladly spoke when spoken to and often glanced surreptitiously at Mister Litton, who kept his own eyes firmly on his plate, though he stole a look at Jack once in a while.

"Will you have more, Mister Litton?" Grace asked when his spoon hit the bottom of the bowl.

"No, ma'am. Good eating, though, and thanks."

Litton got up, pulled on his hat, and left by the back door. His lantern was visible bobbing through the dark as he made his way to his rooms over the stable, and when Grace turned back to the table, she noted that Enid had watched his leaving, as well, though when Grace caught her eye, she blushed and looked down.

"I understand Mister Litton was wounded in the Mexican war,"

Grace commented. "I have a brother limps like that. He wears a special shoe on his foot."

"My uncle Sean," Jack put in. "I don't know him yet."

"He didn't come with you to the city?" Enid asked.

"No." Grace scraped up a last bite from the bottom of the bowl onto Jack's spoon, then left it for him to finish. "We were all together in New York, but then he went on to Utah Territory and I've heard nothing from him."

"Probably dead," Hopkins stated matter-of-factly. "Being a cripple and all. No place for cripples out here."

Grace winced, but only Enid noticed.

"Took up with those Mormons, did he?" the housekeeper asked around the chunk of potato in her mouth.

"Aye. When we passed through there, I asked after him. Mostly they didn't know who he was."

Grace paused, seeing the tiny, well-run towns clearly in her mind; the citizens of each had eagerly restocked the pioneer wagons with over-priced goods, but no such eagerness was forthcoming when it had come to answering questions about missing relatives who might have joined their number.

"There was one man thought he'd come here with a mining party, another said he'd gone back to New York, and a third said he'd gone up into Canada."

"They're all mad," Hopkins pronounced. "Crazy as loons. Got a nest of them here—Sam Brannan and his. Don't appear to have more than one wife each, but you can't be too sure. A closemouthed, clannish bunch. Prideful. Pride is a terrible sin, Enid—you remember that," she instructed her daughter.

"Mister Brannan is awfully nice, though," Enid ventured, "always puts his head around the corner to say hello when he comes visiting the master."

Grace put down her spoon, considering. "Do you think he might know something of my brother?" she asked hopefully. "Especially if he came out here to mine."

"Doubt it." Hopkins tongued a bit of gravy from the corner of her mouth. "His lot broke with them in the desert long ago. Goes his own way now, does Sam Brannan. Made a name for himself here, and not likely to share it with that other devil, Brigham Young."

"You could ask him anyway," Enid suggested, earning a look of gratitude from Grace. "Next time he comes."

Hopkins scowled at her daughter. "Quit prattling on, Enid. Time to draw the curtains and turn down the beds." She stood. "Enid will bring down the tray from upstairs. We will retire until the doctor is safely in, and then we'll bank the fires and put out the lamps. You are responsible for the stove and the lamps in here, of course."

"Of course," Grace echoed. "Thank you, Missus Hopkins. What time will you want your breakfast in the morning?"

"We rise at six. Breakfast for the servants at seven, the master at eight or nine, depending. Miss Wakefield has her coffee at ten."

Hopkins nudged her daughter with a sharp elbow to the ribs, then jerked her chin at Jack, whose head lay on his outstretched arm.

"Boy's used to sleeping anywhere, eh, Enid? Don't have proper beds in Ireland, you know. They sleep on the floor beside the animals for warmth. That is, until they get enough children to keep them warm, then the pigs have to shove over!" She laughed harshly and jabbed her daughter again.

Grace put a hand protectively on Jack's shoulder. "You've never been to Ireland, I guess, or you'd know we have all kinds of living for all kinds of people, same as anywhere."

"Never been, never will," Hopkins retorted stiffly. "My Richard was killed in that cursed place. Went over as a soldier to help the miserable papists and got his throat cut for it."

"I'm sorry for that," Grace said with quiet dignity. "I lost most of my own family in that time, as well, so I know how you suffer with it. And now, if you'll excuse me, I'll put my boy to bed."

"He's had a long journey." Enid gazed tenderly at the little fellow. "Such a nice lad."

"Lad's a lad," Hopkins declared. "They grow into men and do what they want, with little regard for their mothers. Mind that, missus, and don't waste your affection." She gave Enid a little shove toward the door, then followed her out, and Grace could hear the scolding tone of her voice and the apology of Enid's as both faded away down the hall.

"Going to have a hard time with that one, young Jack," she warned her son in a whisper as she scooped him up into her arms.

Jack roused only long enough to squirm and kick before she placed him on the bed and pulled off his boots, and then he lay like a big rag doll, arms and legs flopping limply as she got the rest of his clothes off him and a nightshirt over his head. There was plenty of bedding, and she tucked the blanket up under his chin, wondering whether he would be warm enough or should she burn a small fire to take the damp off the room.

She decided to wait a while longer and, after kissing his dirty face gently, Grace returned to the kitchen to wash the crockery. She had just finished drying up when she heard Doctor Wakefield's carryall pull into the yard. Through the window, she could see George Litton's lantern held high as the doctor climbed down and then reached back into the seat for something. A moment later, George led the horse and buggy toward the stable and the doctor headed for the house, a bundle in his arms. Grace rushed to the door and flung it open.

"Here she is, Missus Donnelly," Wakefield announced, passing through the kitchen and going directly into Grace's new rooms. "Oh." Seeing Jack sound asleep on the bed, he immediately lowered his voice. "I'll just put her right here, next to him, shall I?"

Grace nodded, her vision swimming. She went to her daughter's side and looked down into a face still very pale but with a hint of pink from the evening ride.

"Mam." Mary Kate reached for her mother's hand. "I didn't want to stay alone. He said I could come to you."

Grace kissed her daughter's fingers. "I didn't much like going off without you, either, agra, though I knew Sister Joseph would stand over you all night long." She looked up at the doctor. "Thank you so much for bringing her to us. Is she all right, then?"

"Oh, yes." He took off his hat and gloves. "Still requires strict bed rest and steady nourishment to regain her strength, of course, but she's going to be just fine. Aren't you, little lady?"

Mary Kate nodded. "Thank you, sir," she said politely. "This is a very nice house."

The doctor laughed. "Well, honey, there's a little more to it than just this. When you're up and around in a week or so, we'll give you the grand tour." He stopped and sniffed the air. "Missus Donnelly, what is that truly delectable smell? It wouldn't actually be my dinner, would it?"

"Chicken pie and still warm, I'm hoping. Will you eat it in the dining room?"

"If you'll put it on a plate for me, just this once, Missus Donnelly, I do believe I'll take it straight up to my room."

"As you like, Doctor. Be back in a moment, love," she whispered to Mary Kate.

She dished up a generous amount of pie, then poured out a large glass of ale from the pitcher. When she turned around, there he stood, waiting expectantly, hands out to receive his plate.

"Thank you, Missus Donnelly." He bathed his face in the steam that rose from the dish, breathing in deeply. "Thank you, thank you, thank you."

"You're most welcome, sir." She had to laugh. " 'Tis I who should be thanking you, though."

"You're quite comfortable in your accommodations?" he asked solicitously. "I see you need a cot of some sort for the boy. George'll take care of that for you in the morning."

"Thank you, sir. And now you really should go and enjoy your meal. Good night, Doctor."

They smiled at each other, then Grace turned and finished up in the kitchen, wiping off the worktable and putting out the lamps, save the one she used to light her way back into her own rooms. She checked on the children, who were fast asleep, and then realized she herself had no place to lay her head. She laughed softly; well, she'd slept in bunks and hammocks and cots, on ships and wagons and steamboats, on the bare ground and, just this past week, in a chair. She looked around the room—there was always the bench under the window, but oddly, she was no longer tired. In fact, she felt a kind of giddy excitement. *It's because we're all of us well,* she told herself. *We're well and we're fed and we're sheltered and I've work.* They had made it; they were here. From Ireland to America, from the Atlantic all the way to the Pacific—they had come as far as they could; there was nowhere else to go. And now her eyes fell on the one trunk she'd brought with her, and she carried the lamp over to it, sinking to her knees and undoing the latch, lifting the heavy lid and propping it open.

She had not looked at many of these things in a great while, and for a moment she simply ran her fingers over the quilt that covered her treasure, breathed in the smell of old memories. Taking a deep breath, she took out the quilt and wrapped it around her shoulders, then began carefully lifting out her precious things one by one.

Here was the fragile burial cloth she'd embroidered to cover Michael Brian's wee coffin; here was Blossom, the soft and love-worn doll Granna had made for Mary Kate, and this she set aside to give back to her daughter; beneath it lay the cashmere shawl Grace had brought back from her honeymoon in Dublin for her gran, who loved fine things. Next to that was a bundle of picture postcards, tied up in a green hair ribbon, belonging to Grace's mother, Kathleen. Grace untied the ribbon and looked at them now, one after the other, touching their soft papery edges and remembering how they'd looked tacked up on the cabin wall. Her mother had loved to gaze upon them—the Mourne Mountains sweeping down to the sea, the cliffs of Kilkee, the grasslands of the Golden Vale, and the sunset at Bantry Bay. She had told her children all the stories of the Ireland she'd loved so deeply, of the sheer beauty of the land and the special people who dwelled thereon.

Setting these aside, Grace then pulled out her mother's old Bible, which Sean had left behind in New York before he disappeared. Inside, on the flyleaf, was a record of Kathleen's marriage to Patrick O'Malley, followed by the birth and baptism dates of her children—Ryan, Sean, and Gracelin—all written in her fine hand. Below these, Gran had added the marriage dates: Grace's to Bram Donnelly, followed by the birthdate of their children; Ryan's marriage to Aghna, followed by Thomsy's birthdate. No deaths other than that of Mary Kathleen's twin brother, Michael Brian, had been recorded—not Gran's or Grace's father, Patrick's, nor those of Ryan's little family; the only date she knew to enter was Gran's. She sighed and opened the book further. Safe between the pages were the papers that showed Mary Kathleen as daughter of Bram Donnelly and rightful heir of Donnelly House upon her eighteenth birthday. That had taken some doing, Grace recalled wryly, thinking of Brigid and her grandson—now Philip Donnelly—who lived a far better life with Bram's brother in England. Grace wondered if Mary Kate would really ever return to Ireland and take possession of the manor; at the very least, it was property she could someday sell, ensuring a personal income so that she might never be dependent upon anyone

In a corner of the trunk was the wooden box Liam had carved for her—*Mother*, it said, and that still moved her, for she'd not been his mother for long, nor as good a one as she should've been. She hoped that Alice and Seamus, his real parents, could see him now, could see the fine young seaman he'd become under Captain Reinders' tutelage.

Inside the box was a daguerreotype of Mighty Dugan Ogue in his boxing togs; Grace looked at this for a long time, rubbing the knuckle of the finger he'd broken while saving her life. Dugan and Tara had been her most loyal friends in New York, and she still missed the sound of their voices ringing through the busy saloon.

Also folded into Liam's box was a letter that Grace took out now and held to her heart, closing her eyes. *Weep for me and then be done with weeping, for I am watching over you as I never could before.* She knew it all by heart, every word; she had carried it on her person for a very long time, but when Jack was returned to her, she'd been able to pack it away. She packed it away now, next to the ring Morgan's sister Aislinn had given Mary Kate—the ring with the piece of Connemara stone— next to the small gold hoops he'd worn in his ears and the thick gold wedding band Lord Evans had presented him with at the moment of their wedding. The band she wore on her own hand had belonged to his mother, and she had never taken it off. Would never take it off, un- less . . . She shook her head, tired now, but peaceful.

She put her precious things away and closed the trunk carefully, then stood, the quilt still wrapped around her shoulders. She turned down the lamp, and darkness filled the room, along with the steady, gentle sounds of sleeping children. Her children. Nothing was more precious to her than they. She kissed them both gently and stroked their hair, then curled up in a chair beside them, watching over them as she al- ways did, until the darkness of night gave way to morning's light.

Six

The day he limped into town and saw the Pacific Ocean, Sean O'Malley knew that he had come as far as he was ever going to go. This was the end; he felt it. No matter how many more years he lived, he had finally arrived at the rest of his life.

San Francisco was a sinner's paradise, all the more recognizable from the perspective of a fallen Saint, and Sean breathed a sigh of relief—the struggle was over; he would simply give in and enjoy the ride down. Even the smell was appropriate: fresh sea breezes and pine skating along the surface of a civic stench of raw sewage, pools of stagnant water, raw lumber, acrid tar—the smell of a city in the making, the smell of success. Did it dry your throat? Make you thirsty? Step into any saloon any hour of any day: Whiskey poured as if from pumps so that dusty miners just in from the fields might slake their thirst immediately, might begin spending their money within the first moments of their arrival in the City of Gold. They drank like none others Sean had ever seen, they gambled with a vengeance, they whored every night, fought like sailors, cavorted, rioted, mobbed. And then they banked what was left of their money, picked up guns and ammunition and fresh supplies, and headed back into the fields for months of backbreaking work, their places at the bar taken by the next round of miners dusty and dry, the next group of emigrants ready to go. Sean watched them from his place at the end of the counter, from his table in the back, from the window of his boardinghouse. The ebb and flow of humanity was fascinating to him; you never knew what the tide might bring in.

From the direction of the sea, what washed up on the shore were

Irishmen the like of which Sean loved best—"Sydney Covers," the locals called them, as they were convicts from Australia, criminals of a seditious and political ilk, the Young Irelanders of home. Sean was not one of this crowd, not anymore; he had failed his own people in more ways than one and so he kept to himself. But he could not help listening to their talk, though it made him so sick for home he drank more than ever.

From his stool at the end of the bar, he soon learned that a steady stream of convicts from the penal colonies in Van Diemen's Land were making their way first to Hawaii and then to San Francisco, where they received a hero's welcome. His old friend Terence MacManus—though a Liverpool native, still one of Smith O'Brien's greatest supporters—had landed in San Francisco in 1851 and hadn't been able to turn round without having a glass pushed into his hand. The extradition treaty between Britain and the United States was gleefully ignored by American judges when it came to political prisoners, and each escape from the penal colonies was heralded from coast to coast. MacManus had stayed in San Francisco for a while, trying his hand at the shipping business, but had been no match for the East Coast traders, and now word was he'd taken up ranching. Sean privately wished him well, even lifted a glass each time his name was mentioned—or the names William Smith O'Brien, John Mitchell, Thomas Meagher, Morgan McDonagh, but not Sean O'Malley . . . he choked on that drink. When his own name was raised in the company of these great men, he simply hung his head in shame, glad that he'd come to the end of the road and no one would know him again.

Though they were tagged "Covers," most of the Irish in town settled their own quarter south of Market Street, near the industries and St. Patrick's Church, avoiding contact with the English convicts from Australia, rowdies who made Sydney Town nothing more than a nest of arsonists, looters, and robbers. Sean stayed away from both areas, stayed away from their pubs and saloons, their restaurants, shops, brothels, and casinos. This was little hardship; there were literally hundreds of other places to go.

With his remarkable memory, Sean had quickly become a creature of the evening, venturing out at dusk to begin another long night of gambling. He had a particular talent for card games, and poker was his favorite, though it was considered too slow and complicated a way to win or lose money by most of the forty-niners, who preferred craps or the French card games of vingt-et-un and lansquenet. The hands-down favorite, however—whether at the El Dorado, the Blue Wing Saloon, Aquila de Oro, the Verandah, the Parker House—was monte, a fast Mexican card game involving bets placed on whether one card would be matched from the deck before its partner. Bets ranged from fifty cents to five dollars a hand; however, Sean had witnessed occasions in private rooms where they ran as high as twenty thousand dollars, one of these placed and won by the city's best professional gambler, Charles Cora. Cora was a fascinating man who'd been born in Italy, raised in the bordellos of New Orleans, and had married the beautiful Belle, proprietress of the city's most lavish bordello. Cora was a man who never went out, and certainly never gambled, without a derringer at his side; Sean took note and bought a similar gun for himself, though he kept a much lower profile and hoped he'd never have to use it.

Determined to maintain anonymity, Sean had taken the last name of Miner, his own private joke. He'd had no trouble finding lodging, though many boardinghouses reminded him of the terrible rooms in the Irish slum districts of New York City; even with deplorable conditions, rooms were not cheap. He had not wanted to establish residence in a hotel, where more attention would be given him, but boardinghouses were tricky—reputable landlords were loath to rent to a crippled Irishman, clearly not a miner, who did not appear to be gainfully employed and came home reeking of whiskey and cigar smoke in the wee hours of every morning.

Sean had soon found that he was not interested in reputable landlords anyway; more desirable were those in Chinatown. There he'd come to a fine arrangement with Mister Hung Chang-Li, a discreet man from the Pearl River Delta region, seven thousand miles across the Pacific Ocean. The Hung brothers were still working a claim at Wood's Creek in the Chinese diggings, but Chang-Li had used his initial earnings to establish a boardinghouse and a pawnshop—two lucrative propositions in these times, and jobs that did not break the back, as he was fond of saying. Sean enjoyed Chang-Li, whose English was good and whose conversation tended toward philosophical axiom; they often drank tea together from delicate little bowls in the afternoon before Sean went out.

It was a house where men, mostly Chinese, came and went, but there was also a young woman of indeterminate age called Mei Ling. Chang-Li referred to Mei Ling as his slave, but when Sean pointed out that California had banned slavery when it became a state in 1850, Chang-Li allowed that in reality Mei Ling was more of an indentured servant, Chang-Li having assumed responsibility for the cost of her passage in return for seven years' work. She had four years to go and did not appear to resent her status, which was that of lowest lackey in the house. She was very shy and somber, and so exotic to Sean's eye that he found himself watching her as she went about her work, gazing upon her more than he should have. Chang-Li appeared to have no opinions about her other than the largely held view that servant slaves were lazy and underhanded; he often barked at her, setting her to yet another task, even if it was only to fill his sweet pipe and kneel beside him while he smoked it. He cursed her frequently and slapped at her as she passed, bemoaning the fact that he was burdened with the care of such an ox and musing upon the many ways in which she might be trying to poison him.

Although their relationship made Sean uncomfortable, he did not interfere; he knew his days of passionate intervention were over and that, by turning his back on God, he was left with only the dispassionate observation of his own sinful nature, and that of others. It was a study worthy of his scholarship, and he undertook it with grim satisfaction.

So this was his city now, and Chinatown his quarter, his home—a far cry from the Irish country lane into which he'd been born. He and Gracelin had spent their entire childhoods in and around that simple cabin, growing up with a stubborn, heartbroken father and an equally stubborn, though optimistic, grandmother. Their older brother, Ryan, had never seemed part of that childhood, and Sean could barely remember him, could bring forward only a hint of his features and the faint sound of his voice. Dead now, of course: Ryan, his wife, Aghna, their son, Thomsy—as dead as Sean's father, mother, grandmother, sister, niece, best friend, every friend. Oppression, occupation, famine, typhus—the Ireland of his childhood was gone, replaced by a country full of the sick and the desperate, run by an enemy bent on eradicating their past, determined to deprive them of a future. He and Morgan and

Grace had tried to change this path, had struggled for the freedom of their countrymen, but the struggle had been too great; all the good men were gone, one way or another. He'd been a good man once, sent to New York City to work for the cause; but instead he'd abandoned the very people he loved most, throwing them over for a new cause, the finest cause, or so he'd thought—this Kingdom in the Wilderness. Sean leaned forward and rested his forehead against the cool glass of the window, shut his eyes, and tried to forget. If only he had it to do over again, he told himself; if only he'd done it right the first time around.

Outside, the light had faded and the lamps were being lit; it was the ghosting hour, when bad men relished their deeds of corruption, and good men sat haunted by deeds gone bad. Where was he in the mix? Sean wondered. He lifted his forehead from the glass and saw himself mirrored in the window: Neither good nor bad, he was merely inept—perhaps the worst kind of man for the damage they wreak in the lives of those who trust them.

Down in the street below, the party had begun; already he could hear the shouts of camaraderie, of drinkers banding together, gamblers setting out, brawlers warming up, the odd whistle of a woman who steps out of the shadows for just a moment to let you decide. They were calling him, all of them, like revelers from Hell let out for the night. In the dark room, he located his clean, pressed linen shirt and put it on, then the vest and then the jacket, securing his money in the false pocket stitched into its hem. He checked to make sure his derringer was loaded and practiced his quick draw as a way of loosening up his hand. As he left the room, locking the door securely behind him, Sean pulled the fedora down low over eyes just sharp enough to put off the good men, just cold enough to earn an invitation from the bad. At the bottom of the landing, he patted his pockets—money, gun, opium, and whiskey; Sean O'Malley was ready for yet another night on the town.

Seven

The baby was still alive, her beautiful dark eyes locked onto Morgan's face as he walked behind Aquash through the vast northern wilderness. Nearly three weeks had passed since they left the trappers' settlement, and though Morgan was sure no one followed them, still they were watchful, hiding themselves at the first sound of voices on the trail. By the second week, Aquash's wounds had healed and she'd recovered her strength so that they were able to travel for more of the daylight hours. Those hours were diminishing, however, and Morgan had begun to wonder what would happen to them if the Mi'kmaq camp was not found soon. Though the sun was still bright enough to warm them during the day, the nights were getting colder. And longer. He had a taste of winter each time it clouded over and rain fell, though their activity kept them from getting chilled.

Aquash kept the baby tightly wrapped and secured on her back; they stopped every few hours so that she might nurse the infant and take in some nourishment herself. Morgan and Nacoute used the time to hunt small game or, if they were by the river, to fish. There were still berries to be found, and nuts, but no eggs, fruits, or vegetables. Not here. Not in the middle of the Canadian wilderness.

They'd stuck to the river as much as possible during the first week, pulling the canoes up at night, building a fire, making a camp warm enough for the infant, who slept most of the time. Nacoute, his demons buried along with Remy Martine back at the settlers' camp, was more calm and peaceful than Morgan had ever seen; he was quite taken with his tiny sister and held things up in front of her face to entertain her—

a leaf he twirled by the stem, two nuts he knocked together for the sound, eagle feathers picked up off the forest floor, which he tickled along her cheek. Aquash watched them and smiled; she, too, seemed more at peace, and Morgan realized that neither she nor her son had entertained the thought that they might not find their camp before winter. They might not find it at all.

When the river became more treacherous and difficult to negotiate, they left their canoes hidden in underbrush and set out on foot, still following the direction of the river as much as possible. Morgan had begun to think that the Mi'kmaq had moved inland, perhaps to trap or trade, and that their winter camp was going to be difficult to locate. Aquash had not seen her people for eight or more years, by Morgan's reckoning, and had no real idea of their pattern of movement anymore. It was early October now, the geese overhead flew south daily, and the forest creatures were busy squirreling away food for winter. Morgan had quietly decided that he would force them to stop and build a winter camp if they had not found Aquash's people in the next week or so. They could not afford to wait for the first sign of snow; he knew from experience that those first snowflakes could quickly turn into a blizzard that raged for days, and they could not be caught out in the open if that happened. The forest was full of fallen trees and broken branches, and it was not too late to take deer or elk for the hide and meat; also, there were caves pocked into the mountainsides, and these could be made habitable if they could vent smoke from a fire out of the hole. If need be, they could survive the winter, but only if they stopped hoping for a miracle and began to prepare for the inevitable.

Each night, Morgan told himself that they had reached the end of their search, that in the morning they would have to make a camp. But each morning, he could not bring himself to stop the party; he, too, hoped to find their people before winter came, and he hoped to see them settled in so that he might continue south to the States. And yet, they were everything to him, this little band of mother, son, and infant daughter. Theirs had become the tiniest of worlds, with its own rhythm of rise and eat, walk and eat, walk and walk and walk and eat, then sleep and rise again. Even though Morgan spoke only English and a few words of French, and Aquash spoke only Mi'kmaq and a few words of French, and Nacoute spoke not at all, they seemed to have little problem communicating. The silence of the forest, broken only by the movement of animals and the wind, suited all of them, all of them lost in their own thoughts. Often, an entire day would pass with only a word here and there, most of their communicating done through gestures, smiles, the language of the eyes. It suited Morgan. Sometimes he remembered the long, intense conversations with the lads of his youth and he wondered if he would ever be able to hold his own at an Irish table again.

He looked past Aquash's shoulder to Nacoute, who was leading them this morning, then his eyes fell back and met those of the baby. Marie was her name, and she seemed to know already that she was a child of two different worlds; she watched everything around her with the eyes of an old woman, and Morgan was besotted. It was Aquash who had chosen the infant's name, but only after she had made Morgan understand that the name she wanted was that of his mother. She had laid her hand on Nacoute's shoulder, then pointed to herself; then she laid her hand on Morgan's shoulder and pointed up, as if to something above him. It took some repetition, but finally he had understood and said slowly, "Mary, Mary McDonagh."

"Mah-ree," Aquash had repeated, then nodded and laid her hand on the baby's head. "Mah-ree," she said to the little girl, smiling into those watchful eyes.

Now Marie peeked out of her bundled pack, her eyes widening when he smiled and waggled his fingers at her. She cooed and his heart was happy. He had forgotten how much he loved the promise of a little baby. He thought of his mother and all the babies she'd had, all girls save for himself, all little mothers in their own way. His favorite had been young Ellen, so full of life and his faithful companion as he went about the place doing the work that kept them all going. Poor Ellen, he thought now. Her body wracked by starvation and illness, she'd died in his arms on the road to the convent where their older sister was a nun. For two days he'd carried her lifeless body, unable to leave it by the side of the road where so many others lay, bringing it to Barbara, who buried Ellen in the convent cemetery by the garden. They had all died, all his sisters, except perhaps for Aislinn, who'd run off to London before the famine hit. He had hoped to contact Barbara secretly, hoped to find out where Grace might be, but that hope had been squashed the day immigrants from Cork City arrived with the news that there was no one left alive at Sisters of the Holy Rose, all the nuns dead of fever and no one left even to bury them.

He had been ill his first year in Canada, ill to the point of madness, fevers burning his brain and leaving his body drained of all strength. The recovery had been slow, each week tormenting him with its passing. He could only vaguely remember being hauled out of his prison cell by those he thought were guards come to execute him at last. He hadn't cared; he was so sick he knew he'd be dead soon anyway. But instead of killing him, they hid him in a wagon, then smuggled him on board a ship. There had been a priest with him—or a man dressed as a priest; he'd never really known—but within days this man, too, was dead and buried at sea. Somehow Morgan had survived, though there had been many days he begged God in a loud voice to end it now, to bring him home and let him rest, to release him from his misery. But God had other plans. Morgan landed in Grosse Isle and was immediately quarantined. Again he hovered between life and death, and again he begged God to let him go, but the answer was no. Two long years he'd spent there—first in the hospital, then in a kind of recovery house for indigent immigrants, and finally in his own small hole of a room with a debt to repay as long as a ship's mast. In all that time, he'd told no one his real name; he was, after all, still on British soil, and while he certainly wanted to be released from this life, he didn't want it at the hands of his enemies. As his strength returned, he accepted that he would live and set about repaying his debt. The job carting supplies from an immigrant town to the trappers' camp downriver was ideal for him; it allowed for plenty of solitude, which he found he sorely needed, and it gave him freedom to explore the lay of the land. He had nearly paid off his debt and was about to set out for the States when he was caught in the storm that felled the tree that crushed his legs. Aquash and Nacoute had seen him through that horrific time, and though he'd often wondered why this had happened to him yet again, looking into the eyes of the little baby in her mother's pack, he knew.

"Because of you," he whispered to her. *Because you were coming,* he said to himself, *and the Lord has plans. I could not save the lives of my sisters, but He's letting me do something about yours.*

Marie's eyes widened again, and she cooed at him as if she'd heard.

He'd given up the wondering of *why* a long time ago and found peace in knowing that he was simply where he was meant to be. It didn't mean he wouldn't continue south, wouldn't continue trying to find out what had happened to Grace; only that he wouldn't torment himself any longer about when that time would come.

It was getting later in the day now, the afternoon air taking on that damp chill that comes right before darkness falls. Morgan called to Nacoute and motioned that they must stop for the night. Nacoute frowned but then, seeing the weariness on his mother's face, nodded and put down his pack. Morgan lifted the baby's pack off of Aquash's back, then leaned it up against a tree, loosening the laces in order to lift Marie out and hand her to her mother. While Aquash fed the baby, Morgan and Nacoute laid the fire, which Morgan lit with his flint. He'd shot a duck in the morning, which Nacoute plucked, then handed to Morgan for gutting and spitting. By the time their camp was readied and darkness surrounded them, the duck was roasting, droplets of fat sizzling as they fell into the fire.

Outside the ring of light, Morgan thought he saw a shadow moving in the trees. He glanced at Nacoute, who had seen the same thing, and both men stood, Morgan shouldering his rifle.

"Come out and I won't kill you," Morgan said evenly, peering into the darkness.

Beside him, Nacoute quietly unsheathed his knife.

A very long minute passed, and then a man stepped out from behind a tree, hands raised, moving slowly into the light of their fire.

"You are English!" The man nodded enthusiastically.

"Irish," Morgan corrected. "And you are . . . ?"

"French, of course." The small man shrugged good-naturedly. "Père Leon, at your service." He gave a small bow.

Morgan eyed him carefully, taking in the warm winter garb of a trapper. "You're a priest?"

"A man of God, *oui.*" He sniffed the air. "A very hungry man of God, I would say." He looked across the fire at Aquash and the baby, then up at Nacoute; when he spoke next, it was in their language, and they both looked surprised.

Though clearly he was speaking to Nacoute, as the man, Aquash answered and the priest moved closer to hear her. She asked him a few questions, then spoke at length while he nodded, glancing every now and then at Morgan.

"Well." The short priest rubbed his hands together, then turned to Morgan. "That is very interesting, and I am glad to say that I can help you. You are only one day from the Mi'kmaq winter camp," he reported. "You must go back the way you came and then turn west half a day."

Morgan felt a surge of relief and lowered the rifle. "You speak their language."

The priest shrugged. "I have spent many years among these people. And I have learned more from them than they from me." He smiled. "She says her husband is a French trapper, dead now, and you are helping her to go home. And that is her son." He pointed to Nacoute.

"Aye." Morgan nodded. "Will you sit, then? Share our meal?"

"Avec plaisir," Père Leon said enthusiastically, sitting on the log next to the fire. "How long have you been traveling?"

Morgan lifted the spit from the fire and tore a small piece from the bird, which he handed to Aquash. "About twenty days, I'd say." He held the bird out to the priest.

"Merci." Père Leon gingerly tore a piece of the hot meat away, then blew on it. "You have come then from the settlement up near where the river pools." He took a bite of the meat and chewed noisily. "Why did she not marry another man from the camp? They usually do, these Indian brides. They are used to a civilized life."

"Civilized," Morgan repeated. "Is beating your woman a civilized thing, do you think, Father? How about attacking an innocent babe, or treating a mute boy with such cruelty that others do the same? Is drinking yourself blind and destroying your home civilized?" Morgan spat out a bit of gristle. "You'll excuse me, Father, if I don't think that white men are necessarily more honorable than Indians."

"Don't romanticize them, my son." Père Leon wagged his finger. "Indians can be as cruel to their women and children as white men."

"So one is no better than the other?" Morgan asked.

Aquash and Nacoute had stopped eating, their eyes moving from one white face to the other.

Père Leon regarded the young man sitting across from him. "I agree that each man must be measured of his own accord, and that only God can judge what is in the heart. Do you know God, my son?"

"Aye." Morgan leaned forward. "And He knows me."

The priest nodded. "Good. Let me ask you this—will you live with this woman in her camp?"

"I have a wife," Morgan told him. "I don't know where she is, or even if she still lives, but I'm a married man."

"So this infant is not yours?"

"No, Father, she's not." Morgan looked to where the baby slept in her bundle at her mother's feet.

"Then this is a selfless act, taking them to their people."

Morgan thought about that. "Not selfless, no. I owe my life to this woman and her son. I . . ." He stopped, thinking of the accusations Aquash had suffered because of him, of the violence that had occurred, the boy's confusion. "Not selfless."

Père Leon nodded slowly and resumed chewing his food. Morgan and Aquash shared a long look, but he could read no fear in her face or apprehension about the man sitting at their fire. She spoke then, her voice light and soft after the gruffness of the men's.

"She asks will I take you south with me, to the border. She says you want to go to America. To find your wife."

Morgan looked at Aquash. "I do want to find my wife," he said. "But I'll not leave her here. I'll see her to camp first, and then I'll find my way."

"Very difficult to navigate through the wilderness," Père Leon said. "Men become lost and die alone."

"I've died a couple of times already. I'm not afraid."

The priest looked around at each face in the firelight, and then he spoke to Aquash, who listened intently, then smiled in relief.

"I told her I will take you all to the Indian camp, and then you and I will leave together for the border." Père Leon leaned forward. "I think I will like to travel with a man who is not afraid. And I think we will have many things to talk about."

"Thank you," Morgan said, and then he looked at Nacoute, whose eyes struggled with sadness. "Tell him, Father, that we will talk more when we've reached the camp. I won't be going anywhere 'til he's ready for me to do so."

The priest spoke to the boy, who nodded slowly, then got up to move closer to Morgan. Sitting beside this man who had seen him through so much, Nacoute longed for words to thank him. Instead, he put his hand on Morgan's knee and gripped it, not looking anywhere but into the wavering flames of the fire.

Morgan felt the tension in the young man's hand, looked down and saw knuckles torn and scratched, ragged nails, the dirt. He covered that hand with his own, staring like the boy into the flames.

"It'll be all right, son," he reassured softly. "It's going to be all right now."

Eight

San Francisco was so far removed from the small shanty and tent city of Grace's imagining that she sometimes wondered if she was even in the right country. No longer the Mexican harbor town of Yerba Buena, the San Francisco of October 1852 was quickly becoming one of the most magnificent cities ever built, and the energy that surged up and down newly planked streets, in and out of fireproof doors, around and through the paved marketplaces and plazas, was catching. Grace felt the excitement every time she descended into the bustle and sweep of a city built on sheer optimism.

It was so different from New York City, which had seemed permanent and well established by the time she'd arrived; San Francisco was a city in the midst of a glorious rebirth. The city fathers had determined that San Francisco would burn no more; no more loss of commerce and real estate threatened investors, and now they poured their money into elegant and substantial fireproof brick and stone buildings, any one of which would be remarkable in any country for great size, strength, and beauty. Most of these incredible buildings were situated around Portsmouth Square, the original plaza of the Spanish-Mexican era, and along Battery, Front, Sansome, and Montgomery Streets; there were also many fine brick buildings in Stockton Street. Elegant private houses were being constructed at North Beach, Mission Bay, Pleasant Valley, and Happy Valley. Rincon Hill was being developed into seventeen elegant brick homes centered around a floral park, to be enclosed by a locked iron fence—all this designed by Englishman George Gordon—and residents would have the only keys.

Grace had overheard Doctor Wakefield and his friend Doctor Fair-fax discussing the advantages of moving into a more ostentatious house, one closer to the splendid United States Marine Hospital being built on Rincon Point; Wakefield would serve on the staff of this illustrious modern facility and was excited about the advancements of medicine he knew would be possible there, but he liked his domicile upon the hill, with its view of the city and the bay beyond—it afforded him the privacy he felt was needed in caring for his sister and was also removed from the pressures of his work. Grace had not ventured out so far as Rincon Point, though she had promised Jack and Mary Kate that they would see it once Doctor Wakefield took up offices there.

Each Sunday afternoon, as Mary Kate grew stronger, they explored a different part of the city, witnessing firsthand the erection of grand homes, hotels, restaurants, theaters, public houses, the new library. Wooden structures were being replaced with those of polished Chinese granite, brick, and stone, all with exterior window shutters and doors of thick wrought iron. The streets, too, were in transition as better grades were established; those in the lower part of the city were in the process of being raised several feet above their former height, while those on high ground were being lowered, sometimes fifty feet, all in an effort to make the streets run parallel and perpendicular so that the city could be better navigated. The original streets, many of which had yet to be improved, had begun as dirt roads, were later covered with planking, and eventually laid with cobblestones, macadamized paving, or even square-dressed blocks of granite and whinstone. Wagonloads of materials rumbled up and down the streets and alleys; workmen on scaffolding hauled up buckets by rope pulley; the sound of hammer and chisel, ax and saw, rang out through the city until nightfall, when it was replaced by raucous laughter, the policeman's whistle, the smash and clatter of saloon brawling.

Their visits into the city were always stimulating but left them tired, and Grace was always glad to climb the hill at the end of her Sunday. She paused now, halfway up, mindful of Mary Kate, whose cheeks were pink from the brisk air, but whose eyes were weary. A child's hand in each of hers, Grace turned and looked back out over the bay, at the ships anchored there, at the steamers coming into port, the fishing junks with their daily catch, and the rowing boats ferrying passengers back and forth. She knew the *Eliza J* was not among them, could not be among them yet, and still she looked for the ship she loved best of all.

On market days, when Grace came down the hill on her own early in the morning, she ran to one of the twelve wharves, each one extending like a long finger into the bay. In the beginning, she had often lost as much as an hour there, mesmerized by the off-loading of an amazing amount of cargo — millions of pounds of flour and meal, barley, butter, and tea; thousands of barrels of pork and beef, whole hams, Carolina rice, rice from the Orient; thousands of cases of candles, soap, boots and shoes, coffee; tons of coal; barrels of rum; kegs, casks, hogsheads, and pipes of every liquor imaginable, including champagne from France. Most of it for California, some for Oregon, and always her heart ached for Ireland, which knew none of this bounty, received no shipments such as these, continued to scrape by on oats, potatoes, and cornmeal.

Grace tore her eyes away from the sunset. "Time to get home before darkness swallows us up. Are you ready, then, children?"

Mary Kate smiled and nodded, but Jack dug in his heels.

"One more minute, Mam," he pleaded. "Just 'til she sinks in the sea! Look! Look!" He pointed to the giant fireball now slipping out of sight.

Grace waited a moment, then said, " 'Tis gone now, Jack, and time to walk on."

"Oh, all right." He kicked at a rock in the road, but Grace knew he wasn't really mad.

As they approached the house, Grace saw a dim light shining from Abigail's room, but that was all. There was no light on downstairs, not in the dining room or the large drawing room on the other side. Around back, the kitchen was dark, and Grace was surprised—surely Enid would be lighting the house by this time. Above the stable, Mister Litton's room was also dark, but this was expected; the man disappeared every other Sunday, and no one saw hide nor hair of him until Monday morning, when he would appear for his strong cup of coffee, eyes rimmed red from drink. *We all have our own demons to fight,* Grace reminded herself.

Once inside, Grace lit a lamp, then sent Jack to the pump to fill the kettle while she stoked the stove. There was a pot of stew ready to heat, upon which Grace placed the quick dough that would become dumplings. As dinner warmed, they removed their coats and scarves, hung them in their room, then set the table for supper. The night was chilly, so Grace laid a small fire in the hearth in their private quarters to take the damp off the room. At table, they all ate heartily and, when they were through, Mary Kate unfolded the newspaper to read parts of it aloud to Jack as Grace cleaned their dishes, the sound of their voices in the warming room a comfort to her.

The first time Grace had asked at the newsagents for the paper, he'd had a nice laugh at her expense, asking which one of the twelve she preferred: eight were morning papers, he'd said, and three were evening, one in German; he also had two French papers out three times a week and six other papers out once a week—three being religious, one French, and one a Sunday special only. It had taken Grace a moment to digest this information, and then she'd chosen the *California Star,* as its editor was a friend of Doctor Wakefield, and she'd stuck to it, though only the Sunday edition; rarely did she have time during the week to read, though she liked to know what was going on in the world and scanned the pages for mention of Ireland or New York City.

"Mam." Mary Kate's soft voice broke her mother's reverie. "There's the bell. That'll be Miss Wakefield."

Grace pulled a long face of mock horror and the children laughed, especially Jack, who kept asking her to do it again. The bell became more insistent and was followed immediately by the crash of spilled china.

"Better go," Mary Kate said soberly. "Missus Hopkins isn't here, I think. Or Enid."

Grace nodded, wondering where on earth the two women had gone. They never took a half day on Sunday if Grace was going to be out, and they'd not said a word this morning, either one of them.

"Jack, help your sister put away the dishes. Then get yourselves to bed. I'll be back to tuck you up."

The children nodded dutifully, and Grace left the warmth of the kitchen for the dark cool of the hallway and the foyer, where she lit the lamp that sat on the little table at the foot of the stair. After adjusting the flame, she started up cautiously, shadows looming behind her.

"Hopkins!" Miss Wakefield's shout was followed by an angry rant and then the solid thump of a body falling to the floor.

Grace took the stairs two at a time, rushed down the long hallway, then knocked quickly at Abigail's door before pushing it open.

"It's Missus Donnelly, ma'am. Hopkins isn't—" Grace stopped.

Abigail lay on the floor, her dressing gown disheveled and stained with wine and sickness. The smell was awful, but before Grace could get to a window, the woman heaved again, trying to rise. Grace moved quickly to help, but Abigail fought her off.

"Where's Hopkins?" the young woman slurred. "I want her!" She wobbled to her feet and turned, falling against the side of the bed. "Hopkins!" she shouted again, then began to mutter incoherently.

"Please, Miss Wakefield," Grace began gently. "Let me help you back into bed. You're not well."

"Get out!" Abigail waved her away drunkenly. "Don't want you. Or your brats. How dare you! Out!"

Grace ignored her, coming farther into the room, when suddenly she heard the sound of horses coming up the drive, followed almost immediately by the good-natured shouts and laughter of men dismounting their rides. She moved quickly to the window and looked out; Doctor Wakefield was home and he'd brought a number of friends with him. Grace's heart began to pound.

"Hopkins!" Abigail called again, clutching at Grace's shoulder in an attempt to shove her out of the way.

From the driveway below, Wakefield looked up; Grace yanked the curtains closed, then spoke urgently to the young woman.

"Hush now, miss, before your brother's guests hear you."

Abigail's eyes went wide and she clapped both hands over her mouth.

"Aye, he's coming in the house now," Grace warned. "With Doctor Fairfax and a few more beside. Hopkins isn't here, nor Enid. 'Tis only me to see to you, and them as well." She paused as they both listened to the sound of the doors opening and Wakefield's call for Hopkins.

Abigail's eyes filled with tears and her hands fell limply to her sides. "I'm ill," she whispered. "Tell them. I'm ill!" Her voice became frantic and she clutched at Grace's arm. "I can't go down!"

"They're not expecting you." Grace kept her voice low and reassuring. "But if they ask, I'll say you're unwell."

"Can't go down." Abigail seemed to speaking to herself as much as to Grace. "Can't see them." She stopped and stared at herself in the mirror, put her hands to her face, and shook her head slowly from side to side. "Oh, no. Oh, no, no, no . . ."

"You don't have to see anyone." Grace turned the woman from the mirror and guided her gently toward the chair by the washbasin and pitcher. "Don't worry, now. I'll take care of it."

Making soothing sounds as she would to an anxious child fresh from a bad dream, Grace removed Abigail's robe and peeled off the damp, stained nightdress. In the light of the lamp, Abigail's body was more shadow than light, and Grace breathed in sharply. Ireland had had more than its share of walking skeletons, but those had been people with no food, let alone a servant to cook for them three times a day; did the doctor know how much his sister had deteriorated? Grace wondered. And there was something else, she saw now, something not quite right; this was not the body of a pampered young debutante who'd never seen a day's work in her life. No, this body was nicked and scratched, its skin a lunar landscape of pocks and small white scars; this skin was dry and cracked, scabbed over in some places, while others were newly encrusted with sticky beads of blood. Not only this, but her bosom had withered to nothing and the skin around her belly and hips fell in silvery, puckered folds. Shocked, Grace lifted her eyes to Abigail's and met there a fearful yet resolute gaze before Abigail wrapped her arms around herself and turned away.

"You're very thin, miss," Grace said gently, wringing out a cloth in the washbasin, *and you look as if you're trying to claw your way out of your own skin.* "Can you not eat more than you do?"

Abigail shook her head. "Oh, no," she moaned softly. "No, no, no. How can I? How can I ever . . ." She began to weep, chin sagging upon her skeletal chest and hanks of lank hair falling over a face she now tried to cover with her hands.

"Never you mind." Grace gently peeled Abigail's fingers away. " 'Tis all right now," she whispered, wiping away the tears and crust. "I'm here to help you."

"Help me." Abigail repeated as if momentarily considering the inconceivable, and then she looked at Grace with eyes that knew better. "There is no help for me. I am . . ." She stopped and her shoulders slumped even further, her mouth hung slack, and she stared into the dark corner at something only she could see.

Grace had witnessed the unhinging of a mind once before in her life, and so she recognized now that Abigail Wakefield had more in common with Bram Donnelly than a weakness for drink.

Troubled, but determined to get the woman cleaned up and into bed, she finished washing Abigail, then rubbed her with a towel to get the blood moving again. After securing her charge so that she'd not fall out of the chair, Grace quickly opened and closed drawers until a clean nightdress was located, which she then pulled over Abigail's head and tied at the neck. Finally, a muslin cap was fitted over the woman's matted hair, and she was helped back into bed.

"Go to sleep now," Grace whispered, pulling first the sheet and then the blanket up to Abigail's chin, smoothing it around her battle-weary body. "I'll open the window just a bit as the air's gone bad in here, and you'll be needing a bath come morning, but all's well for now."

"Where is she?" Abigail murmured even as her eyes began to close. "Where could she be?"

"I don't know," Grace told her again. "But the minute she comes in, I'll send her to you straightaway."

Abigail's face relaxed then, and she sighed, her lips parted in the hint of a smile. She must have been lovely not too long ago, Grace thought, before whatever demons she faced had sucked the life out of her.

Afraid that Abigail, in her sleep, would be sick again and choke on it, Grace rolled her over onto her side so that her cheek rested on the very edge of the bed. Satisfied that the poor creature was out of her misery, at least for the length of her sleep, Grace blew out the lamp and left the room. When she got to the bottom of the stairs, Doctor Wakefield came immediately out of the drawing room, closing the doors behind him.

"The children said you'd gone upstairs. I take it my sister has taken a turn for the worse?" he asked carefully, his face clouded with concern.

"She's taken a turn for the bottle, more like," Grace reported.

"No, no . . ." Wakefield shook his head in protest. "It's the laudanum. Sometimes she gets confused and takes too much, or takes wine on top of it—for her nerves—and—" He stopped as the look on Grace's face hardened.

"I've seen plenty of drunks in my time, Doctor, and that woman upstairs is as drunk as they come, medicine or no."

He stared, and Grace could see that he was trying to formulate some kind of explanation.

"I'm passing no judgment, sir," she said before he could speak. "Only don't go telling me what I know to be true is something else beside. 'Tis no sin to be weak," she added. "And truly your sister suffers some madness."

"Abigail is not mad," he insisted firmly. "Troubled, perhaps. Yes, I'll give you that. A drinker, most likely. But not mad."

The library doors opened again and Doctor Fairfax poked his head into the hall, male conversation booming out behind him.

"Wakefield!" he demanded, more than a little drunk. "Where've you gone? Oh, hello there, Missus Donnelly." He waved at her congenially, then frowned at his friend. "Wakefield, where are your manners? Feed and water us at once, sir, or we shall revolt!"

Wakefield looked baffled for a moment.

"Refreshments coming right away, Doctor Fairfax," Grace announced in her most professional servant voice. "I've some of that cheese and those biscuits you liked so well last time you were here."

"Best news I've heard all night. Thank you, Missus Donnelly; you are far more civilized than your illustrious employer." Fairfax pulled his head back inside and rejoined the others.

"Thank you," Wakefield echoed Fairfax's sentiments gratefully. "Thank you very much, Missus Donnelly."

" 'Tis my job, sir. Go back to your guests, and I'll be in with a tray quick as I can. Miss Abigail is sleeping now," she added quietly, "but I'll keep an ear out for her."

He nodded, relieved, and straightened himself up, raking his hair back into place with his fingers before reentering the library, where he was met with a cheery hurrah.

Grace hurried into the kitchen and was tying an apron on over her dress when Hopkins came through the back door, cheeks flushed and eyes dark with trepidation, though her tone was aggressively defensive.

"The master is entertaining? He said nothing about it to me or I never would've gone out! Did he wake Miss Abigail?"

"Yes, he's entertaining," Grace stated. "And no, he didn't wake her. She was well up . . . and well drunk by the time I got home."

"Of course she wasn't drunk," Hopkins retorted scornfully. "You Irish. Miss Abigail takes medicine for the headaches, and . . ."

Grace held up a hand. "I've already been through this with the doctor. Miss Wakefield's headache remedy has backfired. I got her cleaned up as best I could and into bed. She'll sleep for now, but she'll be wanting a bath in the morning, and the room will need a good scrub and airing out."

"I don't take my orders from you. How dare you . . . ? Where is Enid? Why didn't she attend Miss Abigail?"

"I've no idea where your daughter is," Grace replied evenly. "And I doubt Doctor Wakefield knows, either, but we could certainly ask him."

Red-faced, Hopkins planted her hands on her hips. "My position in this household is absolutely secure, if that's what you're implying."

Grace shrugged. "Perhaps you'll be wanting to take a little better care of your mistress, then, as she's looking the worse for it."

"Miss Wakefield is my business," Hopkins warned. "You keep your nose out of it."

"Oh, I don't think so. Not after what I saw tonight. Not with you disappearing whenever you like."

Hopkins opened her mouth to reply but was stopped by the sound of the back door opening and closing softly. They both turned as Enid came tiptoeing in; when she saw them waiting, she froze and the color drained from her face.

"Where have you been, you wretched girl?" Hopkins demanded. "You know better than to leave the mistress alone!"

Enid swallowed hard. "She was asleep! Sound asleep! I just went out in the moonlight to sit by the pond. Only for a moment, Mother, I swear to you! I was gone but a moment!"

Far longer than that, Grace thought but said nothing that might add to what would clearly be the girl's forthcoming misery.

Hopkins crossed the room in a fury and grabbed Enid by the ear, twisting it as she dragged her daughter after her.

"She was up!" Hopkins hissed. "And ill! The master's come in with guests—anything could've happened!"

Enid yelped with pain and tried to apologize.

"I don't want to hear it." Hopkins twisted harder. "You'll pay for this, you stupid girl, and don't think you won't."

"That's enough," Grace admonished. "Missus Hopkins, go check on your mistress. And, Enid"—she took the girl's arm and withdrew her from her mother's grip—"help me lay out these trays for the doctor and his guests. They've been waiting long enough."

Enid nodded miserably, a hand to the ear that was now bright red. Grace could feel the fury coming off Hopkins in waves, but she ignored it, and the housekeeper finally turned on her heel and left the kitchen by the back staircase.

"Where were you really, then?" Grace put two wedges of cheese on a dressed platter. "Because I know you weren't out sitting in the moonlight."

Enid fumbled the loaf of dark bread, dropping it onto the cutting board, but she said nothing, just picked up the serrated knife and began to slice, focusing all her attention on the task.

"If that's how you want to play it, then fine," Grace told her. "But we can't all be out of the house at the same time. If you're going out, I want to know. Do you understand me, Enid?"

"Yes, ma'am." Enid's hand stilled, but she kept her eyes on the bread. "It won't happen again."

"Good. That's all I'm asking. For now," she added pointedly. "There—does this look right for that crowd in there?"

Enid stepped back and nodded at the sight of the two trays with their plates of thin black bread, cheeses, a large piece of smoked salmon, pears and small apples, a bowl of walnuts.

"Take it in, then," Grace directed, but at that moment Hopkins returned in her dark dress, white apron, and cap.

"Follow me, Enid." Hopkins picked up the first tray. "And do as I do. Keep your eyes lowered and curtsy when spoken to."

"Yes, Mother." Enid picked up the second tray and followed her out of the kitchen.

Grace built up the fire in the stove and put the kettle on, knowing the doctor would certainly call for coffee or tea. Then she slipped across the narrow hall and into her room to check on the children; both lay quietly in their beds, Jack sound asleep but Mary Kate still awake.

"Hello, love," Grace whispered. "I'll be a while yet. The doctor has guests in."

"Shall I help you, Mam?" Mary Kate rose up on one elbow. "Jack's dead out, so I could, you know."

"Thanks." Grace smiled at her and sat down on the edge of the bed. "Missus Hopkins and Enid are back now, so I'm fine."

"Was Miss Wakefield sick of the drink?"

Grace looked at her in surprise. "How do you know about that, then?"

Mary Kate bit her lip and picked at her blanket. "I was looking round the house last week, late like . . . I know I'm not allowed," she added quickly, looking up. "Only I wanted to see the library."

Books, Grace thought. *Must get the child more books.*

"She came in, more on the quiet than I, ate a part of the lunch you'd left on the desk for him—stuffed it all in her mouth!" Mary Kate shook her head, incredulous. "Then she drank down two glasses of the doctor's whiskey, quick like, before she saw me hiding behind the chair."

"Caught you, did she?"

"Aye." Mary Kate nodded, ashamed. "Took me by the arm and said you'd be out of a job if I ever came in there again or told anyone what I'd seen."

"And where was I, then?"

"Looking for Jack and Scout down by the pond. Sorry, Mam." The little girl bowed her head contritely.

"You know better than to shame us like that." Grace waited a moment for the words to sink in, then asked, "Did she frighten you, agra?"

"Aye." Mary Kate's eyes were wide in the dim light. "It reminded me of something. The way she grabbed my arm and all, brought her face right into mine, her eyes all wet and the smell coming off her . . ."

Your father, Grace thought. "Never mind. Put it out of your head, but don't cross paths with her again. She's troubled, that woman, and drink only makes troubles worse."

Mary Kate let her head fall back onto the pillow.

"Go to sleep now." Grace kissed her cheek and smoothed her soft hair. "I'll see you in the morning."

Neither Enid nor Missus Hopkins returned to the kitchen, so Grace decided to serve the coffee and tea herself. She carried the heavy tray down the long hall to the drawing room doors, which were ajar; open-

ing one side a bit more with her foot, she entered the room and was
met with a blast of heat that immediately flushed her cheeks.

The men were grouped together in the far end of the room, near the
fireplace, and conversation was going strong. Grace quietly made room
on the sideboard for the teapot and coffee urn, surreptitiously glancing
around to see who was in attendance. She recognized a few of them.
There was Doctor Fairfax, of course, who leaned against the mantel
with a handsome pipe in his hand. Fairfax came up to the house regularly now and reported that meals at Wakefield Heights were far superior to those at the best restaurants in town; he and Wakefield were
great friends and spent hours at the doctor's desk, poring over plans for
the new Marine Hospital and discussing the best way to lure more
qualified doctors west in order to force out the hundreds of quacks who
still continued to dispense their questionable remedies. Fairfax was in
favor of inviting graduates from the new Women's Medical College in
Pennsylvania, but Wakefield was opposed—he had no faith in the skills
of these "doctoring ladies" or in the Quaker group who'd established
the college. Their conversations always fascinated Grace, who often lin-
gered when she served the men, in order to listen to their opinions.

The man standing next to Doctor Fairfax tonight was "Honest
Harry" Meiggs, complete with enormous cigar and puffed-up cravat.
Grace knew from the papers that Meiggs had become a very successful
lumber dealer with a wharf and a mill up at North Beach, and was currently trying to buy up all available land around there in anticipation
of the continuing growth boom. Wakefield had joked that Meiggs was
courting him like a fervent suitor, in the hope that he would join the
growing list of speculation partners, and he seemed to tolerate the man
in good humor, enjoying a bravado that was alien to his own nature.
Grace noticed that Meiggs always gave her the once-over whenever she
entered the room but beyond that paid her no mind, which was fine by
her—she disliked him instinctively; he reminded her of the land agents
she'd known in Ireland with their notions of superiority.

She didn't know the tall man who kept tugging at a thick lock of
brown hair, but when Meiggs addressed him as "McCabe" and asked
him about business at the packed and popular saloon he frequented,
Grace realized he must be James McCabe, owner of the El Dorado.
Now she took a closer look at him, curious to see the man rumored to

have set his mistress up as head of a fancy bordello. Grace's own brief experience with the fallen ladies at Molly O'Brien's in London meant that she harbored no ill will toward such women, only pity that they should have no other way to live but this. McCabe looked respectable enough, though of course looks were often deceiving, especially in a town of new money, but Grace felt sure that the doctor would not have entertained him at home if the man had proved unfit for good society.

Next to him was Edward Kemble, editor of the *California Star,* and Grace reminded herself to try for a quick word with him if time allowed. Kemble had come over on the *Brooklyn* with Sam Brannan, and Grace wanted to know whether he could help her make inquiries after her brother. She had seen notices in papers, posted by those seeking information on the whereabouts of relatives, and this, she'd decided, was to be her next course of action.

The last familiar face was William Shew, a favorite of both Doctors Wakefield and Fairfax, and a good friend of Mister Kemble. Shew operated the Daguerreian Saloon, and his images of miners in the field were gaining him fame across the nation, as was his new series about the burgeoning city in the West. He'd shown Grace some of his images and she had dared to share the visions she sometimes had when looking at recorded faces; intrigued, he'd invited her to come to his studio with the offer of making her own image or that of her children. She had agreed and now they were friends, of a sort. He caught her eye now, smiled, and nodded.

The last two men in the group were without doubt the doctor's latest acquisitions—two young medical students only days in from the East. Both wore the newest fashionable attire and were smoking cigars, an air of youthful exuberance about them that would fade into humility as they experienced the limits of their medical knowledge. But for now, they were as giddy as young pups, and Grace wasn't the only one enjoying the energy they brought into the room.

Quietly inquiring as to their preference for coffee or tea, Grace poured out cups and began handing them around. She took her time—the discussion had just touched on slavery and the state of the South, in light of a new book by Harriet Beecher Stowe, and Grace wanted to hear what the gentlemen thought of it. She'd read a number of editorials referencing *Uncle Tom's Cabin, or Life Among the Lowly* and was as fascinated as the rest of the country appeared to be. Though the book was selling like hotcakes, she felt certain that Doctor Wakefield would most likely not be buying a copy, and she looked forward to joining the nearly completed Mercantile Library, though ten dollars to belong and one dollar a month dues seemed a lot; she must do it for Mary Kate, especially, she reminded herself, and her wage here allowed room for such luxury. It was at times like these she felt intensely the absence of her brother. Not only would he have purchased straightaway a copy of the newest controversial book; he would have read it cover to cover and digested it in such a way that his conversations would have enlightened her own reading. He would have glowed in a room such as this, she thought with a pang of longing.

"Times are changing, Wakefield." Kemble's voice drew Grace's attention, though it was the doctor he attempted to draw into conversation. "Your beloved South is going to be dragged kicking and screaming into the future, I'm afraid, whether they like it or not."

Wakefield lit his own cigar, then shook out the match. "And what kind of future do you envision that to be, Edward?"

"The future of equality." Kemble stood up and moved toward the fireplace. "The future of payment for labor instead of payment for human beings."

Wakefield nodded, and Grace pretended to fuss with the bread plate, wanting very much to hear his reply.

"First of all," the doctor began thoughtfully, "it is *not* my beloved South. As you well know—most of you, anyway—I am not in favor of slaveholding, but neither am I as ignorant as some who have never lived among the Negroes. One cannot simply set free a people who have been cared for like children all their lives."

"Why not?" asked one of the younger doctors. "Why not give them the freedom to live life as they choose?"

"I happen to agree with Doctor Wakefield," Meiggs interjected, coming into the circle. "Let's say, for instance, that you owned a flock of sheep—what would happen if they were suddenly sent out on their own? Could they feed themselves, get their water? Could they defend themselves against predators? They could not." This last comment he directed toward the young doctor. "They could not survive in a world for which they had not been prepared."

"And whose fault is that?" Kemble asked quietly.

"No one's," Wakefield argued. "You are assuming that these people *want* to be prepared, that they are *capable* of being prepared."

"Surely, Wakefield, as an intelligent, learned man, you're not saying that the Negro is so inferior he can never learn to live productively on his own?" Kemble asked. "What about Frederick Douglass, Sojourner Truth, Dred and Harriet Scott . . . what about our own William Leidesdorff?"

"Anomalies," Wakefield insisted. "Most have enough European blood to negate the more base African blood, but it doesn't mean their essential characters are not still coarse and ruthless for all they've altered their outward bearing. Who do you think sells them into slavery in the first place?" He did not wait for an answer. "Their own people! In Africa! Negroes are not opposed to the condition of slavery—in point of fact, they foster it."

"How so?" Kemble flicked his cigar butt into the fireplace.

"You know as well as I do, Edward, that free Negroes don't hesitate to buy Negro slaves, to put them to work on their own farms, in their own businesses. What does that say about their character?"

"He's correct." This affirmation came from the second young doctor. "I don't know how many of you gentlemen have ever spent time around Negroes, but I can attest to the very low character that is common among them. They can be good and decent people," he conceded. "But, given the odd exception, they will never contribute to society what the European has—in fact, given a free hand, they can only bring the rest of us down."

"California recognizes your complaint, Mister Kemble," Meiggs offered. "And, while the good citizens have permitted the Negro his freedom, in their wisdom they have withheld the privilege of homesteading, voting, holding public office, and schooling their children with ours for the very reasons given by Doctor Wakefield. With freedom comes responsibility," Meiggs concluded. "And the Negro is simply not ready to assume as much."

The ignorance of brilliant men often staggered Grace, especially in light of the fact that they governed the lives of so many. She had turned and opened her mouth to speak when her eyes fell upon Doctor Wakefield, and she was instantly reminded of her place. She bit her lip hard, recalling other drawing rooms and other conversations into which she had entered, often to great satisfaction, but this time it could cost a very lucrative living and the well-being of her children. She felt a knot in her stomach at the realization that she'd entered the realm of compromised values; she was now no better than the men with whom she so strongly disagreed.

"If there's nothing else, sir?" Her voice was tight with resignation.

"Thank you, no." If Wakefield noticed her red face, he did not comment. "Gentlemen, some of you know my new cook, Missus Donnelly. For those who don't, this remarkable woman is late of Bleeding Kansas, the great cities of Boston and New York, and before that—Ireland. She is the one responsible for my renewed interest in gastronomy and the added girth that has resulted therewith."

The men guffawed and raised their glasses good-naturedly.

"Hear, hear!" Fairfax cheered, tossing her a wink.

William Shew met her eyes and made a discreet half bow in deference to her clear agitation. Grace forced herself to acknowledge their cheers with a smile, then hurried from the room, turning to pull the doors closed behind her.

"And not so bad to look at in the bargain, eh, Wakefield?" Meiggs ribbed.

"None of that," Grace heard the doctor reply sternly.

The trays could be collected in the morning, Grace decided; it was late and the day had been endless. Yearning for the comfort of her own bed, Grace passed through the kitchen and entered her own private quarters, closing the door behind her and sighing with relief.

The fire was low but the room was warm, and soft, rhythmic breathing came from the beds of her children. Grace took off her apron and then the dress beneath—it would have to be laundered, she saw now—removed her boots, her small clothes, and then her stockings, relishing the last bit of heat from the embers on her bare body.

She longed for a bath and was suddenly reminded of the beautiful soaking tub at Donnelly House, the first and last she'd ever known. Granted, the big tin tub she filled early every Saturday morning in the Ogues' kitchen behind the saloon was a luxury compared to the not-much-bigger-than-a-bucket tub she'd had in Kansas. There was a tub here for her use, and the children got their baths every Saturday night so as to be clean and sparkling for church come Sunday morning, but it was a sit bath, though she'd not complain—not after river bathing on the trail; at least the water was warm. The doctor bought himself a bath in town every few days, and Abigail was reported to have a lovely tub upstairs in the bathing room, but Grace would never spend so much as a minute soaking there and refused to allow herself to even think about it. The doctor was paying her quite a bit of money, but everything was so expensive in San Francisco; still, she might look into the price of a larger tub, one she could keep down in the cellar and bring up to use on evenings such as this, when her body longed for sleep but her mind was too restless.

Though the fire was nearly out now, Grace could not quite bring herself to leave it. Thinking of poor Miss Wakefield's devastated body, she looked down at her own, noting with satisfaction the new pounds put on now that she was not walking ten, fifteen, twenty miles a day and sleeping on the hard ground at night. The extra weight felt good; she had always been strong and sturdy and had not liked how her ribs had begun to show, the way her collarbone had stuck out and her cheeks had sunk beneath their bones—it reminded her too much of Ireland during that last, terrible year, when even the trees had been stripped of their bark, the grass pulled up by the handfuls and stuffed into desperate mouths, dirt eaten, anything to ease the pain of empty bellies. No, Grace thought, she preferred to keep weight on, wanted her children plump, with round arms and legs, soft bellies, chubby cheeks. Both Jack and Mary Kate had gotten too thin during the grueling walk from Kansas to Oregon, and Mary Kate had lost even more weight with her illness, but all that was changing now. The children were every day more robust and healthy; their eyes sparkled; their hair grew out dark and thick; they laughed more now and quarreled, always preferable to the heavy silence of defeat, of exhaustion. With a sigh, the embers breathed their last and Grace shivered in the coolness.

Her nightdress was warm from where Mary Kate had put it near the fire screen, and gratefully she tugged it on over her head, letting its warm folds spill down over her breasts, her hips, to her ankles. Next she wrapped a blanket around her shoulders and settled into the rocking chair, then began pulling the pins out of her hair, shaking it loose. When it had all come undone, she took up her brush and smoothed it, piece by piece, until she could run her fingers through it, lifting it from her scalp in heavy handfuls. She had lost hair during the famine years, and several teeth—though not in the front, thank God; the teeth would never grow back, but the hair was thick again and of good color. It was all vanity, when, of course, she should simply be grateful to have a life at all. She shook her head, pushing away the guilt that always threatened to come with the realization that she had lived while so many others had not. Instead, she let herself feel the weight of her body, its physical presence in the world, the fact that it was here.

Grace let the brush fall into her lap, trying to remember the last time her body had been held by another. In New York, of course, with Peter. And before that, one night—mere hours—with Morgan. She never dwelled upon her nights with Bram, though she did not regret them, as one had given her Mary Kathleen. She thought of the single, pitiable woman upstairs—Abigail Wakefield had perhaps lain with a lover, the loss of whom had ruined her. Why was it, Grace asked herself, that some were able to carry on despite the blows life dealt them, while others were crushed and lay down, waiting for death? She remembered the weight of her own grief when Morgan died, and then—with shame—her breakdown in New York when she'd thought Jack dead, as well. Had Dugan not wrested the knife from her hand—Grace allowed herself to touch briefly upon the terrible despair that had overwhelmed her—would she have really taken her own life? Mary Kate would have been orphaned, though she knew Dugan and Tara would have lovingly raised the girl, and Jack would have remained with Julia in Ireland; Grace would never have known Peter as her love, nor come to San Francisco to be his wife. Everything would have been otherwise—not worse, only different. And she was suddenly glad to have survived it, to be here, now, in this warm room with both of her beloved children asleep in their beds. She had survived it because of her faith and because of her friends; did Abigail Wakefield have either of those things? Grace suspected that the answer was no, and so she took the poor woman into her heart at that moment, and later, as she knelt by the side of the bed to give thanks, she named Abigail in her prayers as one who needed comfort.

In bed at last, Grace listened to the sounds of the men outside her window calling their farewells, departing with a slow clip-clop down the steep road back into the town, back to their own homes, wives, and families, if they had them. She heard Doctor Wakefield close the heavy front doors, knew then he was on his way up to bed. In the morning, Grace would serve his breakfast, then make up a tray for Abigail, carrying on as if the day before had held nothing out of the ordinary. And perhaps, for this household, it had not. But for Grace, everything was out of the ordinary and had been for as long as she could remember. Every morning she awoke as if she'd been holding her breath, and every night she closed her eyes knowing that the day had brought her closer to—what? *When Peter is here, I will know what to do,* she reassured herself in the dark. She wrapped herself around Mary Kate, pulling the snug little body close to hers. *This one is growing up,* she thought, and her eyes filled with tears—growing up with no real sense of what was home, what was a father, what was regular family life.

"I'll make it up to you," she whispered against the soft, curling hair. "To you and Jack, both."

Come home now, Peter, she prayed. *'Tis time.*

Nine

Captain Reinders lay drenched in sweat, his groans no less nor more than those of the other men in the tent hospital on the shore of Flamingo Island. He was getting better, though—in lucid moments he knew this to be true—and he urged First Mate Cole Mackley to sail north without him, to take Liam and the crew of the *Eliza J* on the fastest run for home they could make. God forbid that Liam should fall ill as well, and die down here in Panama. Reinders knew that he would survive, that he would see San Francisco Bay once again, and the beautiful harbors of the Pacific Northwest, but he could never face Grace with the news that he'd lost Liam, the boy they'd both taken on as their own.

Go, he'd ordered Mackley. *I'll come when I can.*

Mackley had promised solemnly, but still the *Eliza J* sat anchored offshore, losing money every day, losing its passengers to other ships—those damned steamers he hated so much for their noise and smoke—her crew waiting and watchful, having refused to a man to leave their captain in this godforsaken country with its unrelenting heat, torrential rains, screaming monkeys, giant insects, malaria, and dysentery; "Reinders" would not be one of the names recorded in the ever-growing cemetery that already housed a thousand dead, including most of the American Fourth Infantry, who'd fallen ill just months before.

In the evening, when the heavy heat abated, Reinders was able to stagger to his feet and, with the help of an orderly, make his way painfully to the front of the tent, where he looked out to the place his ship lay anchored, waiting for his return. His ship. Along with his boy.

The two things he loved most in the world; two of the three, he corrected himself. Each evening, he stood and watched the sun set on her magnificent masts, the sails tightly furled, sheets coiled and ready, the crew busy with maintenance chores—swabbing, tarring, stitching, repairing, polishing, sanding . . . anything and everything to keep their hands busy while they waited.

Reinders had borrowed a telescope, and now he raised it to his eye, focusing the lens, running it slowly aft to fore. He stopped midship; there was Mackley on the bridge, his own telescope glinting in the sun as he trained it on the island and then the tent in front of which his captain stood. Reinders lifted his hand in greeting and, a moment later, Mackley saluted in return, the boy beside him doing the same. Reinders trusted Mackley to look after Liam, but still he longed to see the boy himself. Finally, exhausted by the effort, he lowered the telescope and signaled to the orderly, who helped him back to bed.

At night, Reinders felt more awake, more alert and focused, than he did during the day; the hours stretched out before him minute by long, cool minute, giving him more time for reflection than he might ever have wanted, time to consider what was now worth living for and what, if anything, was to be gained by the ending of his life on this island. Nothing, was the obvious answer, and the answer to which he clung. Nothing was to be gained by dying here. This was no noble cause; there was nothing heroic in transporting goods and people from Panama City to San Francisco Bay. He wondered why he was even still in this game—certainly those damned steamers were the transport of choice among the moneyed; true, there were still fortunes to be made in importing, and the *Eliza J* could take far more cargo than could her rivals, but these runs had become dull. There, he'd admitted it at last—running his ship to the south had become routine, and routine was anathema to an adventurer. Even Mackley had made noises about joining another crew, though Reinders had ignored him; he couldn't imagine running his ship without the man who'd been by his side for so many years.

But Mackley was a courting man these days; he'd met a woman, the daughter of a cavalryman stationed up at Fort Vancouver on the Columbia River. Those were the runs he wanted to make—north, to Fort Vancouver, and farther, to the land that was about to become Washington Territory. There were settlements up there, in Seattle and at New Whatcom, that had caught Mackley's fancy. "And mine," Reinders admitted, then cursed himself for mumbling aloud, as the orderly was looking sideways at him again. He had to get well, had to get well rid of this place before they locked him up as a madman.

Reinders let his mind wander to the northern territories, to the islands and waterways that had quickened his heart in a way nothing had done since he'd come to the West. His first runs had been up the coast and then inland, where he sailed Captain Puget's spectacular sound until he reached the bay and the timber mill. This land lay in a pocket between the rugged Cascade Range and the imposing Olympics; on a clear day, it was simply the most beautiful territory Reinders had ever seen in his life. Mount Rainier rose like a god behind smaller mountains carpeted with dense forests that flowed down to the very edge of the water.

Out of this wilderness, settlements had been carved, and his favorite was New Whatcom—a colony that lay farther north of Seattle, in Bellingham Bay—a bold town of loggers and fishermen, their wives and families; a town that bristled with a bright industry, somehow noble in the face of such a rugged existence. He'd struck up a friendship with the Eldridges, Edward, a former seaman, and his wife, Teresa, who'd come over from Ireland during the famine; the two had met aboard Edward's ship, much as Peter and Grace had, though the Eldridges were married now and had a little daughter, Isabella. Over dinner in their cabin one night, Reinders had talked about Grace, and Teresa had shared her own experience, reminding him again how strong these Irishwomen were, how brave to build new lives not just once, but two times, three . . . however many it took to secure a future for their children.

Through the Eldridges, he'd also met Rolf and Astrid Sigurdsen, a young married couple who'd fled the famines in Norway and come overland to the West. At Edward's suggestion, Reinders had decided to invest in New Whatcom and had established a general store, which Rolf and Astrid ran as his partners. It was the first time he'd actually done something on his own with his own money, and his business partner, Lars, had been pleased with his choice of investment. It was a good store, and the Sigurdsens ran it well. Reinders was always glad to see them when he came up—glad to see her, he amended, Astrid. He sighed now and rolled over. Rolf had drowned early in the summer while fishing, leaving Astrid to run the store alone. Reinders had fully expected her to pack up and go back to any relatives she might have—she lost the child she'd been carrying shortly after Rolf's death—but she let him know in no uncertain terms that she planned to stay on and that she hoped he would still honor their partnership, as the store was making money. He'd made arrangements to have a cabin built onto the back of the store to make it easier for her, and he thought of her often. She reminded him of Grace in many ways; though they looked and sounded nothing alike, the two women shared a faith that seemed to see them through all kinds of catastrophe, and both had the gift of humor, which he readily admitted was lacking in himself. Yes, he thought now, she was a good woman, Astrid; he needed to get up there to make sure she had everything she needed to run the store. Winter was coming and supplies were always short.

There were Indians in New Whatcom, but the Lummis were prized for their knowledge and willing assistance to the settlers and, in return, were treated respectfully by those who now occupied part of their land. He'd seen the number of Indians along the lower Columbia decline with the advent of pioneers and the smallpox and measles they brought; even the sweat lodge—used to cure almost every ill that plagued them—was useless and, in fact, seemed to bring death even more quickly. But north of the Columbia, Indian life was still thriving, and in New Whatcom it was a colorful part of everyday life.

Reinders closed his eyes now and tried to muster the feeling of those cool, salty breezes, the scent of fir and cedar, tried to hear the lush sound of the wind in the trees, the call of fat gulls, the soaring magnificence of the eagles. Would he see it again? Would he sail those waters alongside orca whales and porpoises, taste the fresh salmon, giant crab, clams, and mussels that were her bounty? "Yes," he told himself, and this time he knew his voice rang out in the tent, but it didn't matter. Yes, he would go there again, and he would take Grace with him. He would get back to San Francisco, see Lars, then head up the coast to the Willamette settlement; she would have arrived there by now, barring any setbacks. She was with Lily and Jan, and theirs was a large wagon train that had left Kansas in plenty of time—no Donner Party horror for them, though he shuddered to think of all the other things that could go wrong. No, he told himself. Grace had wracked up all her suffering early in life—nothing else would go wrong. He would sail up the coast and see her; it might be awkward, he knew, but they had written to each other regularly and, of course, they had Liam in common. Liam would be with him, and that would make their reacquaintance easier. When she was ready, he'd take her up north and show her the jewel that was New Whatcom. When Liam had first seen this part of the country, he'd said how much like Ireland it was, especially County Cork, the part that Grace was from. Reinders had not realized how much he wanted her to love it, how important it was to him, but the hours lying awake on this cot had made that clear. People called it God's country, but he didn't really know what that meant—either the entire world was God's country, or nothing was. Though he now acknowledged the existence of God, he still didn't have much faith in Him; there was too much chaos in the world, too much disaster and cruelty to allow for any kind of omnipotent plan. But if he was ever stirred by the presence of a greater being, it was when he sailed into the bays of the Pacific Northwest—the sight of that land always moved him profoundly.

Feeling as though he had come to a kind of resolve, Reinders closed his eyes and smiled as the sight of the harbor and his little store swam into view. There was Astrid come down to the shore to watch him row in, her skirts tucked up away from the muck, her hair tightly braided and coiled upon her head. Grace would like her; they would all be friends and neighbors—the Sigurdsens, the Eldridges, the Reinderses. He and Grace could build a house up there; Grace had always wanted to live by the sea, he remembered—it was one of the things he loved about her.

A sense of calm washed over him then, and the last thing he felt was the swoop that comes before dropping away into sleep. It must have been the deepest, most restorative sleep he'd had since coming to the island, because when he awoke, he knew he'd turned the corner. Peter Reinders was well.

Ten

From far away, Barbara Alroy looked much older than she was; her once dark hair was now completely gray, and she stooped ever so slightly, though it was from constantly picking up small children and carrying them on her hip, rather than an advancement of years. As one drew closer, her true age became apparent in skin that had retained the tautness of youth and in eyes whose light still shone despite the hard years of famine; though her face was lined, it was as much from laughter and joy as from the struggles of survival. She was a striking woman, Barbara, with the strong dark handsomeness of all the McDonaghs. Had she been able to stand for a moment beside her brother, the resemblance would have been uncanny. She still missed Morgan with a fierce ache that made her hands clench into fists and her teeth grind together, but she did not indulge in the romantic notion that he had somehow escaped Ireland and was imprisoned in Van Diemen's Land, or was working in Canada, or living among the wild Indians in America. Morgan had been one of the most beloved heroes of the Young Irelander rebellion, and his stature had grown to mythic proportion, which was why each rumor she heard was bigger and more grand than the last. As much as she longed for him to be alive and living anywhere, anywhere at all, she knew that it was as the priests had said—Morgan had died in prison, beaten to exhaustion and sick at heart as well as in body. Barbara was every bit as strong as her brother had been, and she refused to torture herself, accepting instead that she would see him again, but in the next world.

She stood now in the doorway, wiping her hands on her apron, watching as a handsome carriage with trunks tied onto its back made its way slowly up the hill toward the schoolhouse that a dozen children, including the twin boys she had with Abban, called their home.

"Abban Alroy," she called over her shoulder, "are you expecting a visitor today? For one's come calling."

He looked up from his mending—a pair of small trousers gone out in the seat—and shook his head. "Not I, Barbara," he said. "But perhaps the queen herself has sent along a load of supplies, seeing as how we're caring for her orphans and all."

"You better come, then," Barbara ordered. "As you know, I'm not home to the queen."

Abban laughed, then set aside the mending and got out of the chair with the aid of his crutch. It had been three years since he lost his leg, but he still missed it, reaching down at night to scratch a shin that wasn't there. Having hobbled his way across Ireland with Barbara, from Cork City to Galway, he had learned to maneuver up, over, and around anything that might lie in his way, and now he moved with the speed and grace of a man who had the use of two good legs instead of one, and could dance well besides.

"Nice carriage." He shaded his eyes from the weak autumn sun. "Good horses, as well. Is it Julia, do you think? Back from London already?"

"Her letter said she'd be in Dublin for Christmas and see us after," Barbara reported. "But look—there's an arm waving out the window!"

They both stepped out of the doorway and into the yard as the horses swung the carriage round to the gate. Children stopped playing and stared, as did Gavin Donohue, the young man who helped about the place; visitors were rare, visitors in grand carriages more rare still. As one body, they moved silently to the fence and climbed the rails, straddling posts and beams, heads poking over and under, waiting to see what grand creature would emerge from such a conveyance.

" 'Tis Julia after all!" Barbara exclaimed, rushing to the gate. "Julia!" she called. "We never expected you!"

Julia stepped down from the carriage and embraced her old friend. "Good to see you, Barbara. How are the boys?" She eyed the youngsters gawking on the fence. "Hello, Gavin!" She waved to the young man, who swept off his hat and bowed as if to royalty, making her laugh.

"They're upstairs sleeping with the young ones," Barbara told her.

"And did you bring your wee girl with you?" She tried to peer into the carriage for Julia's year-old daughter, but Julia put a hand on her shoulder and turned her away.

"She's with my father at the Dublin house."

"Brave man, your da. Staying home with a crawling infant."

Julia laughed. "Ah, now, he's mush in her hands, completely useless. Only wants to dandle her on his knee and make the most ridiculous sounds. I left a nurse to look after the both of them." Her face grew serious. " 'Tis a quick trip I'm making, Barbara. Hello, Abban."

He shook her hand warmly, then kissed her cheek. "Always good to see your face, girl, though we hadn't a clue you were coming."

"It was all very last minute." Julia took both their hands, her eyes traveling from face to face. "I've brought you a surprise. A *true* surprise," she added. "Someone you've not seen in a long time."

They looked at her, bewildered, and watched as she moved away from the carriage door. A young woman emerged, familiar somehow to Abban though he didn't know her; Barbara, however, gasped, and her hands flew to her mouth.

"Do you know me, then, Barbara?" the young woman asked gently, eyes hopeful and wary both. "Your troublemaking, runaway, good-for-nothing younger sister?"

"Aislinn!" Barbara flew forward and wrapped her arms around the young woman in a fierce embrace. "Oh, Aislinn, my darling girl. Of course I know you. Of course I do." She held her sister at arm's length to look at her again, then hugged her more tightly than ever. "Oh, thank God! Thank God you're alive!"

The two women wept and laughed at the same time, as Abban looked on incredulously and Julia stood grinning.

"Abban!" Barbara drew Aislinn to him. "This is my sister Aislinn, gone away these many years to London!" She looked at Aislinn again in wonder. "And come back again! Oh, dearest girl!" And she began to cry in earnest, overcome with joy.

"Let's go inside," Abban suggested, taking the arm of his distraught wife and leading the others into the house. "Sit down. Sit down, please, and I'll fire up the kettle."

Aislinn was a younger version of Barbara, Abban realized, only the hair was lighter in color, and her face and figure more full. Certainly, her dress was that of a lady, and there were rings on her fingers, silver earbobs, and ivory combs in her hair. Barbara had never worn a new dress in all the days he'd known her, hadn't a piece of jewelry to her name save the ring he'd put on her finger, wore her hair in a simple braid down her back like a young girl, and yet she was the most beautiful, elegant woman he knew.

"I'm afraid we've not much to offer in the way of comfort." He waved his hand over the one great room scattered with chairs and stools, a large plank table in the center. "But you're welcome to it."

"Please don't apologize." Aislinn's voice was thick with emotion as she settled herself in a rickety wooden chair. "My dress is the way I used to live. Not the way I want to live now."

"And how is that?" Barbara asked quietly, drying her eyes.

"With you, Barbara. And with your husband. If you'll have me."

"Oh, aye!" Abban didn't hesitate. "There's no question of that. You're family and you've a home with us as long as you want it."

"You may not want me once you know how I've lived," Aislinn told him honestly. "I'm not proud of it, but I can't change it now, and I don't want to lie to you about it."

Abban and Barbara shared a look over her head.

"Did you marry Gerald O'Flaherty, then?" Barbara asked quietly, sitting down beside her sister. "And have you left him?"

Aislinn was quiet for a long moment, gathering her courage, and then she spoke. "Gerald never intended to marry me," she confessed. "I bore him a child but could not care for it on my own and gave it up."

Barbara reached for Aislinn's hand and held it.

"The next year was hard and I cared not for living. I was kept by a married man, wealthy and titled. He was good to me, and I was sorry when he died. The jewels, my rooms, and the money were my own, and I thought I might go on living a quiet life in London." She shook her head, saddened. "But I was too much alone, and my ghosts haunted me. From Julia, I knew you were alive and doing good work here, and so I hoped . . . perhaps . . ." She stopped, determined not to cry again.

Barbara turned to Julia, astonished. "You knew she was alive? All this time, you knew it?"

"I'm sorry, Barbara," Julia apologized. "I ran into her quite by chance the first year I went to London to raise money, and she begged me not to tell anyone what had happened to her."

"I didn't want to shame you," Aislinn confessed. "I knew I could never come home."

"Our mam loved you, Aislinn," Barbara assured her. "She wanted you with her but said 'twas best you lived away than died at home. Not a day passed, she didn't remember you in her prayers."

"And I, her," Aislinn said quietly.

"Was it you, then, sent us the money for this place?" Abban asked.

"I met Julia in Liverpool before Grace sailed. When you left the convent later on, I asked her to do it in her own name."

"So Grace knows you're alive?" Barbara was stunned.

"She told me about Mam and the girls, and that Morgan had died . . ." Here she paused again. "I knew she'd left the baby with you, and she said I didn't know you very well if I thought you wouldn't welcome me home again without a word said."

"Always thinking of others." Barbara shook her head. "She was in a terrible way when she left here, weak and exhausted. I worried she'd never survive that trip."

"Oh, aye, but she did. She went to Lord Evans in prison before she sailed for America. Do you remember, Julia?"

Julia laughed ruefully. "How can I ever forget? That was my first and last experience with prostitutes."

"What?" Barbara and Abban asked at the same time.

"Another time," Julia promised. "That's a story for a long night and a bottomless glass."

"I could use a glass of something myself, right about now," Barbara admitted. "But I don't think I'm ready for any more stories. And I've got to get the little ones up from their nap." She stood, still holding Aislinn's hand, and turned to her husband. "Will you check the big ones in the yard, Abban?"

"Should I come with you, then?" Aislinn asked. "Seeing as you've still got hold of my hand."

Barbara laughed with her, and Abban delighted in their resemblance.

"While you do that, I'll make our tea." Julia stood now, too. "I know my way around this place well enough."

Barbara led Aislinn up the stair to a wide dormitory set under the eaves. One half of the room was lined with cots for the nine older children; the other side had makeshift cribs for the five young ones, who were just now beginning to stir.

"Look here." Barbara leaned over the nearest crib.

Aislinn stood beside her, looking down at two boys sleeping in a tangle of arms and legs, dark-haired like the McDonaghs, but with Abban's nose and chin.

"Meet your nephews," Barbara whispered. "Declan, there, with the freckles. And Nally, after our da, bless his wild soul."

Aislinn put her arm around Barbara's shoulders. "Aren't they the most beautiful boys you've ever seen? How wonderful for you, Barbara. What a miracle they truly are."

"Oh, aye. Boggles my mind to think on it—the hunger and sickness were so terrible, and yet, without it, I'd never have found my Abban. I wouldn't have left the order, gotten married, and become the mother of these two lovely creatures. God has blessed me. Despite everything. Oh, Aislinn, I'm sorry," Barbara said quickly. "Sure and they must look a bit like your one."

Aislinn nodded. "I tried to get him back once, but they'd not tell me where he was. They said he'd have a better chance at life without me around his neck, and they were right."

"Their intent was right," Barbara told her. "But had they known your heart, they would have rushed to put him back in your arms."

"Thank you," Aislinn whispered. " 'Tis all right. I'm at peace with it now. Sometimes I imagine him growing up with a mam and da who dote on him, who play with him, and teach him things . . . and I'm glad for it. I'm glad he'll grow up well."

Barbara put her arms around Aislinn and held her. "We've lived through some times, Sister, have we not?"

"We have, Sister," Aislinn murmured. "We have."

"I'm so very glad you're here. That's all that matters now."

Aislinn's grip tightened. "I can stay, then?"

"Can you cook and clean, wash clothes and mend them?"

"I'm a little out of practice," Aislinn admitted, "but I'll do my best."

"Good." Barbara laughed. "Then the job of beloved sister is yours."

*   *   *

At the end of the visit, Abban walked Julia out to her carriage. "You're welcome to stay with us, girl, start out fresh in the morning."

"Thanks, Abban, but I've got to get as far as I can today. I had no idea Aislinn would be coming back from London with me, and I felt I owed it to all of you to bring her out right away."

"You can stop atoning for the past any time now, Julia," Abban gently pointed out.

"I don't think I can, actually," she admitted.

"How's our young Jack doing? Have you heard lately?"

"I almost forgot!" She reached into the pocket of her skirt and withdrew an envelope. "Letter from Grace. He's well. Loves Kansas. Cowboys and Indians and all that."

Abban shook his head. "I can hardly imagine such a thing, myself. What a life they're leading out there."

"She's thinking about moving farther west, to the coast, to a place called Oregon Territory."

"Is that where the sea captain is? Will she marry him at last, do you think?"

"He's south of there, but I don't know how far. And yes, I think she's ready to marry now." Julia thought about it for a moment. "It's a busy life, but she sounds lonely in her letter. Tired, as well. She's never really gotten past losing Morgan, and I don't suppose she ever will. But I think she wants to try."

"Not a day passes, I don't think of him in some way, remember something we did, or a thing he said. He's not a man fades easy from the mind."

"Or heart." Julia put on her bonnet and tied it under her chin. "Listen, what do you need in the way of supplies? I've got a meeting with the Quakers in Dublin, and also the Catholic Charities."

Abban called up the eternal list he held in his mind. "We could use seed for next year's garden. And another shovel—spading's hard work in this ground," he explained. "Also clothes for the bigger ones, especially dresses for the girls, and boots. We'll take any books, as most of them are learning here with Barbara. Slates'd be nice for their writing. Anything, really, Julia—anything a'tall would be put to good use."

"I'll see what I can do." She shook his hand. "Do you get much news of the world out here?"

Abban shrugged. "The odd paper comes our way now and then, usually wrapped round a fish. I know Meagher and MacManus escaped the colony and got to San Francisco."

"Aye, Terence stayed, but last I heard Thomas went on to New York City and was joining the army."

"You don't say!" Abban looked delighted. "Always had a keen military mind on him, that one. Wish he'd come on back here, but never mind—he'll show those Americans what the Irish are all about. He'll be a general before they know what hit them." He laughed. "And what about Smith O'Brien? Has he escaped, as well?"

"Still out in Van Diemen's Land. He's not well, by all accounts, but Jenny and the boys sailed out to live with him, you know."

"That'll be some comfort. I don't suppose anyone's ever heard what happened to Sean?"

Julia shook her head. "I think that's one of the reasons Grace is going farther west. She'll travel through Utah Territory and, if he's still alive, maybe she can find him."

" 'Tis a vast place," Abban marveled. "Like looking for a needle in a haystack, I suppose. And if he'd wanted to be found, he would've been by now."

"I just don't know. So many people have simply disappeared for one reason or another."

"But some are found again, as well." Abban looked back over his shoulder to where Barbara and Aislinn stood talking in front of the window, each with a twin riding on her hip. "Thank you, Julia."

"Thank yourself," she replied. "I just run around the country shaking people down for money. You and Barbara do the hard work."

" 'Tis a job I'm glad to do after all's been said and done." He put out his hand. "I've kept you long enough. You'd best go on while the light's still good."

"Good-bye, then, Abban." She shook his hand warmly. "I'll see you soon."

"Kiss little Aiden for me. Aiden Elizabeth Wilkes," he sounded it out slowly. " 'Tis a strong, strong name you've given her."

"Aye, she'll need it with me as her mam!"

They both laughed, and then Julia climbed into the carriage and gave the order to her driver. Barbara and Aislinn rushed out to the gate, and they all watched the carriage go back down the road, Julia waving to them from the window.

"Well." Abban turned to Aislinn after Julia's carriage had rounded the last bend before disappearing from sight. "Shall I take your young nephew, there, and give you a chance to settle in?"

"If you don't mind, I'd like to hold him a while longer." She picked up Nally's chubby fist and kissed the curled fingers.

"Then you go right ahead." Abban tussled the boy's hair. "I expect you'll be chasing him about the yard with a broom soon enough—he's a handful, our Nally. Takes after his grandda, I hear."

"Aislinn was always good with our da. Maybe she'll have the same effect on his namesake." Barbara winked at her sister.

Aislinn laughed and twirled the little boy around in her arms, then lifted him high to see the look of sheer delight on his face, and when it appeared, something burst free in her heart, and she held him again tightly in her arms. She had not been surrounded by so many children since her childhood, when she'd been one of nine in a neighborhood where almost every house had as many, and it was a crowded, chaotic, familiar feeling that washed over and around her, bathing her in peace.

That night, they all gathered around the table   Abban, Barbara, Declan and Nally, their auntie Aislinn; the hired help, Peigi O'Reardon and Gavin Donohue; six more boys in addition to the Alroy twins and six girls, ranging in age from four years to thirteen—faces flushed from being outside in the cool autumn air, eyes sparkling in the light of candles and lanterns, all on their best behavior for what must surely be an honored guest, so beautiful was the woman in her shimmering blue gown. Barbara passed the bread—she always made sure to have plenty of that—while her husband ladled out the potato soup, and when everyone had food in front of them, they all looked to Abban at the head of the table to lead them in prayer. When it was done, they still sat quietly, eyes wide.

"Go on, now," Barbara urged. "Pick up your spoons. It's not like any of you to be shy. 'Tis only my sister, Miss McDonagh. She's going to live with us now, but I promise she won't bite." Barbara's eyes twinkled.

There was a long pause as they all considered the fact of Missus Alroy having a sister and that this glamorous creature was going to live with them in the old schoolhouse.

Maeve, the wise eight-year-old at the opposite end of the table, over-came her shyness and asked, "Have you lost all your family like us, miss, and that's why you've come?"

"Aye." Aislinn put her hand over Barbara's. "All but my sister, and she's been kind enough to take me in."

"Mister Alroy and missus are good at caring for folk." Maeve looked to her surrogate siblings for confirmation, all of whom were nodding in agreement. "Welcome then, miss, and we're glad to have you."

"Welcome, miss," the children repeated shyly, each one giving up a smile of encouragement to their newest member.

Aislinn squeezed Barbara's hand, not daring to look at her for fear of spilling tears. Instead, she let her eyes travel from face to young face, seeing in them the images of her lost brothers and sisters, her neighbors, her baby.

"Thank you, dear children," she said to them all. "It's good to be with family again."

"And friends," Gavin added, his eyes meeting hers over the table. "You've friends now, as well, Miss McDonagh."

His steady gaze was uncomplicated; Aislinn saw only the strength and clarity she had missed in people. "I see that I do, Mister Donohue, and I'm glad for it."

"My friends call me Gavin"—he grinned now—"when they're not calling me the names I can't say at table."

The older children sitting on either side of him laughed and shoved into him affectionately.

"Gavin was beat up by the guards," Maeve offered, proudly. "For smashing a store window and stealing food. They put him in jail."

The young man's face reddened, but he did not hang his head. "Stealing's wrong, Maeve, and I'm sorry for it." He shrugged slightly. "Best to leave some things behind, wouldn't you say, Miss McDonagh? Get on with the living instead?"

The table was silent; Abban and Barbara exchanged a look that held in it all the things of their own they'd left behind.

Aislinn set down her spoon and put her hands in her lap. "Easier said than done, Mister Donohue. But I'm going to try my best."

"Gavin," he reminded her quietly.

"And I'm Aislinn." She smiled at him. "Now pass the bread."

Eleven

All Saints' Day dawned wet and cold, marking the end of their warm autumn weather. Rain splattered against the windows and dripped from the eaves, flattened the long brown grass, filled the road with puddles, and turned the yard to mud. Grace found that instead of dampening her spirits, this weather that was familiar from her youth somehow revitalized her. She had never minded rain, didn't mind it now, so long as the cold was not so great. It could rain every day until Christmas and she'd have no complaints, just no snow, please, and none of those icy blizzards she feared so greatly.

Grace pushed the heels of her hands more deeply into the bread dough, kneading it until it was silky and smooth, and then she placed it in a crockery bowl near the fire to rise. Wiping her hands on her apron, she glanced at Jack, who sat on the mudroom steps, plucking the first of four fine ducks. Doctor Wakefield, who enjoyed a day of sport now and then, had bagged them on an outing with his friend Doctor Fairfax. Litton had established a blind for them on a lake up the valley, just an hour's ride from here, and there they'd waited for the unsuspecting birds, firing upon them as they lit upon the water, then sending the dogs out to bring them in. Scout had remained in the stable, still recovering from the birth of her litter, but Doctor Wakefield had been proud of the new dog, a fine black Labrador retriever, who had worked tirelessly the day long, reveling in the cold and muck of the marshland.

Jack had watched them ride out in the morning, watched with a longing that had not gone unnoticed by the doctor. Wakefield had bent down and solemnly promised the little boy that he would take him out on one of these trips, show him how to shoot and run the dogs. Jack had insisted that he already knew how to shoot, but Wakefield had laughed and pointed out that gentlemen did not hunt with pistols. Stung, Jack had hung his head, but Wakefield had restored his dignity by putting him in charge of Scout and her pups. Jack had embraced the task with great enthusiasm and now spoke of the burgeoning puppies with an owner's proud air.

"How are the birds coming along, son?" Grace asked him now, smiling at his industry.

"Fine, Mam," Jack answered, surrounded by feathers—in his hair, on his jacket, stuck to his chin, floating around the mudroom. "I'm getting 'em all in the sack, as you said."

"Aye." She laughed. "I can see you're trying. Remember—the more you sack, the softer your pillow."

Reminded of that, he bent his head over the task and plucked with even greater deliberation, spitting out the odd pinfeather that attached itself to his tongue.

"And how're you coming along with those?" Grace turned her attention to her daughter, who sat at the table, a bowl of freshly scrubbed potatoes at one elbow, a pile of thick orange carrots at the other.

"Oh, fine," Mary Kate said, scraping the carrots; the paring knife slipped suddenly and marked her finger, drawing blood.

"Pay attention, there, girl," Grace admonished, seeing now the other nicks and cuts on her daughter's hand. "Are you writing stories in that head of yours again, or are you peeling carrots for our dinner?"

"Peeling carrots." Mary Kate smiled apologetically. "But, Mam?" Her hands paused. "Do you suppose Captain Reinders and Liam might be the prisoners of terrible pirates?"

"Pirates?" Grace frowned. "Why would you be thinking that?"

"Well." Mary Kate set the knife and carrot down. "You know how pirates love gold and treasure and all that."

"So I've been told."

"And them in the hills, they're digging nothing but gold still, aren't they, Mam?"

"Aye. Get to the point, girl."

"Well, what I'm thinking is that a smart pirate would be laying in wait out there beyond the harbor, ready to attack an innocent ship and rob it of its treasure. And once they'd gotten it, they'd—"

"Kill the crew!" Jack stood in the doorway, eyes wide, holding a half-plucked duck by the neck. "Run 'em through with their cutlasses!" He thrust his free hand in the air, making the gesture.

"All right, that's enough," Grace scolded. "Captain Reinders and Liam have not been captured by pirates, let alone killed by them." She shot Mary Kate a warning look. "And you know better than to spin a tale like that in front of Jack."

"Ah, Mam." Jack shook the duck at her. "You don't know nothing 'bout pirates."

"Jack McDonagh." Grace put her hands on her hips. "You get yourself back to work, now, boy, and I don't want to hear another word out of you about what I do or do not know."

He scowled but went back to his stool and sat down. "Yeah, well, you don't know Calico Bill or Captain Kidd," he muttered.

"Oh, and you do?" she replied, then instantly regretted taking the bait.

"Aye! Mary Kate's been reading out to me, and we know all about them scurvy bastards."

"Jack!" Even Mary Kate was shocked. "Mam, I never did teach him anything like that," she insisted.

Grace bit the inside of her cheek very hard, determined to put the fear of God into her precocious young man.

"Young Jack," she warned darkly, "if you ever talk to me like that again, I'll tan your backside and give you nothing but porridge to eat for a fortnight."

He glowered and kicked the chair leg.

"And no more stories at bedtime," she added. "No books, no stories. For an entire year."

Jack was instantly contrite. "Sorry. Sorry, Mam." He looked to his sister. "Sorry, Mary Kate. You'll read still, won't you?"

"Only if you behave, Jack," Mary Kate said, sounding very much like her mother. "Now get back to your work."

They all resumed their tasks in a heavy silence—Jack plucking with a grim stoicism, Mary Kate slicing vegetables, their mother snipping dried herbs and grinding spices to season the fowl—when suddenly Grace burst out laughing, unable to hold it in any longer.

"Pirates!" She shook her head and wiped her eyes. "I don't know which of you's the worst. I really don't."

Jack and Mary Kate hesitated, then began to laugh as well, relieved at the dissipation of tension in the room. The children lived for their mother—they were happiest when she was happy, lightest when she was light, least anxious when she moved about with purpose and direction.

"I want you to know this." Grace was still smiling, but serious now; she turned so that both of the children could see her face. "Liam and the captain can take care of themselves wherever they are. They don't know we're here in San Francisco, or they'd've come back straightaway. But we're fine until they do come back—do you understand me?"

Mary Kate nodded, then Jack did the same.

"We've a roof over us and warm beds. And plenty to eat," Grace added this last for her daughter's sake. "Are you both happy here—for now? Are you, Mary Kate?"

"Oh, aye. Doctor Wakefield says I can have books from his library."

"That's right," Grace confirmed. "And you, Jack, are you happy enough here?"

Jack shrugged indifferently, but then his face brightened a bit. "I'm in charge of the puppies," he announced. "And maybe I'll get one of my very own."

"So we're fine for now," Grace stated. "And when Liam and the captain return, well . . . then we'll decide what to do from there."

Mary Kate put down the paring knife. "Will you marry him, Mam?"

Jack's hands paused over the bird, waiting for his mother's reply.

"I'm thinking I might," Grace answered carefully. "Will you want a da, do you suppose?"

"Is he a hero, like mine?" Jack asked.

Grace thought of how Peter had overseen the rescue of Lily's children from South Carolina. "Aye," she told the boy. "He is."

Mary Kate lowered her eyes, her hands limp on the table. Grace saw this and came to the table immediately, sitting down close beside her so that their shoulders touched.

"Your da was a good man as well, Mary Kate. 'Twas the terrible times turned his character." She took her daughter's hand. "He had many fine qualities and you've got the best of those," she said firmly. "Never forget that you're the granddaughter of Lord Donnelly, and when you're eighteen, you shall inherit the manor house and lands back home in Ireland."

"But you loved Jack's da best," Mary Kate pronounced. "You loved Morgan most of all."

"I loved your da, too, and I wanted to be a good wife for him." Grace paused. "When Bram Donnelly died and Morgan asked me to marry, I saw then that I'd always loved him—since we were children, only I never knew it."

"And then he died." Mary Kate knew the story well.

"Then he died," Grace repeated. "But you and I went on. We came to America, we got Liam and lived with Uncle Sean, we went to Boston to live with Lily, and now we're here in the West."

"Do you love Captain Reinders like you loved Morgan and my da?" Mary Kate asked.

Jack had come into the doorway again.

"I think I do. I . . ." She hesitated. "There are many kinds of love, you know. 'Tis hard to make sense of them all."

"I'll not take a husband," Mary Kate resolved firmly.

"And why not?" Grace was surprised.

"Too sad when they die."

"Nor I," Jack piped up. "No husbands for me."

Grace and Mary Kate looked at each other and had to laugh.

"No *wives*," Mary Kate told him. "Boys marry wives."

"Oh." Jack frowned, hating to be corrected, and retreated to his stool.

Grace picked up Mary Kate's hand and kissed it, then pressed it against her cheek, thinking of what to say to this young girl.

"Well, they don't always die, agra," she reminded her gently. "You can't have the promise of a long life with them, but you can always hope for one. A little time is better than no time a'tall, don't you think?"

Mary Kate shrugged her little shoulders.

"What of the children you have together?" Grace pressed.

"Then everyone is sad," the girl said simply. " 'Tis too hard to care for the babies with no husband to help you. You could marry another man only for the help of him, but you'd still be sad." She kept her eyes on the table. "You'd still cry at night for the one you loved most of all."

The impact of those words forced Grace to sit back in her chair and take a good look at her daughter, at the child she'd towed halfway around the world, through misery and mayhem, the child who had grown even wiser than Grace herself had suspected. She thought hard, knowing she would have to be honest if her daughter were to have any faith at all in the future.

"Your life, agra, will not be like mine," Grace began. "I couldn't protect you from all that happened to us, and I'm sorry for that. Very, very sorry." She bit her lip, feeling the rise of emotion in her chest. "But you cannot be afraid of what *might* happen. A heart cannot be locked away, and truly you are strong enough to love someone with your whole heart. You are." Grace smiled into her daughter's eyes. "Haven't you lived through more in your nine years than most people in their lifetimes? And I cannot wait to see what you'll make of it all, what you'll become in the world, because you are"—she sought the word—"magnificent."

Mary Kate's eyes filled with tears and she let her mother hold her.

"Love does not run out," Grace promised quietly. "You'll always have enough, no matter what happens. Only you have to believe 'tis there; you must have faith in it."

"I love *you*, Mam," Mary Kate told her. "And Jack. I love Dugan and Tara and their Caolon. And Lily and Jan, Sam and Ruthie, Mary and Sol, all the Frees. And I love Uncle Sean."

All the people we left behind. Grace closed her eyes.

"And most of all, I love Liam. I miss him, and what if I never see him again?"

"Me, too," Jack said suddenly, having come all the way into the room. He pushed himself between Grace and Mary Kate, putting an arm around them both. "What if I never see him again, too?"

"Well, now, Jack, you've never actually met our Liam. Nor Captain Reinders." Grace squeezed his shoulders. "Only heard tell."

"But that's how!" Jack insisted. "The captain brought you over from Ireland, and Liam's mam died so he's our brother now, even though he lives with the captain!"

"Well." Grace kissed him. "That's about as right as it gets."

"So I miss them, too." He leaned his head into theirs. "I love plenty of folk, Mam. I promise."

Thank God for Jack, Grace thought again as she and Mary Kate laughed and the little boy joined in, glad to have cheered them all up.

"All right, now, you two." She gave them each a quick hug, then stood up. "Can't sit here chatting the morning away. Back to work for all of us, and then we'll have a nice cup of tea and some of that apple pie from last night. What say you, then?"

The children cheered, then resumed their tasks, and Grace made an excuse to slip away for a clean apron. She closed the door to their room behind her, went to the window, and pressed her face against the cool glass. The burden of the past with all its trials did not matter if it meant a better future for her children; they were healthy and bright, the finest companions a person could wish for, and she would have the privilege of knowing them all her life if she raised them well enough now *Grant me the wisdom, Father,* she prayed. *Help me to do what is best for them in all things.*

As if in answer, the clouds above the hill parted and a single shaft of light streamed down to the muddy yard, illuminating for a moment the glistening grass, the moss on the stable roof, the chickens running in their pen, the rippling pond down the back lane. The possibility of starting anew, of doing better, occurred with every fresh moment, and this gave her hope. She returned to the kitchen to check on the children, then decided to get a platter for the ducks from the dining room sideboard, but when she pushed open the door, there stood Abigail Wakefield in bare feet, her skin pale and her hair undone.

"Miss Wakefield!" Grace put her hand to her heart. "You gave me a start. Is there something you're wanting from the kitchen?"

Abigail regarded her with wary, bloodshot eyes. "Tea," she ordered hoarsely.

"I'll bring it straightaway. Is Missus Hopkins not with you, then?"

"On an errand." Abigail did not look directly at Grace, but over her shoulder. "In town."

"You should've rung for me," Grace told her. "You'll catch your death, standing there in the cold."

"No." Abigail's eyes clouded with anxiety, though they remained unfocused. "I'm not ill. I just . . . want . . ." She sighed and turned away, moving slowly back down the hall.

"Tea. Aye, miss."

Grace resisted the urge to take Abigail's arm and help her up the stairs, so much did she resemble an old woman, but instead returned to the kitchen.

"Jack." Grace poked her head around the corner to where he still sat on the mudroom steps. "Wipe off your hands and go fill the kettle at the pump, will you, love?"

"Aye, Mam, but where were you?"

She lowered her voice to a whisper. "Having a word with Miss Wakefield out in the hall."

Mary Kate turned around to look at her mother, her eyes as wide as Jack's. "Was she angry, then, Mam? 'Cause she had to come down?"

"Did she yell at you, Mam?" Jack demanded. " 'Cause, you know I'll . . ."

Grace shushed them both. "She wasn't angry and she didn't yell. She's not a mean person, really, just . . . sad, I think."

"Why?" Mary Kate tipped her head to one side.

"Well, I don't know, exactly. But perhaps we could soften our hearts a bit toward her, what with Christmas coming round and all. What do you think?"

Mary Kate considered it for a moment, then nodded. "I could give her over to God when I pray." She paused. "But will I have to, you know, speak to her or anything like that? Will you want me to, Mam?"

"No," Grace agreed. "Best to stay as we are—out of her way."

"I'll quit spitting in her teapot," Jack offered soberly.

"Jack! You never did!"

"Twice," he admitted, holding up three fingers. "Sorry, Mam."

"One of these days, boyo, you'll be in for it." Grace shook her head, wondering why her inclination was always toward laughter instead of anger over Jack's antics.

"All right, Mam, all right. Just not right now, as I'm going to help Mister Litton. After I get water," he added, swaggering out the door like a little man.

A few minutes later, he struggled back in, lugging the heavy kettle with two hands. She relieved him of it and put it on the fire, then made him put on a jacket and cap before he went back out to join George, who stood waiting near the garden gate.

"Be good now, and mind Mister Litton."

"Ah, Mam, I'm always good, aren't I?" He looked up at her with such complete innocence that again she had to smile.

"As good as you can be, our Jack." She buttoned up the jacket, then hugged him quickly and let him go.

"Do you want to go out, as well?" she asked Mary Kate, who still sat at the table.

"I'll help Enid feed the chickens in a bit," the girl replied, then looked up, puzzled. "Where is Enid?"

Grace shrugged. "With her mother, perhaps," she said, then leaned forward and whispered dramatically. "Out on another one of their mysterious errands."

"Maybe Enid has a lover," Mary Kate whispered back, giggling.

Grace let her mouth fall open in pretended shock. "And what would you be knowing of such things, young lady? And besides, why would she be wanting her mother along?"

"Maybe the lover has a father," Mary Kate imagined. "And he's Missus Hopkins' lover! Maybe they work in a big house, as well, and the four of them meet in the plaza! For a rendezvous!"

Grace laughed. "That's quite a word for a little Irish miss. What's it mean, then, and where did you come by it?"

Mary Kate sat up proudly. " 'Tis French for 'a secret meeting,' and I got it from *The Count of Monte Cristo*. Doctor Wakefield told me how to say it."

"Aren't you a clever girl?" Grace praised. "But I don't know that I'm so keen on your reading all about lovers and rendezvous and the like. Can you not find yourself a nice story of dogs or rabbits, or girls living quietly in the country?"

"There's no quiet living in the country, Mam," Mary Kate reminded her soberly. "You know all that happened to Jane Eyre."

Again Grace laughed and shook her head. "Never should've read that one to you, but 'twas a long, cold winter, the last." She put her hand fondly on her daughter's head. "Aye, you remind me of your uncle Sean with your thirst for books. Your father had a good mind, as well. You get it from them."

"You're the one reads to me every night and puts books in my hand, talks to me about the stories and all," Mary Kate pointed out. "You're the one I want to be as clever as."

Moved, Grace kissed her cheek, then went to the stove to get the hot water.

"I better get this up to Miss Wakefield. You go on out when you're ready, then, and mind you put on your warm jacket and hat."

Mary Kate nodded and finished up her chore while Grace quickly made the tea and, at the last moment, added a small piece of the apple pie to the tray.

Walking carefully, she carried it down the hall and up the narrow back stair, then down the upstairs hall, stopping in front of Miss Wakefield's door. She set the tray down on the small table and rapped quickly, then opened the door, picked up the tray, and entered the room.

Miss Wakefield had gone back to bed, and the room was stuffy and cheerless, lit only by whatever weak and watery November light slipped through the haphazardly drawn draperies. It was enough light, however, to show up the dust and disarray, and Grace wondered why Abigail did not insist upon it being cleaned more thoroughly.

"Your tea, miss." She set the tray on a writing table that sat before one of the long windows. "Shall I pour it out for you?"

Abigail opened her eyes and sighed. "Yes." She picked up a small ornamental timepiece from her bedside table. "Is this the correct time? Eleven o'clock?"

" 'Tis," Grace confirmed. "Are you feeling better this morning, Miss Wakefield? Could you eat a bite?"

"Hopkins has not returned?"

"Not yet." Grace poured a splash of milk into the china cup, then added a stream of hot, black tea. She brought this over to Abigail, who took it more gratefully than Grace had expected. "Would you care for a piece of last night's apple pie with it?"

Abigail looked at the plate, tongue wetting her lips, but she shook her head.

"Begging your pardon, Miss Wakefield, only there's nothing to you but skin and bones. You can't ever hope to get well again if you don't eat."

"I'm not trying to get well."

Grace was surprised. "Well, there're quicker ways of going than starving yourself, you know. Your medicine there." She indicated the blue laudanum bottle sitting in its little saucer on the bedside table beside a glass of water. "I'd say that's more than enough to do the job."

Now it was Abigail's turn to look surprised. "You can't possibly understand," she said finally.

"You're right. I saw more starvation in Ireland than I ever care to see again—why would a person do that to themselves on purpose, do you suppose?"

"I . . ." Abigail looked confused. "I don't have to explain myself to you. You're no one to me."

"True enough. But maybe I'd leave you alone about your meals, if I knew what you were doing here. Quit sending the tray up, and all. Make it easier for you."

Abigail shook her head. "I don't want it to be easier."

Grace waited, but when no other explanation was forthcoming, she spoke again.

"So, I'm to keep making up your meals and you'll eat only enough to keep yourself alive until the next day, and we'll keep on doing this for . . . what? Another year, at the most, and then you won't be around to deprive yourself of anything." She paused. "Sounds to me as if you're paying penance, Miss Wakefield, and that's very Catholic of you and all, but—"

"Hopkins is not Catholic," Abigail interrupted.

"Ah." Grace nodded. "I thought she might have something to do with it. I don't know what she's convinced you of, miss, but I'm here to tell you that you cannot make up for anything you did yesterday by starving yourself today."

Abigail closed her eyes and pressed her fingertips into her temples.

"The headaches are from lack of nourishment," Grace informed her. "Drink, laudanum, and no food. You can't think straight on that. Eat this one thing," she enticed, holding out the plate. "And see if you don't feel a wee bit better."

"I don't want to feel better!" Abigail's eyes opened and she slapped the plate out of Grace's hand. "Get away from me, Satan. I won't be tempted by you."

Shocked, Grace knelt down and cleaned up the pie, the broken bits of plate. When she stood up again, Abigail was spooning a generous dose of laudanum into her mouth. Eyes on Grace, she swallowed, put the spoon down, and leaned back against her pillows. Within moments, her eyelids closed to half-mast and her mouth sagged open.

Grace put the mess of food and china back on the tray, then glanced back at Abigail, who seemed to have entered a twilight state. The room was overly warm and close, the smell of sickness and decay cloying. Grace went to the window and pulled back the heavy cloth, then the sheers behind, pushing the material all the way to either side and tying it off. Glancing at Abigail once more, she surreptitiously lifted the sash just enough to allow for an exchange of air. The outside breeze was crisp and damp and immediately alleviated the stuffiness of the room; Grace took a deep breath. It was a dark day and would only get darker, so she lit the lamp on the writing table; with the hem of her apron, she wiped off the dusty, water-ringed table and straightened up the books and papers that lay thereon. Ink had splattered on the blotter and the pen drawer was ajar; it stuck when she tried to push it back in, then closed with a loud snap.

"What are you doing?" Abigail demanded, suddenly sitting bolt upright. "Get away from there. I didn't tell you to do that."

Grace felt herself blush, and her heart was pounding wildly.

"Yes, miss," she stammered. "I'm sorry. I only wanted to set it right," she said more firmly, having collected herself. " 'Tis dusty in here, ma'am. And none too clean."

"You're not the housekeeper." Abigail's voice was slurred and her eyes began to glaze over again. "Where's Hopkins?"

"Gone to town, you said."

Abigail struggled to keep her eyes open. "Want to see her," she murmured. "I do."

"Here I am." Hopkins stood by the open door, and Grace had the distinct feeling that she'd been listening in the hall long before she announced her presence. "It took longer than expected, miss, but here I am now. You may return to your kitchen, Missus Donnelly," she added, narrowing her eyes.

Grace looked from one woman to the other, then picked up the tray and left without saying anything to either one. Behind the closed door, voices rose behind her, and though she couldn't hear what they were saying, she could tell that it was Hopkins who was increasingly angry while Miss Wakefield's anger was almost immediately dissolved into pathetic pleas and crying. She shook her head, not knowing what to make of it, then retreated to her kitchen, where Enid sat at the table, staring at nothing, hands clasped in front of her.

"Enid! Have I not said you mustn't go off like that? I don't mind looking in on the mistress, but you're to tell me. Else, I'll have a word with the doctor, and before the day is out."

The young woman's eyes cleared and she looked up at Grace. "Please don't do that, Missus Donnelly. It won't happen again. Today was . . . well, Mother had an errand for Miss Wakefield and I was needed . . . in another place . . . for something."

Grace sat down across from her and looked her firmly in the eye. "You're a very bad liar, Enid," she said quietly, "which speaks well of your character. I don't know what's going on around here, but that woman upstairs is in a bad way and 'tisn't only nerves did that."

Enid's eyes went wide, and then she looked down.

"Where were you, Enid?"

"To church." She hesitated. "And then to see—"

"Enid!" Hopkins stood in the doorway, her face red with anger. "Get back to work at once, girl! Right now!"

Enid jumped to her feet and rushed from the kitchen, her mother glaring as she pushed past. When the door had closed, Hopkins came well into the room, hands at her sides balled into fat fists.

"You don't know the half of how things lie around here, missus, so don't go upsetting the balance," she menaced. "Keep to your kitchen and you'll keep your job. Trouble that poor woman upstairs and you'll get trouble yourself."

"I'll keep to wherever I like," Grace said calmly, standing up. "You can bully your daughter and Miss Wakefield, but you'll not bully me." She paused for good effect. "What kind of religion is it, Missus Hopkins, says God demands endless suffering for the sins of your past?"

Hopkins clenched her jaw. "You don't know what you're talking about."

"Here's what we're going to do now," Grace informed her. "That woman upstairs is going to start eating again."

Hopkins shook her head. "I have nothing to do with that. She's addle-minded; you've seen it yourself. And she drinks—I admit that. Now you know the truth. You think I have some power over her. That I force her to starve." She lifted her hands in a gesture of helplessness.

"But she'd be dead if not for me. I'm doing the best I can by the poor demented creature, God pity her."

You're a better liar than Enid, Grace thought, *but I don't believe a word of it.*

"If you can't get her to eat, then I'm taking over her care." Grace held up her hand to stop the housekeeper's protest. "Once Doctor Wakefield sees the state she's in, he'll know something must be done."

Hopkins' face reddened with suppressed fury, but she nodded reluctantly, and when she spoke again, the forced contrition in her voice made Grace even more wary than before.

"You're right." The housekeeper looked pained as if the burden had been too much for her. "Something must be done or she'll waste away to nothing. I've been to church about it this very morning. But the mistress doesn't like you, Missus Donnelly. And she can't bear your children. Your presence only makes things worse. You must promise not to disturb her in the future."

"Then don't leave her alone without telling me," Grace countered. "And while you're up there, you might clean that room—it smells to high Heaven. The whole house is wanting for a good spit and polish; you might try giving Enid a hand once in a while."

The mask slipped, and Hopkins' eyes glinted with her true brittle anger, but just as quickly she resumed her act of contrition.

"Miss Abigail has demanded so much of my time," the housekeeper simpered. "Poor Enid has had to bear the brunt of the work, and you know how inept she is. And now, what with the doctor entertaining more, well . . . I can see we've fallen behind."

"To say the least." Grace wasn't giving her an inch. "But Christmas is coming now, so I want you to see about cheering the place up a bit. Mary Kate and I'll give you a hand now and then if you're so hardpressed, though it seems Miss Wakefield sleeps much of the time."

"She does," Hopkins allowed. "Though it's a fitful sleep and I hate to leave her unattended."

"Which is why you left her alone this morning?"

"I only go out when she insists. Only when she insists."

"Then leave Enid with her, and tell me," Grace said. "That's how we're going to run this household from now on. Now, if you'll excuse me, I've a meal to prepare."

Hopkins gave her a ghastly smile, one that obviously hadn't been used in years, then bowed rustically and backed out of the kitchen, leaving Grace to wonder what had just occurred. She shook it off and set her mind to the tasks that lay before her, losing herself in the simple pleasure of familiar work.

By late afternoon, the loaves were out of the oven and sitting on the sideboard cooling, and the ducks were spitted and roasting over the fire, the scent of which was driving the dogs mad—Grace had to hold them back with her foot every time she opened the back door. Jack had returned from the pond as wet as if he'd actually gone swimming, so Mary Kate had dried him off and changed his clothes, and now both children sat before the hearth, playing draughts.

Enid had been noticeably absent from the kitchen all afternoon, and Mary Kate had seen to the chickens without her. So they would all sit down to dinner at the long table, and Grace knew it was bound to be an awkward meal. She could not let go of the day's conversations, and of her time spent with Abigail. She felt drawn to the woman and yet was also deeply troubled by her. Despite Hopkins' protestations, the housekeeper clearly had a hold over her mistress and it was an unnatural hold, at best. Grace was beginning to understand that she must have a further conversation with Doctor Wakefield to make sure he knew how poorly his sister fared in Hopkins' care. And yet, the household had been like this for . . . how long? Years, Hopkins had said. They had functioned this way for a long time, and who was she to come and change things? Hadn't she promised to maintain a peaceful home life for the children, and didn't that promise outweigh any obligation she might feel to her employer? *Aye,* she told herself. It did. She would try to keep her nose out of whatever odd routine had been established, though Missus Hopkins need be none the wiser. Grace liked the fact that the housekeeper might be wary enough of her to stay out of her way, and if she could get a clean house for the doctor in the bargain, then that was good enough for now. Grace stood and stretched her back, hands behind her, pressing down on her hips. Whatever the truth was, Hopkins was ultimately right—it wasn't Grace's concern, and she needn't go out of her way to make it so.

Twelve

Abigail Wakefield woke in the middle of the night, her heart pounding. She hated the dark, but the fire never lasted an entire night and they never left a lamp burning in her room—not even a candle or matches—for fear she'd stumble against it and catch the entire place on fire. Hopkins put all the lamps out herself before retiring each evening, leaving Abigail to face the dark alone should she wake after the embers had burned themselves out. Usually, she swallowed enough laudanum, wine, whiskey, or a combination thereof to ensure she slept through the night, but lately it hadn't been working; lately she awoke despite the fog in her head and lay there in the dark, fighting desperately against the memories that would not be silenced once they realized she was vulnerable to them. They marched across her mind's eye in a steady progression, whether she wanted them to or not, and the worst was when a single scene froze, forcing her to examine its every corner.

The worst, of course, was the hanging. The lesson, they called it back home: *We're going to teach that boy a lesson,* they'd say; *that black nigger, that yellow gal, that mulatto chile* . . . all of them needed lessons, it seemed, all of the time. The lessons were usually administered in the form of whippings—for laziness and thievery (notorious among Negroes), lying (born to it, all of them), debauchery (they couldn't help themselves, but still a good master would try to beat it out of them)—but runaways and horse thieves might find themselves hobbled, though owners hated to damage their own property, and transgressors who had committed even greater evils got the noose. Thomas had gotten the noose, the ultimate lesson in *Thou shalt not.* Lynching was what it was, Abigail knew—hanging a man who never set foot before a judge, who was never found guilty, who was tried and sentenced and executed in the dead of night, under cover of darkness, the executioners masked to protect themselves from . . . what? They were cowards, Abigail knew. Lynching was the act of cowardly men.

Lynched, she thought. To hang a man from a tree and leave him there to swell and rot like overripe fruit. She knew it happened on plantations all through the South, but usually women were protected from the sight of such brutality—white women, anyway. Abigail had never seen a lynching, though she'd stumbled across the aftermath once or twice and had imagined how it happened. But this time, this time they made an exception—did they suspect, she often wondered, or were they merely so full of pride that they wanted to share their vengeance with her? After all, they were doing this for her, weren't they? They were avenging the honor of a daughter of the South whose innocence had been corrupted by a man who, though free, was no more than the lowest animal in their eyes; what that man had done to one of theirs was not only wrong—it was evil. Evil. The word they used. What they said to her—she'd been ruined by Evil. She parted her lips now, in the dark, heard the crackle of dried spit in the corners of her mouth, felt the split in her lower lip reopen, probed it for blood with the tip of her tongue, thought of forbidden fruit, what they said to her. It was all so very horrible, and her hands fumbled for the bottle beside her bed, desperate to drive it away because it could not be undone but nor could it be borne.

She had screamed. Screamed and screamed and screamed until they yanked the wagon out from beneath him simply to stop the echo of her screams crashing through the hot, fetid summer night. They had looked at one another, those men, unnerved by her shrieks, but taking it as proof of the madness she'd suffered at the hands of her attacker.

They had been eager to avenge her maidenhood—oh, yes, so eager and willing to put this presumptuous Negro in his place, his place in the ground—but then they could not meet her eyes the next time they saw her; could not meet her eyes at a dinner party or on the dance floor; could not look at her in church, where they went to pray for protection from Evil. She'd begun to realize that they could not look at her without thinking of her body being overpowered by that young Negro buck, and it shamed them because they considered themselves civilized men. But it excited them, too—oh yes, it did—and she knew it and they knew it.

Her father could not look at her; her brothers brushed past her on the veranda, in the hall; their wives made every excuse to leave the room when she entered. The slaves, once friendly, now kept their eyes on the floor and answered her reluctantly, if at all, when she spoke to them; she had taken one of their own—she knew that this was what they were thinking—a free man, a promising young man, a man who was going to make a difference someday. What had she been playing at, this wealthy white girl, tempting a poor Negro boy? Didn't she know they'd lynch him? They'd had no right, of course, to lynch anyone, especially a free man, but—and here a dry, joyless laugh escaped her—white men could do as they pleased in the South. Maybe white men could do as they pleased anywhere in the world, but she didn't know anything about the rest of the world, only about the South. Only about the men in the South. And because she knew about them, about the power they held over everyone in their worlds, the slaves were right—what had happened was her fault. It was *her* fault.

And when she realized that, the world tipped sideways and she fell off. She could no longer eat at dinner parties, could not even lift her fork; could not dance, for its requirement of lightness was something she had lost forever; could not follow the service in church, so filled was her heart with the begging of God for understanding, for forgiveness, for redemption. But God had known it was her fault, too, and her words had fallen on deaf ears. She'd done everything she could think of in order to atone, but how could anything make up for the loss of a human life? She'd proceeded with a plan that only proved how really stupid, foolish, and ignorant she really was—no wonder God could not, or would not, bring her relief.

But He had brought Agnes Hopkins, and Hopkins had shown Abigail the way to redemption. God did not want her prayers, her words, her petty atonements—that was too easy; God wanted proof of Abigail's remorse, evidence of her suffering, before He could relieve her guilt, before He would forgive her. And so she had put away that which she loved most in the world, that which she had fought so hard to keep, put it away in a safe place until she could claim it with a cleansed soul.

And she had spent years making her penance, had given up the world, starved herself, suffered the necessary abuse heaped upon her by the one doing His will, had given herself over so that her own stubborn pride and sinfulness might be torn from her. But now, as she was finally drawing near the prize, a devil had entered the house in the guise of a simple cook, determined to wrench her away from God's servant and win her soul for Satan, thereby to be separated forever from those she loved.

Abigail's heart began to pound, and she sat up, clutching the blankets in her bony fingers, eyes wide in the dark. She would have to be wily to pass this last test; she would have to summon every ounce of strength left in her decimated body and fight until blood oozed like sweat from her pores. *Help me,* she whispered into the gloom, *help me lest I be forever damned.*

She listened for a moment to the hiss and whisper of the dark, listened until it began to make sense to her. *Yes,* she answered the voice in her head. *Yes,* she nodded, faster now, the end in sight. *Thy will be done. Be done at last.*

Thirteen

Morgan awoke suddenly to a stillness he knew well, and to a crisp, clean scent in the air that undercut the close smell of smoked meat. He lay for a moment, orienting himself, looking up toward the top of the birch-lined *wicuom,* out through the hole at the peak, where tendrils of smoke from the rock-ringed fire pit escaped. Lying there in the dim light, he could also smell the fragrance of the fir boughs that covered the floor of the *wicuom,* over which the women had laid mats of woven reeds, and then fur robes. Because winter was coming, they had begun to line the walls of the *wicuom* with reed mats as well, and a collar for the smoke peak had been made ready for installation at the first sign of bad weather. Morgan took another deep breath, then rolled over and squinted at the shaft of light coming through the door flap. Yes, he was right. The bad weather had arrived.

Père Leon, snoring contentedly, lay buried beneath his own fur robe next to Morgan on the men's side of the *wicuom.*

"Father." Morgan shook the priest's shoulder until he snorted and rolled over. "Wake up, Father," he said quietly. " 'Tis snowing."

Père Leon opened his eyes immediately and looked at his new friend.

"Huh," he grunted, mumbling something else in French, then threw off the robes and crawled over the older sleeping men to the flap. He pushed it open, and Morgan saw even more clearly that, though the snowfall was still light, the ground had already been covered.

Around him, thirty members of Aquash's family still slept; above them all hung long sausages of moose intestines stuffed with fat, meat, and berries, the scent rich and flavorful in the close environment. Morgan's stomach rumbled and, outside, the dogs began to whine for their breakfast.

Père Leon crept back and, shivering, wrapped the warm robe around his shoulders. "We must go today," he said decisively, "or stay for the winter. Which would not be so bad," he added, sniffing the fragrant air.

Morgan shook his head. "I must get to America."

"Then dress yourself, my friend, and say your good-byes." Père Leon called to Aquash, who woke immediately and came to him. He spoke to her, pointing to the flap, then nodding as she replied.

She went to Nacoute's place among the men and roused him, waking the others in the process. Grunts and yawns were replaced by a few words here and there as the Indians woke up and greeted one another, dressed and checked the weather for themselves, then gathered their children and began to prepare food for the morning.

Morgan pulled on his pants and stepped from the *wicuom* to relieve himself in the woods; the sky was gray and bright, snow flurries swirling around him. Squirrels were running madly up and down tree trunks, storing away what might well be their last food supplies before winter, and a pair of foxes, their pelts bright against the snow, moved stealthily past, eyeing the man who eyed them back. The forest was muffled this morning, and there was a sense of urgency in every flash of wildlife he saw. Shivering, Morgan returned quickly to the tent, passing Père Leon, who was on his way out. He reached for his shirt, but before he could put it on, Aquash stopped him. She pointed to a pile of Indian garments she had placed on his blanket—winter clothing, it appeared—and he watched closely as she demonstrated the order in which each piece should go on.

She handed him a pair of thick moose-hide leggings that had been painted up the side with triangles, circles, and scallops mostly in black but with a touch of yellow, red, and white around the cuffs; the Mi'kmaq wore these leggings under loincloths, but Aquash had attached them to a seat so that they more resembled the European trousers to which he was accustomed. Over his thin linen shirt, she helped him pull on a long tunic of sealskin that would keep him warm and dry, also painted, though not as intricately as many he'd seen in the camp. His boots were long worn through and his woolen socks threadbare, so he was grateful for the fur-lined moccasins she handed him; they were long, a tube of skin from a moose leg, sewed across the toe, rubbed with seal oil so that they were both supple and water-resistant. Around these she wrapped bands of leather to keep everything in place. And last, she handed him a robe of rich warm beaver fur that had a belt at the waist and fell to just below his knees. For his head, there was also a cap of beaver with flaps to cover his ears. He recognized the cap; he had seen Aquash working on it last night, stitching the pieces together with a bone awl and strands of dried animal sinew, just as she had the moccasins.

All the while she dressed him, Aquash did not meet his eyes, and Nacoute stood nearby, holding Morgan's gun and knapsack, his baby sister bundled near his feet. Now that the moment had come, Morgan struggled with how to say good-bye to these three people for whom he'd come to care so deeply. Sensing his anxiety as she sensed every emotion that floated around her, Aquash finally looked up and laid her hand upon his cheek. She smiled reassuringly at him, then took his hand and led him out of the tent, Nacoute following.

Although Morgan had met many of the Mi'kmaq during the past four days of celebration, he had not thought there were as many as this; it seemed that more than one hundred gathered now in the clearing between the *wicuoms,* the men glancing at the sky and nodding, their women calling out shyly and smiling at him.

"They have all come to bid us good journey," Père Leon told him. "Here is their headman, Aquash's grandfather."

An elder, dressed in his finest robe, came forward and put his hand on Morgan's shoulder, looking deeply into his eyes and speaking slowly. Morgan did not avert his gaze even as he listened to Père Leon translate.

"He says, thank you for bringing Aquash and her children home to her people. You are a good and brave man, and your name will be one of honor among them."

Morgan shook his head. "Tell him it is Aquash who was brave, Nacoute who showed courage."

Père Leon spoke to the old man, who listened and then motioned for Aquash. She came to him, the baby, Marie, in her arms, and Nacoute by her side. And then he spoke to Morgan again, peering so closely into Morgan's eyes that Morgan was sure he could see into his soul.

"He says that Nacoute and Aquash have told him the story. He knows the story."

The old man nodded, his eyes never leaving Morgan's face.

"You have given him back his beloved granddaughter, his great-grandson, and his new great-granddaughter, and for this, he will sing of you every year when the first snow falls."

When Père Leon finished, the old man smiled and stepped back, and Nacoute took his place. Morgan had to fight the urge to embrace the young man, a move he knew would be wrong in front of all these braves. Nacoute reached into his tunic and pulled from it a leather pouch on a strap; this he removed and opened, pouring out its contents into Morgan's hand. Morgan turned it over and felt its smooth edges—it was the carving of a bear, done in bone, possibly of the bear itself. He listened as the headman spoke again and Père Leon translated.

"He says this is Nacoute's spirit-helper, the great and mighty bear who wants only to be left alone in peace but will fight to the death for her cubs." The priest paused while the old man spoke again. "Though the boy cannot talk, the old man understands what you are to him. Nacoute has said through his mother that there is only one man he thinks of as his father, and that man is you."

Morgan regarded the young man before him. "Tell him"—he stopped and cleared his throat. "Tell him that he honors me, and that I could ask for no finer a son." He wrapped his fingers around the bear and brought his fist to his chest. "I will carry him always here."

The priest translated, and all the heads in the crowd that listened so raptly began to nod with pleasure.

Morgan put the string around his neck and tucked the pouch into his tunic. Aquash stepped forward and kissed his cheek; he kissed hers in return, and then the baby, and then there was a rush of gifts—a moose bladder filled with creamy fat, a sharp hunting knife in a coyote-tail sheath, a pipe with a stone bowl and a pouch of native tobacco, a hemp bag of smoked salmon, two long moose sausages, a birch-bark container for holding and boiling water, and pieces of chert and iron pyrite for sparking a fire.

Overwhelmed by the generosity, Morgan turned to Père Leon.

"Say to them that they are like the people from my country far, far away, and I pray that the God of my people will bless them."

Père Leon translated his words, and the Mi'kmaq cheered in the way that was their own, waving the travelers off. Morgan waved farewell to Aquash and Marie but could not find Nacoute in the crowd though he scanned it again and again.

"Let's go, my friend." Père Leon tugged at his arm. "We've miles to go before dark."

Morgan took one last look at the camp, knowing he would never see such a thing again, nor people like these, and then he turned and followed the priest into the wilderness. As they walked, he became aware of a shadow flitting among the trees behind them, though he could never quite see it, however fast he turned around. A trick of the light and snow, he told himself, but finally Père Leon turned around, laughing.

"It is the boy," he said quietly. "He will follow us a while longer and then he will turn back. It is how he sees you safely on your way."

They walked an hour, the boy's presence felt behind them, and then came the eerie sound of a whistle or pipe. Morgan turned, and Nacoute stepped out from behind a tree, the small pipe in his hand. This was good-bye now, and Morgan knew it. He raised his hand and kept it in the air until the boy raised his, as well.

"Good-bye, son," he called, his voice ringing out in the wilderness, but the boy had already turned toward home.

Fourteen

It was not a long process, daguerreotypy, but holding still once the artist had disappeared beneath his great canvas hood was absolutely necessary, and so it was a feat of heroic endurance for Jack, who seemed to think that it also required the holding of his breath.

"Done!" William Shew reemerged, looking pleased. "That will be a very nice portrait, if I say so myself." He patted his mussed hair back into place.

"Phew." Jack blew out a long stream of air and shook himself all over like a dog just out of water. "Is it over, Mam?" he asked, panting.

"It is for you and your sister," Shew told him. "But I'd like one of your mother alone. I'm willing to spring for chocolates next door, if you'll mind your sister the entire time?" He turned and nodded encouragingly at Grace, soliciting her acquiescence.

"That's very kind, Mister Shew, but you've already been so good to us and we've taken up so much of your time." She shot Jack a warning look and the protest he'd been about to utter died on his lips.

"It's my pleasure, Missus Donnelly, really. They've been simply delightful, and it will give them something to do while I arrange you. Children?" He reached into his vest pocket and pulled out a half-dollar, which he pressed into Mary Kate's hand. "That should cover just about anything you'd like. When you've chosen your treats, you can enjoy them on the bench right out front there until we're done in here."

"Thank you, sir," they both uttered with barely suppressed, wide eyed delight.

Jack was quite certain that Mister Shew was now the best man he'd ever known. Next to Mister Litton, of course. And Doctor Wakefield. Those three were the best. His mouth was watering.

"Off you go, then." Shew ushered them out the door, laughing, then returned immediately to Grace. "I wanted some privacy," he confessed. "To make something really splendid. Stay seated for just a moment, will you?" He disappeared into a small closet, and Grace could hear him rummaging around.

She swallowed hard. *Oh, please don't let him ask me to take my clothes off,* she prayed. He'd been so good to them all and she liked him so very much, but now she was anxious and wondered if she'd been naive in accepting his offer of making a family portrait. He'd told her he intended to display it in his next exhibition, after which he'd make a gift of it to her; she'd been excited about that—it would be the first and only image she had of her family, a record of who they were: Irish Americans in San Francisco, state of California, November 1852.

"Here we are!" Several silk cloths were draped over his shoulder, and he carried a mirror in each hand.

"Oh, please, Mister Shew," she began.

"It will be magnificent," he said, ignoring her feeble protest. "It is my gift to you, Missus Donnelly, in thanks for sharing your unique gift the last time you visited my gallery. Do you know," he continued, "I have been quite inspired by your insight. I am recording the city still, yes, but not just its prominent citizens. Emigrants, Missus Donnelly, I am recording the flood of emigrants that wash up on this shore. For posterity!" He lifted a finger in the air to make his point. "And I haven't forgotten what you said about the Indians, either," he added. "I'm planning a journey to the interior even as we speak. Their ways shall be recorded so that we might always know how they lived before they joined the rest of civilization."

"Well, that's not exactly what I said, Mister Shew, though I'm happy you'll see them for yourself."

Grace shifted on the hard stool. She had brought Mary Kate with her to the exhibition, knowing the child shared something of her own gift of vision. In New York, except for Mathew Brady's gallery, it had seemed to leave her—too crowded, she'd thought, for visions of passing spirits—but on the trail from Kansas to Oregon, she'd seen them almost everywhere she looked. The first time had been when she thought their wagon train was simply catching up to another, but when they began passing through it, passing through the very people who walked and the animals who pulled their wagons, she knew that no one else was seeing what she saw. Though mile upon mile separated one wagon train from another, Grace's experience was of one long trail of humanity, peopled by the spirits of those who had died along the way. She was not afraid of these spirits—she'd been allowed glimpses beyond the veil for as long as she could remember.

She learned, too, not to comment on the Indians that rode past, be they hunting parties, war parties, traders, or migrants, nor could she trust Mary Kate, who saw them sometimes, as well; only after Jack whooped and pointed them out could Grace know that these were living Indians and not the spirits of those gone on ahead. The prairies were full of such spirits—the woods sheltered them, the hills were alive with their rustling energy—and they were generous, pointing out to her the hidden creeks and bubbling streams that saved her children from drinking muddy, sulfurous water; they led her to rabbit and gopher holes when she needed fresh meat, showed her hidden nests full of eggs, warned her of snakes and quicksand, prairie fire and thunderstorms, guided her across scorching desert, and helped her cross the dangerously swollen rivers. She had garnered something of a reputation among the hundred others of their party, had known they whispered suspiciously about her uncanny luck. Only Lily had known what it was Grace could see, and Lily had told no one, though she'd followed Grace implicitly.

San Francisco was not so full of souls, though Grace suspected the hills and desert land beyond were more heavily occupied. She and Mary Kate had not been able to resist Mister Shew's gallery, and both had learned the stories of the Chinese people in those images, not from Shew himself—who knew nothing—but from the eyes that bespoke their souls.

Letting Mister Shew believe that the insight she gained came directly from the artistry of his images, she shared with him the importance of recording human beings in all their diversity. He had already begun such work by taking images of the Chinese, and these were invaluable, she'd told him. And there were still so many others, she'd pointed out— the Californios on their rancheros, those whose land was being taken from them now even as they had first taken it from the Indians; the exotic Chileans, Peruvians, South American Indians; the Negroes, especially the Negroes who were tasting freedom in a way their parents had never dreamed, though their acceptance even in the Free States would be generations in the making; the American Indians in their spectacular dress, so many different tribes—the Paiute, Nez Percé, fierce Sioux and Apache, Shawnee. This time was passing more quickly than any other time in history, and it would be gone, lost to mankind forever, if it were not recorded by a sensitive and dedicated artist.

True enough, she told herself then, listening to her own internal voice. He was an artist unlike any other, and she would trust that what he wanted for her was important for reasons she had yet to understand.

"Would you take off your jacket, please, Missus Donnelly?" he asked, his equipment ready and waiting.

Grace bit her lip but unbuttoned the jacket and allowed him to help her out of it.

"And now—" He hesitated, his hands hovering though he knew that touching her would be inappropriate. "What I want, Missus Donnelly. I mean, what I envision for your portrait, is . . ."

"You'd best just have out with it," Grace told him, "before we both jump to the wrong conclusion."

"You are a very beautiful woman," he began.

Grace's hands went to either side of her face and she shook her head. "When I was young—"

"I can only imagine, Missus Donnelly," Shew interrupted. "How breathtaking you must have been. But it is not youth that interests me so much as it is a life farther along the path of experience. To me, the smooth perfection of youth pales in comparison to the depth of beauty that can only arise through the very act of living."

Grace let her hands fall to her lap, where they worried one another anxiously.

"The lines you have accumulated upon your face—those across your forehead and here, at the corners of your eyes . . ." He reached out gently with one finger and touched the spot. "And here, by your mouth. These are more alluring to the artist because they speak of a life hard won—the mixture of elation and grief and every emotion in between, of marriage and childbirth, affirmation and disappointment, struggle and triumph." He touched her cheek now, and she looked up into his eyes. "There is a history etched upon your face, Missus Donnelly, that is unlike that of anyone else, and it fascinates me. I catch a glimpse of it, there, in your eyes, but I can never know all you have experienced. I can only honor it in the way I know best—by recording it, as it is today, in this moment of your life, a moment that is suspended between the past and the future. This will be one of my finest portraits ever recorded, Missus Donnelly. Please trust me to do you justice."

Grace nodded imperceptibly, moved by the grand sweep of his speech.

"Because I wish to portray you as a woman of her century in a way that is also timeless, I will ask you to take down your hair and let it fall freely about your shoulders. And then to remove your blouse to the waist of your skirt, so that you sit only in your chemise." He paused to gauge her reaction. "I am asking more than I have a right to, I know that."

Grace studied his face for a moment, intent upon understanding him and not being played a fool, and then she nodded.

"The buttons are in the back," she said quietly. "I'll need help."

He came around behind her and started at the top, sliding each button out of its catch with a delicate dexterity. How long since she'd felt the touch of a man upon her body? Grace closed her eyes and willed her heart to settle itself; William Shew was not a lover, nor did she wish him to be.

"All undone." His breath upon her neck brought every nerve in her body to attention; the feeling intensified as he gently pushed the blouse forward off her shoulders, watching as she slipped her arms from the sleeves, the garment falling in a pool of gentle folds at her waist. He rested his hands on her shoulders, which were bare but for the straps of the simple white cotton chemise. "Shall I take down your hair?" he said so quietly she barely heard him.

"I will," she murmured. "I can do it."

He left her side and returned to his camera obscura, though his eyes never left her face and the warmth of his hands remained upon her skin. Grace kept her own eyes lowered as she raised her arms and felt in her hair for the pins that held it in place, removing them carefully, one by one, dropping them into her lap. When she had done, she shook her head gently, letting the heavy hair drop down upon her shoulders, feeling its cool weight against her flushed neck and back. Finally, she allowed herself to meet his gaze.

"Exquisite," he breathed. "The shade of your hair in this light, your skin, those eyes . . . if only I could capture you in all your colors, if only I could paint." He shook his head. "But it would not do you justice."

He gathered up his mirrors and selected a piece of dark green silk, which he then hung on the wall behind her, positioning the mirrors so that her head and shoulders were illuminated by additional light. He stood back and surveyed her with an artist's impartiality, and then he was behind her once again. Grace found that it was hard to breathe as he turned her sideways, his hand again on her shoulder, the other on her thigh. Next, he lifted the hair away from the front of her face, settling it behind her shoulder; on the other side, he brought the hair forward, his fingertips brushing the bare skin of her bosom just above the low neckline of her top. It was excruciating, and she wondered if he realized how terribly he stirred her. Finally, he was satisfied and bid her not move a single muscle until he was through. Twice he recorded her image, and twice she felt a surge of light pass through her.

Grace felt as if her blood ran hot, pulsing from one part of her body to another, and that this heightened state must surely be visible to the man who studied her now, who approached as if to warm himself near the emanating glow. Again he stood behind her, and again she felt herself become weak, though instead of touching her, he gathered up the folds of her blouse and held it in such a way that she might easily slip into it, after which he brought it together in back and began to do up the buttons. He had nearly reached the top when he paused for just a moment, then lowered his mouth to the side of her neck, pressing his lips there for the most brief of tender moments. It was over so quickly that Grace wondered whether she had imagined it, so stirred did she find herself, and completely overwhelmed.

Without a word, he gathered up her hair and plaited it, then reached into her lap for the pins and secured it to the back of her head. And then he was done. When he had lifted the shade and taken a seat on the stool near his instrument, Grace finally found the courage to meet his eyes, though she was still without words.

"It will be remarkable," he pronounced soberly. "You are remarkable." When Grace did not reply, he peered at her more closely, concerned. "Are you all right, Missus Donnelly? I do apologize most sincerely if the experience has left you in any way troubled."

"No, Mister Shew." Grace found her voice but felt herself near tears for some reason she could not explain. " 'Tis exhausting, though. I'd no idea 'twould be like this."

"Actually"— he regarded her for a moment, a smile at the corners of his lips—"I have *never* experienced a sitting quite like this. I hardly know what to say, Missus Donnelly, except to thank you. I do believe we have created a masterpiece."

"That will be your doing," she said, beginning to relax. "You're the artist, Mister Shew. I'm honored to be included in your work."

He was still looking at her with a slightly dazed expression. "I took two," he told her. "Two portraits. One of them, I will give to you with the portrait of your children. The other . . ." He paused. "The second one, I'd like to keep for myself. For my private collection. If you've no objection."

"None," Grace said immediately. "You've charged me nothing a'tall for this, and I know the value of your time and talent. I'd be pleased to know you have it." She felt a twinge of pain in her shoulder and winced. "Could I stand up now, do you think? I'm getting a bit stiff."

He jumped to his feet. "Oh, of course! Please," he proffered a hand to assist her. "You must be more than ready to retrieve your children and go home."

She nodded, feeling more than a little light-headed, and held fast to his arm as he escorted her to the front door, grateful for the fresh air that swept through the room when he opened it. She stuck her head out and was happy to see that Mary Kate and Jack sat dutifully on the bench, heads together over a bag of peppermints, feet swinging merrily. She turned back to her host and extended her hand.

"Thank you, Mister Shew," she said warmly. "I'll be looking forward to seeing them when you've done setting them up."

He nodded but did not release her hand. He glanced up and down the sidewalk, then pulled her just inside the doorway.

"Missus Donnelly," he began, his eyes searching hers. "Do you think you might accompany me to dinner one night? Delmonico's is very fashionable; we could even hear a concert afterward— if that pleases you."

Grace bit her lip, loath to admit even to herself that she was tempted.

"I do understand your situation," he continued. "Wakefield has said you've formed an attachment but that the gentleman in question is currently away. If it is not a formal engagement, does that not leave you free to accept a social invitation?"

"I am free," Grace allowed. "But, that said, I don't think it would be right somehow."

"I can promise that I will not press any case other than friendship. I would so much like to know you better." He did not step any closer, but Grace felt the intimacy between them increase.

"Perhaps if there were others in our party," Grace conceded. "Perhaps if the children came along, or even just Mary Kate. I'd be more agreeable to such an outing as that."

Shew nodded, relieved, and kissed her hand before releasing her. "The theater, then," he suggested. "Your daughter would enjoy that, I think, and I know I would enjoy attending with the two of you. I shall arrange it and send word to you at Wakefield's."

Grace's smile was a little unsteady, unsure as she was whether or not she had just entered into something more than she should have. She said good-bye to him politely and left him standing in the doorway, watching as she collected her happy, sticky children and shepherded them down the street. She was distracted all the way home, and the children took full advantage, pausing in front of every window that interested them, darting to the corners ahead of her, surprised when she did not call them back. What had happened to her this morning? she asked herself, reliving each minute of her time in the studio. Why had it unsettled her so completely that she now felt unalterably changed? She looked around her at the city, at the sunlight reflected in a hundred windows, up at the gulls tossing overhead, down into the animated faces of citizens who hurried about their business, and then she realized what it was—suddenly, she did not feel old and tired, as if all her life lay behind, the future for her children alone; suddenly, she felt lovely again—truly lovely, desirable even, with every hope of a future to call her own.

"I'm young," she whispered to herself, acknowledging the hum of her body, the lightness of her heart.

She grabbed Jack up by both hands and twirled him around her, laughing at his delighted squeals, then set him down and swept up Mary Kate, determined to bring a smile to her face, as well. When she was done and both children were wide-eyed and grinning, she knelt down before them and took one of their hands in each of hers.

"Be happy," she said to them then. " 'Tis a beautiful day, we're all together, and life is long. Be happy," she repeated. "And never forget how wonderful it feels."

Fifteen

Always the great strategist, Sean had memorized the layout of San Francisco within a week of his arrival, traversing the streets and alleys on his horse, making notes on the map he'd bought, and so he knew exactly how to get from Delmonico's on O'Farrell Street to Ah Toy's luxurious parlor house in the alley off Pike Street in the Chinese district. That first week had been the only time he'd traveled San Francisco by daylight; now he was strictly an occupant of the nighttime city. Still, streets lay out the same by day as by night, so finding the famous brothel was no trouble at all.

He lay back in the soaking tub, eyes closed, as steam rose around him and his muscles began to relax. Tonight was a big night, and he'd already had a fine meal at Delmonico's, a walk for his digestion, now a bath, and then an hour with one of the girls. This was a Chinese house, so he'd requested a peasant—no bound feet for him. The first time he'd come to Ah Toy's, they had sized him up as a man of exotic appetite and had shown him to a room where sat upon the divan a lovely woman in an extraordinary gown. Though he'd been relieved of his virginity in the first week of his arrival to the city and had made the rounds of many parlor houses, Sean was by no means a worldly man and was therefore unprepared for what his first Chinese woman offered. Her appearance alone was enough to excite him—the long dark hair, white-powdered face, and brightly painted lips, her slim, pale body beneath the silk robe—and he had no problem moving into her delicate arms. But as their fondling grew more heated, she nudged him with her foot and he took hold of it, kissing the little silk shoe and then unraveling the strange stocking. The sight of what lay beneath had shocked him, and he still did not like to think of it, had tried to put out of his mind the broken, deformed foot, toes curled round to the heel. Later, he had learned from Chang-Li that this was a rare delight—the lily—a courtesan's most erotic offering, but he could not imagine pleasure between a man and woman that depended upon such painful sacrifice. He had become aware of these women and had since caught glimpses of them being carried from room to room, or hobbling painfully on the arm of a servant. His own affliction, the shortened leg and twisted arm, made him especially sensitive to theirs, but his was the result of an accident, not the intended outcome of loving family members who broke the foot of a child, then bound it tightly so it would never grow, considering this a beautiful and desirable attraction for a future husband. He simply could not wrap his mind around this and had made it quite clear that bound feet were not what he wanted when he came in for a woman.

But this degradation he considered an anomaly; he had not witnessed the cruel side of prostitution, though if he were to be honest with himself, he knew it existed. He had seen the battered faces of girls who quickly closed their doors, had heard screams in the middle of the night, had stared into guarded eyes when he asked after a girl who was no longer there. He told himself that this was simply a rare hazard of the job. Most of these girls—whether in the best parlor houses off Portsmouth Square or the slab shanties of rebuilt Little Chile or the backroom dives of Sydney Town and Clark's Point—were here by choice, in this town to make their fortune just like the miners they serviced, the entrepreneurs, the gamblers and businessmen. This was a city of opportunity, and these women were making the most of it—the houses he frequented were clean and well run, the women he bedded seemed to be enjoying themselves while at the same time experiencing a measure of independence and good money. Most likely, he supposed, they left here with a hefty bankroll and were able to establish themselves in other towns, where they would enjoy a life of pleasant anonymity, assuming the identity of widow women or spinsters.

This was what he told himself as he reclined in his steaming tub in an upstairs room in the back of Ah Toy's parlor house, listening to the grunts and groans of happy customers, the polite laughter of the girls.

His own girl would come in shortly to dry him and then lead him to the bed that lay behind a silk curtain in the softly lit room. Most gamblers he knew liked to visit the brothels *after* the cards or dice, capping off a perfect night of vice, as it were, but Sean preferred to *begin* his night this way instead—it relaxed him completely, left him languid and comfortable with a sense of well-being that served him well at the card table. He could see tension building in the other players as the night proceeded, knew they would find their release long after it was too late to do them any good; he played so well and so confidently that he'd begun to believe that this was the secret to his success, unwanted though success may be.

Tonight was important, which was why he'd dined at Delmonico's. There were any number of good French restaurants in San Francisco— the Poodle Dog, Maison Doree, Merchand's, Jack's Rotisserie, all with their twelve-course meals that took hours to eat and their private wine reserves that took hours to drink, and of course, their private floors and even more private rooms for those whose romantic inclinations were inspired by such repast—but Delmonico's was Sean's favorite. The right price always bought him a private table in the back where he could observe without being observed.

Most of the men in there tonight had begun hours earlier, following the cocktail route from Ernest Haquette's Palace of Art, to the Grand Hotel's Hoffman Café, to the Palace Bar, and, eventually, to Johnny Farley's Peerless Saloon, where they downed buckets of champagne, Gold Rush Sazeracs, and the new-style iced cocktails. Well oiled by the time they arrived for dinner, these men were not shy in conversation, and Sean learned a great deal about the inner workings of city politics.

This was a city that loved its food and thought nothing of spending five or six hours over dinner; Sean enjoyed the bounty after years in Utah, with its beans, buffalo, beef, and salt pork. Tonight, among other things, he had sampled jellied shrimp, crab legs in creamed sherry sauce, a delicious piece of venison, and potatoes unlike any he'd ever tasted in Ireland. Working his way through the steak and well into a bottle of whiskey, Sean had listened to the conversation, watched the pontificators, smelled the cigar smoke, and thought of better days in Ogue's saloon, where an Irishman would pick a fight with the devil himself just for the sake of good argument. Some of these men were

Irish— Sean could hear it in their voices, could almost place the county from which they'd come if they were new enough—but there were also Germans, Norwegians, Chileans with their strong good looks, French, and Italians. Plenty of priests were dining out on the goodwill of their parishioners, as well, and Sean watched them most carefully. From his place at the bottom of the morality scale, he found it much easier to tell the good from the truly bad. After all, he knew the truly bad now, rubbed elbows with them all night long, laughed with them over a bottle, and listened to their stories; he had come to know which daylight citizens were really nighttime in disguise and which nighttime dwellers still carried the light of day in their hearts. Mostly good citizens tonight at Delmonico's, he'd allowed, but a nice mix of schemers in the lot, as well, like that Harry Meiggs, who owed money to everyone in town and was bound to go under any day now, and James McCabe, who sat with his usual cronies, as well as Sam Brannan, who stopped at their table for a quiet word with McCabe.

Sam Brannan was a name everyone in San Francisco knew, though Sean had heard it mentioned long before he'd ever gotten here. Brannan was famous—or infamous now—among the Latter Day Saints, for having brought over two hundred persecuted Mormon men, women, and children from New York to Yerba Buena on the *Brooklyn*. This new land on the West Coast was paradise, Brannan had written to Brigham Young; this was the new Kingdom in the Wilderness. Young, however, ordered the *Brooklyn* emigrants to cross the mountains into Utah with the greatest of haste. Brannan refused and remained in San Francisco along with half the original party; some went up the hills north of the bay to cut lumber, others went to work in Sutter's Fort at New Helvetia, and another twenty families hiked up the Stanislaus River in the San Joaquin Valley to found an agricultural colony called New Hope. Brannan himself had built a mansion on the corner of Portsmouth Square, and owned a prosperous general store up at Sutterville, as well as the *California Star*. Some of those original renegade Mormons had gone to work for James Marshall, who was building John Sutter's mill on the south fork of the American River; these men were there when the river revealed its first yellow sheen of gold. Though Sutter and Marshall had sworn their laborers to secrecy until the claims could be staked, it was Brannan who'd made the news public by marching up and down Montgomery Street, waving a vial full of dust, and proclaiming in his loudest voice, "Gold! Gold! Gold on the American River!" Sean knew all the stories, had been interested to see the man himself, and had been surprised at how young Sam Brannan was for one who had accomplished so much.

Brannan had been among the most formidable vigilantes in the early days of San Francisco proper and had facilitated more than a few lynchings, and he still swaggered through town quite certain that the respect he was given was indeed his due. He was one of the powerful men in San Francisco, those whose word was law, and Sean avoided him like the plague. He wanted nothing to do with Mormons, founding fathers, newspaper owners, or vigilantes; Brannan was all of those things and worse—he was a Saint who'd remained a Saint, even as he lived the life of a sinner. Sean was an interested observer but had no intention of meeting the man himself. Ever. What if he were wooed out of this pit, brought back into the light, and made a success on top of it all? Well, he would just have to make sure that didn't happen. There was a way to the bottom of this hole and, one way or another, he would find it.

Perhaps he would find it tonight. Certainly, he would be pushing what had been the most extraordinary luck. He'd been warned away from the El Dorado, McCabe's gambling palace, after winning too much—far too much—in the past week. What could he do? Sean smiled to himself—'twas a gift, one that made him laugh in the middle of the night as he undressed in his rooms and emptied his pockets onto the bed. Here, he'd come to sink into anonymity and disrepair, and instead he was wealthier than he'd ever been in his life! Men parted respectfully when he walked into the saloons at night, and barkeeps gave him his first couple of whiskeys on the house! Arrah, he was disgusted with himself. He'd meant to stay away from the very public gambling at the El Dorado, but it had simply been too hard to resist, and he'd spent night after night at the place, throwing the dice now and then to kill time, but mostly playing cards; letting others take the small pots, waiting for their guards to drop until the table was awash with cash, which Sean then collected.

He would have kept on, had he not been tipped off by one of the girls in Irene McGready's parlor house. McGready, a good Irish Catholic, was McCabe's former lover and business partner, the two having parted ways years ago. Rumor had it that McCabe had not defended his mistress's honor when she was snubbed at a social gathering, but whatever the reason, she had never forgiven him for it. Biding her time until he visited her with a change of heart, Irene took her revenge in the form of a haircut, first drugging McCabe, then shaving his head to the scalp so that he was forced to slouch around town in a too-large hat until the hair grew out again. Needless to say, she was delighted with Sean's enormous winnings at the El Dorado, particularly during a time when McCabe needed ready cash for property investment. Not only was Sean cleaning out the house on a regular basis, rumor had it that the properties he was picking up here and there in the city were really being purchased by a Chinaman. When Chang-Li had approached Sean about the difficulties a Chinese man faced trying to buy property, Sean had readily agreed to a scheme that would be profitable to both men. It seemed Sean couldn't turn around without making money in this town.

When word reached Irene of McCabe's keen interest in the nattily dressed Irish gambler and real estate speculator, she advised Sean to lie low until McCabe took another one of his long trips to the South, where he managed other gambling interests. Sean had taken her advice and had stayed in his rooms for the past four days, but last night he'd visited her parlor and learned that McCabe had indeed left on a steamer that afternoon. Thus, the celebratory dinner at Delmonico's, which turned out to be cautionary as well, for there the man sat, eating with his cronies. Had Irene purposefully set him up? Sean wondered again. Was she hoping that Sean would be accused of cheating, that a *code duello* would follow? Dueling seemed to be the entertainment of the day, it was true, but if she thought Sean was gentleman enough to defend his honor, she was sadly mistaken. He drank, he gambled, he whored—he shrugged his shoulders—there you had it: no honor left to defend. Certainly nothing worth killing a man over. Maybe, though, it would be a nice way to die. Pistols at dawn. How romantic. Sean laughed. And so he was going to the El Dorado anyway, just to see how this next page of his life turned out. Maybe he'd be alive tomorrow, and maybe he wouldn't.

The door opened, interrupting his reverie, and a girl came in with a soft piece of toweling, which she used to pat his face and hair. He stood and she wrapped it around him, pressing it against the moisture on his body, kissing his bare arm. She led him to the bed and waited for him to recline before removing her own robe, letting his eyes wander over her slender figure, the smooth skin and long limbs; she shook out her silky black hair and he reached for her then, pulling her down on top of himself.

He took his time—there was never any rush these days—and enjoyed her completely, pausing to kiss her neck, her throat, her lips, and to whisper to her like any good lover, though whether or not she understood, he didn't know. The irony of his life never ceased to amuse him, and it was not lost on him that the small crippled Irish boy who once sewed nappies for a living and couldn't get a girl to look at him twice, let alone kiss him, was now a man who knew his way intimately around a woman's body and could please her as thoroughly as he pleased himself. Who would have thought that the two things Sean O'Malley was best at in the world were cards and women?

After they'd finished and had lain a short while in silence, the girl rose and put on her robe, twisted her hair and put it up, then bowed politely to him and left the room. Sean rose and dressed himself, then opened the lid of a black-tasseled red silk box and laid the money within; on top, he left a packet of tea and a porcelain cup as a gift. If his time spent with a girl had been slow and languid, and there had been intimacy between them instead of just sex, he always left a token of his appreciation. The Chinese girls, he knew, valued the black or green tea of their homeland, combs for their hair, pieces of silk. Not so different, really, from the Mexican or Spanish girls, or from the French, although if he'd been pleased by a Peruvian—cholo, mulatto, or Creole, it didn't matter—he left the cigars they prized. It pleased him to do this, and he hoped they somehow thought well of him, though he supposed they were most likely laughing up their sleeves at the foolish romantic Irishman.

Now on the street—fed, freshly bathed, and sated—Sean considered his options. *Might as well arrive in style,* he told himself and hailed the first cab he saw. It was an open carriage, and the night was cold, but the sky was crisp and clear, scattered with a thousand stars and a crescent moon, so Sean climbed in.

"Where to, governor?" the coachman asked.

English, Sean thought. Can't get away from them even here. "The El Dorado," he replied. "No rush."

The coachman turned to look more closely at his passenger. "Relaxed, are we tonight, sir?" He winked lewdly. "Partaking of foreign delights, eh?"

"There's a tip if you don't talk," Sean replied shortly.

The coachman was unruffled. "Right you are, sir. The El Dorado, it is." He turned and started up the horses, then spoke over his shoulder. "Place is hopping tonight, sir. Dropped off several gay parties on me rounds. Now, one gentleman in particular—"

"The tip," Sean reminded him.

"Right." The coachman pretended to lock his lips and throw away the key, then turned his concentrated effort toward driving.

Sean enjoyed the ride across town, the light spilling from windows as they passed through neighborhoods, more light and the bodies of men spilling through windows and doors as they moved toward the center of town, with its saloons, theaters, and restaurants. When they were still a couple of blocks from the El Dorado, Sean stopped the cab, got out and paid the man, then handed him what would probably be his biggest tip all night.

"Thank you, sir. My pleasure, sir." The cabbie could barely believe his good luck; usually the big money, if any was to be had, came at the end of the night from those who'd done well at the tables, and were drunk beside. He'd never been made by a sober gentleman going *into* the saloon. "And the best of luck to you tonight, sir," he continued. "Want a cab home, just send a runner for one Randall Dawson. That'll be me, sir. Randall Dawson. Know this town like the back of me hand, I do. Get you anywhere you like. And fast."

Sean considered this bit of information. "Good," he decided. "Be waiting here at two a.m., Mister Dawson, and I'll double that tip."

The coachman's eyes went wide with this unexpected good fortune.

"Wait for me," Sean repeated. "No matter what."

"Absolutely, sir," Dawson fawned. "Here at two. Waiting. You can count on me, sir."

"I am," Sean said, then started off in the direction of the El Dorado.

There was no missing this most lavish of all saloons: the sidewalk without was crowded with miners and gamblers waiting for room—any kind of room—to become available either at the bar or at any of the tables that offered faro, craps, roulette, rouge et noir, monte, and—Sean's favorite—draw poker. As Sean approached, a number of the outer circle stepped back and made room for him. He had affected a certain look for his gambling nights, and it paid off at times like this. He wore his hat at a rakish angle in order to show off the braid that hung just past his shoulders; he'd run a dye of black tea and boot polish through his dark blond hair, raking it with his fingers, then braiding it so that it stayed out of his way. He sported a mustache and a scruffy goatee, also rubbed with black, and he kept a Chilean cigar clamped firmly between his teeth. Always the same white shirt, open at the neck, with a dark red silk cloth knotted loosely at the base of his throat. Over this, he sported an embroidered Mexican vest and the best silk-lined jacket money could buy; his trousers were light cotton, tailored to fit perfectly into the tops of his polished riding boots. He knew he cut a baffling figure, one that was hard to pin down—was he part Chinese? Mexican? European and Indian from South America? No one ever guessed there was Irish in the mix until he opened his mouth, and even then, only if he allowed the brogue to show or was more than halfway down the bottle. He enjoyed playing the part of whatever it was he was playing at— he would die in anonymity, that was for certain, for who the hell was Sean Miner?

He confidently worked his way through the crowd, nodding in the direction of those men who nodded at him, but never looking them directly in the eye, until at last he was in the great room itself. The most impressive thing about the El Dorado, he often thought, was the presence of the formidable guards McCabe had placed shoulder to shoulder around the tables. They stood with their legs slightly apart—the fierce mustachioed Mexicans, their serapes covering *pistolas,* and the godlike Peruvians whose ponchos served the same purpose—eyes shaded but alert as they watched vials of gold dust, bags of nuggets, coins, and scrip change hands. He watched them now, looking for the slightest change of expression or shift of posture when they saw him move into the room, but they gave away nothing, and so perhaps he had been wrong. Perhaps he was not so threatening as he'd thought and no one cared if he took the house for all she had, as long as he did not do it every night. The enormous bar stood all along one side of the room, every inch of it packed with miners, travelers, adventuring men. No women, though, only the daring creature up in the balcony who played her fiddle for the entertainment of the crowd, and even she was guarded by a Mexican who barred the top of the stair. Sean picked his way to the far end of the bar, beneath the balcony, and signaled the barkeep—one of three working the counter tonight—for a whiskey and a pint. The whiskey for courage, the pint for thirst.

He tossed off the whiskey and was working his way through the pint when a place opened up at a table, "Gentleman Jim" Ransom, a crony of sorts, shoved away the man who tried to take it, then waved Sean over. Obviously Gentleman Jim was tired of the riffraff and wanted a challenge, Sean decided as he obliged.

"What, are you drinking or gambling tonight, Miner?" the stout man growled.

"Both, if it's anything to you," Sean replied amiably, taking his seat and plunking his bankroll down in front of him.

All motion at the table stopped, Gentleman Jim's cigar nearly falling from his lips, as they stared at the wad in front of Sean.

"You're outta your mind." Ransom tapped off the ash of his cigar. "What, did you rob a bank?"

"Didn't have to," Sean said easily. "Not after the few hands we played last week."

The other men immediately looked at Ransom, who was known for his quick temper, but when he laughed, they joined in, too, and an air of excitement settled around the table. Only the house dealer appeared nervous; Sean could see the slightest tremor in his hand as he shuffled the cards.

They played for a couple of hours, weeding out the amateurs—including a young doctor just out from the East whose confident boasts had died on his lips after a single hand—drawing the more skilled players as the game went on. Spectators kept a respectable distance from the table, aware that they were in the presence of high-stakes players, and the guards kept a regular eye on the piles of cash that now sat before each man. McCabe's manager appeared from his back room every now and then to take a turn around the room, and twice he paused directly behind Sean, watching the play. Sean heard a low hiss escape from his lips when the house lost yet another hand. This dealer wasn't even par-

ticularly good, Sean thought, and was surprised that he'd not been replaced by one more seasoned. They took a break to stretch and relieve
themselves, have a drink, and shake the tension out of their shoulders,
and then they settled in again. Lighting a fresh cigar, Sean caught a
glimpse of McCabe and his cronies entering the saloon at last. The man
moved smoothly through the room, then flipped up the bar and went
behind to have a word in the barkeep's ear. The barkeep nodded and
motioned to one of the guards. Sean fanned out his cards and pretended to consider his hand, though he kept an eye on McCabe from
under the brim of his hat. Carrying a fresh bottle of whiskey, the guard
was coming over. When he got to their table, he plunked the bottle
down on top of the pile in the middle.

"Compliments of Senor McCabe," the guard said smoothly, a false
smile on his face. "And then, *adios, amigos.*"

"We're still playing." Sean reached out and moved the bottle to one side.

The guard shook his head. "No. You are done, senor. Show your
hand, have your drink, then go."

Sean shrugged and set down his hand. "Full house, gentlemen."

The others groaned and threw down their cards; the dealer paled and
narrowed his eyes.

"Drink?" Sean offered the bottle to the man on his left, then picked
up the pile of cash and added it to what he had in front of him.

"Maybe we'd best wet our whistles somewheres else," Gentleman Jim
suggested, eyeing the guard. "Seems we've worn out our welcome here.
One of us, at least," he added pointedly.

Sean looked past the guard to where McCabe stood, leaning on the
back counter behind the bar looking back at him. Sean lifted his glass
to the man, then picked up his cash and slowly counted it before rolling
up the entire wad and slipping it into the inside pocket of his jacket,
making sure his pistol was well seen by any man who might be considering the possibility of robbery.

"Don't come back." The guard put a heavy hand on Sean's shoulder.
"Last warning."

Sean shook it off. "Don't remember a first one, *amigo,* but I get your
meaning. If the house is out of money," he said loudly, "then so be it."
He laughed and shoved past the ring of guards toward the door, feeling
McCabe's eyes on him all the way.

Once they were outside, Ransom let out a tense whistle. "You're a strange one, Miner. Baiting the big man himself like that."

"I don't like to be threatened." Sean looked up and down the street, still full of men even at this hour.

"Guess not," Ransom allowed. "Still, McCabe's no one to mess with. And he hates to lose money."

"Shouldn't be in the gambling business, then."

Ransom laughed. "Never seen anyone play cards the way you do, friend, and I'm one of the best." He leaned in conspiratorially. "What's your angle? You let me in on this and we'll clean this place up. Hell, we could *own* the El Dorado, that's what you want. Really live it up!"

Sean shook his head. "Not interested in living," he said, and then he laughed, feeling the whiskey. "And there's no angle. Just turned out to be something I'm good at."

"You sure?"

"Oh, yeah." Sean started down the sidewalk, then stumbled, drunker than he'd thought. "See you round."

"Wait." Ransom took his arm. "Better let me help you, son, before someone comes along and relieves you of that bankroll." He steered Sean down around the corner and up a darker street, to the alley that ran behind the El Dorado. "Uh-oh," he said as a group of men appeared.

Sean reached for his pistol, but his movements were sluggish, and when he tried to yell, the words came out slurred and nonsensical. *Drugged,* he realized then from somewhere in the fog of his brain. *That last drink was drugged. And I'm about to die.* He started laughing.

"You're one strange fella," Ransom pronounced, feeling around in Sean's jacket for the money. "Remember, I gave you a chance. Been my partner and I'da hid you for a while, then made us rich." He pulled out the wallet and opened it. "Oh, well. I make money this way, too."

The men now stood in a circle around Sean, though through his eyes it was a circle that spun and wavered and simply would not stay in focus.

"Took my cut," he heard Gentleman Jim say as if from far away. "Rest is for you boys. McCabe says leave him his legs so he can run out of town."

And then the beating began, but oddly, Sean felt little. He heard the meaty thwacks of fists landing on his body, felt the impact of blows against his face, smelled the copper scent of his own blood; he offered little resistance—what was the point? It was a meet and right end, after all this time.

Then suddenly it was over, the men scattered with a round of gun-fire. Strong arms slipped under his own and heaved him up and into a carriage.

"Two o'clock on the nose, governor. You can count on Randall Dawson."

The thick cockney accent would have made Sean smile had any of those muscles worked properly.

"Always carry a bit of protection, I do. Nothing but ne'er-do-wells this time of night. Rob you blind, did they?"

Sean mumbled something, tasted fresh blood in his mouth.

"Never you mind, governor. We'll get you home. I know you're good for it. I can tell a gentleman by looking at him. Where to, now, sir? Better hurry before those thugs change their minds."

Sean made a great effort to concentrate his energy on moving his mouth. "Chinatown," he managed. "Stockton Street." And then he slumped back in the carriage, barely conscious.

Dawson found the house as directed and was paid generously by Chang-Li, whom Mei Ling had immediately summoned. When the driver had gone, they got Sean up to his room and on the bed. They opened his clothes and examined his wounds, Mei Ling bathing them and applying strong-smelling ointments before bandaging him. Sean was sure his face was battered, and the increasing pain in his sides told him the thugs had broken a few ribs. True to their boss, they hadn't damaged his legs beyond a few well-placed kicks, though his hip was beginning to throb. Mei Ling's cool fingers probed the knots and bruises that covered his exposed torso and, embarrassed that she should see him like this—not only beaten but with his crippled arm and leg exposed—he lifted his head. A blast of pain tore through his temples and he moaned, unable to say anything, unable now to even open his eyes. The moaning continued, and then a weeping that mortified him even more when he realized it came from his own lips.

Chang-Li spoke quietly to Mei Ling in the corner of the room, and then Sean heard the door open and close. When she returned, it was with a long-stemmed pipe, which she handed to Chang-Li. He put the stem in his mouth and lit the contents of the bowl, pulling in until it was well fired, and then he placed the stem between Sean's cracked and bleeding lips. Gratefully, Sean pulled on the pipe. A little more, and the terrible pain in his body began to ease; more still, and a feeling of well-being washed over him. One eye was swollen shut, but the other he managed to open just enough to see Chang-Li leaving the room. Mei Ling, however, remained, and when he looked at her, despite the cut that opened afresh, she came and stood beside him, smiling.

"You sleep now," she said gently. "You not die."

The sadness that overwhelmed him at those words must have shown in his eyes, as hers suddenly creased with concern and her smile faltered.

"*Not* die," she repeated as if he'd misunderstood. "Better soon."

He closed his eyes so as not to confuse her further and offered the ghost of a smile for her reassurance. *How funny,* he thought. It was going to be much harder to leave the world than he'd imagined.

Sixteen

After a very busy week of restocking the pantry with preserves, Grace and the children were feeling more than a little cooped up, which was why, when the sun came out Thursday noon, she informed Missus Hopkins that she was taking the children down into the city. The doctor was out and would be until late, and Abigail was still asleep; there was plenty of food either stored or warming, and Enid had agreed to make up Miss Wakefield's tray for the light luncheon she now ate daily.

While the children got their coats and hats, Grace pulled tonight's bread from the hot oven, setting two of the three loaves on the rack to cool. The third loaf she wrapped lightly in a piece of cloth; she placed the bundle in her marketing basket, then sent Mary Kate to the cellar for a small pot of honeyed butter, which she put in her pocket, not wanting it too close to the warm bread.

"Do you remember what to do?" Grace quizzed Enid before going out the door.

"Pea soup on the stove—give it a stir now and then," the girl repeated dutifully. "Bread beside. Drippings in the bowl. Part of a ham in the cold box, cheese and apples, molasses cakes for afters."

"If your one wakes hungry, give her the broth instead of soup," Grace directed. "Easier on her stomach."

"Yes, ma'am. There's Mister Litton with the wagon!" Enid nodded toward the open door, hands automatically tidying her hair, smoothing her apron. "Good of him to take you down the hill."

"Aye. And we'll get a ride back up with him, as well, once he's picked up the rails." Litton was building a fence around the back of the property now that the hill was becoming more populated. "See you later."

Enid followed them out, smiling shyly at George as Grace climbed up next to him and the children scrambled into the back.

The afternoon air was brisk, and a breezy wind sent flocks of white clouds sailing across the sky. Out on the bay, smoke streamed from the steamers coming into port, and already-anchored ships tossed among the whitecaps. The wagon moved cautiously downhill, mindful of puddles that might be deeper than they appeared and of the layer of slippery mud that lay upon the drying road.

Mister Litton was silent, as always, and Grace thought she might take advantage of the situation by encouraging a little conversation. Though he ate with them every night, he offered little in the way of give-and-take and rarely met any eye that sought out his. If spoken to, he'd answer with a gruff monosyllable. Only Jack had succeeded in learning anything directly, and that only because he trailed Litton relentlessly as the man made his rounds of an afternoon, badgering him with comment and question alike.

"You've been very patient with our Jack, Mister Litton," she said now. "I wanted to thank you for letting him tag along while you're at your work. I hope he doesn't slow you down too much?"

"No, ma'am." Litton kept his eyes on the road.

"You can always just send him in to me if he gets out of hand."

"Yes, ma'am."

"Because I know he has a lot of questions about things. Likes to know how things work and all. He's a talker, our one."

Mister Litton glanced at her sideways out of the corner of his eye, and Grace had to laugh.

"Seems to run in the family, you're thinking."

He turned his attention back to the horses. "Gee up," he encouraged, but he smiled ever so slightly.

"Do you have family of your own, Mister Litton?" she asked, one hand keeping her hat in place.

"No, ma'am."

"None still living?"

"None as own me."

Grace looked at him, surprised as much by what he'd said as by the fact he'd offered something personal.

"But you were a soldier," she pursued gently. "You fought in the war. Do they not think that honorable?"

Litton shrugged. "Not the way I come to it."

"You are not the man you once were, Mister Litton. 'Tis safe to say you've redeemed your character in more ways than just the one." Grace paused. "Does your mother live?"

"I couldn't say."

"Aye, that's too bad. And did you care for her, then?"

Litton's hands tightened around the reins. "I turned out poorly. Wasn't her fault."

Grace bit her lip, thinking. "I'll tell you something, Mister Litton. Something I'm not proud of." She swallowed hard and lowered her voice. "When I came away from Ireland, Jack was left behind."

Litton glanced over sharply, then away.

"He was newborn, and sickly. My da was to bring him out, but then a letter come saying both had died."

Grace looked over her shoulder now, just to see the top of Jack's head, to know that he was really there.

"The guilt nearly killed me, but wasn't there Mary Kate to live for?" She paused, remembering. "And then a miracle—another letter saying he was alive, after all. A friend had taken him in, and 'twas she brought him all the way out to America to me."

"Huh." Litton glanced at her again.

"The world was set right the day I knew my lost boy was found. Mothers can't help but love their children, Mister Litton. We think about them all the time."

Litton was silent as they rounded the corner at the bottom of the hill and headed toward the waterfront, and she hoped she had not brought up in him a host of painful memories. He was quiet for so long that she thought perhaps she should apologize for speaking out of turn, but then he hunched even further over the reins and cleared his throat.

"I don't read nor write so well," he stated. "I wouldn't know what to say to her."

Grace was careful not to look at him. "If you should ever want to send a letter, Mister Litton, I'd be glad to write it out for you. 'Twould be a private matter between the two of us."

Litton nodded slowly as the wagon pulled up in front of the house next to the hospital where Sister Joseph lived with her nursing order. Grace jumped down before he could help her; she lifted the children from the back and agreed upon a time to meet—two hours from now, right here—and they waved as he started the horse up again. She knocked on the front door and asked the nun who opened it if she might see Sister Joseph. The door closed, but then, just as quickly opened again, this time revealing Sister Joseph.

"Well, and if it isn't my favorite little Irish family." The nun beamed. "What're you doing here on a Thursday afternoon?"

"We had to stretch our legs, and so we've brought you a bit of home." Grace lifted the towel that covered her basket.

"Soda bread!" Sister Joseph clapped her hands together.

"Warm from the oven. And a pot of fresh butter, as well. I thought we might have our tea with you, if you're willing."

"I'm going out." The sister looked crestfallen. " 'Tis my afternoon for seeing to the Mulhoney family, and they count on me coming."

"We'll leave this for you, then." Grace handed over the loaf and butter pot. "Which way do you go? Maybe we'll walk a ways with you."

Sister Joseph looked down at the children's expectant faces. "Sure and I'd love to have your company. 'Tis down along the wharves—wait a moment and I'll just get my things." She disappeared back into the big house while Grace and the children stood on the front stoop.

"All right, then?" Grace asked as they waited. "We'll walk a bit, then stop on our own for tea—what do you say?"

"Can I have a sticky bun?" Jack licked his lips expectantly.

"Never ask." Mary Kate elbowed him. " 'Tisn't polite."

"Of course, you may ask," Grace told them both. "Only first say 'please'."

"Please can I have a sticky bun, please?" Jack tugged at her sleeve.

"We'll have to see what's out today. Might not be sticky buns on Thursday, but I promise we'll get something nice to eat."

Grace rested her hand on his head and gave him a smile, and then Sister Joseph emerged in her great black cloak, a large basket full of foodstuffs over her arm and a string bag full of apples in the other hand.

"Carry that for me, young Jack—there's a good boy," the nun praised, handing over the heavy basket.

Brother and sister each took one side and carried it between them, following their mother and Sister Joseph down the sidewalk toward the boardinghouses near the wharf.

"Who are the Mulhoneys, then? Your other favorite Irish family?" Grace teased.

"Favorite *big* Irish family." Sister Joseph laughed. "Originally from County Kerry. Worked as sharecroppers in Kentucky, but Mister Mulhoney cared not for that. Sold up what little they had and brought them all overland, intending to mine, then get a bit of farmland to the north." She sighed. "Grand plans, but he died two weeks upon getting here. I met Margaret, his wife, in hospital. Thin little thing, with four children, and another coming any day now."

"How're they getting by? On that, you're bringing them?" Grace took the bag from Sister Joseph, who was huffing a little now.

"Aye, and what little's left from selling their possessions—didn't bring much, I'm sure. Margaret says everything of value went on the other end to buy the wagon and team in the first place. Sure and it wasn't near enough to take them back to Kentucky, and too late anyway what with her being so far gone and all." The nun stopped and leaned against the wall of a big stone building, hand to her heart. "Wait a minute while I catch my breath, will you?"

"Are you all right, then?" Grace saw the beads of sweat across her brow. "Do you want to sit down on the steps here?"

Sister Joseph shook her head, sipping mouthfuls of air. "Don't get out enough, I guess," she confessed sheepishly. "That, and being so very ancient, you know."

"You're not ancient!"

"Forty-seven at Michaelmas! Been with the Sisters of Mercy over thirty years, I have, and wouldn't know any other way of living, though it does wear a body out." She pushed away from the wall. "All right, let's get on with it."

They started off again, but at a slower pace, and Grace decided to walk her all the way to the door. They were on the waterfront now, the wind a little sharper, the air more damp than up on the hill; the faces that peered out through grimy windows were also sharper, more wary than those in the boardinghouses just off the plaza, Grace recognized hunger when she saw it.

"She's lived frugally," Sister Joseph continued the story. "But there can't be much left. The older boy works a job here and there, and there's a girl same age as your Mary Kate, runs errands for an old fella lives upstairs. Gets two bits for that. She'll look after the baby once it comes, then Margaret'll go out to work. Honest work, I hope. In a town full of men, 'tis no easy thing turning down the ready money that's sure to be offered her, if you know what I'm saying."

"I do." Grace nodded grimly, having met an Irishwoman in the market just last week who'd told her confidentially that miners would gladly pay a dollar just to have a look at her private place. The woman had insisted she'd never done it herself, but knew of others, fallen on hard times, who supported their families quite adequately in that manner; she wanted Grace to know that there were fortunes to be made.

Grace's thoughts were interrupted when Sister Joseph abruptly halted the party in front of a battered, mildewed door upon which she rapped.

"Will you stop in?" the nun asked over her shoulder. "I'm sure Margaret would take comfort in the company of another young woman, and yourself a mother and all, like her."

Grace hesitated only a moment. "Aye." She glanced at the children. "We'll all come in and say hello to them. Have a wee visit. Hear me, children?"

Mary Kate and Jack nodded.

"Ah, there you are," Sister Joseph said by way of greeting to a very little girl who opened the door. "Will you let us in, Laurie? I've brought a friend for your mother, then."

The little girl stepped aside to let them pass, and Grace entered a room that got only darker, the window in the front giving them their only natural light. As her eyes grew accustomed to the dimness, Grace saw that it was one room with pallets along one side, a small grate for cooking and heat on the other, a table and stools in the middle, and a rocking chair in the corner. Margaret Mulhoney struggled to rise from the rocking chair, her swollen belly making every move difficult.

"Please don't get up," Grace protested, setting the basket on the table. "I remember well how that feels."

The woman sank back into her chair with a sigh of relief. "Thank you," she said with effort, then smiled at the nun. "Hello, Sister, good of you to come."

"Hope you don't mind, Margaret, but I thought you might like a bit of company, so I asked Missus Donnelly to stop in." Sister Joseph began unpacking the basket, setting food on the table.

As if drawn by a magnet, Margaret's children came from all corners to gather around her, their eyes lingering on the bread and cheese, the sacks of beans and oats, knob of bacon, apples, and onions. Sister Joseph spoke kindly to them, calling each one by name and introducing them around.

"Pleased to meet you, Missus Donnelly," Margaret said, then suddenly winced and closed her eyes, pressing her hands to her belly.

"Is it kicking at you, then?" Grace pulled a stool over beside Margaret's rocker and sat down.

" 'Tis nearly my time." The woman's eyes filled with tears, which she brushed away before the children could see. "You know how 'tis." She managed a weak smile.

"Oh, aye. Weepy all the time. Or fit to be tied," Grace added. "Is there anything I can do for you, Missus Mulhoney? Do you have what you need for the baby?"

"The sisters have given me diapers and such," Margaret said gratefully. "And Davey—he's our oldest—he'll run for Sister Joseph when the time comes."

"Might have to carry me back." Sister Joseph smiled at the tall boy with the grim face. "Seems I'm slowing down some in my old age. Can you do that, Davey? Ride me on your back?"

"I'll try, Sister," he promised soberly. "I'll try my best."

They all laughed, and then the door burst open.

"Ah, Rose, there you are." Sister Joseph waved the bread knife at her. "Just in time for tea. Take your coat off and have some bread and butter. This is Missus Donnelly and her children, Mary Kate and Jack."

"How do you do?" Rose dipped a shy curtsy, her eyes cutting glances at Mary Kate.

"Were you out for Mister Smith, then?" The nun handed her a thick slice of bread.

Rose clearly wanted to eat immediately, but good manners won out.

"Aye, Sister. He needed oats," she reported dutifully. "Porridge for the boy."

"An imbecile," the nun explained to Grace. "Saw him once when I knocked to look in." She shook her head sadly. "One of the worst I've ever seen, and I told the father of a place for such as them, but he got angry and threw me out! Loves the boy, it seems, and more's the pity. Best to let them go sometimes, though we're all God's creatures, true enough."

Margaret's hands tightened protectively around her belly, and Grace gave her a sympathetic look; she remembered the anxiety that came before birth, the prayers for a healthy baby and the worry that it might not be so.

"Here's two bits, Mam." Still chewing, Rose went over and handed the money to her mother, then rested her hand on the mound for a moment. "I feel her," she whispered, eyes wide.

Margaret smiled and caressed her daughter's face. "Rose is quite sure we'll be welcoming a wee sister. She's my little helper, and what would I do without her? Or any of them?" she added, looking at the faces of her children, who watched her with love.

" 'Tis nice they're company for one another," Grace replied. "Mary Kate and Jack only have each other up where we are. If you're of a mind, Missus Mulhoney, we could pay you another call sometime. When the baby's come, perhaps. I could bring a meal and we could celebrate. I know the sister's still got a few jigs in her."

Sister Joseph laughed and tapped a few slow steps.

"I'd like that," Margaret said earnestly. "Very much. We all would." She took her bread from Sister Joseph and looked at Grace. "Won't you have something to eat now?"

"Thank you, but we had a bite right earlier on." Grace shot Mary Kate and Jack a warning glance; the last thing she wanted was to take food out of the mouths of this struggling family. "And we'd best take ourselves off now, before the hour gets late. But thanks for having us in, and 'twas a pleasure meeting you all."

"I'm off, as well," Sister Joseph announced, wrapping up the loaf and setting it to one side. "But I'll see you again tomorrow, Margaret, or before, if Davey comes a-knocking."

"Thank you, Sister." Margaret rose now and waddled awkwardly to the door, her fist in the small of her back. She put out her hand. "Nice meeting you, Missus Donnelly, and we'll see you soon enough. When this one's howling instead of kicking." She patted her belly.

Grace laughed and they shook hands, the children took leave of one another, and then the door closed.

"Puts me in mind of the rooms in Liverpool," Grace said as they walked away down the street. "And parts of Dublin. New York was the worst, though. Worse than anything I'd ever seen in my life."

"Oh, aye," the nun agreed. "We were at the mission in Five Points before they shipped us out here. You know, we were poor growing up, but it never seemed as such. Maybe as everyone had nothing, no one of us missed anything." She paused. "You'd think the wealthier the city, the better cared for its people. Only 'tisn't so. Every man's out for himself, and the cruelest poverty's to be found in the grandest of places."

Grace sighed. "There's so many need help—the Mulhoneys, that old man upstairs and his son, all their neighbors running about half-dressed . . . where do you start?"

"With the one in front of you," Sister Joseph declared. "And if that's all you can do, so be it. Better to do something about the one than sit and wring your hands over the many. If there's anything I've learned in my years, 'tis that."

"Sure and I've been the one more times than I can count," Grace said as much to herself as to her friend. "I'd like to help you with the Mulhoneys, if you don't mind. I'm being well paid by Doctor Wakefield, and I could share it out 'til she finds work."

"Take care of your own family first," the nun reminded her. "Then see where the Lord leads you. Maybe He's got other work for you. But I won't say no on Margaret's behalf. She's a good woman and deserving."

They turned the corner, the children prancing up ahead, and down the block was the hospital.

"We're here already!" Grace was surprised, then concerned as she saw how exhausted the nun appeared. "You should go in and lie down a while now. You're worn out."

"I'm a bit more tired than usual," the nun admitted as they stopped in front of her building. "But will you not come into the parlor for a cup of tea? Jack never got his sticky buns, did you, boy, with all that running around and do-gooding?" She grinned at him.

"That's all right." Jack was temporarily humbled by his experience at the Mulhoneys'. "I don't need anything." He and Mary Kate sat down side by side on the steps, elbows on knees, chins in their hands.

"We won't come in, but we'll wait here for Mister Litton, if you don't mind," Grace said. "He'll be along anytime now."

"How's he getting on up there?" Sister Joseph started up the stair with Grace's help. "I had hopes for that Hopkins girl, but no, eh?"

"Not for lack of trying on her part, but she can barely get two words out before he's mumbling something and taking himself back to the stable. I don't know what he's so afraid of!"

Sister Joseph laughed, "Poor Mister Litton. He doesn't think himself deserving of any happiness or even that there's any happiness to be had."

"Believe me, Enid would gladly try to change his mind about that," Grace told her. "But her mother's got everyone in that house dancing on a string, including the doctor's sister, I might add."

"How d'you mean?"

"I don't know exactly, but she's got that poor woman paying penance for something!"

"Well, you know, dear . . ." Sister Joseph began.

"Not with Hail Marys and Our Fathers," Grace clarified. "Miss Wakefield is slowly starving herself to death, and I can't for the life of me figure out why."

Sister Joseph was still for a moment, thinking. "Atonement, most likely. She inflicts suffering upon herself in order to prove something to God above."

"Over a ruined engagement?" Grace wondered. "There must be more to it than that."

"Martyrdom can become a way of life. Makes them feel powerful, in a strange sort of way—their own private battle with the Almighty." She frowned. " 'Tis prideful, though, to think that. Didn't His son suffer enough for all of us, and doesn't He forgive us in that name?"

"Maybe you could pay her a visit?" Grace suggested.

Sister Joseph shook her head. "I offered once to do just that, but the doctor thought it would only trouble her more. They're not Catholic, you know, not churched much a'tall, really."

"Doctor Wakefield sometimes attends the Methodist Episcopal

Church over on Powell," Grace informed her. "The children and I rode along once, though we've been going to Grace Cathedral, which is grand, and we'll visit St. Mary's once 'tis finished. But Miss Abigail has never been to my way of knowing."

"And he has no clergy coming to see her? Bring her the sacraments?"

"No, but Hopkins reads the Bible to her. I hear them. They pray aloud together, as well."

"Better than nothing, I suppose. But hear me now. Don't go troubling yourself over something you can do nothing about," the nun admonished. "She's been a long time in her decline, long before you got there. That Hopkins isn't interfering with you and the children, is she?" She looked down at the bottom of the stoop, where Mary Kate and Jack were playing a hopping game with stones.

"Not anymore. We had a few rows, the two of us, and then she pretended to feel sorry over it." Grace shook her head, still baffled. "But we have plenty to eat and warm beds, and you'd never even know Mary Kate had been ill, she's so full of life again. That's all that matters to me."

"Well, there you have it. Any word from your captain?"

"Not yet, but I left a card with that nasty butler, saying where we'd set up house."

At that moment, Litton's wagon rumbled around the corner and made its way down the street, the back piled with neat stacks of boards. He nodded at the children, who shouted their hallos and chased down the sidewalk to where he pulled up the horses.

"Sister." Litton doffed his hat and nodded respectfully to the nun.

"Nice to see you, George," the nun greeted him cheerily. "Glad to hear all is well. Mind you get this family home in one piece, now!" She turned to Grace and kissed her cheek. "Good-bye, agra. Lovely to see you, and mind you leave off the worrying over what goes on upstairs. Good-bye, dear ones." She took first one face in her hands and kissed it, and then the other.

Grace and the children crowded into the front of the wagon, and George called to the horses, urging them to make this last trip up the hill toward home. They were tired, all of them, and silent, lost in their own thoughts all the way through town and up the hill, the rocking of the wagon lulling them into a drowsy ride. When at last the horses pulled up at the back of the house, Mister Litton again cleared his throat and mumbled something that Grace didn't catch.

"What was that, Mister Litton?"

"I'll write. To my mother. But not tonight," he added quickly.

Grace resisted the urge to pat his arm, and instead gave him an encouraging smile when he glanced over at her.

"That's fine, then, Mister Litton. Just fine."

She climbed down from the wagon seat and helped Mary Kate off, then Jack. The tired children walked slowly toward the kitchen door, but Grace stood a moment longer.

"You tell me when." She looked up at Mister Litton, who kept his eyes on the horses. "Anytime a'tall."

Litton nodded, and she expected him to drive the horses back toward the stable, but he didn't; he sat still, reins dangling in his hands.

"She was always good to me."

Now Grace did pat his hand. "Tell her so. When you write her."

Litton turned his head and Grace was moved to see the depth of his doubt and yearning.

"Thank you, missus," Litton said then, and Grace could have sworn he almost smiled.

Seventeen

Chang-Li had increased his wealth considerably in the past year, and so had decided to host a banquet in honor of the God whose birth Americans celebrated with a feast day late in their month of December. This was also a time during which gifts were exchanged, and Chang-Li, priding himself on his knowledge of all things American, had made a list of appropriate recipients, as well. This year, he would also include the *fan qui* boarder with the unpronounceable name whom Chang-Li now addressed as Mister Sung. The intelligent and Caucasian Mister Sung, though clearly disinterested in personal improvement or well-being, had proved an invaluable asset in the business world of European San Francisco, and Chang-Li knew that it was in his own best interest to look out for the man; Chang-Li understood that their destinies were intertwined, even if Mister Sung did not.

Thanks in part to Mister Sung, Chang-Li had quietly accumulated several large properties in and around the city. Though the name on the deed was Sean Minor, Chang-Li and Mister Sung had signed a separate agreement that acknowledged their partnership, a partnership that allowed Chang-Li to buy out Mister Sung for a modest commission when such a time as Chinese ownership of properties became acceptable. Mister Sung appeared to take a great deal of delight in subverting what Chang-Li called "the difficulties of Chinese advancement" and what he, Mister Sung, called "those prejudiced bastard sons of bitches." Chang-Li laughed to himself now, thinking of the glee on Mister Sung's face each time they successfully bid upon and purchased another property; oh, he did find enjoyment in the odd young man, despite said man's proclivity for prostitutes, excessive gambling, and opium.

Mister Sung's growing affection for the sweet pipe was of minor concern to Chang-Li; there was no danger as long as the man did not become indiscriminate about his choice of dens, the criminal element always on the lookout for a drugged *fan qui* to roll. And, of course, Mister Sung had garnered something of a reputation in the darker corners of the city, despite his attempt to maintain a low profile: he'd won too much money, too publicly, at the bigger gambling houses, earning the ire of the powerful Mister McCabe, a man with whom Chang-Li had once wished to do business. That opinion had changed, however, as he came to know Mister Sung over porcelain cups of amber tea, over the companionship of their pipes of an evening. Mister Sung, it was quickly apparent to Chang-Li, was brilliant. The man spent too much money on prostitutes and opium, but—and it was an important but— he never ran out; for every dollar he spent, he earned twenty more, the doubloon turned into golden double eagles before Mister Chang's very eyes. It was a gift; not only had the gods smiled upon Mister Sung, but they had delivered him into the hands of Chang-Li, a wise man himself and one who understood the nature of such a gift. Unlike the Californios, who squandered the gifts bestowed upon them, who used up the men in their charge, then discarded them in favor of new blood, Chang-Li treasured the gift of Mister Sung. He prized Mister Sung. He was determined that Mister Sung should abandon the path of self-destruction, for this was not his destiny; Mister Sung's destiny was a life as brilliant as his mind, and Chang-Li would help him to realize this.

And so to the problem of what to give the man who could have anything he wanted and wanted nothing at all, who had everything for which to live and wanted only to join the ancestors. It must be a most special and important gift, a gift to honor their partnership, to cement the bond Chang-Li wished between them because Mister Sung was the best thing that had ever happened to Chang-Li since finding passage to America. There was, of course, the House of Good Fortune, but Mister Sung was already a partner in that venture, as well. A minor establishment in a sea of pawnshops, under Mister Sung's sharp eye it had quickly become a gold mine better than any out in the desert. Customers preferred doing business with a white man, even if he did wear his fair hair in a long queue like a Chinaman and hid his opium-sensitive eyes behind green-tinted spectacles. It had taken him a relatively short time to understand the value of certain objects, of mining tools and weapons, furniture, clothing, and jewelry. Guns and precious stones quickly became Mister Sung's specialty; he'd understood from the start that most of these things were stolen, the act of pawning merely a pretense, the profit to be made upon resale enormous. This game, too, had delighted Mister Sung, and now he spent his late mornings and early afternoons in the shop, rubbing elbows with a different class of profiteer.

Chang-Li looked up as Mei Ling entered with his luncheon—a bowl of steaming rice flavored with slivers of fresh salmon cooked in sesame oil. There were dumplings, too, and a bowl of clear soup. A feast. He rubbed his hands in anticipation as she placed a tray before his favorite chair and arranged the food in a manner she knew would please him. He got up and crossed the room, thinking how foolish people could be. The Californios liked to say that all Chinese people dined on rats, but Chang-Li always pointed to the proliferation of these rodents in the city as proof that no one was eating them. Chang-Li would never admit to his American friends that as far as he was concerned, rat filled an empty belly as well as any other meat; these *fan qui* had obviously never known hunger like that which had come with the war and famines in China, or they would not say one kind of food is lower than another. Look at the jungle Indians from the South who ate baked monkey and breast of parrot—here, monkey and parrot were pets, along with the bear, the wolf, the fox, and all kind of birds! Chang-Li sat down in his chair and sighed; he did not understand this concept of pets. A bird in a cage, yes—that was for music. A fox on a leash, no—that was for nothing.

Mei Ling pushed the tray closer to Chang-Li, poured out his tea, then bowed to him and left the room. Chang-Li watched her go, his head tipped to one side as he considered something he had not before. It was true that Americans did not keep slaves, except in the southern part of the Union, which had been sorely disappointed when California elected to be a Free State instead of slaveholding. Still, everyone knew this did not apply to the Chinese, who maintained a tightly knit community and kept their business to themselves. Indentured servitude was not against any law, and the line between that and outright slavery was easily blurred, especially when no one in authority particularly cared. Chinese slaves knew no other way of life and depended upon their masters to care for them. Mei Ling had always been a slave, someone had owned her before Chang-Li and someone would own her after. That someone could be Mister Sung, if a better present could not be found.

Chang-Li held his bowl in one hand, ivory chopsticks in the other, lifting to his mouth the savory rice he enjoyed so well. What Mister Sung enjoyed was living outside the law, and so perhaps he would find the gift of Mei Ling as delightful as a stolen ruby necklace or falsified mining deeds. Perhaps she would be the perfect gift.

But then his hand paused midair, and he frowned. Mei Ling had been with him from the very beginning. Her previous master—an old, old man who should never have set sail with no sons to look out for him—had begun to die on the crossing and had exchanged Mei Ling for Chang-Li's promise to return the old body to Canton, there to be buried among the ancestors. Chang-Li had kept his promise, with help from the benevolent society, and had then kept the girl—his first slave, and a sign from the gods that he was destined to prosper. Would he anger the gods, thereby altering his prosperity, if he gave the girl to Mister Sung?

He set the bowl and chopsticks down and thought about this. Mei Ling was a form of company, this was true, and she warmed his bed on those nights when he wanted a woman but was too tired to go out. Best of all, she brewed his tea perfectly and prepared his meals in the style he liked most of all. On the other hand, Chang-Li was ready to marry, and he had witnessed too many times the discord of a house in which wife and slave were jealous of each other; too many times not to know that when he did find a wife and brought her home, Mei Ling would have to go elsewhere. If Mei Ling belonged to Mister Sung, Chang-Li could still see her now and then, could get her to cook for him the meals he loved, for what if the wife or the new servant was not as talented? Still, he did not foresee marrying in the very near future. There was time yet.

No, he decided, this was not a decision to be made lightly. He would have to give it considerable thought, would have to consult the astrologer and spend time at the joss house of his fellow Confucianists. Also, perhaps he might visit the Taoist and Buddhist temples; there were many wise men in the city, and certainly Chang-Li should not rule out any options.

And in the meantime, for additional good fortune, he would continue his private tradition of offering at the sacred houses of the Holy Romans and the First Presbyterians, the Emanu-Els and the First Congregationalists; he would present tokens of his esteem to the mayor, the city inspectors, the policemen who patrolled his quarter, the bankers at Wells, Fargo, Adams and Company. He would put away the yellow squares of silk that fluttered over his doorway, replacing them with festive red and green, and in the front window of the House of Good Fortune, he would place a small wooden barn where the gods Mary, Joseph, and Jesus would stand, surrounded by sacred animals.

Chang-Li nodded, pleased with himself for having arrived at so many good decisions, and finished his meal in peaceful contentment. He was going to enjoy himself this year. This American feast day was his favorite; he had even learned some of the songs. Setting his chopsticks to one side, Chang-Li clapped his hands and began to hum merrily.

Eighteen

"**A**h, Missus Donnelly, you do spoil us around here." Wakefield rubbed his hands in anticipation as Grace set a tray down on his desk. "Is that what's been driving me mad all morning?"

"Sorry about that, sir. 'Tis brown bread steamed in molasses." She handed him the plate. "I learned to make it in Boston. Thought you'd like it with your coffee."

He took a piece and tasted it as she filled his cup. "Delicious," he said around the bite in his mouth. "Pure ambrosia."

"That's what you said about last night's apple dumplings," she teased. "And the two are nothing alike."

"Perhaps not in appearance," he allowed. "But each is so perfectly made as to inspire rapture."

"Ah, go on with you." Grace laughed. "I could put a bowl of cold porridge down and you'd say the same."

"But you never would. And for that I am eternally grateful." He took a sip of his strong, black coffee. "Sit down. Have a cup of coffee with me."

Grace shook her head. "I'll have my tea with Enid in the kitchen."

"Please. Just for a moment. I wish to speak with you about something important."

Grace sat down in the chair across from him, sure that she knew what was coming.

"If it's about William . . . Mister Shew, I mean. I know he's your friend and all, only I don't feel right about going on."

"Poor William." Wakefield chuckled sympathetically. "He's quite smitten, but I expect you know that already."

Grace sighed and bit her lip. "He's a fine man and good company. He treated Mary Kate and myself to a wonderful meal at a place called Delmonico's, and then he took us to see Lola Montez do her spider dance. They say she's really Irish, Miss Montez—born in Limerick. Is that true, do you know?"

Wakefield's eyebrows went up. "I have no idea, but her dancing is quite—titillating, I'm told. I take it, though, you weren't swayed by William's charming choices. He has the pick of the ladies, you know— didn't you go riding with him last Sunday?"

"Aye. He took us all out in his carriage, and it was so clear and nice. He wants to go again next Sunday, but . . ." She looked down at her hands.

"But you feel your understanding with Captain Reinders does not encompass a friendship with Mister Shew," Wakefield clarified. "Not to mention the fact that Mister Shew is interested in pursuing a friendship more deep than the one you had imagined. Am I right, Missus Donnelly?"

"Oh, aye," Grace agreed fervently. " 'Tis my own fault. The poor man. So good to us, and I told him about Peter, so I thought 'twas all out in the open. And I admit I enjoyed his company. So much. So very much. But then, he—" She stopped, feeling herself blush to the roots of her hair.

"Say no more, Missus Donnelly. Artists are passionate by nature and William is no exception. In his defense, I will say that the sight of a lovely young woman in an open carriage on an autumn day shakes even the best man of his resolve." He smiled at her. "Shall I have a word with him on your behalf?"

"No, sir. Thanks for the offer, but I'll speak to him myself about it next week when I go down to see the exhibit."

"It's quite remarkable," Wakefield reflected. "That portrait of you is . . . well—" He broke off. "I have to admit, when I saw that, I did wonder if poor Captain Reinders had a rival on his hands."

"Was I wrong to sit for it, do you think, Doctor?" Grace asked frankly.

"No, Missus Donnelly, I do not, though certainly I am no judge of these things." He laughed again, this time at himself. "I do know that William Shew will leave behind a true record of history and that you, madam, are a deserving part of that. There are two similar portraits, I believe he said. What will you do with yours?"

Grace didn't hesitate. "I'll have it framed for Peter, for Christmas, if he's returned by then."

"And if he hasn't?"

"Then it'll be ready whenever he does."

"Right and fitting," Wakefield pronounced. "At any rate, it wasn't your many suitors I wished to discuss, Missus Donnelly, but your daughter." He leaned back in his leather chair. "She is a frequent visitor to my library."

Grace's stomach tightened. "I'll have a word with her about that, sir. She's been told not to bother you."

"She's no bother," he said quickly. "Very polite and respectful, that girl. Very intelligent, I'll have you know."

"Aye." Grace blushed again, though this time with pride. "Smart as a whip, and only had a bit of schooling here and there."

"That's what I wanted to speak with you about," he said. "She should be getting regular lessons."

Grace nodded soberly. "I suppose that's right, but she already reads better than most grown people, writes well in a fine hand, and can figure her numbers with the best of them."

"Do you play chess?" he asked suddenly.

"I never have," she replied, eyeing the board on the end of his desk and wondering if he was about to offer her a game.

"Mary Kate does," he announced. "I showed her a few basic moves one afternoon and then we played ourselves a game. She understood it immediately. Chess is very complex," he added. "Mathematical. Women are usually quite challenged by mathematics."

"Are they, now?" Grace kept her voice neutral, though the comment irritated her—her gran had run a business that called for keeping accounts, and her mam had handled the household money until the day she died. She knew plenty of women who figured as well as, if not better than, men. Sometimes the good doctor struck her as a bit limited in his thinking.

"Yes, they are," Wakefield continued, oblivious to her darkened eyes. "Which means your daughter has a rare mind. One that deserves more than just a rudimentary education. She could go far, you know."

"Not as far as medical college, though, seeing as how she's a girl, and all. Isn't that right, Doctor?" Grace asked, then regretted the sharp tone in her voice.

Wakefield winced and put his hand to his heart. "Direct hit, Missus Donnelly. Not only do you keep me well fed, but humbled, too." He set his cup down. "I don't believe that women—as a rule—have as great an intellectual capacity as men, that's true. But I'm not so limited in my own thinking as to ignore the possibility of an exception. I believe your daughter, Missus Donnelly, is an exception. Perhaps not medical college, but certainly some form of higher learning."

"I agree she's very bright. But I don't know that more schooling is the right thing for Mary Kate."

Wakefield frowned. "I must say I'm surprised. You're clearly an intelligent, forthright woman—why wouldn't you want your daughter to be educated?"

"I do want her to be educated," Grace insisted. "But sending her to school's no good."

"I don't understand."

Grace regarded him frankly. "Well, Doctor, we're Irish, as you well know—poor emigrant Irish, and it's not served us well in the schooling of my children. Mary Kate's first master, in Boston, was an Englishman with his own way of doing things. Mary Kate spent most of her time standing in the corner until her speech improved, Irish accents being an affront to the man, I suppose." The muscle in her jaw twitched. "I went to get her early one day and there she stood, tears running down her face. I lost my temper with that daft eejit of a man, and he expelled her—too stupid to learn, he said to her face."

Wakefield set down his coffee cup, shocked. "That's terrible."

"Oh, aye. But she wanted to learn, so I took her to the nuns, where they think better of the Irish." Grace paused. "Though we're Protestant, you see, and Mary Kate found herself standing in corners again for asking questions no good Catholic child would dream of asking. After she got her hands welted up, we quit the place, and I began teaching her at home."

"Well, that's understandable, but—"

"Oh, there's more," Grace interrupted. "In Kansas, we started up with Miss Woodruff, a brittle thing who—for reasons I never could un-

derstand—disliked little girls. Especially foreign little girls. Mary Kate
had learned by now not to ask questions, so she wasn't whipped like the
others, but she didn't learn anything either. 'Twas a long year, but then
come a young man who was happy to teach, and they all adored him,
Mary Kate included."

"Well!" Wakefield picked up his cup again to drink. "There you have
it!"

"But then we left Kansas to come here."

"Oh." His hand paused midair, and then he set his coffee aside once
again. "I see. I really do see what you mean." He leaned forward
earnestly. "She's reluctant to try it again, but perhaps there is a way to
educate this child outside of a school building, at least for now." He
paused, thinking, and then his face brightened. "What would you say
to a tutor? One who came here, say, three or four mornings each week?"

"A tutor? Here? Well, that's a fine idea, Doctor, but . . ." She hesitated.

Wakefield stood up now, excited. "I would, of course, assume all cost
for this enterprise," he insisted. "And we might even launch Jack in the
bargain."

Grace shook her head. "Thank you, sir, but I don't see our Jack sitting still for copying out letters and numbers of a morning when he
could be out in the stable jabbering away at poor Mister Litton. Maybe
when he's a bit older, we'll give it a go."

Wakefield laughed. "Don't underestimate your young son, Missus
Donnelly. He also shows signs of intelligence."

"Well, of course he does, but . . ."

"It's all in the approach with that boy," Wakefield continued, warming to the challenge. "If we tell him that Mary Kate is to receive her lessons with a tutor here in the study, and that he is not—under any
circumstances—to disturb them, because he is too young to go to
school . . ." He grinned. "I do believe he'll expend considerable energy
insisting quite the opposite. It's all a matter of pride with him."

"I see you've made a study of our Jack." Grace laughed, but then became serious again. " 'Tis very kind of you, Doctor, and I don't know
what to say to you. I wouldn't want to be further obligated"—she hesitated—"under the circumstances, you know."

"Oh." Wakefield crossed to the fire and stood with his back to it. "I

see. And I say to you again, Missus Donnelly, that when Captain Reinders returns from Panama, you are under no obligation to remain here.
None. Though I shall be very sorry to see you go. But in the meantime," he added, "why not give the children something useful with
which to occupy their time?"

He's right, Grace thought, but still she felt reluctant. "I'll have to
think about it—"

"What on earth is there to think about?" the doctor retorted. "Unless you're raising your children up to be kitchen help and stable masters? Is that all you want for them?"

Grace bristled. "I want them to be happy, whatever their station in
life."

"But education will give them more choices; don't you see, Missus
Donnelly?"

"I know that, Doctor. Of course I know that." She sighed. "I don't
know why I'm getting upset, here."

"I don't know either. It's not as if I suggested sending them into a
factory or out to the docks."

They looked at each other then, and laughed.

"Ah, forgive me, sir. I'm used to looking out for my family all by myself, I guess." Grace smoothed her skirt. "But I'd be happy for the
chance to school Jack and Mary Kate, and I'm grateful to you. Again."

"Good!" Wakefield rubbed his hands together briskly. "Excellent! I
think I know just the man, met him the other night at Kemble's dinner party—Hewitt's his name. Came out to write a book about the city
but needs gainful employment in the meantime. I shall call upon him
this very day!"

Grace smiled at his enthusiasm. "Thank you, sir. But could I ask—
why would you do this for us, for the children of your servant?"

Wakefield considered the question. "Well, I guess I don't think of you
as my servant, Missus Donnelly. You're a bit too formidable for that."
He winked. "I think of you as a partner of sorts, and I appreciate all
you've done around here. This house is warm and comfortable for the
first time since Abigail and I arrived. The lamps are lit when I come
home at night, and waiting for me is a warm dinner better than I could
get in any restaurant." He nodded. "Even Abigail seems a bit improved;
Hopkins says her appetite is better and her manner is less . . . anxious."

"Oh, sir," Grace warned, not wanting his hopes to be too high, "I've nothing to do with that."

"Don't underestimate the power of your presence, madam. When you set a tray in front of a person, believe me, that person feels compelled to eat!" He laughed. "And I'm grateful to you for weathering the storm that is Hopkins," he added wryly. "It is a relief to have a balance in the atmosphere. Better for Abigail, too."

"I wonder sometimes, sir, if it wouldn't be better to hire a proper nurse for your sister?"

Wakefield shook his head. "Abigail won't hear of it, though I've asked her to at least consider a lady's maid. Someone like the girl she had when we first arrived. If only for a . . . lighter presence in her daily life."

"She had another maid in the beginning?" Grace was surprised.

"A sweet girl," he replied. "Abigail had two slaves at home, whom—much to my father's chagrin—she freed before leaving, so she hired this girl when we got here. Untrained, of course, and Hopkins didn't like her, so she didn't last long, but a cheerful girl nevertheless. Listen." The doctor leaned forward. "I want to get Abigail a special present for Christmas. What would you suggest?"

"Oh, sir, I don't know your sister at all." Grace bit her lip, considering the request. "Before her troubles at home, what gave her the most pleasure?"

Wakefield hesitated only a moment. "Her pianoforte. She loved that instrument. Played and sang for hours at a time. She had a beautiful voice," he added wistfully. "I'd forgotten that."

"Would that be something you could do for her, then?"

"I suppose so. But I have to say, Missus Donnelly, I don't think Abigail will ever make music again. It's just not in her anymore."

"You know best, sir. But perhaps a diversion will help turn her mind to other things than that which causes her sadness."

"Her sadness," Wakefield repeated. "Growing up, Abigail was not the delicate, nervous creature you see upstairs—she was headstrong and demanding, and our father adored her. After our mother died, he perhaps indulged her too greatly." Wakefield looked down at his hands, laced the fingers together in his lap. "She was quite publicly engaged to a very powerful man in our circle, who later changed his mind in favor of another woman. His cousin, I believe."

"And for this she was cast out by her family?"

"Indeed, you *have* been on the receiving end of gossip." Wakefield's voice was suddenly weary. "Do you know the story, then, Missus Donnelly?"

"No, sir. Not the truth of it, at any rate."

"Then let me clear it up for you. There were other . . . circumstances, of course, and Abigail was humiliated. It broke her spirit completely, and by the time I returned from my studies in the North, she was not the sister I remembered. Father could not control her erratic behavior and planned to have her committed." He closed his eyes briefly, then opened them again but did not look at Grace. "I persuaded him to let me bring her here instead. I had wanted to come for some time, but needed money, which involved the dissolution of property—never a good thing as far as planters are concerned. However, for this, Father did what he had to." He smiled ruefully. "So, you see, I have benefited from my sister's tragedy, while she continues to decline." He stopped now, embarrassed perhaps, or contemplative; Grace wasn't sure.

"You did what you thought was right," she offered gently. "You didn't abandon her to the care of strangers. Whatever she suffers, at least she's not alone."

Wakefield nodded, his eyes searching her face.

"And she may yet come to peace, though it take years. You can give her that, can you not?"

"I can give her all the time in the world. The rest of her life."

"Then have faith that the great physician Himself is at work, and don't despair. And in the meantime," Grace continued, reiterating his earlier advice, "why not provide something useful with which to occupy that time?"

Wakefield smiled then, and some of the gloom fell away from his face. "Wise counsel, Missus Donnelly. Quite right. In the name of gainful occupation, the children shall have their tutor, and Abigail shall have her piano."

"It'll be a very happy Christmas around here, Doctor, with all that. The children will be so pleased."

"Thank you, Missus Donnelly. For your discretion. And for your kindness. You have again reinforced my earlier opinion regarding your status in this household."

"We do what we can, sir. As our friend Sister Joseph is always quoting, 'Worry adds not a single hour to the length of your days.' "

Wakefield laughed. "I could almost convert because of that woman."

"She's a treasure," Grace agreed. "And now you'd best let me pour out a fresh cup of coffee as I'm sure that one's stone cold."

"I'll do it myself. I've kept you long enough. And here"—Wakefield opened a desk drawer and rummaged through it until he found an envelope, which he handed to her—"I've included a little extra in the housekeeping money this month. We've never had a proper Christmas here," he explained. "And I thought, especially with children in the house, we might establish a new tradition."

"Wonderful, sir." Grace slipped the thick envelope into her apron pocket. "But I don't know how you do it in the South."

"And I don't know how you do it in Ireland," the doctor replied. "But what does it matter? Do it anyway you like, as long as we have good food, good drink, Christmas trees and caroling, friends calling, presents . . ."

"Goodwill toward man," Grace added with a smile.

"That most of all, Missus Donnelly," he said and looked out the window. "That most of all."

Nineteen

"You look awful." Lars Darmstadt leaned against the mantel, puffing on one of his favorite Chilean cigars. "You're half the man you were before you left. Must've been a terrible bout."

"It was." Reinders sat in the big comfortable chair near the fireplace, a brandy at hand. "I had to take a cab from the wharf, and even that short ride has done me in."

"Where's Liam? Up in his room?"

Reinders shook his head. "Stayed on the ship with Mack. They're off-loading and seeing to repairs."

"How's the old girl holding up?" Darmstadt moved away from the fire and sat down across from his old friend and partner. "I know you're dying to tell me."

"I'll give you the blow-by-blow another time, Lars. It's all I can do to keep my eyes open."

"Another time? You mean you don't want to review every hoist of the sail, every knot she picked up, how well she weathered the voyage? Dear boy! You *have* been ill!"

"Who's been ill?" Darmstadt's wife, Detra, sailed into the room, and then the smile on her face evaporated. "Good Lord, Peter! You look simply dreadful."

"Thank you." Reinders smiled wearily. "It's now official. If you'd seen me a month ago, however, you'd be raving about my glowing good health."

Detra inspected him more closely. "Malaria?"

Reinders lifted his glass.

"You've lost a lot of weight," she appraised. "And I suppose you're weak as a kitten. How on earth did you make the trip back up?"

"Mack and Liam saw to everything. They made sure I stayed in my cabin, and—to tell you the truth—I didn't put up any kind of fight. Liam's going to make a fine captain one day," Reinders added proudly. "He navigated that ship beautifully."

"Well, all I can say is that I'm glad you're home safely. And you're staying home for a while now, aren't you? Isn't he, Lars?" She looked to her husband for confirmation.

Darmstadt laughed. "I hope so, my dear, but you know Peter. He does whatever he wishes. What do you say, Captain? Home for the Christmas holidays, then?"

"Yes." Reinders leaned his head back against the chair and closed his eyes.

The smiles on their faces faltered, and Lars and Detra exchanged a worried glance, unused to seeing their old friend so complacent.

"Oh." Peter's eyes struggled back open and found Detra. "Have you seen the mail? Is there anything from Grace?"

"I haven't had a look at anything yet; we've only just gotten back ourselves, and the household is in a bit of disarray."

She went out into the hall and spoke with the housekeeper, who returned a moment later, bearing a basket full of newspapers, magazines, and envelopes. With a word of thanks, Detra set the lot on her writing desk and began sorting through.

"Ah!" She held up an envelope with Peter's name scrawled across the front. "Here's something," she announced, bringing it to him.

He recognized Grace's handwriting and opened it immediately, reading it quickly while Lars pretended to be busy with his pipe and Detra feigned interest in a new magazine.

Reinders turned it over, saw there was nothing on the back, and then the hand with the letter fell into his lap. He looked up at his friends, who had stopped all activity in order to hear the news.

"She's in San Francisco!"

"Here?" Lars leaned forward. "When did she arrive? Where is she staying?"

"Going by the date on this, she got here in September." The captain's forehead creased with concern. "She says only that Mary Kate is ill—

was ill, I guess now—and is in the hospital, and that she'll leave word again once they've found a place to live." He turned to Detra. "Is there anything else from her?"

She looked through the pile again, then shook her head.

"Lars, call Arnott. Ask him if she's been here." Then she turned to Reinders and whispered, "I don't like that butler. He's off-putting."

"He's a snob," Reinders said bluntly.

"Hush, the two of you." Darmstadt rose from his chair. "I like a man who's off-putting—such a benefit when creditors come to call." He headed toward the hall. "Arnott!"

The butler appeared so quickly he might well have been standing behind the door. Peter and Detra nodded at one another knowingly, their suspicions confirmed.

"Ah, good, there you are." Drawing himself up to his full height, Lars was still inches shorter than the hulking butler. "Arnott, has a Missus Donnelly stopped here in the past months? She would have asked to see Captain Reinders."

The butler frowned and looked at the tips of his shoes, as if trying to recall such an incident.

"A number of women called for the captain, sir. I don't remember a Missus Donnelly in particular."

"A lovely young woman," Darmstadt prodded. "Perhaps with a child alongside? Irish?"

"Ah, yes. Irish." Arnott looked up, his tight lips betraying a certain disdain. "A beggar woman, sir, extremely dirty. Wearing *trousers*. I suspected a claim upon the captain and did not encourage her further."

"Trousers?" Darmstadt looked over his shoulder at Reinders.

"But you took her letter?" Detra asked.

"Yes, madam. I put it with the others."

"And there has been no further word from her?" Darmstadt resumed control of the interrogation.

"Yes, sir. She wished to report her living arrangements with another man." Arnott darted a quick glance at Reinders. "Wakefield is the name she gave, sir."

"*Doctor* Wakefield?" Darmstadt clarified.

"I believe so, sir. She may be a domestic in that household. It was difficult to understand her manner of speech, sir."

Darmstadt eyed him warily, acknowledging the slight. "That's enough, Arnott. You may go."

"Very good, sir." The butler bowed. "Excuse me, sir, but Cook wonders how many for dinner."

"Three most definitely." Detra spoke up. "Possibly five, if Master Kelley and Mister Mackley join us."

"Very good, madam." Arnott bowed again and left the room.

"Blast him," Reinders cursed, smacking the arm of the chair with his fist. "Arrogant, sniveling little ball—"

Darmstadt cleared his throat noisily.

"Excuse me, Detra. Too long at sea," Reinders apologized. "Who is this Wakefield, Lars? Do you know anything about him?"

"Rowen Wakefield." Darmstadt crossed the room and stood before the fire. "Old money from the South. Good man, though, is my understanding. Excellent doctor. Set up the cholera clinic down by the waterfront; saved thousands during the epidemic. Runs it as a general ward now, and he's on the board for the new Marine Hospital out on Rincon Point."

"So she met him in the clinic, most likely," Reinders surmised. "Had no idea where I was or when I might get back, so she took a place in his house. The children must be with her."

"He's a very reputable man," Darmstadt reassured him. "Highly thought of in every quarter. I'm sure she's in good hands."

"That may be the cause of his anxiety, dear," Detra informed her husband. "We must send word to Missus Donnelly that Peter has returned. Get the writing box, Lars."

"No." Peter attempted to rise from his chair. "I'm going over there to see her myself. Right now."

"Sit down." Darmstadt's weak push on Peter's shoulder was all it took to collapse the man. "You're not in any condition to go anywhere." He went to the desk, got out paper and pen, then brought them to Reinders. "Write to her and ask her to come first thing in the morning."

Detra nodded encouragingly. "He's right, Peter. Give her some advance warning. After all, it's been a very long time since the two of you laid eyes upon one another. She'll want a chance to bathe and change her dress, do up her hair. Prepare herself."

"She's not like that."

"She's a woman, isn't she?"

An image of Grace came flooding back—standing on the deck of the *Eliza J* the morning they'd buried Liam's mother at sea; exhausted and stoic, she'd kept her head held high, a protective arm around each child, supporting them in their grief.

"Not like any woman *I've* ever known. Present company excepted, of course," he added gallantly.

"Write your note, dear boy." Detra smiled gently. "Then get a good night's rest. No woman wants to see the man she loves looking as if he is upon death's door."

Reinders was too exhausted to protest, though suddenly he yearned to see Grace, to hear her voice, feel the touch of her hand. He thought again of the afternoon they'd spent together before he'd left New York, the way the setting sun had filtered through the curtains of his room, bathing her skin in a warm glow, her lashes dark against her cheek as she slept; how many times had he revisited that room, that bed, the woman upon it? He shook his head. Too many to count. He picked up the pen.

> *Dearest Grace,*
> *I can hardly believe you are here at last. . . .*

Lars waited until Reinders had finished his missive, then handed it over to the errand boy to deliver at first light.

Too worn out even to eat, Peter allowed himself to be helped up to his room, where he undressed and lay down upon his bed. He'd thought he might lie awake for hours, thinking of Grace and the future, now that she'd come, but the feather bed was unbelievably soft after months on a hard plank, and he sunk into it, reaching down for the duvet, his eyes closing before he'd drawn it even halfway up.

Reinders awoke, in what felt like only minutes, to the sound of a commotion downstairs, of loud greetings and laughter, and then the pounding of boots on the stair, before his chamber door was thrown open.

"Peter, she's come!" Lars announced. "She's downstairs even as we

speak. What a charming young woman she is! I had no idea!" He
clapped his hands together with great satisfaction. "All these years and
I never pictured someone as lovely as that. You haven't done her justice,
Peter," he scolded good-naturedly. "What on earth she sees in you, I'll
never know, but you'd better get down there before she comes to her
senses. She's not wearing trousers, by the way," he added, a note of disappointment in his voice. "Don't know what Arnott was on about
there. No trousers," he repeated, and then his face brightened again.
"But the most lovely green skirt and neatly trimmed jacket, and a wonderful hat . . ."

Reinders lay, unable to move, stunned as much by the verbal barrage
as he was by the fact that she was actually here, a mere floor below, and
he was still in his nightclothes.

"Get up right now!" Lars went to Peter's wardrobe and began rummaging through the possibilities. "Here." He held out a clean white
shirt and a pair of fairly new breeches. "Put these on. Everything's going
to be too big, but these will do. C'mon, man—you're not going to let
a little malaria keep you away from that beautiful creature, are you?"

Reinders sat up and swung his legs over the side of the bed, closing
his eyes again as a wave of dizziness nearly tipped him back over.

"Sorry, old man." Darmstadt laid the clothes on the bed, reversing
his enthusiasm immediately. "Of course. Take your time. Shall I send
Arnott up to help you dress?"

"No," Reinders growled, eyes still closed. "Do it myself. Need fresh
water, though."

"I'll have the girl bring it up right away." Darmstadt went to the
window and drew back the curtains.

Reinders winced against the bright light. "What time is it?"

"Not quite ten. We've breakfasted, but I'll have tea sent into the parlor for you and Missus Donnelly. Detra and I have to go out."

"Since when?" Peter pulled the nightshirt off over his head, then
reached for his undervest.

"Since we thought you might like a little privacy," Darmstadt admitted sheepishly. "Detra's idea, of course. You know women."

"I'm not so sure I do." Reinders buttoned up the white shirt, then
stood to put on his breeches.

"Just be yourself," Darmstadt advised. "Actually, pretend to be me.

I've always had wonderful success." He grinned. "See you downstairs in a few minutes, then?"

Reinders nodded. "Soon as I'm dressed."

It took much longer than a few minutes, Reinders noted, as he finished bathing his face and brushing his hair; he wished he'd had time to shave, but the beard would have to do. The smallest of tasks still left him exhausted, but his heart was pounding at the thought of seeing Grace, and he hoped she wouldn't be disappointed. Had he aged so much? he wondered, looking at himself in the glass. Certainly his hair had been thicker and longer in New York, and his face marked less by time—when had those creases that lined his forehead appeared? Or the wrinkles at the corners of his eyes, around his ears? He had to admit he'd cut a better figure back in those days and, of course, he hadn't resembled the walking cadaver he was now. *I look like an old man,* he suddenly realized, then clenched his jaw, refusing to participate in such vain foolishness. He looked like what he was—a seasoned sea captain in midlife, one who had been recently beset by terrible illness. A few weeks' rest and good food, the presence of the woman he loved, and he would regain his vim and vigor in no time. Resolve firmly in place, he left the room and made his way slowly down the stairs, pausing only a moment outside the parlor before pushing open the doors.

"Peter!"

Grace leapt to her feet and Reinders braced himself, sure she was about to rush into his arms, but surprisingly she did not. Instead, she stood with her hands awkwardly by her sides as if suddenly unsure how to act around him, and this only increased his own uncertainty.

"It's good to see you, Grace," he said politely, frustrated by his own stubborn reserve. "How have you been?" *How have you been? How have you been?* Reinders could've bashed himself in the head—was he reverting to the tongue-tied bumbler he'd been when they first met?

"Well, I"—Grace hesitated, took a step forward, then stopped—"I'm fine, Peter. And you?"

There was an awkward pause as Reinders opened his mouth, but nothing came out.

"Well, then." Lars rose from his chair and Detra followed suit. "You must excuse us, Missus Donnelly, as my wife and I have previously scheduled and unavoidable business." He took Grace's hands and held them warmly. "It has been an absolute delight to meet you at last, my dear, and I know we shall all dine together very soon."

Detra took up Grace's hands when Lars had released them. "And I look forward to meeting your children," she added graciously. "We're so very glad you have all arrived safely."

"Thank you so much. I'm happy to have met you, as well. Peter has always spoken so highly of you both." Grace found Reinders' eyes, and then she, too, was at a loss for words.

Lars and Detra made a hasty exit, murmuring their farewells, barely noticed by the two left behind. When the door had closed, a silence wrapped around Peter and Grace, broken only by the ticking of the mantel clock and the crackle of a freshly laid fire.

"Are you well?"

"You've been ill."

They spoke at the same time, then laughed self-consciously.

"I *have* been ill," Reinders admitted. "And I'm afraid I have to sit down now or risk falling flat on my face."

"Oh, Peter! I didn't realize . . . Let me help you." Grace's concern overrode her shyness and she came quickly to his side, wrapping one arm around his waist to steady him, his arm over her shoulder, as she moved him toward his chair.

He closed his eyes and felt the warmth of her body beside his, her solid presence. *I only want to kiss her,* he thought. *I should kiss her now, and then we'll be as we were.*

"Aye," he heard her say and felt the press of her lips against his.

He returned her kiss, lightly at first, and then—as she pressed herself against him—with greater urgency, not wanting to stop, losing himself in the deliriousness of this moment out of time. He wrapped his arms more tightly around her and dropped his mouth to her neck, breathing more heavily now, his head swimming.

"Ahem." Arnott, tea tray in hand, cleared his throat pointedly from the doorway.

Startled, Grace and Peter stepped apart, Grace now flushed with embarrassment, Peter with irritation.

"Shall I bring this in, Captain?"

"Put it over there." Reinders jerked his chin toward Detra's writing desk. "That will be all."

Arnott took his time setting out the cups and saucers, the teapot, and the plate of scones Detra had ordered. There was a smirk on his face that Reinders didn't like, and finally the captain had had enough.

"That'll be all, Arnott," he repeated tersely. "Close the door on your way out."

"Very good, sir. I'll say you're not to be disturbed." The butler bowed languidly, then crossed the room and went into the hall, reaching back in for the doors, which he pulled closed with agonizing slowness.

"He reminds me of that Boardham," Grace noted. "Your old ship's steward. Remember him?"

"How could I forget?" Reinders ran his hand over the top of his closely shorn hair. "He caused us all a lot of trouble. Got away with murder, the cowardly bas—" He glanced at Grace. "You remember Tom Dean? From the ship?"

"Aye. He was one of your best, you said. But you know, Boardham got his own back in the end," Grace reported grimly. "Washed up on shore with his throat cut. Dugan sent me the article out of the paper, just so I'd know he wasn't still out there looking to cause us misery."

"Those were the days, eh?" Reinders shook his head ruefully, then lowered himself into his chair. "Forgive me, I have to sit. I'll have to build up my strength if you're going to kiss me like that."

Grace blushed to her hairline. "Will you have your tea, then, Peter? Shall I bring it over to you?"

Reinders nodded, and she set up on the small table by his chair, crowding the top with two cups, saucers, and the plate of scones. Next, she carried over Detra's smaller writing chair and put it close to the captain's. She sat, and they looked at each other in silence, hardly daring to believe they were actually in the same room, neither one knowing where to start.

"You look tired, Peter," she began, hesitantly. "And you're so very thin."

"Malaria." He put a hand up to his face, felt the hollows beneath his cheekbones, the scratchy stubble. "Sorry I'm not cleaned up properly."

"I like you with a beard. You were sporting one the first time we met aboard ship in Liverpool. Do you remember?"

"I do. And you were sporting indignation." He laughed. "Nothing but trouble, right from the start."

Grace ignored his teasing. "Then, when I saw you again in the city at Lily's stall, you'd shaved it off and I hardly recognized you." She reached out tentatively and stroked the side of his face. "Though I'd know you anywhere now, with or without it."

Reinders caught her hand and kissed the tender flesh of her palm; he'd forgotten how much he loved that hand, the square shape of it, the long fingers—it was a hardworking hand, a hand capable of great strength, of holding on. Pressing his lips even more tightly against the fragrant skin, he closed his eyes and felt tears stinging behind the lids. What was the matter with him, he wondered, that he was so easily overcome?

"You're worn out, is all," Grace assured him, gently withdrawing her hand. "You've had a hard time of it, Peter. I can see it in your eyes. But you're home now. And I'm here to take care of you."

He turned away, embarrassed by his show of emotion and by the fact that it was she who comforted him rather than the other way around; this was not the reunion he'd imagined so many times.

Grace sensed his discomfort and changed the subject. "Was Liam ill, as well?" she asked, knowing he'd respond to any question about their boy. "Is he here with you now?"

"No." Reinders faced her again and accepted the cup of tea she poured out for him. "To both questions. Strong constitution, that boy—he and Mack are the only reasons I'm sitting here." His hand shook slightly as he lifted the cup. "He's a fine seaman, Grace; you'd be so proud of him. They're down on the ship right now, taking care of business."

"I can't wait to see him. And Mary Kate is beside herself, quite sure you'd both been captured by pirates. She and Jack discuss it daily." Her eyes sparkled. "You'll like Jack."

"From your letters, I already do." His smiled faded. "I'm sorry I wasn't here when you arrived, Grace. To help you. I know how brutal the overland trip is, and I thought about you all the time. You must have been exhausted, and then Mary Kate getting sick, and Jack to take care of." He sighed. "I just can't believe I wasn't here . . ."

"And how were you to know, then? 'Twasn't 'til we'd passed through Utah Territory that I began to think Sean might've joined the miners out here. Mary Kate falling ill was like a sign from God, and that's when I knew for sure we were coming. But not before then, so how could you've known?"

"Sean's here, then? You found him?"

Grace shook her head. "I've been asking round, though. Plenty of Irish passing through here—Mormons, as well—and one day somebody'll have something to tell me about him."

"Have you taken out notices?"

"Aye. Edward Kemble at the *California Star* is helping me out with that, and I've been down to the school Sam Brannan runs. He said the Utah group's been sending Saints down to mine, mostly to Mormon Island, but unless they come into the city and look him up, he never sees them. Still, he offered to write a couple of letters to some of his folk living up there now." She paused and sipped her tea. "Do you know William Shew, has the Daguerreian Saloon? He invited me to look through his images of miners in the field, see if I can't pick Sean out, but there was nothing. He's found a few more, though, so I'm going back, end of the week, to try again."

Reinders was staring at her, mouth open, and then he tipped back his head and laughed.

"What's so funny, then?"

"Those are noteworthy men," he said admiringly. "And you've got them all on the lookout for your brother! How on earth did you meet them?"

"At Doctor Wakefield's house. They come for dinner now and then. I'm cook there," she added. "Did you know that? That I'm hired on?"

"Maybe you'd better start from the beginning." Reinders set his cup aside and leaned back in the chair.

Grace hesitated—he looked so tired—but when he promised to eat a buttered scone and take another cup of tea, she agreed. Knowing there'd be time for details later, she told him briefly about joining the wagon train in Kansas and heading out along the Oregon Trail, the months of coping with mud and flooded rivers, then heat and dust, and finally the narrow mountain passes before coming down into the valley. Finally, she told him about Mary Kate's increasing lethargy and the decision to come by steamboat to San Francisco, of finding the hospital and meeting Sister Joseph, of learning that the *Eliza J* was in Panama, and of receiving Doctor Wakefield's offer of employment.

"So you're head of the kitchen staff?"

"I *am* the kitchen staff." Grace laughed. " 'Tis a small household, though, only the doctor and his sister, who's"—she thought for a moment—"sickly. There's a housekeeper and her daughter, and an outdoor man. Mary Kate helps me now she's better, and Jack likes it well enough for the horses and the dogs, though he misses Kansas and all the gun fighting."

"How about you?" Reinders asked. "Are *you* happy here?"

Grace considered the question. "Aye. 'Tis a good enough place for us. The wage is generous—more than generous—and our rooms are warm and comfortable. Also, there's a teacher for the children, comes to the house and all."

"He hired a tutor?" Reinders was skeptical. "Why would he do that?"

"Well, you know—paid or prairie—school's not worked out well for Mary Kate, and she's a smart girl, Peter. You'd not believe what goes on inside that head. Anyway, he saw that in her and took an interest. He thinks Jack's bright, as well, and when he offered, I'd no reason to turn him down, though it struck me as odd. He's a kind man, Doctor Wakefield is."

"So I've been told." Reinders frowned. "I guess I should be grateful to him. It could've been a lot worse for you—San Francisco is a rough town."

"Aye, but what a city," she said fervently. "I pictured tent saloons and iron houses, brown hills and mud to your knees, though I knew from your letters it'd been built up after the fires. The China people call it *Gum San,* Gold Mountain—I think of it that way now, what with all the money going into buildings and houses and the like."

"The architecture may be more grand, but brown hills and mud have remained a permanent feature," he reminded her.

She laughed. "After Oregon and all that lovely green, 'twas a shock to find you were right about there being no trees a'tall. Only, I was taken with it anyway, with the spirit of the place—something to be said for a city that rises up and rebuilds itself over and over again. 'Tis like the emigrants themselves. I knew right away the children and I could make something of ourselves here."

"You've made something of yourself in every place you've ever lived,

Missus Donnelly, so why should San Francisco be any different?" Reinders smiled at her affectionately, noticing again those incredible sea-colored eyes, that lively mouth. "I've missed you, Grace. It's good to be with you again."

"I've missed you, as well." She left her chair to sit on the edge of his; he was so thin, there was more than enough room for two.

He wrapped his arms around her and pulled her to him, so that she rested against his chest, her head beneath his chin.

"Grace," he whispered in her ear. "Have you come to marry me?"

She stiffened for a moment, then turned her head and kissed him, feeling the tension in his body as his fingers slid into her hair and held her there, until she drew away to collect herself.

"Yes," she told him, looking into his eyes. "As soon as you're well, as soon as you see the children, meet Jack, and—"

Reinders kissed her again, stopping the flow of words, halting the invasion of the real world into this fragile and delicate moment. Gracefully and with practiced ease, he shifted his own body and then hers so that she was completely enfolded in his arms. His embrace intensified, his hands moving over her body, and she found herself responding, remembering now the passion that lay just beneath his composed veneer. But suddenly he stopped and leaned back, dizzy and short of air.

"Peter! You're white as a ghost!" She laid her hand against the side of his face, his forehead, feeling now the cool clamminess of his skin. His shirt was damp to the touch and clung to his chest and shoulders. "Close your eyes, now," she urged. "Take a deep breath."

She got up and quickly fetched a glass of water from the decanter on the sideboard, then watched with concern as he drank it all down. Slowly, his color began to return and his breathing became more regular. Feeling better, he patted the seat beside him as if intending to take up where they'd left off.

"Are you daft, then, Peter?" she chided gently. "Because there won't be any more lovemaking, I can tell you that. Not until you're better."

"That's quite an incentive." He smiled wanly, then closed his eyes again and exhaled.

"The place for you is back in bed. Alone," she added sternly. "Though a hot brick might be good company."

He didn't argue, and that caused Grace even greater concern. She helped him up to his room, pulled off his boots, and left him dozing on the bed, though it was difficult not to remain by his side. On her way out, she spoke to the butler and made sure he understood that Captain Reinders must be looked in upon regularly, then attended to when he awoke. She would come back the next day, she had promised, for a brief call, but wouldn't bring the children until he was up to such a visit.

Once home, Grace changed out of her better clothes and into her everyday dress and apron, talking to the children as she did so. They were eager to hear all about the captain and Liam, though Grace could only tell them that Reinders had been terribly ill and was still recovering, and that she'd not yet seen Liam, who was working aboard the ship.

There was a great deal of work to be done in the kitchen, so Grace was kept busy throughout the long afternoon, stopping only to serve afternoon coffee to the doctor in his study. Wakefield, too, was very interested in the outcome of Grace's visit to Reinders, and finally asked her outright if she planned on leaving them now. Grace assured him that she would remain, at least through the Christmas holidays, as the captain had been weakened by malaria and would need a great deal of time to get back on his feet; certainly, he didn't need the stress of a household with children during the holidays. Wakefield seemed relieved to hear that Grace would continue working, and thanked her profusely; she was surprised herself at how relieved she felt that her life would not take yet another sudden change, but one that would be made gradually.

At table that evening, she fielded questions from Hopkins, not wanting to discuss her personal life with the obnoxious woman, but she did let Enid and George know that she and the children would remain with the Wakefields into the New Year, and perhaps longer, depending upon the captain's progress. Talk turned then to Christmas, and the forthcoming preparations, when suddenly there was a loud knock on the back door and all conversation halted. Litton rose immediately to his feet.

"I'll see to it," the stableman said gruffly and picked up a lamp to light his way into the mudroom.

The rest of the diners sat still, straining to hear as Litton inquired after the purpose of their backdoor visitor. A moment later, he was back.

"It's a young man, Missus Donnelly. Name of . . ."

"Liam!" Mary Kate burst from the table and threw herself into the open arms of the young man who had followed Litton into the room.

"Hello, little girl!" Liam grinned from ear to ear as he picked her up and twirled her, then kissed her cheek. "Hello, *big* girl!" He set her down. "And where's me mam, then?"

Tears of joy sprung into Grace's eyes as she hurried around the side of the table to embrace him. He clung tightly to her for a moment, though now it was her head that rested against his shoulder instead of the other way around.

"Thank God you made it." He kissed her cheek with a loud smack. "I'm so happy to see you."

"And I, you." She returned his kiss, then stepped back to have a good look at this person who'd left her as a boy of nearly twelve and was now a young man of fifteen. "You're a giant, Liam Kelley!" she exclaimed, wiping her eyes. "Life at sea agrees with you, then!"

"Oh, aye." He laughed. " 'Tis a great life. You look well," he told her, then put his hand on Mary Kate's head. "Both of you. But where's young Jack? Hiding behind your mam's skirts, are you? C'mon, now, boy, let's have a look at you!"

Jack came around the side of his mother shyly, though unable to take his eyes off the strapping young man. "Are you Liam who went to sea? Because I already know about you."

"I know about you, too." Liam bent down and offered his hand, which Jack shook solemnly. "Nice to make your acquaintance at last, young Jack. Your exploits are famous aboard the *Eliza J.*"

"What's 'exploits'?" Jack asked warily.

"Adventures," Liam explained. "All the things you've done in your life so far that's grand."

"Like I came out here in a covered wagon?"

"Oh, aye," Liam acknowledged soberly. "Though I've not yet heard the tale of that one. You'll have to tell it to me one night."

"What a surprise, Missus Donnelly." Hopkins stood stiffly at the table. "And who would the father of this one be, pray tell?"

"This is Liam Kelley, son of Seamus and Alice Kelley," Grace told her evenly. "We made the crossing together, and he lived with us in New York after his family perished. He's my adopted son and the ward of Captain Reinders."

"How do you do?" Enid dropped a little curtsy.

"This is Enid Hopkins, Liam," Grace introduced. "She and her mother over there work for Doctor Wakefield, as well. And by the door is our own Mister Litton, stable master and groundskeeper."

Liam tipped his head respectfully to the ladies and shook hands with Litton, then put his arm around Grace's shoulders again.

"Pleased to meet you all," he said warmly. "I'm sure we'll be seeing plenty of one another as long as me mam is working here."

"How nice for you." Hopkins turned to her daughter. "Come, Enid. Time for evening rounds." And then she left the kitchen without so much as a backward glance, but Enid managed to offer them all an apologetic smile as she hurried out behind her mother.

Mister Litton mumbled something about the horses, nodded toward Liam, then grabbed his cap and disappeared out into the dark yard. With everyone else gone now, Grace settled Liam at the table and got him a plate of dinner, watching with motherly satisfaction as he ate every mouthful.

"Oh, that's grand, then!" he pronounced with a hearty sigh. "Everything tastes the same at the Darmstadts'. Even our cook on board is better than the one we've got at home, and he only knows three dishes—boiled fish, fried fish, and fish stew!"

Grace and the children laughed, all crowded around him at the table.

"You know you're welcome here anytime, agra," Grace told him. "Always a place for you with us."

"Will you not be coming down the hill, then?" Liam pulled the napkin out of his collar and put it on the table. "To live, I mean, when you and the captain marry?"

Jack and Mary Kate held perfectly still, only their eyes shifting from one face to the other in anticipation of the answer.

"Sure we will," Grace allowed. "Though not 'til he's had time to recover himself again. He didn't look well, Liam, and I was worried for him."

Liam nodded. "Aye, he was the worst I'd ever seen. Me and Mack were afraid for a while there we'd have to bury him on that island, and I was beside myself over it."

Grace's heart fell at the thought of Peter dead, along with all the others she loved.

"He told us to go on without him, but all of us, the entire crew, were agreed—we weren't leaving him down there in that jungle."

"Were there savages?" Jack asked breathlessly.

"No. Only Indians. But insects as big as your hand." Liam stretched his fingers out to show the length. "And snakes, long as from here to the stable out back!"

Jack's eyes were wide with horror. "Could they eat you?"

"I never hung round long enough to find out," the young man admitted. "Mister Darmstadt has a collection at home—butterflies, moths, insects, and the like. All in a glass case. The captain brings them back for him. Snakeskins, as well, and we have a parrot in a cage."

"A parrot!" exclaimed the children excitedly.

"Aye, and it talks." Liam grinned. "You'll see it when you come." He turned to Grace. "Will the doctor let you off to have dinner with us tomorrow night?"

"I'm sure he will. He's very good to us, and he knows we've been waiting all this time for the two of you to return."

"That's grand, then. The captain'll be pleased. He was cursing himself for not being in better form when you came this morning." Liam laughed. "I better get back, then, and let Missus Darmstadt know about tomorrow night." He kissed Grace on the cheek and stood up. "Can Mary Kathleen walk me round to the front, do you think?"

"Please, Mam?" Mary Kate asked, her eyes shining.

"Well, and why not?" Grace patted her daughter's cheek. "Get your cloak is all, as it's turned cold out there. Jack, you give me a hand with the dishes, eh, son?"

"Aw, Mam." He knocked the toe of his boot against the table leg.

"We'll have a man's day out soon enough, young Jack," Liam promised the boy. "I'll give you the grand tour of the ship that carried your mam and Mary Kate to America. And me, as well."

"I've never been on a real ship," Jack confessed wistfully.

"And how is it you got to this country, then, son?" Grace teased.

The little boy scowled. "Doesn't count if I can't remember it," he told her.

Grace sighed affectionately. "Say good night to him now. He'll be back, I promise you."

Jack said good night reluctantly, then began to clear the dishes as Mary Kate and Liam slipped out the back door. Once outside, Mary Kate wrapped her cloak around her shoulders and put up her hood.

"Cold." Liam looked up at the star-scattered sky, his breath hanging in the damp night air. "Beautiful, though. 'Tis better than Kansas, or not?"

Mary Kate thought about it for a moment. "In Kansas, you could see for miles and miles. There was more sky," she decided. "But no harbor."

"Landlocked." He pretended to shudder. "Horrible, then."

"Not horrible. Just different." She smiled and took his hand. "This way." She led him around the far side of the house, along the path that wound down toward the driveway.

There were no lamps on in the front rooms of the house, so the night was even deeper and they could see more clearly the city that fell away below them, the small sea of flickering lights that gave way to the darkened harbor.

"I love it here," Liam admitted shyly. "Reminds me of Dublin. Only without the green." He laughed. "Do you remember anything of Ireland, a'tall, Mary Kate? Do you ever think of it?"

Mary Kate nodded. "I remember the folk—Granna at our cabin. And Grandda at the convent when Jack was born. There's a smell reminds me sometimes, when peat's burning, I think, or 'tis damp, or the sea." She paused. "Mostly, though, my stomach hurts when I think of Ireland, so I don't too often."

"Mine, too. Dublin was terrible. Folk lying in the alleyways, dead or dying. Me mam was desperate to get us out. I was scared a lot of the time." He kept his eyes on the city below. "Were you?"

"I had me mam," Mary Kate said simply.

"Aye, you did." He let go of her hand and put his arm around her shoulders instead. "Captain says she's the bravest woman he ever knew. He didn't like to think of her stuck in Kansas, though. Too hard a life, he said; too much work for a woman alone."

"She was tired all the time," Mary Kate confided. "And sad, as well.

'Twas onions, she said, but who peels onions in the middle of the night? I was glad when we decided to come away."

Liam gave her shoulders an affectionate squeeze. "It's all going to be fine now," he reassured her. "She'll marry the captain and he'll build you all a grand house up north."

"Up north?" Mary Kate looked up at him, puzzled.

"Aye, the captain's bought a general store and some land up the coast in New Whatcom. He wants to make the harbor there his home port and move you all up."

"Will you be living with us?"

He shook his head. "I'm keeping my room at the Darmstadts', but I'll be seeing you whenever we make a run up."

Mary Kate frowned, her eyes wide in the dark. "But I don't want to go off again! We only just got here, and I like it." She thought of Mister Hewitt and then of Rose Mulhoney. "I have a teacher here, and a friend. I have a friend." Her eyes searched his face, then filled with tears. "And you, you're . . ."

"You're crying!" Liam was aghast at what he'd caused and hugged her immediately. "Ah, don't listen to me, girl. What do I know anyway? Nothing. Nothing a'tall." His arms tightened around her. "You're the first one ever said I could make something of myself, and now I have and wanted you to see it, and instead I made you cry! Please don't cry," he begged.

As they stood there, Liam remembered the night after they'd buried his mother and sister at sea, when he'd lain down on his bunk, exhausted and numb, willing himself to die along with them. At that lowest moment, Mary Kate had crawled in next to him, put her head against his chest—just like now—until his arms had gone around her and he'd realized he had something to hang on to. She had willed him to live, and her will had been strongest, for here they both were—alive and well, half a world away from where they'd begun.

"I'll take care of it," he promised her then. "You're not to worry anymore, now, Mary Kate, do you hear me?"

She nodded, then pulled away from him, dried her eyes with the heels of her hands, and reached deep into her skirt pocket.

"I have something of yours." She handed him a bundled handkerchief, then watched as he carefully unwrapped it. "I didn't send them in the mail, because things get lost," she said soberly. "And, anyway, I knew I'd see you one day."

" 'Tis Mam's hair comb." He looked at it in wonder. "And Siobahn's wee sock. How did you come by these?"

"The day you left for your da's, remember? You told me to keep them safe as you'd be coming home for them."

Liam's thoughts flew back to that terrible summer in New York, back to Seamus and the filthy slum in which he lived—Seamus, who'd deserted Liam's mother and sister, Seamus the drunk, Seamus, who'd taken Liam away from the very people he'd come to love . . . Seamus, who'd made up for it all in the end by giving his own life for Liam's.

"I do." He touched the scar on his cheek, the one left by Boardham's knife, then looked at the meager possessions in his hand again, all that was left of his mother, his sister. "You saved them all this time?"

"And this." Mary Kate handed him a mumblety-peg knife out of her other pocket. "Mister Marconi said I was to give it to you, but he thought 'twould be in Boston. Most likely, you're too old for it now."

"I used to call him an old garlic eater." Liam was embarrassed now at the thought; he took the small knife and turned it over in his hand, then frowned as if in pain. "He was good to me, Mister Marconi. I didn't deserve how good he was."

"Yes, you did."

Liam looked at the things in his hands, then at Mary Kate. "Thank you," he whispered, hugging her again. "Thank you, Mary Kathleen." He let go and wiped his eyes. "All right, we're even now—couple of old saps. Funny, isn't it? The *Eliza J* brought us all the way across to America, and there she sits tonight—out there in the harbor—with you and me on this hill, peering out at her. I don't know quite what to make of it all."

"It's the plan." She nodded quietly. "Mam says we're meant to be here. We don't always have to know why."

"But what if the plan's meant to take you up north?" he asked. "Would you go?"

"No." Mary Kate was positive. "We're to stay here. I know it. I'm always going to live here. For my whole life."

Liam looked at her, at the way she met his gaze. "Me, too," he said.

They stood a moment longer, the young girl and the boy to whom she was heart-bound, arms around each other as they looked down upon the youthful city, each on the verge of becoming. Their eyes shifted from the glittering sky to the glowing city to the moonlit harbor and back again, and they breathed in the cold winter air, while upon their shoulders rested the hands of a thousand Irish ancestors, steadying them for the work of the future, for the dream that was America, the land of the free; for America, home of the brave.

Twenty

When Sean walked into the parlor and saw Chang-Li modeling his prized dog-fur jacket in front of the mirror, he knew the time had come to say good-bye.

"Ah, Mister Sung! Please to sit." Chang-Li motioned to one of the great wingback chairs in front of the grate, taking a seat in the other. "Sail tomorrow, so must discuss business now before leaving to Canton."

"The bodies are here, then?" Sean was surprised by how quickly time had passed since they'd learned of the deaths of Chang-Li's brothers; shot, both of them, a week ago, and robbed of their gold.

"Ah, yes, yes." Chang-Li nodded. "Already on ship."

"It's good of you to take them all the way back home. 'Twill be a long journey for you, Chang-Li, and I'm sorry for your loss."

Chang-Li shrugged. "It is their destiny. Brothers will be returned to ancestral burial and so to not wander alone. And Chang-Li"—he touched his own chest lightly—"will take opportunity to find good wife from high family name. No good Chinawoman here for important Chinaman to marry. Must get from own country."

"I guess that's right." The few single Chinese women in San Francisco got their living as laundresses or cooks, or in the nighttime trades; Chang-Li clearly had higher aspirations. "She might not be so comfortable having a *fan qui* boarder about the place; is that what you wanted to speak with me about? Should I start looking for other rooms?"

"Ah, no, no. Chang-Li make arrangement for new wife house. Mister Sung stay in *this* house, stay here long time, see to House of Good

Fortune and other business. Make much money for Chang-Li and Mister Sung." He smiled encouragingly. "Yes?"

"You'll be gone a long time, Chang-Li." Sean thought with longing of the increased hours he now spent with his pipe, the intimate relationship he had so painstakingly built with his addiction. "Things may have changed by the time you get back." *Most likely I'll be dead,* he thought. "Could you not leave Mei Ling in charge of the place? I'll help her out, of course, as long as I can."

Chang-Li shook his head vigorously. "Mei Ling is slave! Mei Ling is girl! No good for business—only clean house, wash clothes, serve tea." He stopped himself then, and forcibly changed his expression. "Mei Ling is very *good* girl," he now emphasized. "Work hard. No argue. Follow every order."

Sean stared at him, baffled by the about-face, but Chang-Li had regrouped and now pressed his case from another angle.

"Time is come for Great American Feast Day," the landlord announced, fingertips pressed lightly together. "Celebration of birth of God called Jesus."

"Christmas?" Sean blinked. "Are we talking about Christmas now, Chang-Li?"

"Ah, yes. Time of many foods and presenting of many gifts."

"Well, I suppose that's one way of looking at it, though I'm not so keen on the holidays myself, anymore."

"Yes, yes." Chang-Li ignored him. "One time, Chang-Li have long talk with Reverend Hopkins of San Francisco Bible Society. Say many good omen at time of birth, say to Chang-Li all men perfect now to Father God because Son God live perfect life as man."

It took Sean a moment to wade through the syntax, but then he understood. "Aye, that's true," he agreed, though uncomfortable with finding himself in a conversation about the God whom he had so mightily disappointed.

"Yes, yes. Very good God. Sit in highest place." Chang-Li indicated the shrine, which did indeed include a religious card with the face of Christ; it clearly occupied the place of honor among all the other gods Chang-Li worshipped, complete with a special offering bowl of food and smoking joss sticks.

"Didn't your Reverend Hopkins tell you about the first commandment?" Sean couldn't resist, knowing Chang-Li prided himself on his knowledge of all things he considered American. " 'Thou shalt have no other Gods before me'?"

Chang-Li raised an elegant finger. "This God *is* highest. All other gods *after* this God!"

Sean chuckled, wishing he'd been privy to the conversations about religion that must have occurred between Reverend Hopkins and the enthusiastically philosophical Chang-Li.

" 'Love thy neighbor,' " Chang-Li continued. "Also commandment, but is very hard. Many neighbor is bad. Many neighbor try to take from Chang-Li. But not Mister Sung." He gave a single nod over the tops of his fingertips. "Mister Sung is very special friend to Chang-Li. Share destiny in many ways."

"For your sake, Chang-Li, I hope not." Sean smiled wryly. "But, since you mentioned Christmas . . ." he stood up. "I know how much you were looking forward to having your feast, and now you've got to postpone all that."

Chang-Li shrugged; life simply was what it was.

"So I wanted to give you your present now."

Sean went to the doorway and around the corner into the hall, then returned with a large beribboned box, which he handed to his landlord, his partner, and somehow now, too, his friend.

Chang-Li's mouth formed a small O of surprise, but he opened the gift with grave dignity, then abandoned dignity in favor of sheer delight when he saw the superb black silk stovepipe hat that lay inside.

"It's from fashionable New York City." Sean was grinning now. "What do you think? Try it on."

Chang-Li placed it carefully upon his head, then stood gingerly and examined himself in the mirror above the mantel, turning to view first his left profile, then his right.

"So handsome," the landlord pronounced. "Finest style. In Canton, neighbors will think Chang-Li American High Man, invite Chang-Li to marry daughters." Smiling with pride, he returned carefully to his chair, lowering himself slowly, head held steady so as not to unbalance the magnificent hat.

"I knew 'twas made for you and you alone, the minute I laid eyes upon it. Happy Christmas, Chang-Li." Sean pulled out his pocket watch and glanced at it. "And, now"—he looked out the window—"if there's nothing else . . . ?"

Chang-Li eyed him shrewdly. "A man must have pleasure, but too much pleasure may ruin a man. Stay longer, Mister Sung; still business to discuss." He gestured toward Sean's chair. "The mist-and-flower ladies will wait; the sweet pipe will not smoke itself."

Sean sat down again, abashed, but in good humor. "Point taken, Chang-Li. The nice thing about being on the decline is that it takes so little effort to reach the bottom. Just a bit of leaning in that direction, if you know what I mean."

Chang-Li studied him carefully from beneath his new stovepipe, and then clapped his hands together sharply. Sean thought he was calling for the tea tray, but when Mei Ling appeared, her hands were empty.

"In honor of birth of American God, Chang-Li has gift for honored neighbor, for partner, for friend."

Now the landlord motioned Mei Ling forward, urging her impatiently until she stood beside his chair, hands clasped in front of her, head bowed respectfully.

Sean looked from Chang-Li to Mei Ling and back again, shaking his head as the reality of the gift dawned upon him.

"Mei Ling hard worker, cook for Mister Sung and wash clothes," Chang-Li pronounced. "Mister Sung stay here, very comfortable, see to House of Good Fortune; Mei Ling do all thing. Belong to Mister Sung now." He sat back, delighted with his presentation of the gift. "Happy Christmas!"

Though stunned, Sean was careful to think before he spoke, wishing to insult neither the man before him nor the young woman who served them so quietly day in and day out.

"I'm honored by such a gift, Chang-Li," he began cautiously. "But I cannot accept it. One person cannot own another in America . . . in California," he revised quickly as Chang-Li, well versed in the laws of the South, leaned forward and opened his mouth. "The state of California outlawed slavery in 1850, as you well know."

Chang-Li swatted this comment away as if it were nothing but an annoying fly. "In China, some girl slave, some girl wife. Each girl have destiny. And so it is."

"This is not China," Sean reminded him respectfully, though firmly.

"Whatever arrangement lies between you and Mei Ling, I've never interfered with that. But, as a citizen of California"—*and as a human being,* he thought, surprised that some remnant of principle remained—"I cannot—I will not—own another person."

Chang-Li stroked his chin, his eyes stormy with annoyance. "New wife bring own servant, not want Mei Ling." Then his eyes cleared and he shrugged. "So Chang-Li will sell Mei Ling to Chinaman know value of good slave, give Mister Sung good horse instead."

Sean knew full well how savvy Chang-Li could be when it came to getting what he wanted, so he let several minutes tick by before deciding to call the man's bluff. He was about to tell Chang-Li that he wanted neither horse nor slave, to go ahead and sell the girl, if that was how little she meant to him, when he noticed Mei Ling's shoulders tighten beneath her tunic, the line of her jaw flexing as she gritted her teeth. *What did* she *think about this?* he wondered suddenly. *Had she ever had any say at all in the direction of her own life?* Sean changed his mind in that moment.

"Wait." His voice rang out in the stillness of the room.

Mei Ling's jaw did not relax, but she stole a quick peek at him from the corner of her eye.

"You want me to stay on here and run the business for you, and so I'll agree to it—but only upon one condition." He paused for good effect. "That you release Mei Ling from her obligations to you. In other words, Chang-Li, give the girl her rightful freedom and I'll double your wealth by the time you return with your new wife."

Chang-Li's face remained impassive, but Sean knew he was interested by the ever-so-slight arching of one eyebrow.

"Let Mei Ling stay in this house for now, and if she chooses to work for us, then pay her what you would any servant. If she doesn't, she's free to hire herself out wherever she wants. Either way, her free time is her own and she can come and go as she pleases." Finished, Sean leaned back in his chair.

Chang-Li's eyes traveled the seam of the ceiling as he considered the proposal before him. Mei Ling, it appeared, had quit breathing altogether. Sean kept his face a mask of indifference, afraid to admit even to himself how important this had suddenly become.

Finally, Chang-Li nodded. "There is wisdom and good fortune in such a bargain as this. The service of Mei Ling remains, but not as slave to feed and shelter, and so, of no annoyance to new wife. And still, protected."

The look on Chang-Li's face allowed Sean a glimpse of the bond that connected the two of them, one more complex than that of simply master and slave.

"Question." Chang-Li lifted a slender finger in the air. "Why Mister Sung not make free Mei Ling himself?"

Sean thought for a moment. "If *I* did it, then you might never really consider her a real person."

A flicker of annoyance flashed in the landlord's eyes, but he did not let it settle.

"You would treat her as you always have," Sean continued. "She would only be a slave pretending at freedom."

Chang-Li considered this statement. "It is so," he pronounced at last. "And so, it will be as Mister Sung says."

The landlord looked at his now-former slave girl and spoke to her in their language, and Sean noted that Chang-Li was making an attempt to moderate the sharp tones of command he had previously used with Mei Ling to something closer to civility. Encouraged by this, Mei Ling raised her head and met her master's eyes, though shyly and with great hesitation, her answers to his questions consisting of one or two short sounds. Twice she glanced at Sean and then quickly away, and finally Chang-Li asked her something to which she nodded.

"Mei Ling understand now." Chang-Li informed him. "Choose live here, work for Mister Sung. All thing as before, only Chang-Li pay now."

"Ah, but you get me in the bargain, Chang-Li, and we're making money hand over fist, are we not?" Sean looked at Mei Ling and thought that her stance seemed not quite as subservient somehow, that her posture had altered, even if only by the slightest degree. "You did the right thing, Chang-Li."

"Open door and bird fly out." The landlord shrugged. "Perch on top of cage only."

The image rankled Sean a bit, but he wasn't about to push his luck, and besides, his head was pounding—it was time to bathe his sensibilities in something more potent than tea.

"Well, this bird is leaving the cage altogether." He stood and looked around for his hat; Mei Ling got to it first, snatched it up, then brought it to him with head bowed, subservience back in full force.

"Mei Ling prepare food now," she said in her quiet voice.

"Not for me, Mei Ling." Sean settled the hat on his head and, adjusting the brim, pulled it down low. "I'm going out."

"Mei Ling wait."

"I'll not be back 'til late." He saw uncertainty on her face and was puzzled. "Well, leave it on the table, then. I'll eat when I get back."

Mei Ling said nothing, and Sean exchanged a glance with Chang-Li, who merely shrugged, though his eyes suggested an amusement at some private joke. Irritated, Sean turned back to Mei Ling.

"I don't want to find you sitting in the kitchen, waiting for me," he chided more aggressively than he'd intended. "Take yourself out for a walk, why don't you?" he tried, sounding angry instead of noncommittal. "Do whatever you want, then! You belong to yourself now, for God's sake!"

The sharpness of his voice startled Mei Ling, and she looked up at him hesitantly, eyes filled with uncertainty.

"Mei Ling wait," she repeated shakily, then lowered her head and rushed from the room.

"She *does* understand she's a servant now, and not a slave, doesn't she?" Sean focused his frustration on the landlord. "That she can do as she likes with her own time?"

"Ah, yes." Chang-Li was clearly enjoying Sean's discomfort. "Mei Ling choice as paid girl is serve Mister Sung. Mei Ling no understand 'own time.' "

Sean wanted a drink in his hand this very minute; he licked his lower lip and felt the bump of the scar that remained from the beating, thought of the young Chinese girl who'd tended him so gently.

"Oh." The frustration drained away, leaving him tired. "Well, was she never free, then? Is that it?"

"Belong to old man, then Chang-Li take in trade. Before that"—the landlord lifted his hands helplessly—"many father, many mother, sell youngest daughter for food," he explained. "Is great honor to save all of family in this way."

In trade, Sean thought, the reality of Mei Ling's life coming into sharp focus; *sold*. He thought of Grace's friend Lily Free and of the children Captain Reinders had rescued. "How old is Mei Ling?"

"China year different," Chang-Li told him. "All China people one year older on New Year. Mei Ling not know; maybe"—he rattled numbers off in his own tongue—"maybe, in America, Mei Ling twenty year."

Twenty years of submission would certainly preclude developing a mind of one's own, Sean realized, and he saw now that brokering Mei Ling's release from slavery was only the first step in making her truly free; when the bars of her cage had been removed, so had all context for the life she had lived therein.

"Well, I'll help her, then," Sean resolved and instantly wondered how he was going to manage to teach a vulnerable young woman about the possibilities of freedom while, at the same time, continuing down his own path of enslavement; impossible to do both. "When did you say you'd be returning from China, Chang-Li?"

"When time is right," Chang-Li pronounced sagely.

Sean rubbed a hand wearily over the scruff of his beard and mustache. "You did this to me on purpose, didn't you, Chang-Li? Wait"—He held up a hand to stop what he knew was coming—"I know, I know. The path unfolds and takes us where it will. Well, I don't believe that, Chang-Li. We all have choices."

"And Mister Sung has made one."

"I've made a lot of them, Chang-Li, and believe me—only a handful were any good." With those words and the image they evoked of his sister's face, Sean knew he was only minutes away from smoking his way into oblivion.

"Not to worry," Chang-Li said confidently. "This choice fit in that hand. Happy Christmas, Mister Sung, happy Christmas."

Twenty-one

It was the afternoon before Christmas and the children were so excited that they rolled over and around each other like a couple of puppies. In the morning, the kitchen had been filled with the rich smell of weeks of delicate baking—butter cookies, yeasty orange rolls and biscuits, tarts and pies with various fillings—but now the roasting chickens were overpowering the sweet scent with their meaty aroma. Grace had prepared weeks before a fruited cake that had been steeping in the doctor's good brandy; the pudding had also been soaked and was bound in muslin in its container, waiting for tomorrow, when it would be steamed and served with a creamy sauce.

The doctor had invited his good friend Fairfax for the meal, which would be served by Enid so that Grace and the children might spend the afternoon with Captain Reinders and Liam. Grace had been visiting the captain's house regularly and had been delighted with Peter's steady weight gain and the return of his stamina. The Darmstadts would be there, too, of course, but Grace and the children were comfortable with such warm, generous people and always felt welcome in the house.

As the afternoon light faded, she untied her apron and called to the children quietly.

"Let's walk about and see the house in all its glory, shall we?" she asked them, her eyes dancing.

They went out into the great hall and looked up at the banister, which had been entwined with ropes of ivy livened up by holly sprigs. The house itself was shining and clean, and glowed as never before.

Grace had kept on Missus Hopkins to see it through, though it was poor Enid who'd borne the brunt of the work.

In the dining room, the long table had been polished and laid with a thin protective mat, then a snowy linen cloth upon which were arranged two candelabra and a centerpiece of red apples that Grace had dipped in egg white, then frosted with sugar, so that they now resembled the jewels of a king instead of mere fruit. Grace checked to see that the china had been set out on the sideboard alongside the freshly pressed linen napkins and the gleaming silver. Around the room, Mary Kate and Enid had arranged holly and greenery, and vases of long, graceful branches that bore bright red berries.

" 'Tis beautiful," Grace complimented her daughter. "You and Enid did a fine job in here, and aren't I proud of the both of you?"

Mary Kate glowed with pleasure.

"Me and Mister Litton rounded up the holly," Jack quickly informed his mother. "See?" He offered his hands, pricked and scraped, for her examination and sympathy.

"What a tough little man you are," Grace praised, giving each hand a light kiss. "You did a fine job, as well."

Now it was his turn to glow with pleasure.

"Can we see the library, Mam?" Mary Kate asked hopefully.

Grace nodded and led the way, closing the dining room doors behind her. The fire was laid, though not yet lit, a basket of logs to one side and to the other, a basket of pinecones—these would be tossed into the fire tonight when all could enjoy their show of colored flames. The room was filled with the heady scent of pine from the tall, grand tree that stood in one corner, and she breathed in deeply through her nose, enjoying the sharp, clean scent. Liam and Mack had delivered a box of gifts for Lily and her family, and had brought back a number of trees from Oregon, which they sold for a great profit, though they held one back for the captain's house and another for the Wakefields'. The children had strung popcorn, then draped the tree in gentle swoops from top to bottom; interspersed were dark red bows tied from ribbon Grace had gotten in the Chinese market. At the very top, they'd placed a star Mister Litton had cut for them out of tin. Wakefield himself had returned from town with a box of small white candles and their holders, made in Germany, which could be clipped to the tree. These were in place now and would be lit tonight after supper, Wakefield had promised.

Grace realized the children hadn't said a word, and she looked at them now, smiling at the rapture on their faces as they stood stock-still, admiring the tree.

"Wait 'til you see it all lit up. 'Twill be the most beautiful sight."

"Won't it catch on fire?" Jack asked, concerned and excited both. "And burn us all to death?"

Grace bit the inside of her cheek. "Well, it could, and you're right about that. But we'll only light it when we're all here and we'll be sure to put it out when we go to bed."

Reassured, Jack turned his attention to the far corner of the room where a piece of furniture appeared to be draped by a sheet, though a ribbon had been attached to the top, indicating that it was a gift of some sort.

"What's under there, then?" he whispered.

Grace put her finger to her lips to show him it was a secret, then tip-toed over to close the library doors. She crossed the room and motioned them over, then lifted a corner of the sheet.

"Oh!" Mary Kate put her hand over her mouth. " 'Tis a piano, is it not, Mam? Oh, 'tis fine!" She touched the beautiful wood tentatively with one fingertip.

" 'Tis a special present for Miss Wakefield," Grace confided. "The doctor says she used to play all the time before she fell ill. You mustn't breathe a word of it, now," she warned. "Not to anyone, lest she get wind of it and the surprise be ruined."

Both children nodded solemnly.

"And now we'd best get back to the kitchen—it'll be suppertime soon, and then we'll sit in here for a while before bed as a special treat."

"Mam." Jack tugged at her sleeve. "When will I give my present to Mister Litton and them?"

"You already gave a present to Mister Hewitt," she reminded him. "Because you won't see him 'til the New Year now."

Jack frowned, disappointed, and Grace was glad to see it; he liked his lessons with the young master. Mister Hewitt was lighthearted and kind and knew how to interest a little boy who preferred horses and dogs to letters and numbers.

"We gave him a Christmas basket," she said. "You and Mary Kate put in a nice writing pen and a bottle of ink, and I added a loaf of oat bread and a jar of that apple butter he liked so well."

Jack's face relaxed and he nodded. "What about the others?"

"Well, you can put the doctor's gift under the tree tonight, if you like, and Enid and Mister Litton can have theirs anytime." She took his hand. "Let's go now, and you can show me what you have."

She led the children back to the kitchen and opened a window, as it felt overly warm after the cool library. Hopkins was still upstairs helping Abigail with her bath, and Enid was . . . Grace bit her lip and looked out the window, then grinned—aye, there she was, standing by the garden gate, having a word with Mister Litton, presumably about the ham Grace wanted from the smokehouse for Christmas dinner, but really about anything at all that would keep the girl in his presence. They made a handsome couple, Grace thought—Litton was tall and narrow, with long arms and large hands; Enid was shorter, but of the same sturdy build and long limbs. She was surprised that George had remained to talk; usually, he was out of there in a flash, but now he seemed to be in no hurry, nodding at the girl's chatter while he coiled a long hank of rope. Perhaps it was his present to Enid—this bit of his time, the thing she wanted most of all.

"All right, then." Grace tore herself away from the sight and tidied her own hair. "Tell me what you've got and whether it needs tying up a'tall."

Mary Kate disappeared into their quarters, then returned with the large basket that held their gifts for other people, which she set on the table with a heavy clunk.

"I knit these for the doctor, but they might be too big." She pulled out a nicely made pair of dark gray socks that did indeed look too big, but then again, Grace had never actually measured Wakefield's feet.

"And this scarf for Mister Litton."

Grace fingered it, pleased with her daughter's effort. " 'Tis fine work, Mary Kate. The red'll suit him what with all the gray and brown he wears. And did you knit one for Enid, as well?"

Mary Kate frowned and bit her lip, then looked up cautiously at her mother. "I made her a drawing instead," she revealed. "But I'll have to give it to her in secret."

"And why would you have to do such a thing?" Grace asked "Bring it out; let's have a look at it."

Mary Kate scampered back to their own quarters again, and Grace could hear her rummaging around the bottom drawer of the chest, which was where she kept her schoolwork. She returned quickly but held the paper behind her back, reluctant to show it. Grace and Jack exchanged a glance and shrugged their shoulders, neither having any idea what the girl was up to.

"It can't be that bad," Grace encouraged. "You've a fine hand for capturing likenesses."

"Well, that's the problem, you see." Mary Kate set the small square of paper on the table.

"It's Mister Litton feeding the horses!" Jack exclaimed, crowding next to his mother to have a closer look. "And there's Enid with her basket of eggs! 'Tis grand, Mary Kate, grand!"

"Aye, 'tis," Grace agreed. "But I see what you mean—Enid'll be delighted, but her mother might twist her ear off over it."

Mary Kate nodded grimly.

"Why would she?" Jack demanded.

Grace and Mary Kate shared a knowing look.

"Missus Hopkins doesn't care for Mister Litton," Grace explained carefully. "But Enid does."

"Well, sure she does," Jack said, as if it were obvious to the whole world. "He's grand, is Mister Litton. Hopkins is just an old hen."

A laugh burst from Grace before she could stop it. "Jack. Don't speak about your elders that way," she admonished, though she agreed with him completely. "What we mean is that Enid has special feelings for Mister Litton."

"Why doesn't she marry him, then?"

" 'Tisn't that simple. Mister Litton is a quiet man. He . . ." She hesitated, thinking. "Maybe he doesn't know how Enid feels, or maybe he does, but he doesn't feel the same way and doesn't want to hurt her."

"I'll take it up with him," Jack assured them confidently, reaching for his hat. "We'll get it all worked out."

"No, Jack!" Grace sat him down and looked him squarely in the eye. "You mustn't say a word to Mister Litton about Enid nor the other way round. 'Tis not our business and they wouldn't want you talking about it."

"If it's not our business, then why'd she do the drawing, then?"

Grace looked at Mary Kate, not sure how to answer.

"Enid is always nice to us, Jack," Mary Kate reasoned. "She brings us sweets from town, and warns us when her mother's coming so we can get out of the way. I only wanted to do something nice for her, as well."

"Are we both giving it to her?" Jack inquired.

"Aye. And maybe we'll put it in the back of a book so 'tis not out in the open for anyone to see. What do you think?" she asked her brother.

He nodded. " 'Tis a good plan, that," he allowed. "I've a feather for her. A gull's feather," he clarified proudly. "All white and pretty. To put in her hat. And, Mam"—he hesitated—"Mam, can I give my gun to Mister Litton? The gun Jimbo gave me in Kansas? Please, Mam, 'tis the best thing I have."

Grace looked down into his earnest little face and smoothed the hair out of his eyes. "Mister Litton has his own guns for hunting," she told him gently. "I don't think he'd be wanting any others. He was in the war, remember, and sometimes soldiers don't like to think of all the shooting they did."

"Oh." Jack's face fell. "I don't have anything else."

She thought for a moment. "I made a new pillowcase—you could stuff that and give it to him. He'd like that, Jack, he really would."

The boy brightened considerably. "Maybe he'll dream of Enid," he suggested hopefully.

Grace and Mary Kate laughed. Upstairs a door opened and closed, and their happy faces fell.

"Run outside, Jack, and tell Enid that her mother will want the bath water emptied. Mary Kate, you take the presents back to our room and finish tying them up, will you, now?"

"Aye, Mam," both children answered at once and went their separate ways, while Grace turned her attention to supper and the night ahead, her head filled with thoughts of Christmases past.

Her Irish Christmases had been simple but warm, and always there had been good things to eat, things Granna had prepared in the summer and put away so that they would be a bright treat on that special day. Not a churchgoing family after Grace's mother died, they still sang hymns on Christmas Eve and again in the morning after they'd exchanged their homemade gifts. Her brother Ryan always gave their da new tobacco, and so he always smoked an extra pipe on that day, sitting outside the cabin door on the bench he'd made from a fallen log. Grace always received new ribbons for her hair, and this tradition she'd kept up, giving the same to Mary Kate every year. The only time she had not was the year they came across on the *Eliza J;* she had not been prepared for Christmas in any way that year, let alone a Christmas in the middle of the vast sea. She shuddered now to think of that voyage and shook her head at the miracle that they'd survived it when so many had not.

Christmas in New York with Dugan and Tara had also brought a miracle, though not the one Grace had been looking for; she would never forget seeing Peter come into the saloon with two young people behind him, and Lily rising from her place at the table upon realizing that those two were the children left behind in the South, the children she'd been trying to rescue for years. Aye, Grace thought; despite what had happened later in the night, that one single moment had been truly wondrous.

Grace's first Christmas in Boston was also her first Christmas with Jack, and so—another miracle, now she thought about it. The Christmases in Kansas were brutally cold, and yet it was always cozy in their one-room cabin, with the fire blazing and something roasting over it. One Christmas, however, the ice was so fierce that Grace's employer had insisted they not try to get back to their cabin, but take a room in the almost-empty hotel, where they would be warm and safe; there she'd had a bath on Christmas Eve and a fine meal—though she'd cooked it herself—in the hotel dining room with the children.

She had expected to celebrate this Christmas in another cabin, this one beside the river in Oregon Territory; perhaps she and the children would have put the oxen to a sledge and gone through the snowy wood to visit Lily and the family. Did they have snow now? she wondered. She didn't remember Liam saying anything about that, and surely he would have. But instead of Christmas in Oregon, she was spending Christmas in California, here in this lovely, warm house with plenty of food and more money in her pocket than she knew what to do with. The Lord was good, she told herself— mysterious and unpredictable, to be sure, but always good.

There was no snow here, either, nor the promise of it. The climate in this part of the world reminded her a bit of Ireland, with its steady, cool rain and mists, the temperate winds and occasional storms, the fog. She felt a peacefulness here she'd not felt since leaving Ireland, and that alone was present enough on this Christmas.

It was nearing suppertime now, and the chickens were done. She mashed the potatoes and made a rich gravy with the doctor in mind, then quickly boiled the carrots until they were tender. This was one of his favorite meals, and she took extra care to make sure the chicken ran with juices and the gravy was smooth and flavorful. Aye, it was peace she felt as she went about these satisfying tasks, knowing that her family was secure and well provided for, and that she was appreciated for her skills by her employer.

It occurred to her then that this was the only Christmas she would spend in this house; she would be married to Peter by next year, she and the children living with him in his house. She stopped working for a moment, leaning on flour-dusted hands upon the worktable, wondering at the emotion now rising within her, wondering that she should feel a wave of sadness instead of joy. An entirely new way of life lay before her, a better life for her and the children, with a man they loved and a brother Mary Kate and Jack adored. She sighed and shook her head, exasperated with herself, then returned to flouring the gravy. She would not let this be about Morgan, not when she'd nearly mastered the art of putting him away. There had never been any Christmases with Morgan, not one save those of her childhood, when he came tearing down the Black Hill to show Sean what his sisters had made for him or his da had brought back from those long voyages at sea. There had never been a Christmas with Morgan and so, she knew, Christmas should not have any sad memories tied to it. Would not. Not this year. She wiped the back of her hand across her cheek, leaving a damp smear of flour, and turned her mind forcibly to the night ahead and the day to come. She would be with Peter—it was to be their second Christmas together and the first of many more for years to come. She would sit with him and feel the comforting warmth of his hand in hers, the reassurance of sitting beside her dearest friend. Aye, that was what she would turn her mind to now. Christmas with Peter, and the wonderful life that lay ahead.

Twenty-two

Doctor Wakefield and Mister Litton attended church with Grace and the children, while Enid and her mother stayed behind with Abigail. Wakefield had extracted a promise from his sister that she would come down in the morning for the exchange of presents and to enjoy the tree as long as her stamina allowed, and she had agreed, though Hopkins had expressed concern. Wakefield had then reassured the housekeeper—wasn't he a doctor, after all? he reminded her. And wasn't Abigail his own dear sister? She could certainly join them for an hour without damage to either her spirit or her body. Hopkins had tried to protest further, but Wakefield had silenced her by insisting that not only would his sister come down, but Hopkins herself and her daughter would also join them in the drawing room for a glass of punch. Christmas bonuses would be handed round at that time, he added, clinching the deal.

It was cold and breezy, but clear, and they all had red cheeks when they came back into the warm house. While Mister Litton put the horses away, Wakefield went directly to the drawing room to light the fire. He would not light the tree again this morning, as they'd burned out the candles the night before, but it had been a heavenly sight and the children had remained on their best behavior around it, enjoying the glow and scent of it tremendously.

Grace sent them now into their room to change out of their coats and into the new sweaters left over the rocking chair near the hearth by St. Nicholas himself. There were new caps, as well, and mittens, which they'd worn to church, not to mention the small cache of chocolates, fruits, and nuts, which had made them practically delirious.

While they changed—and most likely sampled some of their choco-late—Grace slipped out of her own coat and hat, and stoked the oven, which had died down a little more than she'd anticipated. She set the kettle to boil and added the sliced Christmas bread and butter to the tray she'd laid this morning. When the tea was made, she sent Jack out for Mister Litton, and though George appeared reluctant—twisting his cap in his hands—Grace put him in charge of carrying the tray, and then they all went together into the drawing room.

"Ah, there you are!" Wakefield rubbed his hands together in eager anticipation, and Grace caught a glimpse of the merry boy he had surely been in his youth. "Set the tray down there, Mister Litton. Mary Kate, Jack—come and sit on the divan here by the tree. Missus Don-nelly." He offered a chair near the divan.

"I'll pour out first, sir, if you don't mind." Grace smiled despite her-self at his gleeful enthusiasm. "Will Miss Abigail be joining us after all, then?"

"Oh, yes." He tipped his head toward the disguised piano. "She sim-ply *must* come down, isn't that right, children?"

Jack and Mary Kate nodded vigorously and giggled, Wakefield laughing a bit himself. Grace had never seen him so excited. He left the room, and they heard him call from the foot of the stair.

"Hopkins! Come down now! We're ready for you!"

He came back into the room, his eye falling on Mister Litton. "George!" he boomed. "You sit over here." He pulled out a leather club chair, and Mister Litton glanced down at his trousers, then shook his head. "Oh, come, man. They were clean enough for church; they're clean enough for the chair. You tell him, Missus Donnelly."

Grace laughed. "You'd best do as he says, Mister Litton, for he's a man won't hear 'no' today."

Litton nodded soberly, then crossed to the chair, took out a clean handkerchief from his pocket, spread it on the seat, and sat down. Set-tled, he seemed to relax just a little and began to glance around the room. Grace wished he could have been enticed to come in and enjoy it last night in the glow of firelight, but he'd stubbornly refused, mum-bling with reddened cheeks about a washup and shave before coming into the house proper like that. He certainly looked very well this morning, Grace thought. Along with the stubble, the razor had shaved a good five years off the man's face, and now Grace realized he was much younger than she'd first thought—thirty, if that. His face glowed from the scrubbing and his hair was combed back, his clothes were clean, and he'd even taken a brush to his fingernails. Grace was impressed, and she knew Enid would be nigh on swooning. Suddenly, Enid appeared, her eyes indeed opening wide at the sight of handsome Mister Litton. For his part, Litton acted the gentleman and rose immediately, bowing a little and offering a short speech.

"Merry Christmas, Miss Enid," he said formally. "I hope this day finds you well. And your mother."

Enid's mouth fell open, but she quickly recovered and crossed the room to stand beside him.

"Thank you, Mister Litton," she said warmly, her eyes on his. "Happy Christmas to you, too. So good of you to join us."

"My pleasure, miss." Again he made that funny little bow and then was silent, seemingly having used up all his available language.

Enid didn't mind. She was clearly happy just to be standing at his side, and her smile didn't falter until her mother entered, supporting Miss Abigail on her arm, and shot her daughter a disapproving look.

"Abigail!" Wakefield welcomed her warmly, taking her arm from Hopkins and helping her to a chair near the fire. "Merry Christmas, dear sister. My, you look lovely this morning."

And she did, Grace thought, though it was as if she were a faded picture of loveliness instead of the thing itself. Still, she was dressed in a proper gown with a pretty shawl around her shoulders; her hair was cleaned and brushed, and Hopkins had arranged it well enough, though it was heavier to one side and Grace had to stop herself from going over and repinning it. She wore the delicate silver-and-garnet ear-bobs her brother had given her on Christmas Eve, a simple gold cross at her throat, and a bracelet of charms on her wrist; there was color in her cheeks, thanks to the rouge box, and she'd also applied color to her lips. It heightened the very whiteness of her skin, but without it she would have faded into the color of her dress, which was a creamy white.

"May I get you a cup of tea, Miss Wakefield?" Grace offered.

Abigail nodded but did not look up.

After everyone had been served, the doctor set his cup aside and went to the tree, extracting several small packages, which he handed to

Grace, Hopkins, and Enid. He stood proudly by his sister, a hand on her shoulder, watching with pleasure as his domestics opened their gifts.

"Thank you, sir. Thank you, miss." Enid held up a handsome pair of light-colored kid gloves.

Hopkins did the same, though her gloves were a size larger.

"Very thoughtful, Miss Abigail, very kind of you. Thank you, Doctor," the housekeeper enthused.

Grace's box took longer to untie, but when at last she opened the lid, she gasped in surprise, looking up at the doctor and his sister, then lifting out the silver-backed ivory mirror, brush, and comb that lay within.

" 'Tis beautiful," she said softly, caught completely unaware by the generous gift. "I've nothing like it a'tall."

Hopkins sniffed audibly as if to say 'Of course you don't,' but no one paid any attention to her.

"I enlisted the help of a special little girl to ascertain that very fact," Wakefield said with smug delight. "She remembered that you had a pretty brush in Ireland, but that it was left behind with so many of your things, and that you had never replaced it."

Grace looked at Mary Kate, who was smiling shyly and blushing, and was moved to think the child held such memories.

"Thank you so very much, Doctor," Grace offered. "Miss Wakefield, thank you. Blessed Christmas to you both."

"We're so pleased you like it," Wakefield responded graciously. "And now—George." He handed over a large box to his outside man.

Litton fumbled awkwardly with the ribbon for a moment, then lifted off the lid and eyed the garment within, rubbing the heavy tweed between his fingers. "That's a fine jacket, sir," he managed, red-faced with pleasure and embarrassment. "Thank you, sir."

"And, of course, Abigail and I have a Christmas envelope for each of you along with our thanks for yet another year of good service."

They spoke at once, expressing their gratitude, until Wakefield raised his hand.

"It seems we've forgotten the children!" he exclaimed, pretending shock. "How terrible! Whatever will we do?"

"Oh, no, sir," Mary Kate and Jack said quickly. "That's quite all right, sir. We don't mind."

He grinned and waved them over to his side.

"I'm afraid your gift was rather difficult to wrap up," he explained. "As you know, Scout has been delivered of her puppies and, while they are in great demand around here"—he paused dramatically and leaned down—"you may each choose one to keep as your own."

Mary Kate and Jack turned to one another, their mouths hanging open, their eyes wild with delight. They shrieked and hugged one another, then threw their arms around Wakefield, nearly knocking him over like puppies themselves.

He laughed and extricated himself, then said, "Go on out with Mister Litton now, and he'll help you choose. They're still too young to leave their mother, but at least you'll know which ones are yours."

They ran to Litton, each taking a hand, and practically dragged him out of the room, shouting delirious thanks as they left. Grace noted that although George put on a face of apprehension, he moved quickly and was clearly relieved to escape the society of the room.

"Delightful to have children in the house at Christmas," Wakefield announced, rubbing his hands again. "Delightful day, just delightful. And now, my dear . . ." He turned toward his sister. "If you'll allow me, I have a special gift for you."

"But, Rowen," she demurred, and Grace noted the slur of her syllables, "you gave me my gift last night." She fingered the stones that dangled from her ears. "That's quite enough."

"Merely a decoy, my dear. To throw you off the scent, as it were."

Abigail's eyes followed him as he crossed the room, then widened when he swept off the dustcover and revealed the glowing instrument that lay beneath. He turned to her, beaming with triumph, and then his grin faltered.

"Rowen." Abigail's voice was hoarse. "How could you?" She pushed herself up on shaky arms, then stood, eyes swimming with dark anger and confusion.

"It's a piano!" He stood aside to give her a better view of the beautiful instrument, thinking she hadn't understood. "You love the piano," he insisted. "You played endlessly at home! With such pleasure, I thought, and so I wanted to . . ."

"I will never play again, Rowen. Ever," she told him fiercely, her body trembling. "You know how I feel about such things. Oh, Rowen."

She began to weep, then crumpled into her chair. "How could you do this to me?"

"Abigail!" He rushed to her side, stricken. "Abby," he said softly, falling to his knees, his hands on her arm.

Hopkins moved in immediately. "She's overwrought, sir, as I said. Too much excitement for her poor nerves. Enid," she called the girl sharply. "Help me get Miss Abigail back to her room."

"No." Wakefield shielded his sister. "I'll take her back up in a moment. That's all, Hopkins. You may go."

The housekeeper frowned in disapproval.

"I said, you may go," Wakefield repeated firmly.

Hopkins pinched her lips together, then grabbed Enid by the arm and left the room.

"I don't want her," Abigail whispered. "The cook. Send her out."

Wakefield kept his eyes on his sister's face. "Thank you, Missus Donnelly," he said, excusing her. "Close the door behind you, please."

"Yes, sir." Grace left immediately, though she stood for a moment behind the closed doors, listening to the low murmur of the doctor's voice and Abigail's quiet sobbing.

"Get away from there," Hopkins hissed behind her. "That's private. Go back to the kitchen."

"After you." Grace gestured toward the hall.

In a huff, but unsure about what else to do, Hopkins pushed past her and led the way.

"Well, this is a fine state for a Christmas Day," she announced, sitting heavily at the table. "I warned him. I said it would be too much."

"I think we all need a cup of tea." Grace took the kettle off the stovetop. "Thank goodness the children went out. Poor Doctor Wakefield. Poor *Miss* Wakefield."

"Poor nothing," Hopkins spat. "You don't know what you're talking about. Enid, get me a slice of bread."

Enid darted from the doorway where she'd been standing, twisting her hands and eyeing her mother anxiously.

"Sit yourself down, Enid." Grace waved her back to the table. " 'Tis Christmas, after all, and you've got the whole lunch to serve."

Enid sat timidly, her back to her mother.

Grace set the teapot and a plate of buttered bread slices down on the table. "There, now, we'll have a bite to calm ourselves." She sat beside Enid and patted the girl on the shoulder. "Turn around, now. You've done nothing wrong today."

"Yet," her mother added, spewing bread crumbs on the tablecloth.

"That's enough, Missus Hopkins," Grace rebuked wearily. "Let's set our sights on the gift of the Lord, and quit squabbling among ourselves."

"Easy for you to say," Hopkins scoffed. "You'll be out of this house all afternoon, fraternizing with that captain friend of yours. Got him all lined up, don't you?" she accused bitterly. "Husband number three, is he? Going to get a child by him, as well, I suppose. Maybe it's already on the way, just to make sure he doesn't sail off again."

"Mother!" Enid set down her cup. "Don't say that!"

"Your mother's bad manners are no reflection on you, Enid." Grace put down her cup. "And besides, I can take care of myself."

"Oh, you've made that clear enough," Hopkins said scornfully. "Married for money, married for lust . . . what's the captain, then— married for convenience? Wormed your way in here, meddling where you don't belong, stirring up all kinds of trouble. A piano, bah!" she spat. "*You* put that ridiculous idea into his head, and don't try telling me otherwise. You Irish got no sense. None."

Grace said nothing, trying not to let the words pierce her like the poison darts they were intended to be.

"Stop it, Mother." Enid's eyes had filled with tears.

"And look at you," her mother demanded. "Look at you! Two minutes around her and you forget your place. Don't forget what I've sacrificed for you, girl. What I've done for you."

Enid hung her head, instantly contrite. "No, Mother. I'm sorry, Mother." Tears fell onto the hands in her lap.

"I forgive you. Because I am a good, *decent* Christian woman. Now, go to your room and wait for me there."

Enid got up from the table and left without so much as a glance at Grace, her shoulders slumped in defeat.

Hopkins leaned across the table. "You're a bad influence on that girl, Missus Donnelly. You keep your nose out of our business."

"Keep your business out of my kitchen, then," Grace replied, leaning forward to meet her. "And when you're on your knees at night, Missus Hopkins, try thanking the Lord for the child you've got instead of hating Him for the one you lost."

"How dare you." Hopkins glared, spittle foaming in the corner of her mouth, her hands balled into tight fists.

"You keep asking me that." Grace rose from the table. "So I'll be as clear as I can: You don't frighten me, Missus Hopkins. Not a whit. Not now. Not ever. You're a kitten compared to the lions I've faced in my life—something you know nothing about, by the way."

Hopkins' mouth fell open in outrage, but before she could reply, Grace disappeared into the mudroom. She reappeared a moment later, a great cloak slung over her shoulders.

"I'm going out to see to the children, and then we'll be away for the afternoon. Time's a-wasting and I've got to get the captain all sewn up, don't you know."

Closing the door firmly behind her, Grace stepped out into the cold, damp air and breathed deeply, willing her anger to subside. She was sorry for all of them back there, for the Wakefields and the Hopkinses, for the misery in their lives, whether by their own means or the means of others, and she asked herself if it was worth it. Should she remain in a house with a person as angry as Agnes Hopkins, with a person as troubled as Abigail Wakefield? Were the children affected by it?

Her thoughts were interrupted by laughter from the stable, and she crossed the yard, lingering in the doorway to watch her children unobserved for a moment. Mister Litton stood off to one side, looking down at the two youngsters, who sat in the corner of the stall and laughed with delight as puppies tumbled in and out of their laps, and on his face was an expression Grace had never seen him wear; she could hardly believe it, but it appeared to be true—George Litton was smiling.

For the sake of the children, Grace refused to let the unsettling morning ruin her festive mood, and so she led them both in the loud and off-key singing of Christmas carols all the way to the Darmstadt home, where Captain Reinders and Liam waited eagerly for their arrival.

They sat now in the great room, a fire blazing and trays of food and drink put out on the sideboard. Warm greetings and gifts had been exchanged—a fine leather-bound diary and pen for Mary Kate, a fishing pole for Jack, and for Liam a sextant from Peter and a small illustration of Dublin from Grace—and now Jack was asleep, curled up in front of the fire with melted chocolate in the corners of his mouth, while Mary Kate taught Liam how to play chess on the set she'd gotten especially for him. Mary Kate was lovely, Grace thought, in her pretty blue dress with a matching ribbon in her hair, on her finger the ring her auntie Aislinn had given her in Liverpool; Liam looked fine, as well, in his clean white shirt and dark trousers, his hair slicked back for the occasion. She was proud of them, both of them, and so happy that they were still close. Lars and Detra had retired earlier to their rooms for a rest after dinner, so Grace and Peter were alone with the young people.

"I love my present." Reinders thanked her again, picking up the handsomely framed daguerreotype Grace had given him. "He captured you perfectly—your beautiful eyes, that tilt to your chin. The light around your head and shoulders is . . ." He nodded admiringly. "It's a work of art, really." He looked from the portrait to the woman. "And I'm not even going to comment on the fact that obviously you sat for this alone and half-dressed in a room with a talented, charming man. No, I've decided not to say a word about that at all."

Grace laughed. "I admit I didn't know what he had in mind at first, and I was mortified, but he was always a gentleman and his work is so good. I hoped it would make a fine present for you," she added shyly.

"Thank you," he repeated. "I am honored to accept it. And thank you for my book, as well." He picked up the heavy, leather-bound biography of Lord Admiral Nelson. "I shall begin it at once."

"I thought it might keep your mind occupied while you convalesce. You're looking better, though, and you've put on more weight. I'm happy for that."

"You should be. It's all your doing," he scolded playfully, "that steady stream of fresh bread, pies, cakes, soups, stews, etcetera, etcetera, that finds its way here from Wakefield Heights nearly every day. Not to mention the flowers, drawings by the children, notes from you . . . I'm expecting a band of choral singers and a pretty pony any day now."

"Ah, go on with you." She blushed. "Liam and Detra both said you've no kind of cook about the place to tempt your appetite and, well, if I can't be here every day myself, the least I can do is send on a bit of cheer."

"You could be here every day," he pointed out. "If that's what you really wanted."

Grace bit her lip and looked down. "I do. Only you need your rest. And I've been thinking you're crowded here already, let alone my lot coming to live!" She raised her eyes earnestly to his. "And of course, the children are settled in up on the hill and I don't like to move them yet, especially at Christmastime. Not to mention the wage I'm making. 'Tis madness on their end, but I'm putting by. And then, Mary Kate gets her schooling up there, and Jack, and they like it—did I tell you how well Jack's doing, and who would've thought? But he likes that Mister Hewitt. Mary Kate, as well. He comes up three mornings a week . . ." Her voice trailed off as she ran out of steam.

Reinders had been nodding his head as he listened, and now he pretended to tally up on his fingers. "Rest, crowded, Christmas, wages, school . . . that's at least five good reasons why you can't marry me."

"Yet," Grace added firmly. "Why I can't marry you *yet*."

"But you do still want to marry me?"

Grace hesitated only a second. "Oh, aye, Peter, if you'll still have me. And the children, of course."

He laughed. "Of course the children. Who are you, Grace Donnelly, if not mother to all these children, hmmm?"

She did not fully understand the meaning of what he'd just said, but she smiled as if she did.

"When you're well and on your feet again, we'll talk more about it," she promised. "We're not in dire straits, any of us, and we've time to settle our business before we come together."

"Do you still have business to settle?" he prodded gently.

"No, Peter," she resolved. "I've put it all behind me, and I'm well ready to make a life with you."

"So am I." He reached into his pocket and took out a small box, elegantly wrapped, then leaned forward and put it in her hand. "Merry Christmas, Grace."

Heart pounding anxiously, Grace slipped off the bow and opened the box; the elegant ring was stunning, and she was moved by Peter's thoughtfulness.

"It's an emerald. For the Emerald Isle whence you came. How's that for poetry?"

"Oh, Peter, 'tis beautiful." She looked at her blunt fingers, rough and reddened from kitchen work, the nails cut short. "Too beautiful."

He took the box from her and withdrew the ring, then slipped it onto her finger. "Not nearly beautiful enough," he said and kissed her hand.

She bit her lip, then raised her hand hesitantly, tipping it so that the stone caught and tossed the light from the fire.

"It's my promise to you that we'll marry whenever *you* are ready. You and the children. And in the meantime"—he held up his fingers to count again—"I'll rest, find a house for us, and see if Mister Hewitt will be willing to come there for the children's lessons. I don't know yet what to do about Christmas or your enormous wages, but I'll figure it out."

She got up and kissed his mouth tenderly, then knelt by the side of the chair. "Thank you, Peter. Thank you for everything."

"It's only a ring," he teased. "But if you want everything, I'll get that for you, too."

She laughed. "I don't want everything. Only a home with you and Liam, Mary Kate and Jack."

He nodded, glancing over his shoulder at them. "Mary Kate's a wonderful girl, Grace. You've done well with her. And I like your young Jack, though he seems none too fond of me."

"He'll come round," she declared. "Truly, he's wanted to know you forever. Couldn't wait to hear your letters when they'd come."

"Well, he was quite clear in his opinion that I didn't *look* like a sea captain." Reinders looked down at his own thin frame and laughed. "Granted, even I don't think I'm very impressive these days."

" 'Tis the pirate stories Mary Kate reads aloud," Grace admitted. "I suspect he thought you'd come flying into the harbor with devilish hair full of shells and bones, scars on your face and golden teeth, a great rattling saber at your side."

"Sorry to disappoint him," Reinders said ruefully, running a hand over his clean-shaven cheeks and chin. "Maybe I should grow it back, get one of those hats, an eye patch."

"You needn't work at it. Give him time to get to know you and he'll be in your pocket for the rest of your days. You're great with the boys; look at how devoted Liam is to you!"

"Who would've thought all those years ago when we sailed from Liverpool that we'd end up here together, the four of us. Five," he amended. "I'm glad Liam and Mary Kate are still close."

"They've been from the start," Grace recalled. "When Alice and Siobahn died, he found comfort in caring for Mary Kate and, of course, she adored him. Whisper, whisper, whisper, and only with her did he shed any real tears."

"I remember how little she was then, those big dark eyes watching everything around her."

"Aye, she's an old soul, that girl. She loves Jack truly, but there's a loyalty to Liam that goes even beyond that. Perhaps because of what they survived as young ones."

"I forget, sometimes, what he's overcome. What you've overcome."

"Good, as we're more than that now," she said absolutely. "We're Americans, and hasn't everyone here survived something in order to be here?"

"I didn't."

"Aye, but your folks, now, they did. How's your mam, by the way? Do you write to her as you should?" She grinned.

"Yes, Missus Donnelly," Reinders reported dutifully. "I write my mother twice a year. She sold off half the farm and moved closer to town with my brother and his family. She's getting old now, but she still chides me about not attending church services."

"She's a good mother, then." Grace's eyes twinkled.

The clock on the mantel began to ring out the time, and Jack stirred himself.

"Mam," he said grumpily, rubbing his eyes. "Can I go home and see the puppies now?"

"Aye, Jack. Soon."

"Nice present," Reinders said aside to Grace.

"The doctor saw how good they were with Scout while she carried. Jack especially. Can't get enough of the dogs and the horses, that one. 'Tis the one thing he wanted most, an animal of his own."

"Generous man, your employer. Knows exactly what everyone wants and provides it." Reinders paused. "You don't think . . . Have you considered, Grace, that he might be interested in more than just your domestic service?"

Grace sat up straight and stared at him as if he were mad.

"Doctor Wakefield wants a decent cook for his house, and a house made decent for his friends." High color rose up her neck and into her cheeks. "If you knew him, you wouldn't even think of—" She broke off, frustrated. "What exactly *are* you saying to me?"

"Just that he might have stronger feelings for you than you realize, maybe stronger than he realizes. I just want you to be careful, that's all."

"Well, of course I'm careful, you daft eejit." Grace put her hands on her hips. "Rowen Wakefield is not the kind of man who would *ever* consider carrying on with a servant. And that's what I am in that house, Peter—a servant."

"Grace." Reinders looked at her gravely. "*You* might think of yourself as a servant, but no one else who knows you could ever think of you that way. You're like . . . like . . . some deposed majesty, biding your time until the day you can reclaim your throne."

"Let me tell you, Captain Reinders, that I work as hard as the next with no eye to getting out of it." Grace was really angry now. "I don't know who you think you are saying such a thing to me, but perhaps 'tis *you* don't know me as well as you think."

He put up his hands in protest. "That's not what I said, Grace! Or if it is"— he paused, trying to remember—"it's not what I meant. I don't know what I meant, exactly, except that . . . I guess I'm just uneasy about you living in another man's house. I'm sorry if I offended you."

Grace eyed him warily. "You're not a petty man, Peter." She glanced over at the children, all of whom had stopped playing and were staring at them. "But I shouldn't've gone off like that, either, and I'm sorry for my end." She sank back down onto her knees and lowered her voice. "It's been a long day. A good day," she amended, "but . . . long."

"Grace." Reinders tipped her chin up so that he could see her eyes. "*Is* everything all right up there? It's not too much for you, is it?"

Suddenly, she longed to close her eyes and go to sleep right there and wake up next to him; she longed for the body of a husband beside her and the comfort that body could bring, for the intimacy of talking in the dark, of telling all that was in her heart.

"The work is fine," she said instead. "The housekeeper's a hard woman, hard on everyone, including her own daughter, who does all the work. There's always a quarrel."

"Why does Wakefield keep her on?"

"His sister won't hear of anyone else, but . . . she's unwell, Miss Abigail. Today"—Grace stopped, still not sure what had really happened—"the doctor gave her a piano as a special present, and she gave him nothing but anger and tears."

"What's Hopkins got to do with that?"

Grace shook her head, baffled. "I can't really say, but I know 'tis her making things harder than they ought to be. She'd told the doctor Miss Abigail wasn't up for being with people, and was too smug when the mistress proved her right. Things like that, and then she slips away in secret now and then, not a word to anyone."

Reinders put his hand on her shoulder. "Household servants can live very small and narrow lives, you know that. Take Arnott, for instance—he disappears all the time, always with a good reason, but somehow you just know he's up to no good." He squeezed gently. "You can't let yourself get dragged into whatever drama they've made for themselves. It's too exhausting."

" 'Tis true, I suppose, what you're saying," Grace allowed, though she felt strongly that there was a greater problem at heart.

"See how very useful a husband can be? And speaking of slipping away in secret . . ." Reinders glanced at the children, who'd resumed their play. "Do you see us being alone anytime in the near future? Not that I would ever compromise your morals, Missus Donnelly." He winked.

"Too late for that," she pointed out. "What are you thinking, then, Peter, that we should be lovers again before we're wed?"

The captain was surprised at her bluntness and shook his head. "I've thought of that afternoon a million times, Grace," he confessed quietly. "And I won't deny I can barely stand to wait a minute longer." He stopped himself and laughed shortly. "But in truth, I don't think I even possess the strength to carry you up to bed."

The look on his face intensified the longing Grace already felt. "I think of that afternoon, as well," she admitted. "And sometimes I want only to . . ."

"Lie down together," Reinders finished for her. "I'm glad to know that. But we've waited this long, we can wait a little longer." His words were decisive, but his eyes spoke otherwise. "I don't want you to have to sneak around and make up excuses, especially to the children."

Grace nodded, relieved; her body was more than willing, but her mind was full of trepidation. She did not tell him that her biggest fear was becoming pregnant and the embarrassment she would feel in rushing a marriage that would confirm Missus Hopkins' suspicions of entrapment and convenience. She kissed him now, grateful for his passion as well as for his understanding.

"Soon," she whispered, and kissed him again. "Soon enough we'll be together every night for the rest of our lives."

"Mam!" Jack demanded, standing up and putting his fists on his hips. "The puppy! She's waiting for me! I said I'd come see her tonight, and 'tis night now!"

"Jack, that's rude," Mary Kate chided. "They're talking; can you not see that?"

"They been talking all day!" Jack insisted. "I even took a nap like a good boy, didn't I, and still they're talking!"

"I understand your impatience, young Jack." Reinders let go of Grace and got slowly to his feet. "A puppy is a fine present."

"Oh, aye! 'Tis the best!" Jack enthused. "The best ever!"

Grace sent him a look behind the captain's back.

"But the fishing pole's fine, as well," the boy added, taking the hint about his manners. "Thank you very much, sir."

"You're very welcome." Reinders walked over and ruffled Jack's hair. "I plan to take you out myself as soon as I've recovered my health."

"You might be too old," Jack speculated, ducking the captain's hand. "And anyway I go with Mister Litton. He knows all about the fishing round here."

"Jack!" Grace was mortified by her son's bold tongue.

The boy sighed. "I mean—yes, sir; thank you, sir. Sorry, sir. Sorry, Mam. Sorry, Mary Kate. Sorry, Liam."

"I think that about covers it, son." Reinders laughed. "We'll talk more about the fishing another time, but now you'd better get your mother home."

The captain called for the carriage and they said their good nights in the large entry hall while waiting for its arrival. After he'd seen them safely off, Reinders slowly climbed the stairs to bed, more exhausted than he'd felt in a long time. Although he'd tried to put on a good show for the day, he had to admit that he was still far from his old self.

He was forced to call Arnott for help in undressing and getting into his nightclothes, and the presence of the butler irritated him. What was it about such people? he wondered. The Arnotts and Hopkinses of the world—that they should radiate such smug superiority and barely veiled contempt for others? He sighed and let his head sink into the pillow, and though he'd wanted his last thoughts to be of Grace, they were instead of her little boy, the boy he knew instinctively looked just like his father. Reinders had not anticipated having to win over this child, and it bothered him, as if McDonagh himself had presented one last stumbling block to Peter's and Grace's happiness. "Foolishness," he whispered to himself in the dark—the boy would come around and all would be well. But as he fell asleep, it was uncertainty that circled his heart instead of confidence, anxiety instead of peace, frustration instead of love, knowing that for the whole of the night he would toss and turn, and in the morning look worse than ever. *Ridiculous,* Reinders thought and fumbled for the lamp beside his bed. He lit it and settled himself against the pillows, opening the book Grace had given him for Christmas.

Admiral Horatio Lord Nelson was one of the few men Reinders admired in the world, a hero to any seagoing man worth his salt. Off to sea at age twelve, the diminutive Nelson commenced upon one of the most brilliant naval careers in history—one that eventually cost him an eye and then an arm, amputated without benefit of anesthesia—despite the fact that he suffered from seasickness his entire life and was often ill with dysentery and malaria. Reinders admired the man even more now that he'd had a taste of what Nelson experienced with maddening regularity.

"'I have always been a quarter of an hour before my time, and it has made a man of me,' " Reinders quietly quoted. "But I, Admiral Nelson," he added, looking up from the page, "have always been at least two steps behind, and cannot truly say what that has made of me."

Two steps behind, he thought now, especially when it came to Grace Donnelly, a woman who seemed a century ahead. Would he ever catch up to her, Reinders wondered, ever prove to be the kind of man who deserved such a woman? Admiral Nelson had won the heart of the love of his life, the great Emma, Lady Hamilton; what advice would he give Reinders, if he could?

A man must act decisively, or not at all. Was that Horatio, Reinders asked himself, or yet another ahead of his time?

Quit brooding, Captain, and get some sleep—battles cannot be won with weary heads, you know.

"And mine is definitely weary," Reinders closed the book and turned out the lamp. "Good night, Admiral, if you're there. Thanks for lending a hand with all this."

I've only got the one, the admiral replied, *but it's yours for the asking.*

Reinders stretched out, his eyelids heavy with sleep. "Doctor in the morning," he mumbled and then began to snore.

Twenty-three

Grace woke up late in the night and felt for Mary Kate beside her; the girl breathed regularly and was sound asleep, as was Jack in his cot. She lay still a moment, wondering what it was that had awakened her, and then she realized that someone was outside in the yard or—Grace rose up on her elbows, listening more closely—beyond the yard. It was a woman, crying and pleading, her entreaties matched by the low, urgent voice of a man; Grace was sure it must be the doctor and Abigail. She got out of bed and went to the window, pulling the curtain aside. On the far side of the garden, two figures wrestled in the cold moonlight, the doctor attempting to catch his sister by the arm and drag her back indoors, though she fought him every inch.

Grace went into the mudroom and threw on a heavy jacket over her nightdress, then slipped her feet into her work boots. Outside, the cold slapped her in the face and her breath ached in her lungs. Moving quickly but carefully around the icy puddles, she went around the back of the garden and hurried to where the two people still grappled, Abigail crying out and the doctor cursing now.

"Thank God," Wakefield said when he saw Grace. "Grab her other arm. She's soaking wet. Careful." He was breathing hard. "Got to get her in before she freezes."

Grace did as ordered, though anyone fighting as hard as Abigail was in no immediate danger of freezing, she thought. She waded into the skirmish, surprised at Abigail's strength—*Hell hath no fury* came to mind—and Grace hung on with a grip she knew would leave marks.

"Let go, you devil!" Abigail shrieked, flailing at her new assailant.

Wakefield managed to clap a hand over his sister's mouth, but she bit him and he yelped, releasing his other hand, as well.

Now it was only Grace who had a hold of the woman, and she flinched as a punch landed against her neck, as fingernails raked her cheek. Blindly, she fought for control of Abigail's other hand and caught it right before it scratched her eye. Off balance now, the two women went down with a hard thud, Abigail on top; Grace summoned her might and rolled the woman over, pinning her to the ground, though her head turned wildly from side to side and blood trickled from her mouth.

"Now what?" Grace called over her shoulder to Wakefield, who was frozen where he stood. "Doctor? Help!"

Abigail spit in Grace's face and brought her knee up hard from behind, thumping her captor in the back.

"Hold her there." Wakefield dropped to his knees and felt in his pocket. "Oh, God," he moaned, "It broke. The bottle broke." He withdrew a hand that was dark with what must be blood.

"Abigail!" Grace shook the woman on the ground. "Stop it now! Stop!"

"Get off me," Abigail hissed, then began laughing hysterically.

With his good hand, Wakefield slapped his sister across the face—once, twice, three times, until the laughter stopped abruptly and she turned her head away from him.

"Get off," Abigail muttered, wearily now, all fight suddenly drained from her body.

Grace looked at the doctor, who nodded, and together they helped the demented woman up, each taking her firmly under one arm. Abigail's nightdress was completely wet, and her hair—newly chopped off in jagged clumps—was plastered against her muddy, battered face. Mud streaked her arms and legs and was splattered up her gown. She slumped in their grip, but her emaciated body was as light as a child's, and Grace would have been surprised if no bones were broken, so fragile did she seem now.

"Let's take her straight up to her room." Wakefield pushed open the door and guided them through the dark kitchen, down the great hall, and up the staircase.

"Should I get Missus Hopkins?" Grace whispered, as they sat Abigail down in a chair in her room.

"No. Stay here." Wakefield slipped out the door but was back again in a moment with candles, a lantern, and matches. "Hold her there, don't let her fall off," he ordered as he got light going in the room.

"She needs out of these wet things." Abigail had begun to shiver in earnest. "Shall I do it?"

"I don't want to leave you alone, in case she . . ." Wakefield stared helplessly at this ghost of a woman, his eyes on the shorn mess upon her head.

"Just turn around, then. You're a doctor, after all. Hand me a dry gown out of the bottom drawer there."

Now it was Wakefield's turn to do as he was told. He handed her the gown, then turned around and listened as, with quiet efficiency, Grace stripped off the wet clothes and replaced them with dry. She gently toweled Abigail's assaulted head, noting the ugly nicks in the scalp, the places blood had matted the hair in clumps.

"Help me get her on the bed," Grace directed, and Wakefield came immediately to her assistance.

He lifted his sister easily, then laid her upon the sheets, stepping back while Grace pulled a blanket up over her shoulders. Abigail lay perfectly still, eyes wide and staring at the ceiling, lips moving in silent plea or prayer or curse—Grace did not know which.

The doctor left the room and returned immediately with his kit bag, which he placed on the chair and opened. He withdrew another blue bottle, opened it, poured out a spoonful, and mixed it in a glass of water. Arm around Abigail's shoulders, he attempted to lift her enough to drink.

"Here, dearest." Wakefield put the rim of the glass to her lips. "Drink this now, and sleep."

Abigail's eyes closed as the liquid slid down her throat and her body went limp. Wakefield sat, glass in hand, and then he began to weep.

"Doctor." Grace quietly closed the bedroom door. " 'Tis over now. She'll rest easy and be herself come morning."

Wiping his hand wearily over his face, Wakefield sighed. "I'm afraid she'll never be herself again, Missus Donnelly. Not ever again."

Grace sat down in the chair. "Is it all over the piano, then? I'm so sorry, Doctor. I never thought it'd turn out as it did."

Wakefield shook his head. "It's my fault." He set the glass on the table. "I should've known she wouldn't want anything that brought her out of her misery, anything that might give her the slightest pleasure again."

"But why?" Grace beseeched. "Is it the broken engagement, then? Was she unfaithful and is paying for it now?"

The doctor looked at her for a long time, through her, back to another time and place, and Grace waited quietly for his reply.

"She was not unfaithful, Missus Donnelly," he said, and then his eyes cleared and he saw her. "Abigail was . . . assaulted. By a Negro man we all knew well, of whom we were all so very fond."

The picture suddenly became clear to Grace—Wakefield's hardness toward the plight of slaves, Abigail's pain at having been betrayed not only by the man who assaulted her, but then by the one to whom she was affianced, and worse still by her own family.

"I think I understand."

"I don't know if you can." Wakefield looked down at his hands. "It was my father who came upon the terrible act. Abigail was hysterical, of course, so they put her to bed while they dealt with Tom. That was the man's name—Thomas Eden. We were boys together, he and I. His mother was a slave on our plantation, and when she died, my father allowed Tom's father—a freeman—to buy his son out." The doctor's eyes were pinched with distress. "They beat Tom to within an inch of his life. And then they hung him. In the middle of the night. In front of Abigail. That was my father's idea, and the judge's—they wanted her to know they'd extracted full price for the crime committed upon her."

Grace put her hand to her heart.

Wakefield looked at his sister. "I think it was the hanging that began to unhinge her—she'd never witnessed anything like that in her life. She functioned normally for a while, they told me, but by the time I returned from New York, she had only two states of being—comatose or hysterical." Now he turned his eyes to Grace. "By this time, they all realized she was with child, you see, and they kept her locked in rooms at the top of the house. My father insisted I use my medical knowledge to end this shameful state of affairs before further damage was done to the family name. It was not a *real* child, after all, he told me," Wakefield said bitterly, "but a mongrel, born of forced union between two breeds never meant to mate. It would be a humane act on my part, for the benefit of my sister, who shouldn't have to suffer further pain and humiliation." He hung his head over folded hands. "She begged me not to do it. She was terrified, afraid of dying."

Grace thought of the skin that hung around Abigail's belly, the marks she now knew were from the stretching. "Did you end it?" she asked.

"Do you think me so low as that, Missus Donnelly?"

"No, sir." Grace shook her head. "But people do desperate things in desperate times."

"I told my father she was too near her time and that it might kill her. My father adored my sister—as far as he was concerned, the sun rose and set on her and she could do no wrong. And yet . . ." Wakefield hesitated. "And yet, his heart had hardened against her and I could see in his eyes that her death would be a relief compared to the shame he'd feel every time he looked at her for the rest of his life."

"I don't understand," Grace professed. "How could he turn his back on his own child?"

"You've never lived in the South, Missus Donnelly. We are a society woven together with the strands of a thousand intricate codes. To break even one threatens the entire fabric of our existence."

"But what code did she break?"

"She allowed herself to be raped by a Negro!" he declared. "Worse, she lived. A gentlewoman would have had the courtesy to die from heart failure the moment her dress was ripped from her body, rather than force her family and friends to acknowledge her shame on a daily basis. Such a woman, sullied and besmirched, can hardly be expected to pour out tea at church receptions or go dancing in public."

It took Grace a minute to wrap her mind around such a thing. "What about the baby, then? Was your sister delivered of it?"

Wakefield gave a terse nod. "They sent Abigail and an old midwife up the coast to stay with our grandmother—our Irish grandmother," he added ruefully. "I took them myself. It was a difficult trip, and Abigail gave birth shortly after. I'd returned home by that time, but Grandmother reported that the baby was, mercifully, born dead. The midwife had her orders, I'm sure, but none of us wanted to be party to the murder of an innocent."

"No, of course you wouldn't," Grace acknowledged gently.

"It was Grandmother who suggested I take Abigail west. She felt it was the only chance Abigail had for marriage and a decent family life. My father certainly didn't want her back—wouldn't *hear* of it, if truth be told—so arrangements were made." He looked up at Grace. "I've done the best I can, Missus Donnelly, but I fear Abigail will never recover, and I blame Thomas Eden mightily for that. I hope that man is burning in Hell for what he's done to her, for the lives he's destroyed. I will never forgive him."

Grace sighed deeply, her heart aching for the tragedy of it all. " 'Tis a terrible thing all round," she said at last.

"Perhaps your understanding of the Negro is more broad than it was before," Wakefield suggested.

"I've never thought a man good nor wicked based upon the color of his skin or the country of his birth," she told him. "Not all those caught up in slavery are good and decent people—some are evil, just as there are white men born evil, and Irishmen born evil, Italians and Germans born evil, Chinese—" She stopped. "The man who hurt your sister was an evil man. To excuse him because of his color would be an insult to good and decent people everywhere, of color or no, so I won't do that."

He nodded, his eyes red and awash with tears.

"You should go to bed now, Doctor. I'll stay with her tonight, if you like. I don't think I could sleep anyway."

Wakefield hesitated only a moment, and then he stood up wearily. "I'm grateful to you, Missus Donnelly. Thank you. For everything."

The doctor's words echoed her own to Peter earlier in the evening, and she looked down reflexively at the ring on her finger, Wakefield's eyes following hers.

"Ah," he said then. "I see congratulations are in order. I'm sorry your happy day has ended like this."

"You're sorry over too many things, Doctor," Grace chided. "Don't add this to the list."

"You'll be leaving us soon, I suppose."

"No, sir. I'm afraid you're stuck with me for a while yet, if that's all right. The captain is still getting over his illness, and I'm afraid Jack's not about to leave his new puppy anytime soon." She offered him a small smile.

Wakefield looked relieved. "I'm glad I gave it to him, then. Glad you'll be with us at least into the New Year." He picked up his bag and walked quietly to the door, then turned. "Missus Donnelly, I don't have to tell you that what we talked about tonight is private. I'm not sure how much even Missus Hopkins knows, but I would beg your discretion."

"Of course, sir," Grace assured him at once. "I'll not say a word to anyone a'tall, not even the captain. 'Tis your own concern, as you say."

"Thank you. Good night, then, Missus Donnelly, and . . ." He shook his head apologetically. "And Merry Christmas."

"Merry Christmas to you, as well, sir. Go to bed now, and I'll send a restorative breakfast up to you come morning."

Wakefield picked up his bag, then slipped out, closing the door behind him, leaving the two women alone. Grace bent over Abigail now with motherly concern, noting the pale skin and shallow breathing, the twitching blue-veined eyelids and the spasms at the corners of her mouth, as if her dreams were haunted.

Poor woman, Grace thought, crossing the room and pulling open the curtains; it would be dawn soon, and the start of a new day. Across the city that never fully slept, even on Christmas night, was a man who lay dreaming of her, Grace hoped. She lifted her hand and looked at the ring in the moonlight; it was beautiful, a beautiful gesture and a beautiful gift, the promise of a beautiful life, something that had eluded the sad creature behind her.

Grace remembered the shame she'd felt at the hands of a husband who'd taken her cruelly and knew that other women were just as helpless in their own marriages, but somehow the fact of marriage acted as a shield—others bore no witness to their shame, but neither could their plight be relieved. Grace had known unmarried women who'd suffered rape in Ireland, in New York, in Boston, and in Kansas. Some had been forced to wed the very men who'd assaulted them; others were sent away from their families as if they themselves had committed an unpardonable crime. If these women bore children by such an act, they bore them in profound shame only to raise them in shame, or give them up, or have them taken from them.

Why was it, Grace asked herself, looking down upon the city, why was it that women suffered the price of a crime committed upon them, a crime they could do nothing to stop? Why was sympathy given up by the bucketful for victims of accident, robbery, beatings, even murder, but not for those of rape? Rape was a sin like any other sin, and yet somehow women were thought complicit. Grace shook her head. It must be that rape could not be seen for what it truly was—not an act of sexual depravity, but an act of violence, the same as beating or torture. In fact, torture was the *true* name of rape, because its torment lasted far longer than it took the body to heal; it was, perhaps, the worst of all crimes man could commit, for it robbed the soul of joy and innocence, of trust, of the ability to love freely without fear clinging to hope's hem.

Grace let the curtain fall and went back to Abigail. That, then, was what had happened to this woman, she realized. She had been sinned against and made to feel as if she deserved that sin; and deserving of sin, she had set in motion an act that caused the death of a man she had once known and trusted. These were wounds that no doctor could ever repair; they were deep and everlasting, and Grace knew of only one way to bring about their healing. She sank to her knees beside Abigail's bed, took the woman's cold, frail hand in her own, and began to pray.

T he New York that Morgan McDonagh rode into, the winter of 1853, was unlike any place he'd ever seen in his entire life, and he quickly determined that purchasing a map would have to be his first order of business if he was ever to find his wife among the half million citizens that swarmed these streets. Broadway, Dutch Hill, Corlears Hook, Kleindeutschland, Bancker Street, the Hudson River waterfront—people rattled off names as if he were a tourist, looking to see the sights. But when he asked about the Irish—where he might find them, where they all lived—he met with scornful sneers or warnings to stay out of the Points, especially at night.

The sheer number of people astonished him, the press of humanity, their bark and bite. Even though piles of slush lay pushed up against the curbs, people were everywhere, in all manner of dress and attitude, from fancy prancers to guards with billy clubs, while in the street ran all manner of vehicles, from lowly rag carts and single horsemen to elegant carriages and the long omnibuses that stopped at seemingly irregular intervals.

Morgan himself attracted more than a few curious stares, but not as many as he'd thought he might, dressed as he was in Indian leather stockings and breeches, fur-lined boots, fringed leather tunic, and fur cap, his hair braided down his back and a full dark beard hiding his face. He was lean and hard from the grueling hike down through the wilderness, through New England, where he'd traded furs for a good horse, and into Boston, where he'd left his now close friend, Père Leon. Despite the priest's urging to stay with him at the Brotherhood Mission house and have a bath, a shave, a change of clothing, Morgan had not even considered it. He'd stayed one night, then departed, though he did admit that the sound of Irish voices in the streets had pulled at his heart.

Père Leon had taken up a meager collection for him in the mission so that he might stay in lodgings on the way to New York instead of sleeping in the snow or questionable taverns, and Morgan was grateful. Somehow it had not seemed this cold coming down from Canada, but perhaps it was because they'd been moving all the time, then digging in at night to sleep in their small tent. Here, a cold wind blew in from the sea and the dampness chilled him right through the warmth of his clothing. And he was tired. He knew he was tired. There were times when he'd fallen asleep on horseback, lulled by the regular clip-clop of the hooves, awakened only by the sense of falling off as his grip loosened. He would rest when he found her, he promised himself. He would lie down with her in his arms and sleep for a year, getting up only for food and drink. He didn't think about Sean or Mary Kate or work or money or any of that—only sleep, only lying down with his wife in his arms and sleeping the deepest sleep of his life. But first he had to find her. He looked around, then rode across the street to where a short, side-whiskered man stood hawking guidebooks.

"Maps in there?" Morgan asked from atop the horse.

The man eyed him from top to bottom, taking in the buckskins, the fur, the boots. "Say, mister—what kind of fella are you?"

"Kind wants a map," Morgan replied. "How much?"

"Two dollars fifty."

Morgan pulled back his robe so that the gleaming knife at his side was visible.

"But for you—one dollar even."

Morgan pulled a coin out of his money pouch, checking it carefully before flipping it to the hawker, who then handed up a book.

"Whatcha looking for, mister?" the man asked as Morgan flipped through the pages.

"Man called O'Malley. Sean O'Malley. Heard of him, have you?"

"Shoot, mister, every other Irishman's called O'Malley. Anyhow, that book don't list people's names." He took a step closer, holding up another copy. "It names your eating establishments, your theaters,

Ethiopian Opera Houses, your churches and grand cathedrals; it's got your saloons, your concert halls, dance halls—why, it's got pret'near all the sights a b'hoy or g'hal could want to see in the best city in the world!"

"Saloons," Morgan repeated, shifting his weight on the horse. "Know one owned by Mighty Dugan Ogue?"

"The boxer?" He scratched his chin, thinking. "Sure I do, sure I do. But, mister, that place burned down the summer we had all them fires. Summer of forty-nine, it was, right before the cholera. Killed a bunch of people, but maybe not Ogue himself. Leastwise, I don't recall his funeral and you know there would've been a big one. Hey, mister, you all right?"

Morgan's heart thudded and his vision blurred, then he got hold of himself; he'd not come all this way to accept secondhand news as the truth.

"Where was Ogue's saloon?"

"Down near the waterfront, on Chatham. Page twenty-three in your book's got a map of that neighborhood."

Morgan thumbed to the right page and then held the book down so the hawker could show him where they were now and how he was to travel in order to find the old place. Morgan thanked him and started off in the right direction but was quickly lost again. Despite the mud and ice, traffic in the street was heavy and fast, snarled in places, around upset carts and overturned carriages, and pedestrians seemed to cross anywhere they thought they had a chance. He had to keep an eye out in all directions, and it was exhausting and confusing; he missed the names of streets and boulevards, other landmarks. Anytime he left the main thoroughfares, he found himself in neighborhoods both amazing and frightening; gangs of raucous young men had emerged now the twilight had given way to evening, and they were simultaneously boisterous and menacing to those they pushed past on the sidewalks. Morgan felt again for the knife at his side and decided that he would have to find lodging for the night and a place to feed and bed his horse; it was bitterly cold now, and the poor animal was skittish and exhausted. Up ahead was a stable; he rode the horse in, then dismounted and called for the owner.

"Will you be wanting a stall for the night, then?" The squat man with the pug face eyed Morgan's getup suspiciously. " 'Tis three dollars, but that'll get you water and oats beside."

"You're Irish!" Morgan declared with relief.

The man scowled around the cigar in his mouth. "Half the city's Irish, pal. What's it to you?"

"I'm looking for an Irishman owns a saloon—" Morgan was cut off by a rude laugh. "Mighty Dugan Ogue," he finished.

"The boxer?" The stableman worked his cigar over to the other side of his mouth. "What business you got there, pal?"

"Personal business. One Irishman to another."

The stableman squinted at him through the smoke. "Sure and you sound Irish, but you dress native." He shrugged his shoulders. "Makes me no nevermind. Ogue's place burned to the ground a few years back, but he runs another round the corner from here. The Emerald Isle, he calls it. Hey! Hey, pal—where you going, then? 'Tis the other way!"

Morgan changed his direction, leading the horse along the street, barely able to believe his good fortune. Light spilled onto the sidewalks from restaurants and saloons, snow flurries swirled in the halo of street-lamps, and Morgan's breath hung in the air before him. And there it was, a small but well-kept establishment, the sign above the door creaking gently in the breeze. Morgan tied the horse to the rail outside, where two other horses stamped their hooves and snorted in the chill air. He removed his pack and slung it over his shoulder, then stood outside the door for a moment, looking in, willing himself to calm down—'twas only a starting place, this. Ogue would be able to tell him where Grace and Sean were, he assured himself; they would not be here. But still, his heart held hope.

Morgan took a deep breath and pushed open the door; he was instantly met with a rush of warm air, the sound of Irish voices arguing everything under the sun, and the smell of good ale. The voices nearest him died momentarily as men set down their mugs and leaned back on their stools to have a look at the oddly dressed gentleman who'd clearly come to the wrong address. Morgan ignored them and headed for the bar, nudging through the crowd at one end and waiting patiently until the formidable-looking man pulling drinks saw him and came over.

"I'll have a pint of your bitter," Morgan ordered.

Ogue looked him over, taking in the buckskins, the fringe, the fur. "That how they're dressing in Ireland these days?" he inquired.

"I wouldn't know," Morgan replied evenly. "Been away a long time. You the owner here? Dugan Ogue?"

"Aye." The barman pulled a dark, foamy pint, then slid the glass down to Morgan's waiting hand. "What can I do for you?"

"I'm looking for a man called Sean O'Malley. Do you know him?" Morgan took a long drink, eyeing Ogue over the rim.

Ogue shrugged and wiped up a spill. "Used to. Don't anymore. He left town a few years ago."

"What about his sister, Gracelin?"

Ogue put down the rag and leaned across the bar, eyes narrowed. "What would you be wanting with her, then?"

Morgan leaned forward, too. "She's my wife," he said.

Ogue's bushy eyebrows knit together in suspicious puzzlement. "She's no one's wife, is Grace. Widowed twice over, she is."

"Widowed once," Morgan corrected him. "Her first husband was Bram Donnelly, the father of Mary Kathleen. Her second husband is Morgan McDonagh, who stands before you now."

"But"—Ogue blinked once as if to clear his vision—"you're dead."

"Not anymore." Morgan allowed himself a wry smile.

"No, man, you're not McDonagh! He was a giant of a man! Barrel-chested, long of leg, handsomest fellow alive! And you're . . ." Ogue looked him up and down, then shook his head in disbelief.

"Sorry to disappoint you, friend. I guess I've not aged as well as I might've liked, but I *am* Morgan McDonagh and I can only hope my own wife will still know me."

Ogue frowned deeply. "Where're you from, then, if you're him?"

"Ireland, County Cork, Macroom, the Black Hill."

"Bah," Ogue spat, disgusted. "Everyone knows that."

"Ask me something else, then. Something about Gracelin only her husband would know."

Ogue thought for a moment and then he jabbed a finger into Morgan's chest. "What about her wedding ring, then? What do you know about that? Nothing, I'll bet!"

" 'Twas my mam's," Morgan answered confidently. "Bears an inscription—'Mary and Nally, Evermore.' I gave it to Grace the night we were wed by Father Brown with Lord David Evans as witness. And"—Ogue's mouth had fallen open—"she may have, as well, my own ring which was Lord Evans', thick gold with his signet."

"Wears it round her neck," Ogue whispered, then crossed himself. "Blessed Jesus, Mary, and Joseph! Is it really you, son?"

"Aye." Morgan sighed with relief. " 'Tis."

With a great bark of joy, Ogue leaped over the bar and wrapped the young man in a mighty bear hug, rocking him from side to side.

"Where've you been, boy? Where've you been?"

The boxer stared into Morgan's face again, then turned him around and whistled for silence, waving one arm in the air.

"Folks! Folks, listen to me now!" The room fell silent, every neck craning toward the front. " 'Tis a miracle and only that, God bless him. Standing here beside me is . . ." Ogue paused, his voice choked with emotion. "Our countryman . . . the Great One himself—Morgan Mc-Donagh."

Dead silence filled the room as the news sunk in and jaws dropped, and then a great cheer arose as everyone leapt to their feet and rushed toward Morgan, embracing him, clapping him on the back, touching him, shaking his hand, tears flooding their eyes and running down their faces, Ogue's the wettest of them all. Morgan was overwhelmed as women and men kissed him and thanked him, blessed him and pressed money into his hands, spoke to him though every word was overridden by every other word and he couldn't understand any of it, didn't know why in Heaven's name this was happening.

"That's enough now. That's enough," Ogue roared above the din. "Give him room to breathe."

The patrons fell back respectfully, but not too far, their eyes lingering on the face of the one who represented, to them, all the young sons they'd left behind.

"After all," Ogue continued in his normal booming voice, his eyes merry, "hasn't he been dead now these many years, and not used to close society?"

They laughed then and returned to their tables, their benches and stools, their glasses of ale, talking among themselves with joyful awe and wonderment, their eyes turning again and again to the dark, bearded man who stood at the bar.

"No wonder the Irish come to New York, with a welcome such as that." Morgan smiled weakly.

Ogue laughed and clapped him on the shoulder, half dragging him back up to the bar. "Take a seat, boyo, and have a drink on the house. You're a hero to these people; never forget that." He pulled a bottle of good Irish whiskey out from under the counter and poured a shot for each of them. "Drink this now and collect yourself, for you've a great many questions to answer, starting with this one: Where the hell've you been, man?" He tossed back his drink.

" 'Tis a long story, but . . . where is she, Ogue? Is she here?" Morgan looked back over his shoulder as if he might have missed her in the crowd.

"No, boy, she's not." Dugan leaned on the bar, wondering where to start. "When's the last time you saw her?"

"The night we wed. I know she carried our child, but whether it lived or died . . ." Morgan swallowed hard. "Is she married again? Is that it?"

"Last I heard, she was not," Ogue reported truthfully.

"Where do I find her?" Morgan was on his feet, ready to go.

"She's on the other side of the country, boy. Thousands of miles away from you still." Ogue could hardly bear the look on the other man's face. "Sit yourself back down there and I'll tell you what I can."

Disappointed, Morgan resumed his place at the bar, tossed off his shot, drained the rest of the pint in one long swallow, then slumped over the empty glasses. Ogue reached beneath the counter for the whiskey bottle and found the plate of sandwiches that was his dinner; he took one off the pile and set it before the dazed young man.

"Eat up," he ordered. "You look half-dead."

"Might not believe it, but I'm actually on the uptake," Morgan reported wearily as Ogue refilled both their glasses, then leaned across the bar.

"Here's the story." The barman looked him square in the eye. "Grace and Sean lived with me and Tara—my wife—in the old saloon, 'til it burned the summer of forty-nine. Sean had joined the Latter-Day Saints—fanaticals, they are—and got himself into trouble. He disappeared and we never heard from him, though Grace was sure he'd gone out to Utah Territory." He paused and took a drink, wiped his mouth with the back of a massive hand. "Grace now, she went on up to Boston to live with the Frees; then after Jack come, they all went out to Kansas. 'Twas hard living, though, and in her last letter she'd decided to take the children all the way to Oregon. To homestead. Free land, you know. Hundreds of acres out there."

Morgan had stopped listening after one word. "Children?" His grip tightened around the glass.

"Well, now." Ogue regarded him with a satisfied smile. "Here's a bit of good news, then—you've got yourself a son, Mister McDonagh. John Paul Morgan, he's called, though Mary Kate tagged him Jack and it stuck. Spitting image of you, Grace says." He laughed at the look on Morgan's face. "I guess he takes after you, as well—coming back from the dead, like."

"Jack?" Morgan repeated. "Jack?" He shook his head. "What do you mean, he takes after me?"

"Well, he was sickly at birth and she had to leave him behind, you know. Word come later that he'd died, along with her da. Turns out, though, he was with a Miss Martin—"

"Julia!" Morgan was astonished. "Julia kept him alive?"

"Well, she kept him," Ogue allowed darkly. "Why she didn't write, I'll never know, but your Grace won't hear a bad word, so grateful she was to get the boy back. Your Miss Martin brought him out when he was two years old, and a firecracker already, that one." He chuckled, despite himself. "He's a handful, is young Jack. Can't see how she managed him on a wagon train."

"Are they all in Oregon now?"

"I expect so. We'll hear from her soon enough." Ogue hesitated. "I said she wasn't married . . . but, you know, she may well be, by the time we get her letter."

Morgan paled; Ogue saw it but pushed on anyway, thinking it best to give him the honest truth.

"There's a man been courting her—captain of the ship brought her over, and her friend here in the city. She wasn't prepared to marry, so he went off to San Francisco, but they've been writing all this time and I think she might be going out there to be with him."

Morgan's shoulders slumped in dismay.

"You listen to me now, boy. That girl loved you, and that's the thing kept her from marrying. But the years pass, you know," Ogue reminded him as gently as he could. "They do pass."

"I know." Morgan's head was swimming.

"Jack and Mary Kate, they need a father's hand. And Grace . . ." Ogue thought about it. "She's lonely, you see. Never says in her letters, but we can tell as much. She's grown weary from it all."

Tears burned in Morgan's eyes, but he gritted his teeth and refused to let them fall, afraid that if he began to weep, he might begin to wail, and if he began to wail, then all that was left was to tear this place apart.

Ogue watched as the internal struggle played itself out upon the young man's face. "So where *have* you been all this time?" he asked. "Can you not tell me?"

Morgan realized his hands were tightened into fists and he forced himself to relax them. "Canada," he said. "I've been in Canada."

Ogue poured out more whiskey; if ever there was a night worth killing a bottle, it was this one.

"I barely remember being dragged out of the jail in Dublin. Dying, I was—couldn't move, couldn't speak. Thought I was bound for the pit and there to breathe my last." Morgan licked his lips. "Next thing I know, I'm on the ship and a priest is caring for me, and then he dies. Most of them died. Don't know why I didn't, other than God." He paused and in his mind's eye saw the hands of strangers who'd offered him bites from their own meager supply of food, sips of precious water, a blanket, the comfort of his own language. "We were quarantined on an island, the sick ones, for most of a year. I got out and found work to pay off my debt, then broke my legs." Anger tightened his grip again. "Four years," he said tersely. "Four years, I lost up there."

"You stayed alive," Ogue reminded him, his voice low. "You got yourself here."

"True enough, though not without help." Morgan took another drink. "I came out with a Mi'kmaq family, then met a French priest who led me the rest of the way. Left him in Boston. And now"—he made as if to get up again, swaying slightly—"I'm leaving for Oregon."

"No, son." Ogue shook his head. "Not if you want to get there alive. You're thin as straw, eyes half-sunk in your head, and your hand shakes when you lift that glass. No, son," he repeated. "You stop with us a while, now. Rest, and let us help you make a plan."

"No." Morgan pushed off the bar. "Got to keep going. She's alive, Ogue, you don't understand . . ."

The barman stopped him. "Hasn't the Lord brought you safely this far? He's putting you in my hands for a little while, and I'll do everything I can to help you. Don't lose faith now, boy."

They stared at one another until, from the back of the room, the sweet sound of the fiddle floated above the talk of the crowd. The fiddler warmed up quickly, then began playing the first notes of a song they all knew and loved, a song Morgan himself had sung a hundred times, in a hundred lanes in the land he loved. He turned now to watch, and all eyes fell upon him as one by one the people stood, each voice adding itself to the growing chorus, their offering to him, the boy who'd stood against Goliath. It was beautiful, and it moved him to his very soul, reminding him of who he was and the strength of the people from whence he'd come. And when it was over, though the echo would cling forever to these walls, the people saw that tears coursed down the cheeks of their hero and they loved him all the more, because his heart was like theirs. One by one, they doffed their hats and shook his hand, shyly for Irish, until the room had emptied and was silent but for the sound of the crackling fire.

Ogue stood quietly beside him. "If love were money, my friend, you'd be the richest man on earth."

He handed the key to the barmaid, instructing her to lock up, then returned to his guest, the man he'd looked forward to meeting one day when they'd all got to Heaven.

"We'll talk more in the morning, but now 'tis time to rest yourself, for weary you surely must be." Ogue put an arm around Morgan's shoulders and guided him toward the stair. "Stay as long as you like, son, and, by the way, if I've not said it before—welcome home, boy. Welcome home."

Twenty-five

Sean looked up from his work and peered over his spectacles at the grim woman who stood before the counter.

"Nice to see you back again, Missus . . . ah . . ." Sean hesistated, unable to remember the name she always used.

"Smith," the woman prompted. "Missus Smith, same as always."

"Of course." Sean smiled congenially. "What can I do for you today, Missus Smith?"

She narrowed her eyes as if the question were a trick. "Same as always," she said shortly.

"Of course." He reached under the counter for a green velvet mat, which he then unrolled ceremoniously.

Missus Smith reached deep into her coat pocket and pulled out a packet wrapped in kitchen linen. From this, she carefully extracted a pair of delicate earrings, which she set out on the velvet.

"Lovely." Sean bent over them. "Garnets, are they? In a silver setting." He picked them up and held them so they caught the light. "Lovely, indeed. Must be hard to part with them, though hopefully you can reclaim them in the near future."

Missus Smith nodded and gave a little sniff as if tears were near. "My grandmother's," she lied. "But with Mister Smith still laid up after his mining accident, and most likely his leg coming off soon, well . . . our finances are in no small way compromised. And me with six children." She sniffed again and even pulled out a handkerchief to dab at the pretended tears.

Missus Smith had given him the sob story of her husband's mining accident the first time she'd come in last November, and Sean hadn't believed her, though he'd enjoyed subsequent embellishments to the tale and had never corrected her on the details, such as the fact that last visit—shortly before Christmas—she'd only had four children.

"How much do you want to borrow against these, Missus Smith?" he inquired politely.

In an appeal for sympathy, the woman widened her eyes and batted her lashes, succeeding only in achieving a look of vague lunacy. "As much as I possibly can, Mister Sung. We are down to our last silver dollar."

Sean noted quietly that she was always down to her last silver dollar; everyone was always down to their last dollar, their last half-dollar, their final two bits, when they came to see Mister Sung, the exotic European pawnbroker. Sean laughed whenever he thought of this, his new identity—he'd encouraged, and even added to, the rumors that established him as the debauched son of an aristocratic family, exiled to America so as not to shame them with his gambling, dueling, whoring, and other unmentionable vices. The fact that he'd made a small fortune in cards, scooped up tracts of land around the city, and now ran the lucrative House of Good Fortune in Chinatown with the enigmatic Chang-Li did not surprise anyone who already believed the stories about him; in fact, it only substantiated those stories and fueled the mystery surrounding his purported identity—and that was exactly the way Sean wanted it. Chang-Li's sudden voyage to China and the subsequent transference of Mei Ling to Mister Sung also fueled the proverbial fire. In the first days of their work together in the pawnshop, Sean had insisted to neighboring businessmen and those who cared enough to inquire that Mei Ling was a free agent, that she worked for him now as a paid employee. He soon realized that absolutely no one believed this to be true, and the fact that she remained in Chang-Li's house with him did nothing to change their minds.

Having idled Missus Smith long enough to lower her financial expectations, Sean now set the earrings down and gave her his full attention.

"Five dollars," he proposed.

Missus Smith gasped and put her hand to her heart. "Surely, sir, they're worth at least ten!"

They're worth at least fifty, you old fool, Sean laughed inwardly, *and when your mistress catches on to the fact that you're selling her jewelry, you'll be jailed if not hung.*

"They are very pretty, Missus Smith, but the stones are flawed and the setting is old." Sean let this sink in. "Out of the goodness of my heart and in consideration of your poor children—four, you said?"

The woman's eyes darted wildly, trying to remember. "Five," she decided. "I·mean six. Yes." She sniffed. "Six small children. Just babies. You were saying?"

"I'll split the difference with you." He reached under the counter and into a cash box, and then set the coins out one by one. "Seven dollars fifty," he pronounced, then whisked the earrings out of sight. "You drive a hard bargain, Missus Smith."

She frowned but picked up the coins and put them in her bag, knowing better than to argue further with the savvy pawnbroker.

"Thank you, Mister Sung." She flashed him a quick, hard smile. "You have saved my family from ruin once again."

"And remember, Missus Smith, I will hold your treasures for two months so that you might reclaim them before they are offered for resale to the general public," he reminded her, though both knew she would never be back for things that weren't hers in the first place.

"Thank you so much," she said again. "Good day, Mister Sung."

"Good day to you, Missus Smith, and give my best to Mister Smith and the innumerable little Smiths."

Now she scowled outright, which he enjoyed, then gathered up her bag and hurried from the shop, the bell tinkling as the door closed behind her. Chang-Li had been right in this as in all things—there was good money to be made in the buying and selling of stolen property. Everyone was stealing something from someone in San Francisco; all that was needed was a clearinghouse. Certainly, there were other pawnbrokers in the city, and most likely Missus Smith had used each of them at one time or another as she sold off her employer's belongings—a few here, a few there, so as not to draw too much attention to herself—but these shops were reputable establishments for the most part and their merchandise openly displayed. The House of Good Fortune, on the other hand, was a quieter shop located in one of the little side streets in the heart of Chinatown; to know about it, one would have to have fingers that had already attained a certain degree of stickiness. This was a strictly word-of-mouth establishment, though Sean was happy to pretend that those who came in to sell their merchandise had indeed fallen on temporarily desperate times and only needed a bit of ready cash to see them through. It was a steady stream of domestics and clerks, he'd found, from butlers and parlor maids to shop walkers and junior assistants, hotel boys and laundrymen to carriage drivers and carpenters, not to mention the occasional lady of the evening, most of whom he knew by name; pickpockets and thieves were everywhere, and everyone was getting ahead any way possible. With the amount of wealth floating around this town, no one seemed to think that a few bits and pieces would ever be missed, that they'd ever be caught, and, to tell the truth, few ever were.

There were, however, just enough honorable servants and employees to remind Sean that a moral standard still existed. Mei Ling was one such person—she'd never stolen from Chang-Li and she didn't steal from Sean, not so much as a bowl of rice, though he wouldn't have cared if she did. Sean paid her a wage and made sure she understood that she could come and go as she pleased, but Mei Ling continued to behave as if her life consisted of only one thing—caring for Mister Sung. She worked every day in the shop, learning the business, cleaning and polishing the daily acquisitions, and then she went home and cleaned the house, mended Sean's clothes, cooked his meals, even trimmed his beard and braided his queue. She acted as wife in every respect but one, and though she had made clear her availability, Sean had not brought her into his bed; he went to Ah Toy's for that, though in all honesty, it was her face he sought among the various girls he sampled.

As Mei Ling's competence in the shop grew, Sean spent more time in the back room with his pipe, defeating the purpose of going out at night. He was smoking too much—he knew that; more and more, he wanted simply to lie upon his bed with a woman in his arms, a woman for whom he had not paid, a woman who might possess the ability to free him from himself. Although he wanted that woman to be Mei Ling, he knew she offered herself to him only out of a sense of duty, a sense of destiny, not out of unique longing or a shared desire, and although he tried to convince himself that one more debauchery would make no difference to his already blackened soul, he knew that the risk of engaging Mei Ling's heart, of tying her to such a low man as he'd become, was a greater sin than all the others put together. Because he was, in a way, refusing her, he tried to give her other things instead, to show her that she pleased him, that she was worthy of so much more than he could ever offer.

Sean took out again the earrings Missus Smith had just brought in; they really were lovely, so quiet and delicate, beautiful in their simplicity. He looked under the counter for a small, velvet-lined box, then put the earrings gently inside. There would be an occasion sometime, or perhaps giving these to Mei Ling would create the occasion; either way he would keep the box with him until such a time arose.

"Thank you, Missus Smith." His voice hung in the empty room. "Whoever you may be, thank you very much indeed."

Hopkins kept her hood up as she hurried out of Chinatown, despising the look of the place with its square silk flags and doorway offerings to heathen gods, the harsh sizzle and steamy odor of dumplings fried in sesame oil, the inhabitants who all looked alike and smelled like the fish oil they rubbed in their hair, the jarring tongue that set her teeth on edge with its sliding tones and dissonance. She hated, too, the industry of the place—the laundresses with their basket poles, the shopkeepers who endlessly swept their doorways, the crowded noodle stands and boisterous restaurants—and the fact that, though they bowed respectfully, these people seemed always to be laughing up their sleeves at her. Had Hopkins not exhausted the potential of every other pawnshop in the city, she would not have come at all, though she had to admit that the House of Good Fortune, though it paid out less, was far more discreet in its inquiry and speculation. The police kept a close eye on Sydney Town and Chinatown both, but it appeared that Chinatown paid heavier and more regular bribes—Hopkins had seen lawmen stroll the streets, but they turned a blind eye to customers going in and out of the House of Good Fortune.

Hopkins remained shielded by her hood even after she left Chinatown, heading toward the waterfront. There was always the possibility of recognition, especially as afternoon approached, with more people on the streets, but she kept her head down and her pace up, and if stopped, she would have made the excuse of marketing or errands for her mistress. If hailed in the plaza—especially by Mister Pennywhistle, owner of Pennywhistle Pipe and Tobacco, and a very good prospect for Enid—Hopkins would answer to her real name. But down here along the wharves she was Missus Smith—if she was anyone at all—wife of poor old Mister Smith, who was housebound in caring for their unfortunate son and, by all accounts, devoted to the boy.

Taking care to scurry unnoticed past the small window that fronted the Mulhoney rooms, Missus Smith climbed the dark stair to the landing, walked to the back, and opened the door with her key. It was cold inside, she felt it at once, but any feelings of guilt she might have had were instantly repressed, to be substituted instead by irritation—a much more energizing emotion.

"Harry." Hopkins spoke sharply. "Why is there no fire in the grate?"

A man older than herself, dressed in grimy layers of clothing, rose wearily to his feet. "Hello, Agnes. Sorry. Out of coal since Monday. But we knew you'd come." He turned to adjust the blanket on the body that lay awkwardly curled on its cot. "Didn't we, Wills? We knew Mother'd come as soon as she could."

A moan of greeting came from the lump as it turned itself over, arms and legs spasming, its smile a puddle of drool.

"He's disgusting—can't you keep his face dry? You've only all day to do it, while I work my fingers to the bone."

"Yes, dear," Harry apologized. "I know you do, and we're grateful to you for it. Aren't we, Wills? Aren't we grateful to Mother for bringing us food and coal?"

Wills waggled his head and groaned.

"I don't know why you do that." Agnes turned away in disgust. "He can't understand a word you say, you know. Poor, dumb idiot creature."

Harry shook his head. "Don't call him that, Agnes. I've said it before. I won't hear it. Sickness overtook his body, but I know he's still sharp as a tack in his mind. I know he can understand us, Agnes, and I won't have you saying otherwise. I'm still head of this family."

"Is that right?" she replied, scathingly.

Harry pulled himself up as tall as he could and straightened his vest. "Just say the word, and I'll go out to work. Long as you're willing to stay with him. You can't leave him alone now. He seizes worse than ever. But you just say the word, and I'll go out."

Agnes snorted and started pulling food out of the basket. "You're an old man, Harry Hopkins. Lord knows, you were old when I married you, but at least you could work. There's no jobs to be had for the likes of you. Strong backs only, or strong minds—you don't have either one anymore. Only good for wiping up after idiots, and that's not exactly a booming business, you know."

Wills moaned from the cot and tried to sit up. His father hurried to his side and helped him, pulling the shabby blanket up around the boy's thin shoulders.

"You're troubling him." Harry smoothed back his son's hair. "Why do you come if you're going to talk like that?"

Agnes slammed a loaf down on the table. "Well, forgive me for providing your daily bread, Harry. I guess I'll just get on back to scrubbing the floors and cleaning the chamber pots if I can't say what I like to my own husband in the rooms *I* pay for." She picked up her empty basket.

"I'm sorry, Agnes." Harry immediately humbled himself in the face of her anger. "Please don't go. We're getting off wrong here. We appreciate everything you do— really we do. We'd be lost without you and we know how hard you work for us, don't we, Wills?"

The boy's head was tipped to one side, but he looked from his father to his mother with sharp, clear eyes.

Agnes sighed, a spot of red on each side of her stiff, pasty face.

"Sit down, dear," Harry said soothingly, pulling out one of the two chairs at the table. "I'll get a little heat going and make you a nice cup of tea. Would you like that? A nice cup of tea?"

There was silence as Agnes let her eyes run over the cheerless room with its drab walls and smeary windows overlooking the street and a forest of masts beyond in the harbor. With another great sigh, she unbuttoned her cloak, then sat down, watching Harry lay out the coal and light it. She turned her eyes toward Wills, realized he was staring at her, and frowned at him. She studied the backs of her hands until at last the water had boiled and the tea had steeped.

"Here you go, now, dear." Harry set a chipped mug in front of her. "A nice cuppa. How's Enid? We saw her at"—he glanced at his wife, then away—"before Christmastime, but not since. She's well, then, is she? Getting on up there?"

Agnes wrapped her cold hands around the mug. "Our daughter's not got much more going on upstairs than our son," she said shortly. "But I'm teaching her everything she'll need to know to run her own house. I've got a few prospects lined up. One seems particularly eager."

"Is she being courted, then?" Harry leaned on the table, a smile on his face. "Is he a nice young man?"

Agnes frowned. "Of course she's not being courted, you fool. You can't present a young girl to the men in this society—they'll make all kinds of promises just to get a woman in their house. And Enid is such a simpleton, she'd go with the first one who asked her, and be no better off than . . ." She stopped herself, though it took a determined pressing together of the lips. "It takes arranging," she amended and sipped her tea. "I'm working on it."

"I'm sure you'll find a suitable young man for her. One as she likes and as likes her in return." Harry patted her hand. "Are they church-going men, the suitors, good jobs and all?"

Agnes looked at him as if he were daft. "Of course they're religious. Of course they have good jobs. One of them is rich. Do you think I'm stupid? The last thing I need is a poor son-in-law to support on top of everything else."

Harry winced at the sharpness of her tone, but he pressed on for love of his daughter. "But he'll be a nice man, Agnes. Enid deserves as much."

"Nice men don't marry girls with brothers like that." Agnes jerked her thumb at Wills. "He'll be whatever he is and it doesn't matter, as long as he has enough money to take care of all of us." She stared into her teacup.

"We're doing all right," Harry insisted. "You and Enid, you make good wages up there, and the two of us here are living as cheap as we can. There's no need to marry the girl off unless it's of her choosing, eh?"

"She's not getting any younger, you old fool," Agnes hissed. "And I can't work forever. I'm nearly done up there, one way or the other. Got everything I'm going to from those Wakefields. The well runs dry, you know, Harry. It runs dry."

"Then come home to us." Harry covered her hand with his own. "Let your mistress take care of herself now, or get someone else. You've done enough for her, after all, and it's taken its toll, Agnes. We've got enough saved up to get us by until I find work."

"Don't be a fool." She snatched her hand away. "You can't work, Harry, and even if you could, you'd make nothing. When Enid is married, we'll have her money, plus what I've saved, and then we'll go back to England. I'll buy a house with my sister and we'll take in lodgers."

Harry shook his head. "Wills could never make a trip like that, Agnes. It would kill him."

"He's not going to live much longer anyway," she said, ignoring the stricken face of her husband. "By the time Enid is married, it will all be over. And then we'll go." She glanced out the window at the graying sky. "I have to get back to the house now, or that nosy cook will be at me with her questions."

"Agnes. We have to talk more about this. About Enid and Wills. I won't leave them behind."

"I'm going back to England, Harry." Agnes buttoned up her cloak. "With or without you. As soon as Enid is married."

"Agnes, please . . ." he implored.

She withdrew four dollars from her bag and held the money out to him. "Do you need this?"

He nodded miserably.

"Of course you do." She set it on the table. "And I will give it to you. Just as I have always given you everything since the day we met. Three children, Harry, and I buried the one I loved most. I came with you to a country I never wanted to see, traveled across it at great hardship, and watched my youngest become an imbecile. You didn't want to put him away, Harry. You wanted to keep him with you." She put on her hat. "I went to work so you could do that. I have taken care of everything and everyone, and now I want something in return." She opened the door. "I want to go home, Harry. While I still can."

"You're right, Agnes. You wanted a different life, but you got this one instead. I haven't been the husband to you I should've been, and I know you've done the best you could." Harry's voice was tender with remorse. "You go whenever you're ready, Agnes. The children and I can fend for ourselves, though we'll miss you. You won't go without saying good-bye, though, will you, dear?"

"I'll see you first," she told him, her hand on the doorknob. "I've got to finish things up there, and see Enid settled. And, of course, you'll need money."

Harry came to her side. "You've stood by us all a long, long time." He put his hand on her shoulder. "You do whatever you think is best, and I'll not stand in your way now. I've always loved you, Agnes. I'm sorry."

She did not look at him as he kissed her cheek, but stared out into the hallway. "Rent's paid," she said. "And you got that little Mulhoney brat to run to market for you."

He winced at the epithet but nodded.

"See you in two weeks, then."

Harry stood at the door, watching until she'd disappeared down the stairwell, remembering how young and pretty she'd been when first they met, how puffed up with the importance of having been hired on at the big house. She was bold and exciting, but he was older and should have exercised greater control for her sake; the result of his impulsiveness was marriage on the quick and a son come early. He knew in his heart that she hadn't wanted to marry, hadn't wanted children yet, but she never complained, and oh, she adored that boy—Richard was the true love of her life, always her favorite, even after Enid and William had come along.

In those days, he'd thought himself a lucky man for everything turning out as well as it was—even if she didn't love him, Agnes respected Harry as her husband and the father of her children, and their home was a happy one. But then Richard—seventeen and full of yearning to see the world—joined the infantry, went to Ireland on foot, and came home again in a box. Agnes had taken to her bed and lain there for two months, waiting to die herself and would have—Harry was sure—if not for her sister, Vera, who came and tended her day and night until at last she got up. It was an answer to Harry's fervent prayers, and he'd fulfilled his bargain with God by taking his family to the new land to begin a new life. Agnes had not wanted to go to Boston, had not wanted to leave her sister or the site of Richard's grave, but Harry had insisted, thinking it the best thing for all of them. "Vera will tend the plot," he'd promised, and she had, wanting Agnes to have a new and better life, wanting Agnes to send money home for when they would be together again.

They weren't in Boston a year when William began to sicken; he had seizures, the beginnings of palsy, perhaps it was consumption or tuberculosis—the doctors recommended a drier climate, though they couldn't say exactly what it was that plagued the boy. When Agnes wouldn't hear of going—Wills was, after all, a pale light compared to her Richard—Harry had gone quietly to the reverend, saying he was ready to answer God's call to preach to the heathen Chinese out west. The reverend convinced Agnes to support her husband in this mission, and the church sent them by ship around the Horn. Harry had had great hopes for life in San Francisco and had begun his ministry with fire and enthusiasm, but William had only gotten worse instead of better; soon he could not control his limbs or his speech, and Agnes was sure he'd gone mad. She'd declared that caring for an imbecile was asking too much of her, and she begged Harry to put William in an asylum for such people.

To keep the boy at home, Harry had finally agreed to give up his mission, to live in seclusion while Agnes and Enid took work first in a hotel and then with the wealthy Wakefields. They couldn't know about Harry and Wills, Agnes had insisted; they wouldn't want a married housekeeper with outside responsibilities, especially when the mistress of the house was an invalid and needed special attention. And so he had agreed, out of guilt—for getting her with child and allowing that child to go away from her and die, for moving her to a place full of mud, miners, and foreigners, and for saddling her with a palsied son who'd need her care the rest of his days. He agreed to everything, just as he would agree to her leaving, when the time came, though how they would cope, he did not know. As much as he loved Agnes, as much as he knew he owed her, he simply could not leave his beloved daughter in an arranged marriage and his son to suffer and die alone, with no one to tend the grave. He would cling to his faith, knowing that it was not God who had failed him, but he who had failed God. Young William Hopkins, only twenty years old, would be with God soon enough, and Harry was determined not to fail him in the end.

There was a sound now from behind him, a groan he knew well, as he knew all of the groans that William made—a different one for cold, hunger, joy, sadness, just as a baby had its many cries, all the same to ears who knew it not, but never to those who loved it best.

"Coming, Wills." Harry closed the door on the chilly winter air, putting on a smile and rubbing his hands briskly as he turned to face his son. "Now, how about a meal for the two of us, eh? Looks like we've got a nice loaf here, and some cheese, apples—I'll stew them for you!—

and a lump of bacon. Even some eggs, Willy, old boy! How about a nice boiled egg for your tea?"

Wills groaned and swayed from side to side, but it was no answer to the question; he wanted his father.

Harry sat down beside the young man and put an arm around the wasted shoulders, pulling him close, kissing the clammy forehead.

"I know you're in there, Will Hopkins, and I'll never leave you." He smiled tenderly into eyes that were locked upon his own. "No matter where the road leads, we'll go together, you and I. Even without her, we'll be all right," he vowed. "I promise you that, Wills, and I'll not let you down."

Twenty-six

There were three options, as far as Morgan could see: He could go overland, but he'd have to wait until after the spring rains when there would be plenty of fresh grass and water for his horse; he could sail the seventeen thousand miles around Cape Horn, which meant he could leave right away but would need to raise the 250 dollars passage, and it would still take anywhere from five to seven months before he arrived in San Francisco; or he could travel by small steamship to Panama, canoe up the Chagres River, take pack mules over rugged terrain, then try to book a large steamer out of Panama City to San Francisco—this would take at most two months but would cost nearly 400 dollars.

"Can you work your way over on the ships?" Morgan asked at the breakfast table.

The big man shook his head. "Only experienced sailors," he said around a bite of fried bread. "And only if they're shorthanded, which they never are. Everyone's still trying to go west. Though they must be running out of gold by now, wouldn't you think?"

" 'Tis more than gold draws them." Tara poured more tea into her husband's cup. "New lives, adventure, all that. They say women out there wear trousers," she added.

"Well, darling, they're behind the times, 'cause haven't you been wearing the pants round here for years now!" Ogue laughed and dodged the swat his wife aimed at him. "Isn't that right, Caolon, my boy?"

"Aye, Da!" The little boy grinned from his chair, then stopped when his eyes fell upon his mother's frown. "I mean, no, Da," he said soberly.

Now they all laughed.

"Your one is only a year older than Caolon here," Tara pointed out to Morgan. "Jack, I mean. He'd've turned five last November."

Morgan studied the boy. "Big, for his age, young Caolon. Is Jack big, do you think?"

"Well, we've not seen him since he was two, of course, but aye." She nodded. "He was a good size. They're all big here in America, long as they're not fed that blue milk comes from the stables by the breweries. They add chalk to that, you know, and all manner of nasty stuff to make it white. Better to feed your own the way God intended."

Morgan thought about that. "How was Jack kept alive, with Grace not there to suckle him?"

"They had a woman at the convent lost her own baby," Ogue offered. "And later they used goat's milk. Something wrong with his eyes, though. Sees well enough," he added quickly. "The woman who kept him married a doctor who fixed him up. Wears spectacles now, he does. Looks like a right young scholar, does Jack."

Morgan nodded, trying to take it all in. "Is Barbara still alive, then? My sister? She was a nun at the convent where Grace was meant to go."

"Oh, aye." Tara was pleased to deliver the good news. "We didn't find out until after Jack come, but Julia told us she married and moved to the west, to Galway."

"Barbara married? She left the order?"

"Lot of them have done," Ogue reported. "Left to their own, with so many dead, many just took up their old lives. She married a man called Alroy and they have twin boys, isn't that right, Tara?"

"Aye. Grace writes to them, as well."

"Barbara married Abban!" Morgan was delighted. "And they have sons! That's grand. Just grand." And then, to his embarrassment, his throat closed and tears came again to his eyes. He bowed his head.

Tara reached across the table and covered his hand with her own. "Sure and 'tis a lot of news." She comforted him. "Anyone'd be done in by it."

"Only I was thinking how right it was they found each other. Barbara and I   growing up as we did . . ." He stopped, still overcome. "And Abban. Fought side by side, we did, him saving my sorry behind more times than I can count." Morgan smiled now, remembering.

"There was one time me and Abban and Big Quinn were caught out by a patrol, and Abban, he—"

"Big Quinn Sheehan?" Ogue interrupted. "From County Cork? Great head of hair and sings like one from the heavenly choir?"

Morgan's heart quickened. "Is he here, then? In the city?"

Ogue and Tara exchanged a glance.

"Blackwell's Island," Tara said hesitantly. "In the asylum."

"Got off the boat a year ago. A broken man already," Ogue said. "Come round looking for Sean. Got himself a room, work on the night carts, but stayed to himself, even when drinking."

"Took him over, the drink." Tara picked up the story. "One day he just didn't get out of bed. Wanted to die, most like, but that failed him, as well. We heard he'd been taken out there to live with the paupers. Dugan went to see him."

"He'll not be the way you remember," Ogue warned. "Breaks stone for his keep, spends the rest of the time on his pallet with his face to the wall. Haunted, that one, like most of them out there."

Morgan stood at once. "Which way?"

"Would you quit leaping all over the place, boy?" Ogue thumped the table. "These things take time, you know. You can't just hike yourself on out there and make demands! There's rules about who you can see and when you can see them. Took me nigh on a week last time!"

"You called on that Mister O'Sullivan at the paper," Tara reminded her husband. "Will you try him again?"

"Aye." Ogue nodded slowly. "He knew exactly what to do about getting me in. I'll see him today, if I can." He glanced at Morgan. "Take you with me, as well. He'll be interested in you."

Morgan hesitated, then sat back down. "Why'd he be interested in me, then?"

Ogue set his fork and knife down with a bang. "Son. I don't think you realize who you are in the minds of your people. A hero, that's what you are, the biggest hero come out of Ireland since Brian Boru. Isn't that right, darling girl?" He looked to Tara for confirmation.

"Go on with you." Morgan turned sideways in his chair and crossed his arms. "Never heard anything so daft in all my life."

"Daft or no, 'tis true," Ogue insisted. "You'll have to sort it all out for yourself, but the tales they tell and the songs they sing have made you a legend, boy. A legend. And don't go disappointing the people by making out otherwise," he reproached. "Accept it. Get used to it. Enjoy it, for pity's sake! Haven't you earned it?"

"Not more than any other man over there," Morgan asserted. "All of us fought and starved together, died together."

"Yeah, well, the banner under which all those men stand is called McDonagh, and don't go taking that away from us, Mister High and Mighty." Ogue huffed.

"Oh." Morgan's arms fell to his sides. "Well, I didn't think of it that way. Maybe that's right."

"Aye, 'tis," Ogue swore. "That and a lot of other things, like getting out to Blackwell's Island."

"Sorry, Dugan. Truly I am." Morgan stood up again. "Will we go now to see your man O'Sullivan?"

The barman sighed and looked at his wife, who shrugged her shoulders affectionately.

"Let me finish my breakfast at least, will you?" Ogue shoveled the last of his eggs onto his bread, folded the slice in half, then put the whole thing in his mouth, swallowing it down with a full cup of tea. "Any more of that ham?" he asked Tara, then laughed at the expression on Morgan's face. "Ah, I'm only pulling your leg. Let's go." He stood up and grabbed his hat. "You're going to have to lighten up some, you know, boy, now you're out of the woods."

It was three weeks before Morgan found himself being ferried out to Blackwell's Island with Mister O'Sullivan at his side; three precious weeks, and yet the time had whirled by in a frenzy of receptions, dinners, and speaking engagements hosted by the Irish Emigrant Society and Tammany Hall, prominent Irish politicians and newsmen like Robert Bonner—immigrant printer turned entrepreneur—owner of the *New York Ledger,* and James G. Bennett, editor of the *New York Herald.* It was Bennett who told Morgan that Franklin Pierce had won the presidency of the United States over Millard Fillmore due in large part to the Irish who'd turned out in droves to support him; Fillmore had attached himself to the widespread nativist, anti-Irish, anti-Catholic, anti-immigrant, Know-Nothing movement, and it had cost him. The Irish, Bennett explained knowingly, were moving into politics with a sure hand now, and they knew how to organize. Sure, Hibernians were still depicted on the theater stage as ignorant, hottempered, drunken buffoons, but just look at what they'd accomplished with organizations such as the Laborers Union Benevolent Association, whose membership now topped six thousand, many of them famine refugees, and whose political weight was formidable.

Morgan had been impressed with the fortitude of his countrymen, knowing full well from what they'd come, but he was sorry to have missed those Irishmen he'd known personally. Thomas Meagher was obviously enormously popular and had been issued a personal invitation to the presidential inauguration to be held on March fourth; now, however, Meagher was on the lecture circuit. It had been reported in all the papers that Thomas had been greeted by a militia unit named the Meagher Guard, and in Massachusetts was met with a twenty-one-gun salute along with the cheers of thousands of Irish factory workers. Smith O'Brien, Morgan learned, had been transported to Van Diemen's Land, though it was rumored that men were escaping the place every day. John Mitchel's mother was in Boston and subject of another rumor that had her meeting with Meagher and the presidentelect; Morgan could only hope that this new leader would come to the aid of the Irish rebels who'd been cast far and wide and wanted only to be restored to their homeland.

Despite the outpouring of support and goodwill, Morgan yearned to escape the public eye and resume his private life—he wanted only to get to Grace, only to see Quinn. Although he'd said nothing to anyone, not even to Dugan or Tara, Morgan had come to a decision; if Sheehan was of reasonably sound mind and could be convinced to come, then Morgan would take him to Oregon, even if he had to carry Quinn on his back.

O'Sullivan had finally got an appointment to see Sheehan privately this very afternoon, and he carried the paperwork in his jacket pocket. Quinn had been committed to the asylum but had gotten well enough to warrant a transfer to the workhouse, whose inmates were paupers and the destitute. He could be released for a series of payments; bribes, really, Morgan thought, but technically they were fines and remuneration for his care and housing at the asylum. How much, Morgan had no idea, but in his pocket was a wallet full of cash—every tip he'd made serving beer at Ogue's, every dollar pressed into his hand by those who welcomed him to America, the money he'd got for his knife and his fox-fur robe, the odd bank check slipped into his pocket from some of these American women who'd whispered in his ear offers that made him blush. It was nearly one hundred dollars, and Morgan was prepared to use every penny, if that's what it took to buy Quinn Sheehan's freedom.

The day was dark and the crossing rough; wind gusted against the side of the boat and sleet fell intermittently, soaking the ferry passengers, of which there were few. Everyone was silent, and there was no meeting of the eyes; one of the men was still bleeding from a gash to the cheek, and two of the women were noticeably pregnant.

"Inmates," O'Sullivan mouthed, and Morgan looked again at the swollen bellies of the two very young women.

It was midafternoon by the time they landed on the bleak island, and it took them a moment to find their bearings.

"Welcome to the grand experiment." O'Sullivan removed his hat, dumping water from its brim. "Run by the Association for Improving the Condition of the Poor. Four thousand contributing members," he continued. "Some of the wealthiest and most influential men in New York. All of them concerned with the well-being of the city's unfortunates; translation —'Get the beggars off the streets and out of the sight of decent citizens.' Hence, a two-mile island." He made a grand sweep with his arm. "Shall we go on?"

Morgan nodded, a sense of foreboding having fallen upon him; this was a long way from evening clothes and fancy dinners, from wine and song and speech making. O'Sullivan kept on talking while he led the way up a winding path.

"We'll see the almshouse first, and you'll be interested to know that nearly two-thirds of the seven thousand inmates there are Irish, many of whom were domestics, discharged after years of service, with no children to care for them in their old age."

"So they're in prison?"

"Not prison." O'Sullivan corrected him. "They are considered the respectable poor and housed here as an alternative to Bellevue Hospital. Bellevue," he added, "is nothing more than a rat infested, lice-ridden hole with a mortality rate that is, at best, unnaturally high."

"What about here?" Morgan asked. "Can they leave here if they want to?"

"They can, but if they'd anywhere else to go, they'd not be here in the first place. Blackwell's Island is the end of the road, especially for the elderly." He led Morgan to higher ground. "Now we're facing south, and at that end is the penitentiary. Can't miss it—quite imposing, actually. Fortresslike, one might say. The most hardened criminals are kept there: women in one wing, men in the other."

For a moment, the rain stopped and the clouds parted, sending a beam of light down to that part of the island, illuminating the landscape and a party being escorted toward the prison. O'Sullivan watched them pass, then continued on in a low voice, explaining that these were considered society's most depraved: thieves, rapists, arsonists, murderers—those who had become so debased as to necessitate their removal from society.

Whatever else the women might be, he added, they were also most likely prostitutes—not the protected parlor house girls from the west end of Broadway or those from the elite brothels that never seemed to get raided, but lower-end whores and streetwalkers from Anthony Street and the Bowery, Cow Bay Alley and, most notoriously, Corleans Hook along the waterfront, where sailors, ferry commuters, and dock workers were regularly solicited by the girls they called 'hookers.' "

Many of these girls were simple maids from the countryside, O'Sullivan told him, though a fair number were Irish girls who'd been unable to find work and were desperate to send money home to families they knew were starving to death. Morgan thought of all the young Irish girls he'd known who'd set sail for America with such trust and determination, and his heart fell. O'Sullivan saw the way his young friend was affected by this information and nodded.

"You can hardly blame them," O'Sullivan said empathetically. "Prostitutes are the city's highest-paid women workers, earning in a single night what would otherwise take months. And, in their minds, it's probably a better alternative to staying with a drunken father or husband, or being condemned to a life of monotony and poverty as seamstress or servant. With so few choices and, often, young mouths to feed, who could judge them? Not I." He shook his head. "Certainly, not I."

By society's standards, prostitution was a crime of depravity, O'Sullivan explained, warming to his subject; every new call for reform led to a clean sweep of the streets, even as gentlemen continued privately to subscribe to such handbooks as *Guide to Harems* and *Prostitution Exposed*, to collect private house calling cards dropped off at hotels, or to simply consult the city directory for women listing themselves as "prostitute." However, it was never the men who were degenerate, he proselytized, only the women, and eventually—too careless, too naive, too old—they found themselves booked into Blackwell's penitentiary. The end of the road.

"Down on the tip of the island, there's a smallpox hospital." O'Sullivan changed the subject smoothly. "It's very small, but plans are under way—as plans always are—to enlarge it. I know a number of doctors involved with that project." He turned in the opposite direction. "And up there is the lunatic asylum, a mammoth structure by comparison. This is where our friend, Mister Sheehan, spent his first weeks. Which doesn't surprise me," he added. "Most of the inmates are Irish, though considerably more young women than men." He paused. "I suppose it is because the minds and spirits of women who become destitute are more easily broken. Especially when they've been separated from the anchor of family and friends."

"So, you're telling me that Irish girls either sell themselves or go mad trying not to, but either way they end up on Blackwell's Island?"

"Well, not all, of course. But a great many." O'Sullivan faced him. "Yes, a great many do end up here."

Thank God for Dugan Ogue, Morgan suddenly realized. Thank God he'd taken Grace in, sheltered her, and given her work. He should fall on his knees and kiss the man's feet a thousand times over. *Thank you, God, for sparing her this.*

"Let's move on, shall we?" O'Sullivan ran his hand through his hair and replaced his hat. "The place we want is just up ahead."

The workhouse, he told Morgan, maintained paupers and vagrants; that was where they'd find Quinn Sheehan. Men here were put to work; they labored in the stone quarry, rowed ferryboats like the one he and Morgan had ridden over in, and were loaned out at night to clean the sewers. Sheehan was a quarryman, but he'd been pulled out this afternoon and was waiting in his dormitory.

"Does he know 'tis I coming to see him?"

O'Sullivan shook his head. "He's pretty low, after all. Might not want to see you, even if he did believe you were alive. We're listed as O'Sullivan and Partner, interested parties."

"Interested parties," Morgan echoed, following O'Sullivan up the steps and into the main entrance of the large structure.

Once inside and faced with staff at the front desk, he let O'Sullivan do the talking, preferring to stand back and keep a low profile. They were shown into a small room with benches that Morgan supposed served as a visitor center for those lucky enough to receive such.

O'Sullivan took a seat on one of the benches that lined the walls, but Morgan was too nervous and paced the room instead, finally pausing to look out a narrow window at the bleak landscape beneath a washed, gray sky. At the sound of scuffling boot steps, he turned toward the doorway.

"Gentlemen." The male clerk, or escort, or whatever he was, cleared his throat. "Here's the man you came to see."

Suddenly paralyzed, Morgan could only stare, but O'Sullivan got to his feet at once and went to Sheehan, offering his hand while at the same time dismissing the clerk.

"Mister Sheehan." O'Sullivan shook hands. "You don't know me, but I've brought along an old friend of yours."

Quinn looked over O'Sullivan's shoulder at Morgan, squinting to better see the man shadowed by the weak light coming from behind.

"Who's he, then?"

At the sound of his old friend's voice, Morgan stepped forward and O'Sullivan moved quietly out of the way.

"Do you not recognize me, Quinn?" Morgan approached slowly. "Didn't we grow up together on the Black Hill, and weren't you always causing trouble down in the lanes?" His voice was soothing, calling up the world in which they'd used to live. "You, me, Sean O'Malley, the Neeson boys—we were a pack, then, do you not remember, Quinn?"

Sheehan shook his head, refusing to believe.

"That voice of yours got all the girls," Morgan continued, now standing directly in front of his friend. "Opened every door, and got us drinks on the house." He paused. " 'Oh, Dan, my dear, you're welcome here . . . Thank you, ma'am, says Dan . . .' " The song trailed off as

Sheehan reached out and touched Morgan's arm, his shoulder, the side of his face.

"McDonagh?" he whispered. "Morgan McDonagh?"

"Aye."

"But you're dead." Sheehan yanked his hand away as if burned.

"No." Morgan put his hands on Sheehan's shoulders and looked him in the eye. "Been to hell and back—there's truth in that—but not dead. Look at me, Quinn. See me standing here. We made it."

Sheehan's eyes met Morgan's and cleared, and then a single sob escaped him, a great bark of pain and incredulity, and his knees buckled. Morgan and O'Sullivan caught him under the arms and helped him to the bench, Morgan sitting beside and O'Sullivan moving to bar the door, turning away discreetly from the man who now wept openly against his friend. Sheehan clung to the cloth of Morgan's coat, his desperate grip nearly rending the fabric, but Morgan only moved closer, wrapping his arms around Quinn and offering comfort in the language of their mothers until, at last, the shaking subsided and Quinn rested, his forehead pushed into Morgan's shoulder.

"What happened, Quinn?" Morgan asked gently.

Sheehan sat up and mopped his face with his sleeve, eyes still swimming. "Did you ever go back there? To our village?"

Morgan shook his head.

"I did." Quinn stopped and his eyes creased with pain. "There was no one left, Morgan. No one a'tall. The cabins razed in every lane, and everyone dead or gone away." He shook his head. "I couldn't find any of my own nor any I knew. And then . . . I was so hungry. I took soup, you see, from the Protestants." He broke down again, then whispered in anguish, "I've damned my own soul to Hell."

"No." Morgan put his hand on the man's knee. "That's man's talk, not God's. The only religion God ordered was the caring for widows and orphans, and wasn't I with you time and again when you put what little food you had into the hands of a child who'd no one?"

"But—"

"But nothing, Quinn. You put that straight out of your mind. Who provided that soup in the first place? God, and only God, and don't think He hasn't a few choice words for those took it upon themselves to add conditions to His blessing."

Quinn looked at him, wanting to believe. "They were providing passage for those wanted out, and I took it."

"Good," Morgan declared. "You did the right thing. You came out alone?"

"Aye, thinking Sean was here, or someone. Never knew a place so big as this, though. And they hate us here," Sheehan added quietly. "I didn't know they'd hate us like this, but . . ." He shrugged. "Look at us—poor, raggedy, stupid people, only good for scrubbing floors, cleaning sewers, carting off the dead. I didn't . . . I couldn't . . ." He looked down at his hands. "I lost heart after a while. Thought I'd drink myself to death, but went mad instead."

" 'Tis over now, all that. We Irish are heroes. For this week, at least."

"Maybe," Quinn allowed. "Maybe not. I've no courage left, you see. For going back out to the world."

"Maybe 'tis only this part of the world doesn't suit you," Morgan suggested. "Listen, Quinn—I'm going west. To Oregon Territory. Do you know where that is?"

Sheehan frowned and shook his head.

"Nor I." Morgan grinned. "But I've a map. And a gun. And a horse. But no one to ride with. I want you to come with me, Quinn. To Oregon."

Quinn looked up now, and Morgan caught just a flicker of interest behind the man's wariness. "Why Oregon?"

"Grace is out there."

"Grace?" Quinn leaned forward. "Does she know you're coming, then? That you're alive?"

"I don't know exactly where she is in Oregon. Ogue says I should write this Captain Reinders in San Francisco, but . . ." Morgan hesitated, considering. "The man wants to marry her, Quinn. They may be wed already, but if they're not—well, I don't want a letter from me to hurry him along, if you know what I mean."

"But she's your wife!"

"Aye, married in the dead of night by a renegade priest, witnessed by a man long gone." Morgan let that sink in. "God may recognize it, but the law will not."

"And if they're already married?"

"Don't think I've not considered that," Morgan admitted. "About leaving her to her happiness. But I made that mistake once in my life, and I'm not going to do it again. And then there's Jack. My son," he added proudly. "I have a son, Quinn, and I'm going to shake that boy's hand and kiss his mother one more time, married or no."

"Huh." Quinn slumped against the wall. " 'Tis like a dream, this. I can hardly believe you're sitting here, talking to me."

"Miracles happen every day, my friend. I'm proof of that, and so are you." Morgan stood up. "So, Quinn Sheehan, there's only two choices—will you walk out of here on your own two feet or will I carry you out?"

Sheehan eyed the sinewy frame of his old friend and laughed for the first time in longer than he could remember. "You don't look like you could shoulder my granny, let alone a man breaks rock for his daily bread."

"Try me." Morgan put out his hand.

Sheehan hesitated a moment—a long moment—and then he looked up into the face of the man he'd followed loyally from one end of Ireland to the other, the man whose death he'd mourned every day since learning of it.

"I'll walk out on my own," he said quietly, slipping his hand into Morgan's and allowing himself to be pulled to his feet. "When do we leave?"

"Now." Morgan patted the wallet in his jacket pocket. "Say goodbye to this place, Quinn, for tonight, we'll be singing in Ogue's. And if I've not enough to settle your accounts, well"—he grinned—"I'll just leave O'Sullivan here in your place."

"I think arrangements can be made." O'Sullivan was relieved to see that Sheehan's spirit was on the way to redemption, that his haunted look had been replaced by something closer to hope. "Gentlemen." He held open the door. "This way."

Quinn went first, and then Morgan, followed by O'Sullivan, who put a hand on McDonagh's arm to hold him back.

"I was at a dinner party with your wife once," he began. "When your name came up. There were those who felt that Ireland was a lost cause, and you a sacrificial lamb, but Grace would hear none of it. She said that you loved your life, that life was precious to you, but that sacrifice was the price of freedom and you'd paid that price willingly so that others would not have to. She said you gave your people hope, Mister McDonagh, something to live for." O'Sullivan glanced toward the desk where Quinn now waited, a taller man than he'd been an hour before. "Mister McDonagh," he said quietly, "you do that still."

Twenty-seven

It was Doctor Wakefield who broke the news to Grace that Sister Joseph had died in her sleep. They had all been aware of her slow deterioration—even though she refused to acknowledge anything wrong other than the annoying shortness of breath—but everyone who knew and loved her chose to believe that she had years of life yet. Doctor Wakefield was greatly saddened by the nun's passing and did not attempt stoicism; the thought of her moved him to tears, and he let them fall. Sister Joseph had worked by his side for many years and had been a greater support to him in his work than any male medical assistant; it was the reality of this—after her death—and the subsequent truth that she would have made an outstanding physician, that forced him to reconsider his former stance on "lady doctors." As a tribute to his finest nurse, he quietly funded a scholarship in her name at the Quaker School of Medicine and issued an invitation of residency for one graduate every two years. Needless to say, his colleagues had been floored but in the end had accepted it with humorous goodwill. It did not seem like enough, really, especially when he thought back to that terrible year of cholera and the devotion she'd shown every patient.

Missus Donnelly had attended the short graveside service with him and had introduced him to Margaret Mulhoney, who carried newborn Josephine in her arms. On the way home, Grace had related Sister Joseph's loyalty to the Mulhoney family and revealed that she intended to take that on now Sister Joseph no longer could. Margaret's strength had not returned after childbirth, and there seemed always to be one child or another sick or coming down with something. The family was in dire straits and depended on the kindness of others; Davey managed to find a bit of work on most days, and Rose—the oldest girl—earned money now and then helping the old man who lived upstairs. Sister Joseph had regularly brought them food and medicine, Grace told Wakefield, offering solace to a family far from the caring eyes of relatives and friends.

Wakefield had nodded and taken this mission to heart, as well; he'd told Grace that he would accompany her next time to the Mulhoneys and have a professional look at all of them, see what could be done about their physical health and that of the newborn, and that was how he found himself on a damp day in the dark rooms of a waterfront tenement building.

"The infant is big and healthy, Missus Mulhoney," Wakefield pronounced, handing the child back to her mother. "The others simply need building up with regular nourishment. Once the warmer weather dispels this dampness, they'll be right as rain."

Rose began to cough again, a rough, dry bark, and Wakefield reconsidered his remarks.

"Your oldest daughter, however, should be in bed. Can you manage without her for a week or so?"

"Aye," Margaret declared. "But she'll hear none of it. Won't lie down if others need tending."

"Mister Smith," Rose spluttered. "Who'll look after him? He's sick, as well! And Wills is sick!"

"The old man upstairs has an eejit son," Margaret explained. "They never do go out. Rose runs for their food and all." She turned to her daughter. "Davey'll do for Mister Smith and Wills, Rose; you can't fret yourself over them."

"I'll look in on him, as well, Rose," Grace reassured the girl. "Do as the doctor says and get into bed with your sisters. Look—I've brought a lovely warm blanket for you to snuggle under, and Mary Kate's sent storybooks."

Rose eyed the books suspiciously, and Grace wondered whether the girl could read, having already discovered that Margaret Mulhoney could not; Margaret had confided that her late husband had most of his letters and could figure out most any word, but she herself had never learned, too busy caring for elderly parents, then too busy caring for a husband and babies.

"I'll read to you a bit before I go, shall I?" Grace bribed. "But only once you're abed."

Rose got up slowly and went behind the curtain partition to change out of her dress and into her nightgown, coughing all the while. Grace checked to see whether the kettle was still hot, and set about making a tea of dried mullein leaves to which she added honey, a little whiskey, and the juice of a ripe lemon—ingredients she'd brought with her.

"While you do that, Missus Donnelly, I think I'll go up and have a look at this Mister Smith," Wakefield announced. "Plenty of sickness going around this spring, and we wouldn't want an epidemic of sorts on our hands. Better see what he's got up there."

"Aye, that's fine, then." Grace stirred her restorative brew, the smell of warm lemon filling the air with a clean scent. "I'll be ready to go when you're done."

Wakefield nodded, closed his kit bag, and went to the door. "Which room, Rose?"

"Two flights up and all the way to the back. On this side." Rose pointed to the right, coughing.

Wakefield left and Grace dispensed hot tea, checked to make sure bedcovers were pulled up over vulnerable chests, put fresh bread and butter in the food safe and the rich chicken soup with potatoes on the little coal burner. After that, she changed the baby's diaper, giving Margaret a chance to wash her face and put on a clean apron, then tidied the room so that it looked less cramped and more homey. By the time she finished packing up her own basket, Wakefield had returned, his face tight with irritation.

"Well, he let me in, but not for long. They've got the same chest congestion. Missus Mulhoney, perhaps you could send Davey up with some of this hot drink Missus Donnelly has prepared. It would ease their discomfort."

"Yes, Doctor," Margaret said right away. "We'll do it, and thank you for looking in on us. It's eased my mind considerable to know they'll all get better soon."

"I'll stop in again the end of the week, Missus Mulhoney, but if you need anything before that time just send word to the hospital."

Grace said her good-byes then, too, picked up her basket, and followed the doctor out the door. The fresh air invigorated them both after the stuffiness of the damp rooms, and Grace took a deep breath as they turned away from the harbor and headed up toward the plaza.

" 'Twas good of you to see to them like that. And the old fellow up-stairs, as well."

"Not so old as you might think," Wakefield disclosed. "He could find work and make a life for himself still, if not for the son."

"Bad off, then, is he?"

Wakefield nodded. "Babbles, drools, shakes, spasms—the whole thing. Contracted brain fever five years ago and steadily declined after that, according to the father. Came out west for the drier climate," he added, piteously. "How do they get their living, do you know?"

"Rose says a woman comes every now and again, usually in the early morning, quick like. She asked Mister Smith once, and he said 'twas a charity worker. Sister Joseph thought it must be the mother of the boy or perhaps his sister, hired out or getting along in other ways."

"It's his wife," Wakefield realized. "When he opened the door, I told him I was from the clinic, and he asked if his wife sent me. I said no, I was Doctor Wakefield come about the child." The doctor stopped walking. "He turned very pale and asked if something had happened to his wife, that she hadn't got the child herself. I explained that I didn't actually know Missus Smith, that I'd been downstairs seeing to the Mulhoneys and had learned that Mister Smith and his son were also unwell."

"He must've thought his wife sent you to look at the boy, and when he saw she didn't, was confused. Living alone like he does, with no one but the boy for company, he might be a bit addlepated."

"But why would he think something had happened to his wife?" Wakefield puzzled. "Well, anyway, he did allow me to examine the boy—a young man, by the way, twenty years, I'd say, very frail but not terribly ill, though coughing like Rose." He paused. "When I told him the boy might live another two or even three years, and that he should consider an asylum, he told me to get out! He actually put his hands on me and pushed me toward the door!" Wakefield looked to Grace for confirmation that this was the action of an unbalanced man.

"Well, he doesn't know you, Doctor, and perhaps he was afraid you had some sort of power to take the boy," Grace suggested.

"I would never do that. It's a shame, though, and I pity him, sacrificing his life for someone who doesn't even know anymore the name of the person caring for him."

"Save your pity, Doctor," Grace chided, though not unkindly. "If Mister Smith is the kind of man I think he is, he'd want none of it. He doesn't care whether or not his son knows him any longer—*he* knows his son, loves his son, and is protecting the boy from a world that would have him die among strangers instead of in the arms of his father. To Mister Smith, 'tis no sacrifice to tend his child. 'Tis the greatest gift he can make. Do you think it a sacrifice to care for your sister, then?"

Wakefield shaded his eyes against the glare of the sun off the water. "I am, perhaps, not quite the man Mister Smith must be," he admitted quietly. "I have given up nothing for my sister. Rather, I have gained through her misfortune."

"But you've never married, have you, Doctor? Nor even courted a woman," Grace pointed out. "You don't even entertain that much, and rarely venture out in mixed society. When you do, you suffer the slights of those who would whisper about your sister in their parlors . . ."

"I cannot, in all honesty, call that sacrifice," Wakefield confessed, looking down at her. "Abigail's affliction has meant that I am free to immerse myself in my profession, to pursue my studies day and night, free to circulate only among those of my choosing, free from the social obligations that, frankly, bore me to death."

"Will you never marry? Never make your own home with a wife and children?"

Wakefield let his eyes linger on the lovely hair that blew around her face, the high color in her cheeks, the expression of lively intelligence he found so inviting.

"I like the idea of marriage," he allowed. "But I'm a dull scholar whose passion is rarely aroused by anything other than medical science. And I'm too impatient for polite chitchat. Cut to the heart of the matter—that's my motto. Doesn't go over too well with the debutantes." The doctor started walking again and Grace fell into step beside him. "I would need to find a woman like you, Missus Donnelly, someone to challenge me and keep me sharp, though perhaps just a bit more pliant and adoring," he teased. "Speaking of the latter, how is your accommodating Captain Reinders?"

Grace elbowed him none too easily, and he laughed in surprise.

"That's a terrible thing to say," she scolded. "I'm grateful to Peter for giving us enough time to settle in here."

"Wedding still on for May?"

"Aye." Grace heard the reluctance in her own voice and hoped the doctor hadn't noticed. "He wants the children and me to sail up the coast with him, have a look at this New Whatcom."

"I hear it's beautiful country up there. Unlike anywhere else."

"Liam says 'tis like Ireland in many ways, though he'll not make a home with us there. He likes the city, does our boy."

"You like the city, too," Wakefield mentioned carefully.

Grace bit her lip. "Nothing's been decided yet. Peter's drawing up house plans and I'll go to see the land, but I've not agreed to moving us yet."

"He hopes you will, though."

"Aye. He loves it there. Talks about it all the time." Grace sighed, then caught herself. "But if the children are taken with it, and everyone wants to live there, well, then . . ."

"Then you will make the sacrifice for the people you love."

Grace said nothing, just kept walking with her head down.

"You are very much like Sister Joseph," Wakefield realized. "What is it with you Irish and your eternally bleeding hearts—mother's milk and ancient stories from the cradle on, is that it?"

"Aye." Grace laughed, thinking of her gran. "I could loan you the book we use, if you like."

Wakefield tossed his head back and laughed with her. "I suspect I have that very same book myself, though it is perhaps less worn than your copy." He drew up again, abruptly. "That reminds me—have you loaned out any crockery to the Mulhoneys?"

Grace thought. "Jam jars and pots for soup, but I always fetch them home again when next we go." She held up her basket as proof. "Why are you asking?"

Wakefield scratched his head. "I could've sworn the crockery on Mister Smith's table was ours. A few other things in the room looked familiar, too, so I thought perhaps you'd loaned them to the Mulhoneys, who'd passed them on upstairs."

"I might've misplaced a piece or two," Grace supposed, "though I'm careful with it, as it belongs to you. I'm sorry, if I did. I'll see to its return right away."

"No, no. I don't really care. Just leave it." Wakefield checked his watch. "I'd better hurry if I'm to make the most of this day, and I'm sure they'll be waiting for their lunch up at the house. Shall I hail a cab bie for you?"

"Thank you, sir, no. The walk'll do me good, and I'm stopping for vegetables on my way back up. See you tonight, then."

The doctor tipped his hat and bowed graciously, which always made Grace smile, and then he crossed the street at an angle, causing a delivery wagon to pull up and the driver to shake his fist. Grace laughed and continued on up the hill, stopping to buy produce on the way. When at last she came in the back door to the kitchen, Mister Hewitt and his pupils, having finished their lessons for the morning, were already gathered around the table—Mary Kate and Jack with drawing pencils and paper, their teacher with one of his English novels. Enid stood by the stove, stirring the beans and bacon, head down over the pot, seemingly absorbed in her work.

"Mam!" The children greeted her enthusiastically, and Mister Hewitt waggled his fingers at her over the top of his book.

Grace set her basket on the floor by the washtub, then hung up her coat and hat and tied on a fresh apron. After patting her windswept hair into place, she went to the stove to relieve Enid and there noticed the girl's red-rimmed eyes and pink nose.

"Is something the matter, then, Enid? Have you been crying?"

Embarrassed, Enid refused to look up. "No," she whispered, but a tear slipped down to the end of her nose and hung there for a moment before she wiped it away.

"You can tell me." Grace kept her voice low as she took over the cooking. "I'll not say a word."

Enid sniffed and checked over her shoulder before turning to Grace.

"I'm to be married!" The girl's eyes were wide with anxiety. "Mother has arranged it. I'm promised to Mister Pennywhistle, who owns the pipe and tobacco shop on the square."

Grace stopped stirring. "Do you know him, Enid? Do you want to be married?"

Enid shook her head, tears overflowing. "We went into his shop once. I thought it was to buy a pipe for my father . . . from father's old friend, but it was really for Mister Pennywhistle to have a look at me.

He liked me, Mother says." She wiped her eyes with the hem of her apron. "He wanted to marry me right away, but Mother made him wait until he'd agreed to settle a sum on me. It's for the money," she conceded bitterly. "Mother only wants his money."

"You're of age, Enid." Grace put her hand on the girl's shoulder. "You don't have to marry anyone not of your own choosing. No one can force you into it. You must tell your mother that."

"Tell me what?" Hopkins had slid silently into the room, as was her habit. "Enid? Do you have something to say to me?"

Enid turned and faced her mother with as much courage as Grace had ever seen the girl muster, though her cheeks were pale and her lips trembled.

"I'm not going to marry Mister Pennywhistle," Enid announced. "I don't love him, Mother. I don't even like him very much."

Hopkins' face turned deep red and her hands balled into white-knuckled fists. She took a step closer to her daughter, menacing eyes locked onto Enid's trepid ones.

"Don't be stupid, girl," Hopkins hissed. "You'll not see another chance like this, ever. More women coming here every day now, and soon men like Pennywhistle won't be giving serving girls like you a second look."

"I don't care." Enid held her ground, though she looked as if she might faint dead away. "I don't want to marry him. He's old."

"He's rich!" Hopkins exploded and then worked to calm herself. "You know why you have to do this, Enid," she coaxed quietly. "We all have to make sacrifices. Better to have it over and done with. He'll take good care of you, girl; he'll take good care of all of us. You know what I mean, Enid. You know we're all depending upon you."

"No!" Enid spun on her heel and dashed through the back kitchen door, out into the yard, running blindly down the path toward the pond.

Hopkins turned her fury on Grace. "You did this. You've poisoned that girl against her own mother, and I'm only looking out for her best interests. I can't stay here forever, you know!" the housekeeper ranted. "She'll be on her own! Could've been rich—Enid—and cared for! But you've ruined that now. You've ruined any chance she had for a happy life. You're the devil's own, you are."

"Here now!" Mister Hewitt came to his senses, slammed down his book, and stood up, his finger leveled at the vicious housekeeper. "You're out of line, Hopkins. Way out of line. Missus Donnelly has done you no wrong here."

Hopkins turned her menace on the tutor. "You don't fool me, schoolteacher," she growled. "You're as corrupt as the rest of this house. Don't think I haven't seen you staring up at Miss Wakefield's window while she dresses, or creeping round the stair, mooning outside her door."

Hewitt blushed red to the roots of his dark hair but came around the table with righteous indignation.

"How dare you, madam? I have spoken to Miss Wakefield on the rare occasion she has appeared, once or twice at her open window, where anyone was free to see us. I have also brought some books to her room, with the intention of easing her troubled spirit."

"That's not all you were hoping to ease," Hopkins accused meanly. "I've seen your notes to her."

Hewitt's mouth fell open, aghast. "Poetry, madam. I copied poetry out for her enjoyment."

"It's not natural, that kind of attraction for a sick woman. You're an unnatural man who preys on the weak and vulnerable."

"I refuse to allow my reputation or that of Miss Wakefield to be maligned," Hewitt asserted between clenched teeth. "We will set all this before Doctor Wakefield as soon as he returns."

"You'll find yourself turned out and no character reference given," Hopkins asserted. "You'll be ruined."

"No!" Mary Kate and Jack found their voices.

"Or maybe not." Hopkins reconsidered, in a tone of voice that was unsettling for its eerie patience. "As long as his sister is kept quiet and out of his way, the doctor doesn't much care what she's about. I have proof of that." She grimaced, and everyone in the room shivered to see it. "The only reason you're here, Mister Hewitt, is to keep those Irish brats out of the way while he carries on with their mother. Enjoy yourself this morning, did you, Missus Donnelly? Earn a little pocket money for your wedding?"

"That's quite enough!" Hewitt moved forward, but it was Grace who grabbed Hopkins by the shoulders, turned the woman around, and slapped her face as hard as she could, knocking the stunned house-keeper to the ground.

"Don't you ever insult me or my children again," Grace warned fiercely. "Get up. Get up now, and get out."

"Do as she says." George Litton stepped into the room.

Hopkins staggered to her feet, hand pressed against the red mark across her cheek. "I'll get out," she said. "All the way out. And when that sorry wretch upstairs takes her own life, you'll have to answer to the doctor about why she did it."

Hewitt paled.

"She'll not do anything of the kind," Grace retorted. "She'll be well once you're gone."

"That's what you think." Hopkins smirked. "As for Enid—I wash my hands of that girl. She's your problem now, groundskeeper. Do what you will with her."

Confusion flitted across Litton's face, but then he nodded soberly. "So be it."

"So be it," Hopkins repeated, backing out of the room as if they might attack her otherwise. At the door, she turned and bolted, and they could hear the sound of her shoes on the stair.

The children jumped up from the table and rushed to their mother, locking their arms around her waist.

" 'Tis over now." Grace patted them reassuringly. "Sorry for all that, but don't be troubled. She's a wicked woman and we're well rid of her."

"What about Miss Wakefield?" Mary Kate asked quietly.

Grace bit her lip. "I'd best see to her until Hopkins has left the house. Don't want her to be more upset than need be. Mister Hewitt"—she turned to him—"will you take the children out into the yard for a bit? And will you find Enid, Mister Litton, and tell her that her mother's leaving the place?"

The men nodded in unison and left with the children. Grace took the boiling soup off the stove, set it to one side, and drew a deep breath to collect herself before going up to Abigail's room. After pushing her hair back into place and smoothing her apron, Grace climbed the stairs, then went down the hall; she was about to go in when Hopkins appeared.

"I'll see her first," the housekeeper announced.

"No." Grace kept her hand firmly on the door latch. "You're not to see her anymore. I'll tell her you've gone."

Hopkins considered this, then smiled coolly. "Give her this message, then, as she'll be asking you for it—tell her what's done is done and can't be undone. Eden is lost forever."

"What in Heaven's name do you mean by that?" Grace left the door and moved toward Hopkins.

"Just tell her," the housekeeper laughed, backing down the hall. "Tell her and see what happens." And then she turned and disappeared down the servants' stair.

Good riddance, Grace thought with a sigh of relief, though she entered Abigail's room with trepidation, Hopkins' cryptic message echoing in her ears. She was relieved to see that Abigail still slept, the heavy curtains having muffled all sounds of the world beyond her four walls. Grace decided not to awaken her, to wait until Doctor Wakefield had returned, before telling her that Hopkins was no longer in the house. Although she felt in her very soul that Abigail would begin to revive once the stifling presence of the housekeeper faded, Grace worried that the immediate effect would be far more dramatic. Certainly, she was not about to pass on Hopkins' parting message—"What's done is done and can't be undone," and something about the Garden of Eden being lost; it was wicked, Grace was sure, and meant to push an already troubled woman over the edge, meant to ensure the suicide Hopkins had warned them would happen. Enid would sleep in this room tonight, Grace decided, or Grace herself if Enid was too distraught. No matter what, they would not leave Abigail unattended once she knew that Agnes Hopkins was gone away. Grace was now responsible for the fragile soul that slept upon that bed, a woman unaware that the course of her life had suddenly fallen into very different hands.

Abigail listened for a moment to the silence of the house, the ticking of the clock, the creak of timber as the wind picked up, a cough from somewhere beyond the kitchen. The kitchen, she remembered; that was where the cook lived, the Irishwoman, Missus Donnelly. She paused, her hand on the front latch. It had been Missus Donnelly who drove Hopkins away; she'd admitted as much when she'd spoken to Abigail up in the room! But Abigail didn't care about that—she only cared that Hopkins had left no message, none at all. She'd felt desperate about that, and her brother had come to try to calm her and she'd almost told him everything, confessed everything, but then it had occurred to her—Hopkins left no note because she wanted Abigail to come herself! After that realization, Abigail had only wanted everyone to leave her alone so she could listen to God's voice and figure out what to do. The house was quiet. Upstairs, Enid lay on the floor, sound asleep; Abigail had only to step over her to leave the room.

It was chilly in the damp early morning, and a mist hung over the harbor. Abigail crept carefully down the drive, keeping to the grass on one side so that her footsteps would be muffled. The skyline of the city had changed since she'd taken to her bed, Abigail realized; fires and new development had altered the look of the town, the layout of the streets—how would she find the right room? But then she calmed herself. She would go down to the water. She would find the right building among those on the waterfront, and then she would climb the right stairwell, and then she would find the right room; she would open the right door and Hopkins would be waiting. Hopkins and the child. Abigail's child, Eden. Eden would be waiting for her, and Abigail—at last—would hold the little girl in her arms.

Heart now bursting with euphoria, Abigail picked up her skirts and began to run.

Twenty-eight

The entire house was in an uproar after Enid announced that Abigail was not in her room. Wakefield sat stunned for fully five minutes before asking Enid if she'd any idea where her mother might've gone.

"She may know something about Abigail." The doctor's face was pale with anxiety.

Enid stood quietly, wringing her hands in front of her apron. "To my father," she said at last.

Grace looked at her, startled. "Did you not tell me you had no father, that he'd died?"

Enid nodded miserably. "Mother insisted we keep it a secret. He lives down on the waterfront. With my brother."

"You've a brother, as well?"

"William. He's afflicted." Enid hesitated before going on. "He was always sickly, but then it got worse. Mother said no decent man would have me with a brother like that, and no one would hire us to live in if they knew she was married." Her mouth trembled again. "She wanted Wills put away, but Father wouldn't do it, so she said she'd give them money for food and rent if they kept to themselves. They call themselves 'Smith.' "

Grace and Wakefield locked eyes; there were hundreds of Smiths in the city, but how many were old men caring for afflicted sons?

"I think I've met them," Wakefield told her. "They've been sick lately, haven't they?"

Enid's eyes filled with fresh tears. "Dad's afraid of dying first and then who'll look after Wills? Mother promised him she'd hire a nurse for Wills if I married Mister Pennywhistle." Her face crumpled and she buried it in her hands. "But I couldn't do it! She has Miss Wakefield's money! She doesn't need any more!"

"Money from my sister?" Wakefield stood now, agitated. "I pay the household wages. Why would Abigail give your mother money?"

Enid took a deep breath and opened her mouth, but nothing came out.

Grace sat down beside her and took her hand. "You must tell us, now, Enid," she urged gently. "No one's blaming you. You'll not be in any kind of trouble, aye, Doctor?"

"No trouble," Wakefield agreed at once. "Why did my sister give your mother money, Enid? Was she being blackmailed?"

Enid opened her mouth again, then turned away from him and looked into Grace's eyes, her own filled with sadness and remorse.

"Miss Wakefield had a child," Enid confided fearfully, and Grace recalled the marks along Abigail's belly. "A girl. I never saw it myself, but mother said it was a black baby and had to be hidden."

"No." Wakefield shook his head. "No, that's not right. The baby died at birth."

"She kept it a secret, sir." Enid was able to face him now that the hard truth was out. "She was afraid you'd sell the child away if you knew. Your own grandmother helped her; she sent the baby out with a servant when it was old enough."

"No! It can't be true," Wakefield insisted. "She would never have kept that child, born out of what it was."

"It was born out of love, sir. Mother said the man was a Negro, and when they were found out, he was accused of attacking her. Miss Wakefield was afraid and didn't defend him. And then they hung the man, sir! Before her very eyes!"

Wakefield sat down abruptly.

"Dear God in Heaven." Grace stared at him. "Is she right?"

The doctor's eyes were glazed. "Thomas Eden. We knew him in our childhood. He was my . . . friend."

"Were you there, Doctor?" Grace asked carefully. "Were you part of the lynching?"

"Good Lord, no!" Wakefield appealed to them both. "It all happened before I got there. I never thought for one minute that the story was other than what I'd been told, that they were . . . that she . . ." He reached for the decanter beside him and, with trembling hands, poured a splash into the glass, then downed it in one swallow. "She could have trusted me to help her. She should've known I would never, ever sell her child. Where are they, Enid? Do you know?"

"No, sir. They used to live in a building near to my father, but then the cholera come and the servant woman died. Miss Wakefield didn't know what to do. She was so sick, you know—so Mother found a family outside of town who agreed to board the child, though the price was high."

Wakefield sat, dazed, glass dangling in his hand.

"I'm sorry. I'm sorry, sir. Please forgive me," Enid begged. "I thought Mother was doing right by Miss Wakefield, that we were right to help her keep the secret. But then—"

"Then your mother realized she had her own private gold mine at her disposal," Grace interjected.

Enid nodded forlornly. "Miss Wakefield has her own money. After her grandmother died?" She looked to the doctor for confirmation.

"A trust," Wakefield acknowledged quietly. "Paid directly into her account. I knew your mother drew out for her occasionally, but I assumed it was for women's incidentals, clothing, things she didn't want to bother me with."

"It was for the child's board, but Mother kept raising the price and putting the difference in her own pocket, saying it was her due for all the trouble. She wants to go back to England, you see. Buy a lodging house in Cornwall and live with her sister." Enid looked down, her voice now low with shame. "Miss Wakefield gave my mother everything she asked for. She believed her soul was corrupt, you see, that her lust for pleasure—begging your pardon, sir—had tempted an innocent man and caused his death, and had brought a bastard child into the world. *My* mother let her believe it, told her that if she deprived herself in this life, if she suffered enough, then God would finally forgive her and have mercy on her child."

"Does Abigail know where the child is?" Grace asked.

"I don't think so. She'd ask for it sometimes, cry even, but Mother never gave in. She said she had to be strong for Miss Wakefield because

Miss Wakefield was so very weak, that she was saving the woman from the torments of Hell."

"By making her live out a hell on earth," Grace concluded grimly. "Broken in body as well as spirit. So you think Abigail's gone after your mother now for fear of losing the child forever?"

It was all too much for Enid; she could hardly bear her own culpability in the life she'd just described. The color drained from her face, her eyes rolled back in her head, and she began to slide sideways off the divan. Grace caught her just in time.

"Enid! C'mon, Enid." Grace shook her gently. " 'Tis a shock to us all. But you can help us now. Enid?"

"Enid." Litton's voice came quietly out of the corner where he'd been standing, listening to the whole story, awaiting orders.

The girl's eyelids fluttered, then opened; she turned her head and saw George standing there, saw the compassion in his eyes. He crossed the room, knelt beside her, and took her other hand.

"Time to be strong now, Enid. I'll take you to your dad, and we'll do what we can, eh?"

Enid nodded, trusting him, then allowed him to help her to her feet and escort her to the door.

"Doctor?" Litton stopped. "We'll need you, sir."

"Yes, yes, of course." Wakefield moved quickly, pausing in the hall for his medical bag. He turned, and Grace was right behind him. "You'll stay here, Missus Donnelly? In case she returns on her own?"

"Aye." Grace opened the door for him and handed him an extra coat. "And, sir"— she put a hand on his arm—"if you find her, remember she's been living in a place 'tis dark and cruel. Be gentle with her. We'll sort it all out once she's safely home."

The muscle in Wakefield's jaw jumped as he fought the emotion that threatened to overwhelm him. He nodded tightly, and then he pulled her to him, hugging her fiercely before letting her go.

"Thank you," he whispered, and then he climbed into the carriage, took the reins from George, and urged the horses to make good speed.

Twenty-nine

"She's not here," Mister Hopkins told his daughter at the door, then eyed Wakefield and Litton warily. "You'd better come in. Don't talk loud, now. Wills is having a bad time of it."

The young man lay awkwardly on his cot, moaning, banging his head on his pillow, eyes rolling in his head.

"There, there, son." Harry comforted him, laying a hand on the boy's shoulder. "No more trouble now. Just lie still. Enid is here. Do you see it's Enid?"

The shaking diminished as the young man arched his head back to see his sister. Enid sat down beside him on the cot, rubbing his back until he calmed himself.

"It's all right, Wills," she soothed. "These are my friends. No trouble here."

"You see the way of it," Harry said bluntly, motioning to the chairs at the table. "Please sit down."

Wakefield crossed the room in two long strides and pulled out a chair. "We've met before," he began.

"I know who you are." Harry crossed his arms over his chest.

"And this is Mister Litton, my driver. We're looking for my sister. I believe your wife might know where she is."

"I know nothing of your sister. Agnes came yesterday, saying she'd quit the place for England. Said Enid was set to marry and staying. William and I could stay or go." Harry glanced at his son. "He'd never survive it, she knows that. Left us a bit of money and said she'd write when she got there." He turned to Wakefield. "Are you thinking she took your sister with her?"

"No." Wakefield was positive about that. "It wouldn't serve your wife at all. No, I think Abigail's wandering around trying to find her. Trying to find the child," he added pointedly.

Harry looked at his daughter. "You told him, then."

"It wasn't as Mother said, Dad. He'd never sell the child or put Miss Abigail away. He only wants to help her. But now she's gone missing and only Mother knows where the child is."

Harry crossed the room to the rickety desk, pulled open the drawer, and withdrew a piece of paper. "I thought Agnes was doing right by your sister, seeing as how she couldn't keep the child, being a white woman and unmarried. And so fearful of you." He handed the paper to Wakefield. "The girl lives with a Mexican family on a small ranchero. Sweet child. Stayed here while Agnes arranged it, and I was sorry her mother couldn't know her."

Wakefield stared at the name on the paper. "Eden Wakefield?"

The old man nodded.

"Would Abigail know where this ranchero is?"

"I don't think so," Enid answered. "She knew the first place, of course, but Mother said she wouldn't be tempted to go and see the child if she didn't know where the little girl lived."

"You said she knew the first place," Litton repeated in his low, hesitant voice. "Where was that?"

"Not far from here. Quarter mile south. But it's all been rebuilt since the fires. She wouldn't know it now."

"She's not living in 'now.'" Recalling Grace's words, Wakefield jumped up and rushed to the door. "Mister Hopkins—thank you for this." He held up the piece of paper, then looked at Enid and George. "Let's go."

They raced down the stairs to where the Mulhoney boy stood, holding the harness of their carriage.

"Are you looking for the lady?" Davey queried. "The one as visits Mister Smith? Because I followed her this time and I know where she went!"

Wakefield halted in his tracks, unsure. "Where?"

"To Chinatown, to a shop there. And then to the ticket agent. She

made them cry." The boy jerked a thumb toward the upper story. "I don't like her."

"I want to hear more." Wakefield flipped the boy a silver coin. "We'll be back."

"Yes, sir. I'll wait here, sir!"

Davey watched as the doctor climbed into the carriage and it took off down the narrow, rutted street. *She's in for it now,* he thought to himself and was glad—whoever she was, she'd only made life miserable for those two lonely souls upstairs.

Grace paced the house from kitchen to dining room to parlor to library and back again, looking out every window she passed. Liam had come to the house, expecting a hot meal and a good visit, and instead she'd pressed the children upon him and asked him to take them back to town, to Peter's house for the night. Liam hadn't minded a bit, and Mary Kate had been delighted; only Jack had scuffed his feet, wondering aloud who would feed his puppy. Grace had reassured him and sent along fresh bread and jam for their dinner.

The afternoon was passing now, and the low clouds had trapped the air, making even the outdoors feel muggy and close. Grace had done everything she possibly could in readiness of what she fervently prayed would be Abigail's return. Windows had been opened to catch any breeze that might drift through and, in Abigail's room, the bedding had been changed and turned down; fresh flowers sat in a vase near the bed, and the room was cleared of clutter and debris. The sheets had been marred with hundreds of dots and smears that looked like blood, and this concerned Grace, as it had nothing to do with a woman's monthly flow. She'd found further evidence of outrage in the room—the scissors Abigail had used to chop off her hair hung from a ribbon above her dressing table, still marred with dried blood and hair from where she'd nicked her scalp; the Bible beside her bed was dog-eared, but only in the Old Testament, where entire passages had been underlined with a heavy hand; in the wardrobe, Abigail's finest dresses had been slashed and her silk slippers ravaged; there was no jewelry in any of her cases, only an old-fashioned brooch and a thin gold chain with a simple cross hidden in the very back corner beneath the paper that lined the drawer. When unstopped, perfume bottles revealed the nasty stink of rancid

fish oil; grime lay across her dressing table, its mirror draped with an old piece of stained muslin. Most of this was not obvious to the casual observer, and that which was would not have seemed extraordinary, but as Grace stood still in the middle of the room and considered the consequence of sleeping and waking within these four walls day after day after day, she felt the heaviness of despair settle upon her shoulders, the sharpness of torment pierce her heart, and the prickle of madness behind her eyes. She could not get out fast enough.

Later, as she began to light the lamps, Grace heard the carriage come up the drive. She held open the back door for Doctor Wakefield, who was carrying his sister in his arms.

"Put her in the middle bedroom," Grace directed. "The guest room. Not her own."

Wakefield grunted and passed through the kitchen, then out into the hall and up the stairs. Enid and George stood silently in the doorway.

"I'll go with him," Grace offered. "You two look done in. There's food on the table, and cider besides."

She left them and took the stairs two at a time, reaching the middle bedroom just as Wakefield was laying Abigail on the bed.

"Here, sir," Grace said quietly as he collapsed in the chair. "I'll take care of her now. You go down and eat something."

"She'd never have lasted another night." Wakefield's voice was hoarse with exhaustion. "She's cut herself, you see. With this." He pulled a bloody letter opener out of his pocket and set it on the bedside table.

Grace's heart began to pound as she looked from the instrument to Abigail, saw the bandages on the woman's wrists, noted her shallow breathing, the pallor of her skin. "Where was she?"

"In an old building down on the waterfront. Curled up beneath a stairwell." Wakefield rubbed a hand wearily over his face. "It's all true, Missus Donnelly. Thomas, the child, blackmail—all of it true, and all of it happening right beneath my nose. This is all my fault. I'm a damned fool."

Grace thought about his room at the opposite end of the hall, his study below Abigail's room, his infrequent visits to his sister.

"Aye." She pulled a blanket up over Abigail's bruised bare feet, over her skinned knees and damaged wrists, the battered elbows, over the

dirty nightgown that stuck to all the tiny places she'd cut into herself, trying in desperation to release her pain. "Aye," she repeated. "For all your study of pain, Doctor, you've been blind to your sister's."

Wakefield looked at her, stung, but then he nodded. "You're right. I am the worst kind of physician, willing to treat the symptoms while ignoring their cause."

Grace laid the back of her warm hand against Abigail's cool cheek. "What will you do now?"

"Bring the child to her mother," he decided.

Grace sat down on the edge of the bed and faced him. "Her mother is the one tucks her up each night and greets her each morning, the one feeds and dresses her, plays with her, rocks her to sleep." She stopped, remembering the first time she'd seen Jack, his arms firmly around Julia's neck, the realization that he was very much his own person in the world and not a possession to be returned. "To suddenly take her away from the only family she knows would be cruel. 'Twould be heartless, and you are not a heartless man."

Wakefield slumped. "What, then? Carry on as if nothing has happened?"

"As far as that little girl's concerned, nothing *has* happened. Her world is as 'tis always been." Grace leaned forward. "You can't fix this in a single day, Doctor. 'Twas years in the making, may be years in the undoing, but you must make sure the child's peace is not shattered."

"I don't know anything about these people. Maybe it's not the best place for her."

"Go out and meet them, then," Grace suggested. "Abigail needs time to heal before she sees her child, and besides, sir, you might not be able to . . ." She stopped and bit her lip.

"Say it, Missus Donnelly. You've been right so far. Whatever it is, I can take it. I might not be able to . . . what?"

"Well, sir—'twould be wrong of you to bring the child into this house feeling as you do toward black folk. You might try to hide it, but she'd feel it every day, a hundred different ways, and 'twould hurt her. You've no idea what that's like, but I do. And I've faced nothing compared to her lot."

Wakefield thought about it. "She may be light-skinned," he posed. "Light enough to pass."

Grace shook her head. "Do you hear yourself? Because if you're talking about purity, then we're none of us light enough to pass, though God accepts us anyway. If we were all blind in the world, would it matter to you then?"

Abigail moaned in her sleep and tried to turn on her side; Grace helped her, tenderly resettling the blanket around her shoulders.

"But we're not blind," Wakefield whispered when she was done. "The eyes of society are open wide, and judgment is everywhere."

"Start with yourself, Doctor. You're angry with an entire race over what you thought was the betrayal of one man. But Thomas Eden never betrayed your friendship. You're the one refused to see the truth; you're the one hardened your heart against a man you knew could never do such a terrible thing."

"It was over and done with by the time I got there. I just accepted what they said. And I hated him for what had happened to Abigail, though I never understood it, because . . ." Wakefield's voice broke now. "Because I'd known him all my life. Loved him like a brother. Why on earth didn't he tell me?" the doctor implored. "Why didn't he trust me?"

"Why didn't *she?*"

Wakefield shrugged in defeat.

"Because you're white. Because you're a man. Because you held all the power in their world, and because they couldn't trust how you'd use it."

"They could've trusted me. And as for being a white man . . . I can't change the fact of my birth."

"Nor can any of us," Grace agreed, "especially not that little girl. So why should she pay for the fact of it? Why should any of us pay for how we're born, when how we live our lives is what makes us who we are? Blood is blood, Doctor—you know better than most that you can't tell the color of a man's skin by looking at his blood."

"The little girl's a Wakefield, in other words."

"And an Eden," Grace added. "Her mother gave her that beautiful name to wear to remind her that, in God's eyes, she is perfect just as she is. And if you cannot see that, sir, then you don't deserve to be a part of her life."

Wakefield wiped his eyes on his sleeve. "I want to deserve it," he resolved quietly.

"Then have faith, Doctor. If not in yourself, then in the one who can work great change in any man who asks." Grace paused. "We emigrants know a bit about faith. We set out on little ships for a land we've never seen, all for the promise of freedom and a chance to change the course of our lives. But where is America's promise for those kept as slaves, sir? Can you tell me that?"

Wakefield shook his head. "In the future, perhaps."

"Eden Wakefield *is* the future." Grace put her hand on the doctor's arm. "And if you lift her up before you as the light she truly is, then others will see more clearly what has to be done, and we can all move out of the darkness together."

"You're asking more than you know," Wakefield told her, but Grace could hear in his voice his acceptance of what she'd said.

" 'To whom much is given,' " she quoted, then smiled encouragingly. "Your sister is home, sir, and in time she'll recover; her child is alive and safe, and soon you'll know her. Time is your friend, Doctor, and now"—Grace put out her hand—"it's time to eat something and then to bed if you're to be of any use tomorrow."

Wakefield took her hand and allowed himself to be hauled to his feet. "I don't know what to say to you, Missus Donnelly. Thanks are not enough. Not now. Not after all this."

"Thanks for what?" Grace asked. "For picking a fight with your housekeeper? 'Twas my pleasure, sir. Really and truly."

Wakefield laughed despite himself, then carefully opened the door to let himself out. "I'll let you hire the next one, believe you me."

"I think we can manage very well with just Enid for now, sir. I hope you'll not hold her mother against her."

"No, Missus Donnelly, I will not. After all, no one can change the fact of their birth, only the course of their lives." Wakefield's eyes fell upon his sleeping sister. "Can you stay with her for a few hours? I just need a short rest."

"I'll stay all night, if you like."

"Thank you, but I want to be here when she wakes up. I want her to know that she is no longer alone."

"That's good of you, Doctor."

"It's not nearly good enough," Wakefield allowed wearily. "But it's all I can do for now."

Thirty

Morgan and Quinn sat in the back of Ogue's with paper, pens, and maps laid out on the big square table. Outside the windows, rain poured down and the streets ran with mud and gunk, splashed up by horse-drawn carriages and carts.

"Wagoners cover twenty miles a day, if they're lucky." Morgan tapped his pen against the map. "But I'm thinking we might be able to start with one party, then ride ahead to the next and then the next, as we learn how many days ahead each party is. We could cover a lot more ground that way, make better time. Far better time than if we sailed down round the Horn. What do you think, eh, Quinn?"

Quinn had been staring out the window at the watercolored street, but now he turned and met the eyes of his friend.

"I think I can't do it. I can't go away off somewhere and start all over again. 'Tis best for me to stay where at least I know my way round."

"Right." Morgan put down his pen. "Better to stay in the place that nearly sent you to an early grave. Better to hang around here because Lord knows work's plentiful, the pay's generous, and every Irishman revered for his upstanding character." He leaned across the table, his eyes blazing. "C'mon, Quinn, what do you really think?"

Quinn tried to hold his own, but Morgan's intensity crumbled his resolve and finally, he looked down at the map.

"For the cost of outfitting two riders to go cross-country, you could buy yourself a ticket on a steamer and be there inside of two months," he said quietly. "Two months at most, Morgan, and you could be with your one. I think you're an eejit to be dragging me along."

"Quit playing the martyr, you daft pug," Morgan replied. "I'm not dragging you along. Do you think I have the faintest idea what's out there, what we're up against?" He shook his head. "I need you, Quinn. I'm not going without you, and that's final. So are you going to help me make a plan here, or do we need to step outside to settle this?"

The corner of Quinn's mouth began to twitch, and then he laughed. "Always the big talker."

"Ah, no, that was Sean." Morgan corrected him, and both men fell silent for a moment. "Do you think we'll ever see him again, then?"

"Why not?" Quinn shrugged his shoulders. "You're here, aren't you, so anything's possible."

Morgan's eyes cleared and he nodded. "Right. That's right, Quinn. Don't forget you said that. Anything's possible." He pushed the map closer to his friend. "Now there's two routes we could take—"

"You might want to put that thing away," Ogue interrupted, his big shadow falling over their table. "There's a man here, wants to see the both of you about going west. What do you say?"

Morgan looked up, puzzled. "He wants to ride out with us?"

"I don't know about that. Got his own ideas, this one." Ogue glanced at the well-dressed gentleman standing at the bar. "Bit of a dandy, but I can vouch for him. Will you hear him out?"

Morgan began to fold up the map. "Send him over."

"Smart boy." Ogue popped him on the shoulder, then motioned to the gentleman, who came at once. "Morgan McDonagh, Quinn Sheehan—this is Jay Livingston, friend to both Sean and Grace."

"Very pleased to meet you, Mister McDonagh." Livingston proffered his hand. "Very pleased, indeed. Quite astounding, actually. Your being alive, I mean."

Morgan shook the hand. "Sit down, Mister Livingston. You staying, Dugan?" he asked the barkeep.

"Customers. They never stop coming in. I'll check on you later, though, bring you another round." Ogue left an awkward silence in his wake, but it lasted only until Livingston turned his attention to Quinn.

"Pleased to meet you, as well, Mister Sheehan. Are you also a friend of the O'Malleys?"

"Aye," Quinn answered stiffly. "Grew up near to each other back home in Ireland."

"What can we do for you, Mister Livingston?" Morgan decided to get right to the point. "Ogue says you're interested in coming west with us?"

"No, actually, I have no desire to go west. Too soft for frontier travel, I'm afraid." Livingston smiled ruefully. "And I have a wife and young children."

Morgan regarded him, puzzled. "How can we help you, then?"

"I haven't made myself clear," Livingston apologized. "My interest is in helping *you,* Mister McDonagh. And you, Mister Sheehan," he added politely. "You see, I enjoyed a lively friendship with Sean O'Malley, a man I greatly admired. Through him, I met Gracelin, and my admiration for the family grew. In all these years, I've never met two more remarkable people—Sean, with his brilliant mind and quick wit, and Grace with her . . ." He paused, thinking, then shook his head. "Actually, I never know quite *how* to describe her—kind, fierce, compassionate, tenacious, stubborn . . ." He gave up and shrugged.

"Aye." Morgan grinned. "She's named for the great pirate queen of Connaught. Did you know that?"

"A pirate queen." Livingston considered this. "I believe that sums her up perfectly."

Morgan laughed. "Did you know her well, then?"

"To be honest? Not as well as I would've liked. But by the time I realized that, she was, of course, considering Captain Reinders' proposal of marriage, although I'll admit I was not gentleman enough to let it stand in the way of putting forth my own proposal. Which she turned down most charmingly, I might add. I hardly knew my heart had been broken until well after."

"But she didn't marry him. The captain, I mean." Quinn looked to Livingston for confirmation. "She's not married yet, we're told."

"*Yet* being the operative word," Livingston pointed out. "Which brings me back to my offer—gentlemen, what would you say to a loan in the amount of two steamer tickets to San Francisco, and a stake to set you up in business?" He held up his hand to stop their protests. "You can repay it at will, over time, with interest if your venture is profitable. Or don't pay it back at all. I just want you to have it."

Morgan glanced at Quinn, whose jaw had dropped, leaving him to gape in astonishment.

" 'Tis a sum of money, that," Morgan stared. "Why would you offer such a thing to two men you don't know?"

"Believe it or not, Mister McDonagh, though I offer it as a loan, I consider it repayment of a debt." Livingston pulled off his gloves and held up his left hand, upon which gleamed a solid gold band.

Quinn and Morgan looked at one another and then back at Livingston, who tapped his wedding ring against the edge of the table.

"Do you hear that, gentlemen?" he asked. "That's the sound of happiness, the kind of happiness I could so easily have missed had I not the privilege of Grace's friendship." Livingston turned his attention to Morgan now. "Your wife gave me a glimpse of the true bond that could exist between a man and a woman and, after she left for Boston, I was simply unable to continue finding satisfaction in casual pursuits."

"So you married," Morgan said.

Livingston nodded with pleasure. "I did. She was not the kind of woman I would have ever considered before—not coy and seductive, but quiet and keenly intelligent, passionate in her own way. The kind of woman who would have terrified me in the past." He grinned. "But, owing to the new standard set for me, I fell madly in love with her and managed to persuade her to marry me. And, gentlemen—I am a far better man with her than I could ever have been without."

"So that's the reason you're loaning us the money?" Morgan eyed him suspiciously. "Because you're happily married?"

"Yes," Livingston said simply. "And because the woman who enlightened me deserves to be happily married, as well. Loving my own wife as I do, I know now how much Grace suffered when she thought you were dead. Captain Reinders, though I hate to admit it, would be good to her, but it's you she longs for; I know it. When I heard that you were alive, I realized that here was a chance to do for her what she'd done for me." He paused. "So what do you say, McDonagh? Will you take the money?"

At that moment, Ogue arrived with a tray of glasses, which he dropped heavily in the middle of the table; without a word, he passed each man a glass, then took one himself, picking the tray back up and lodging it firmly under his arm.

"What are we drinking to, then, fellas?"

The three men sitting at the table looked round at one another, Livingston's eyebrows raised hopefully.

"Well, Dugan." Morgan put his hand around the glass and lifted it. "We're going west. Here's to a faster trip than we'd planned."

"Here's to happiness!" Livingston chimed in enthusiastically, lifting his own glass. "And to the love of a good woman, the warmth of hearth and home, the sheer delight of children, and to—"

"I swear to God you must be Irish," Ogue muttered, cutting him off; he then tipped his glass toward the others. "Here's to a safe journey, boys."

Quinn hesitated only a moment, and then he joined the others. "To a new life," he pronounced quietly. "God willing."

Ogue put a hand on the young man's shoulder. "He is, son. He is."

Thirty-one

With Doctor Wakefield's permission, Grace, Enid, and George began the first weeks of Abigail's recovery by stripping the bedding from her old room and carrying the mattress out to be burned. They'd added to the carefully tended fire her old ragged and sullied nightgowns, as well as the blood-mottled rugs and stained runners. Grace had taken down the heavy curtains and given them, as well the rest of Abigail's garments, to the laundress to clean. After George had moved the furniture, Grace and Enid had scoured the room from top to bottom with hot, soapy water; Grace felt strongly that Abigail was through with this room but, painted a cheerful color, with the new draperies and white furniture the doctor had ordered from the east, it could be a very nice room for a little girl, should she one day come to visit.

Wakefield remained at home most of the time, determined to be available every time Abigail awoke, and as their visits grew longer, Wakefield let her know that he was aware of the hold Hopkins had had upon her, that he knew the secret of the child. Abigail was frightened at first, then anxious and ashamed, but Wakefield made sure she understood that he harbored no harsh judgments against her, that he loved her and held himself responsible for the nightmare of these past years. He told her everything he'd found out about Eden Wakefield— where she was living and with whom—and he shared his plans for riding out with George to see the little girl and ensure that all was well with her. Whether or not the child should come to live with them was the question that hung in the balance; both of them were in agreement that each step had to be taken with careful consideration—the priority was the child. As the days passed, Wakefield took his every meal with his sister as a way of encouraging her to eat and regain her strength and, as this began to happen, she also began to trust him enough to reveal the truth about Thomas Eden.

The summer of her engagement to the judge—a man for whom she'd felt not the slightest affection, but of whom her father had greatly approved—she and Thomas had crossed paths, as she was often in town to make wedding arrangements, as well as alterations to the judge's mansion. She and Thomas had never intended more than the careful, respectful friendship that was tolerated between servants and masters, especially those who had known one another as children, but a chance private encounter had made them realize their deeper affection for one another; more encounters, now arranged, led them into love and the beginning of an affair that had almost immediately left Abigail pregnant. They'd considered the alternatives left to them— Thomas' mother was a quadroon, so perhaps the baby would inherit enough of the lighter skin to be passed off as a child of the judge, who was a dark-haired man; this had meant allowing the judge to make love to her, however—something Thomas could not tolerate, even though Abigail insisted she'd do anything to keep their child. But if it turned out the baby was not light-skinned, the outcome would have been terrible.

Desperate, they'd realized they had no choice but to run away together, to go as far north as they could. Thomas was a freeman, after all, and could travel at will, though he rarely left the city, not willing to risk kidnapping by slavers who would then sell him back into bondage in the Deep South, where his claims to freedom would fall upon deaf ears. Travel was risky, and they could not be seen together, so they'd made separate arrangements to go as far as New York City, there to meet up and travel on to Boston. They'd met one last time so that Thomas could give her the purchased ticket and go over the plan again. Anxious and afraid, they'd taken comfort in their passion for one another, and this was how her father and oldest brother had found them, having spied out Abigail's horse tied up behind an abandoned shack on the edge of the property.

The fury on her father's face as he'd absorbed the fact of her deceit and betrayal had terrified Abigail; sure that he had been about to kill them both, she'd begun to scream. Thomas had immediately adopted the role of contrite slave, scrambling away from her and declaring that he'd been overtaken by the devil, unable to control himself, begging forgiveness for his animal urges. Abigail's older brother had scooped her up and whisked her from the room, even as she'd fought him, and then she'd heard the sound of her father's pistol, which had caused her to faint.

She'd been returned to consciousness by her brother's hands as he shook her roughly and told her to get up, to wrap a shawl around her shoulders and come with him in the buggy. Stirred up, but silent, her brother had driven the horses down the dark lanes, turned off into the trees, and pulled up finally in front of a group of men who'd held torches, who'd greeted her with a great show of respect, who'd then held those torches up to illuminate for her the face of the man they'd been about to hang. Abigail had hardly recognized Thomas from the beating they'd administered, and again she'd cried out. The men had received her cries as a sign of her gentility, and this had only increased their rage toward the young man. In the light, she'd been able to see his eyes, to see his love for her, and had been about to scream the truth when he'd shaken his head imperceptibly. And then she'd understood—there was no truth that could save his life. All that was left was to save the life of his child. The end of the rope had been attached to a wagon; the men had applied their whips to the back of the horse, and it had jolted forward, hauling Thomas off the ground and into the air, where his feet had kicked and spasmed and his body had jerked for what seemed like an eternity, and then he was still but for the slow swaying of the rope, the creak of hemp against tree bark.

Abigail sat still for some time after telling her brother this story, and he'd sat in silence beside her, holding her hand, both of them mourning the death of a man they'd loved. Their grandmother had known everything, Abigail confessed, had made all the arrangements to send the baby out with a slavewoman who would be free once she arrived in San Francisco. Abigail had visited them several times, had paid the woman well, and was grateful for the care she'd agreed to give the baby until Abigail could figure out what to do from there. She had thought to find herself a husband of darker coloring and then to adopt the baby, perhaps in the guise of taking on the child of a faithful former servant.

It had seemed possible. But she hadn't counted upon a San Francisco that was barely more than shacks and shanties, hadn't counted upon the lack of social events that made meeting the hundreds of available men nearly impossible, hadn't counted upon cholera.

Hopkins was with her by then, and when Abigail fell sick and could not see to the child, whose caretaker had died, she was so very grateful for the help, so deeply indebted to the woman for finding a temporary home for her child, for keeping her secret. As for how easily she was manipulated and how quickly she descended into a kind of madness, Abigail could feel only shame and bitter remorse. She should never have entered into an affair with Thomas, knowing that he would be the one to pay; she should have stayed strong and coherent when they were found out, and stood her ground until he made his escape; she should have demanded that they cut him loose that night, shot her father before she saw her lover hanged; she should have told Rowen everything when they got to San Francisco instead of continuing the lies and deceit. It had been too easy for Hopkins to prey on her terrible guilt, and the price Abigail had paid for her love was high, though not nearly as high as that paid by poor Thomas.

With Abigail's permission, Wakefield had shared this story with Grace, whose compassion for the woman grew. She and Abigail began a tentative friendship, and Grace shared with her the conviction that God's forgiveness was free for the asking, that it did not have to be earned, *could* not be earned, which made it all the more precious. She told Abigail of the struggles in her own life—the loss of her entire family, including her firstborn son and the husband she loved more than life itself—and she encouraged Abigail to find the strength to ask for forgiveness, and then to have faith in that forgiveness for the sake of the young daughter who would ask so many hard questions as she got older. Grace promised that as Abigail's faith grew, so too would come the strength to forgive those who had trespassed against her, and then she would know peace at last.

In the days that followed, a kind of harmony fell over the house. Enid stepped up to the role of head housekeeper with a competence that even Grace had not expected, further demonstrated in the gentle patience she showed the Peruvian girl they'd hired to train as maidservant. Grace was not the only one to notice Enid's blossoming independence and maturity; Mister Litton was more forthcoming at the dinner table now, and much to the shock of them all—had even managed one night to tell a joke! Enid's shyness had all but disappeared, and she and George spent a part of each temperate evening out in the garden or in the stable, where she kept him company as he put the horses and cow to bed, saw to the carriage. Pressed for details of his youth, George had finally told Enid of his troubled past, and had then shared with her the letter he'd received from his mother in response to the one Grace had helped him write before Christmas. His mother had indeed been grateful to hear from him, had expressed her affection and her relief that his life had taken a turn for the better, that he had been redeemed. Grace had learned all of this when her offer to help him write again had been politely declined, George confessing shyly that Enid was now teaching him to read and would help him write his letters.

Both Enid and George had helped Grace arrange a special dinner party for Mary Kate's tenth birthday at the end of February, and though Liam had attended, Peter had not. Grace suspected it was partly his pride that wouldn't allow him to enter the back door of another gentleman's house and sit at the housekeeper's kitchen table, but she kept her suspicions to herself, letting him make the excuse of an abundance of business details to be discussed now that Lars and Detta had decided to leave for Europe after Peter and Grace were married.

Mary Kate had not minded the captain's absence, had not even seemed to miss him much, Grace thought, what with a full party that included Enid and George, Jack and Liam, and Davey and Rose Mulhoney; even Doctor Wakefield had poked his head in long enough to wish her many happy returns of the day and give her a leather-bound journal in which to write her thoughts. Grace had made a three-layer yellow cake with raspberry preserves spread in between and fresh whipped cream on the top, hot buttered scones, lemonade, and tea—a feast for a girl who valued her food even to this day. Davey and Rose brought her a small box of chocolates wrapped up in a ribbon she could use in her hair, Enid and George gave her a laying hen of her own, Jack presented her with a slingshot and a bag of carefully chosen stones, but Liam gave her the most prized gift of all—a wildly colorful Mexican skirt and vest and a pair of embroidered slippers for her feet. She'd whisked them away immediately, only to return minutes later with them on, twirling to show off the skirt and vest, pointing her toes in the shoes. Though Grace had insisted she keep the skirt for special occasions, Mary Kate wore the vest every day and kept the slippers by the side of her bed. It had surprised Grace, who hadn't realized the child had such an interest in clothes. She was a bit put out, having thought her own gift of three new books would have rated most highly, but really she didn't mind—Mary Kate was ten; she'd reached the age of ten, and she was healthy. She was happy.

Peter had made up for his lack of attendance by taking Mary Kate and Jack on a tour of Chinatown, where they ate bowls of noodles standing up, bought fireworks and kites, and poked their heads into the mysterious Chinese apothecary shop with its misty jars of what seemed to be animal eyes and pickled feet, bundled herbs, burning incense, powders, and potions. Peter had reported that for once Jack hadn't anything to say, simply gazed at the counters with his mouth hanging open. He'd intended to take them both on board the ship, but Jack had stubbornly refused; the boy had developed an aversion to ships and wanted nothing to do with them, a stand his sister quietly supported.

Grace wished with all her heart that Jack would come around to liking Peter, but she knew the number one man in his life was George Litton, followed closely by Mister Hewitt and Doctor Wakefield. Peter trailed a sorry fourth place, and Grace just wasn't sure what to do about that.

Despite the turmoil in the house, Mister Hewitt continued to come three mornings a week, and Grace was impressed with how much learning he'd been able to instill within her stubborn boy; Jack had begun to read on his own and could now count quite ably to twenty. Still, he was always ready to be cut loose after lunch, though Mister Hewitt had made a habit of staying on to visit with Miss Wakefield if she ventured down to the library. Grace noticed that he often had little pleasures to share with Abigail—a lovely yellow lemon to slice for her tea; glistening round red-and-white-striped peppermints from the candy man; the program from the latest play he'd attended, or from a musical event, or a lecture; a woman's magazine, fresh off the boat—anything to catch and hold her interest, to bring her out of herself and give her a taste of the world that awaited her. Mister Hewitt knew about the child—they all did, though it was not something they carried beyond the walls of the house—and he, with his love for and understanding of children, gently encouraged her to think of what a five-year-old might really be like. He often pointed out Jack to her as the boy romped in the yard with his puppy, though he quietly reminded her that young Jack was truly all boy.

At the end of two weeks, Doctor Wakefield had ridden out to meet the Calderons, the family with whom Eden lived, and had explained to them that he wished to continue the arrangement, at least for now, while slowly reintroducing Abigail into Eden's life. Senora Calderon had been especially grateful to hear this, Wakefield had reported, as clearly she was fond of the little girl. There were eight children in the family, the youngest three of whom were being fostered; by all appearances, the Calderons were kind and devoted parents. For Abigail's sake, Wakefield had been relieved to learn that the Calderons had spoken regularly to Eden of her mother, whom they described as an invalid who hoped to recover enough to one day meet her child. That day was coming, Wakefield had said to young Eden, taken by the girl's solemn brown eyes and the mouth that was so like Abigail's.

Senora Calderon and Eden had come out of the house to say *adíos*, and Eden had handed the doctor a sampler that Senora Calderon told him was a copy of one that hung above her bed, a framed prayer that had been in the child's bag the day she arrived. Eden liked to embroider, Wakefield was told, and spent hours a day at it; she had made this as a gift for her mother, though the other woman who sometimes came—Senora Hopkins—had not wanted to take it. That woman would no longer be coming, Wakefield had informed Senora Calderon; he himself would be riding out regularly to see Eden, and they should not hesitate to contact him if they needed anything at all.

The visit had affected him; Grace could tell by the way he sat in his chair that evening, looking out the window, smoking pipe after pipe, hardly moving. She did not bother him but left him to his thoughts, and instead made up a tea tray for Abigail, which she delivered herself. Abigail also sat by the window, looking out, a sampler in her hand.

"Thank you," she said as Grace set the tray down on the little table by Abigail's chair. "Did you see what Rowen brought back today?" She held out the sampler, her eyes red. "Eden made it for me."

Grace sat down across from Abigail and smoothed the linen piece out on her lap. It was the embroidery work of a child, though a child with talent; Grace's expert eye recognized this at once.

" 'Tis very good," she praised. "The letters are neatly done, and the lambs are dear. And the stars above. 'Tis a child's prayer?"

Abigail nodded. "She's copied it from the one that hung over my own bed when I was a child. I brought it out with me so that she might have it."

" *'Jesus, tender shepherd, hear me. Bless thy little lamb tonight. Through the darkness, be thou near me. Keep me safe 'til morning light.' "* Grace looked up. "And I guess He has, then."

Abigail's eyes filled with tears, but she smiled. "I was sitting here thinking about sheep and shepherds, but really it's about the morning light, isn't it? The promise that after the darkness, there will be light."

"Aye." Grace picked up the sampler and handed it back to Abigail. "And you'll be able to see your way more clearly now. Morning light is also the promise of a new day."

"I hope we will always be friends now." Abigail touched Grace's hand. "Even after you're married. I watch you with your children," she added shyly. "You are the kind of mother I hope to be."

"No mother is perfect, you know, miss. We've as much to learn from them as they from us. They humble a person, children do. 'Tis the wonderful thing about them. How they make you see your place in the world."

Abigail nodded, her large gray eyes watching as Grace stood to go. "Could I join you for breakfast in the kitchen tomorrow morning?" she asked. "Would the children mind?"

"They'll be shocked speechless," Grace admitted. "You've got them on the run, you know. Madwoman in the attic and all that."

To Grace's surprise, Abigail burst out laughing, her countenance brightening into youthfulness, if only for that quick moment.

"I guess it must've seemed that way," she said contritely. "But perhaps they'll think better of me after tomorrow."

"See you in the morning light, then."

Grace grinned and left the room, closing the door behind her. She went down the stairs and past the library, where the doctor still sat smoking his pipe, then into the kitchen, which was quiet and clean. Out in the yard, the children were trying to teach their puppies to fetch a stick, but the puppies were having none of it. The evening sun shone halos round the soft fluff of the children's hair; Jack's specs caught the light and threw it off as he tipped his head back and laughed, the way his father had always done; Mary Kate picked him up from behind and twirled him until they both fell down, gloriously dizzy. They would be dirty when they came in, their clothes dusty, faces speckled with mud, bits of straw everywhere, and she would scold them as mothers are wont to do, but in her heart she would cherish this moment, for she knew what it was to be grateful.

Thirty-two

Whenever Mei Ling had the shop to herself and it was a morning such as this—low gray skies, gentle yet steady rain—a delicious sense of solitude washed over her and she experienced a heightened awareness that was almost sensual. The low light lent an intensity to colors that in sunlight seemed flat, less vivid: the dry, brown hills took on a reddish cast and, in some places, revealed the yellow of newest green; the sea, too, revealed its green in opaque chops crested with cream foam; the terns, the gulls, the crows, tossed about against the hills, the water, the sky, drawing the elements together in a single landscape. And in the city, the colored silk flags of Chinatown seemed more rich, more significant; the brick took on deeper shades of red and orange, stone glowed white and gray; lady's parasols, feathered hats, calico bonnets, capes of muslin or velvet—lined in fur or not lined at all—the black lace of mantillas, the bridal white, pink cheeks, red lips, the glistening rings on their hands . . . all of these things, all of this color, spoke to Mei Ling with an emotion that flopped in her belly like a fat fish thrown onto the wharf. She had never allowed herself an internal experience such as this with her previous masters— even Chang-Li; it had seemed too painful to take notice of what the world had to offer, to participate in its beauty like this. But her life with Mister Sung was very different; she did not belong to him. In the beginning, she had not understood what that really meant, could not comprehend a life without the protection and guidance of a master, was afraid of belonging to herself, which she envisioned as coming to the top edge of a waterfall and not knowing how far it fell on the other side—seeing only that the river flowed and then it tumbled abruptly off the edge of the world. Mei Ling had not wanted to fall off the edge of the world, and it was only by attaching herself to Mister Sung that she had begun to see another river altogether, one that continued despite the interruption of falls. Now Mei Ling had landed and this new place was so very beautiful it sometimes moved her to tears, though she kept them to herself.

Would she leave Chang-Li's house, she had asked herself? Would she leave the shop, leave Chinatown, leave the city perhaps, and go to another city? Would she marry? Would she hire herself out for work and live in rooms that were hers and hers alone? Would she have children that she could keep, instead of souls to be released before they could become children? These things she had pondered as she lay in her bed at night, considering what it all meant. And Mister Sung—him she pondered, as well. He was not like the other men she had observed—neither Chinese nor European; she knew he visited the flower-and-mist ladies, that he liked Chinese women in his bed, but he did not take his comfort with her even when she had offered herself to him. He looked at her when he spoke, and the tone of his voice was so patient and so kind, so very personal, that it gave her pain in her heart, and she would withdraw from him back into the lowered eyes and nods of servitude. He did not like this, she knew. He wanted her head raised, her eyes engaged—he wanted to know what she *thought*! This had been very difficult to do, to say what she was thinking! It was far more intimate than anything she could have done to him with her body, and it had been weeks before she'd begun to risk this; she had had to figure out for herself what she was thinking, what she thought about things, what ideas were and why hers should hold any value.

But Mister Sung had been her guide, had engaged her in the kitchen, on the stair, in the shop, in the street. He was pleased with her ability to recognize the value of the things brought in by others who wished a loan of money, to count money and make change, to hold to her resolve once she'd set a price. He would sit on a cot in the back room, behind the curtain, and listen to her, then come out when the customer had gone, and they would discuss the exchange. Often he appeared to be laughing, and sometimes he would pat her on the back or squeeze her shoulders; once he gently tucked her hair back behind her

ear and kissed her on the cheek, though he'd seemed embarrassed by
this and had retreated at once to his back room and his pipe.

Mei Ling put her hand to her cheek now, her fingers brushing the
place his lips had touched. What she felt for Mister Sung was different
from what she'd felt for any other man, and she understood that this
was because she was free to choose him or not. And so the sense of who
she was had begun to emerge, and with it her rebirth into the wondrous
place that was the world.

She stood by the window a moment longer; though shops and
houses, sidewalks and carriages, would later be splattered with mud, for
now the gentle rain showered every bit of the street clean so that it
sparkled and revealed its beauty. Few customers would find their way
into the shop today, she thought, and was pleased. The day would be
her own, the shop her own, and all the things in it. She finished with
her dusting rag and returned to the counter, wiping off the case, sliding open the doors beneath, and reaching inside. Her fingers brushed
the lid of the wooden box that intrigued her so very much, and this she
now withdrew and set on the counter. She had not shown this acquisi-
tion to Mister Sung because she knew it held no value. She had loaned
money for the things the box held, but neither she nor Missus Smith
had bartered a price for the box itself. When Missus Smith had pocketed her dollars for the emerald ring and the ring of green stone that resembled jade but was not, the man's gold signet ring, and the golden
earrings, she had hurried out of the shop, leaving the wooden box behind. Mei Ling had other customers, so the box had gone under the
counter. Only later, after closing up, had she pulled it out to have a second look. It was a simple wooden box with the English word "Mother"
carved roughly on the top. Mei Ling was convinced that this had been
a gift from a son to his mother, and it could not have been the son of
Missus Smith or she would never have left it behind. Although the box
had been emptied of its jewelry, it held personal effects—the image of
a bare-chested man with his fists raised as if in fight, and a letter, its
pages yellowed and watermarked.

In private moments, she set these two things out on the counter
and considered them. The box was given from son to mother—perhaps the image was of this son once he'd become a man; perhaps it
was of the woman's husband, the father of the son; perhaps the letter

was from the son or from the husband; certainly it was from someone the mother had cherished. Mei Ling touched the letter with her fingertips. It was of love—she knew that most certainly. The places where the ink blurred were from teardrops that fell upon reading those words. Mei Ling wished she knew the words—she felt a sadness looking at them, but too her heart filled with a kind of yearning. The contents of the box—the box itself—spoke of family, and this was something Mei Ling could only dream of. Sometimes, out of the corner of her eye, she saw the figure of a man bending over a small child, and this she knew was what was left of her memory of her father; of her mother, she remembered more—the hands that dressed her quickly in the mornings and pushed her outside to play, a tired face looming close up and saying something Mei Ling could not understand, but also arms that had held her on a lap and fed her rice. There had been older brothers and possibly sisters, a younger brother, too, though Mei Ling could not remember them, could not remember their names or the names of her mother and father. Her next memories were of scrubbing floors in the house of the grand mistress, of fanning the mistress on sweltering summer days until the fan dropped from her hand and she fainted dead away, only to be awakened by the sting of the willow branch upon her back. How many years was she with the grand mistress? Mei Ling did not know, they blurred together like the words in the letter that had caught teardrops, but they would have been many, as she had the body of a young woman when she entered the Cherry Blossom House, there to clean up the rooms of the flower-and-mist ladies and to serve, herself, when gentlemen found a need for her. Here, she had learned to set free the souls of children who could not come into the world, because she was no mother; three souls she'd left behind as small shrines in the garden of the Cherry Blossom Street house. Why she had been sold to the old man, it was not her place to ask. His house had been gloomy and full of old grudges, the spirits of ill will and revenge, and he had plotted to escape it by sailing to Gum San, where he believed his good fortune would be restored and his return to China glorious. But he had been too old to undertake such a journey, and Mei Ling had known that his illness would also be his end; she had been relieved when he traded her to Chang-Li for the promise of burial in China—she had not wished to return to the house of gloom and despair with the body of her master. Mei Ling had found the number of *fan qui* in the city to be unsettling and was glad that Chang-Li kept her confined to the house and the limits of the Chinese quarter. He was not a bad master—Mei Ling had two tunics and trousers that were nicely made, new slippers that were replaced as soon as they wore out, and permission to cook as she liked, and so the food was good and plentiful; she also had her own small room in which to sleep and a soft mat for her bed. Also, Chang-Li took his pleasure with her only on occasion and always with care, so that she had only had to free two souls here. He always seemed to know when this had happened and gave her extra money for the apothecary, then left her alone with her sadness for many days together. The last time had been two years before, and Mei Ling wondered if she had used up all the souls that were given her at birth, if no more would come now. This had brought her both relief and distress; sometimes, Mei Ling fanned the fingers of one hand and thought of the souls she had released, the five children she would have if her destiny had been other than that of slave.

But now Mei Ling was no longer a slave. If she bore a child it would not be drowned at birth or taken from her or sold at a tender age; it would be hers to keep, hers to raise and love. She would be "Mother." This is what freedom meant to Mei Ling, and again she ran her fingers over the top of the carved box. When Mister Sung asked again what she was thinking, Mei Ling now had something meaningful to tell him—she was thinking about saving enough money to attract a good husband; she was thinking about having children with him and raising them up in America where they would always be free; she was thinking of the children they would have and how very different their lives would be from the one she had known. This was what she was thinking, she would tell him; this was what she wanted.

Gently, she folded up the letter, slipped it back into its envelope, laid it tenderly in the box, with the picture of the man on top, closed the lid, and tucked it all away beneath the counter, far back where it would be safe, this most precious of treasures—this symbol of love between mother and child.

Thirty-three

" 'T<small>IS</small> gone!" Grace burst into the library, cutting short the awkward conversation of Doctor Wakefield and Captain Reinders, both of whom turned to her immediately. "I kept it always in my trunk, but tonight 'tis gone!"

"What's gone?" Wakefield set down his drink.

"The box Liam made for me. I wanted to wear the ring you gave me, Peter. I kept it in there, along with . . ." Suddenly very white, Grace swayed as if about to faint.

Both men leapt out of their chairs and sprang to her side, though it was Reinders who guided her to a chair, leaving the doctor behind to pour out a glass of brandy.

"Drink this," Wakefield ordered, handing it to her.

"Drink that," Reinders said simultaneously, shooting the other man a wary glance. "Then tell us what's happened."

Grace swallowed the brandy and, when the color had come back into her cheeks, set the glass aside.

"Hopkins must've taken it," she told Wakefield. "She must've thought it held valuables. The emerald is, of course, but the other things . . ." Grace bit her lip in distress. "Oh, Peter! I'm so sorry about your ring!"

"Damn the ring. It's easily replaced. I know what else you kept in that box, Grace, how much it meant to you."

Wakefield looked from one face to the other. "What?" he demanded. "I insist you tell me."

Reinders saw that Grace's eyes had filled with tears and he put a steadying hand on her shoulder.

"Things that belonged to Grace's second husband, Morgan Mc-Donagh. Jack's father. His wedding band, a letter from him . . . and a picture of Mighty Dugan Ogue, a very dear friend of Grace. Am I right?" He looked down into her face and she nodded in surprise. "Liam told me once that you kept your best treasures in that box. He was proud to have made it for you, you see," he explained. "I asked him what treasures, and he told me."

"I'm sorry, Peter," she repeated tearfully.

"For what? For honoring the memory of a man you loved, for keeping his things for his son? You don't have to apologize to me for that, Grace. I know you love me." Reinders stopped, aware of Wakefield's presence. "Is there anything we can do to get the box back?"

Grace shook her head. " 'Tis two weeks since she left the house. We've been so busy, I'd no cause to look in the trunk. Then you asked me to come out, and I wanted to wear your ring." Her eyes filled again. "I don't wear it every day, you see, as I'm working and don't want to ruin it. I put it there for safekeeping, only now—"

"I'm afraid this is my fault," Wakefield interrupted. "Abigail confessed to me that Hopkins sold off most of her jewelry, though she believed the money was going to the child. I asked Enid to see if anything else was missing in the way of household silver and such, and she went over it all. You've been here such a short while," he apologized to Grace. "And you were already doing so much for Abigail, that I didn't want to burden you. It never occurred to me that Hopkins would steal from you, as well."

"You didn't know I had anything worth stealing."

"No," Wakefield insisted. "No, that's not it. I just didn't think of it. I'm so very sorry, Missus Donnelly. Grace. This is quite terrible."

"They were only things," Grace said bravely, though her heart cried out *His things; the only things left of him.*

Comfortingly, Peter gave her shoulder a quiet squeeze, and then he asked, "Where did Hopkins do business, Doctor? Would your sister know? I don't care about the emerald, but maybe whoever bought it also took McDonagh's ring, and we could at least see about getting that back."

"I asked Abigail that very thing when she told me about the jewelry, but she had no idea. I'm so very sorry." Wakefield looked forlorn, but then the expression on his face brightened considerably. "Now, hold on a minute!" He turned to Grace. "After we saw Enid's father, the Mulhoney boy was waiting for us—he said he'd followed Hopkins to Chinatown and then to the ticket agent. I intended to pursue the matter, but after we found Abigail . . . well, everything else went directly out of my mind."

"You think she sold the things in Chinatown?" Reinders brought him back to the point.

"According to Davey, yes. No doubt she took Missus Donnelly's box when she stormed out of here that day, so this pawnshop would be the likely recipient of its contents."

Grace stood up. "Will you take me to the Mulhoneys?" she asked Peter. "And then to Chinatown?"

"Of course." Reinders picked up his hat.

"Let me." Wakefield put a hand on the captain's arm, then instantly removed it when he saw the look on Reinders' face. "What I mean is, I may be able to identify some of Abigail's jewelry, as well. The shop will be closed tonight, but we could go first thing in the morning."

Grace sat back down. "He's right, Peter. 'Twould do us no good, rushing about the city tonight. Nothing for it but to wait 'til tomorrow."

"I know this is all terribly distressing," Wakefield said, "but since there *is* nothing you can do about it tonight, why not carry on with the lovely evening Captain Reinders has arranged? It would be a shame to have that ruined, as well. Could you manage, do you think, Grace?"

Reinders frowned, not at all pleased with Wakefield's suddenly informal means of address.

"There's no need for that. Missus Donnelly is upset and entitled to whatever privacy she may need." He knelt down beside Grace and spoke gently. "We can go to dinner anytime, and concerts are a dime a dozen these days. Get a good night's sleep and I'll call for you in the morning."

Grace looked at him, stricken. "Oh, Peter. You've gone to so much trouble—a table at the Maison Riche and tickets at the American Theater. No," she decided. "We're going out. I won't let Hopkins rob me of this night, as well as of my treasures."

"Well said!" Wakefield smiled at them, relieved. "She is a most remarkable woman, wouldn't you say, Captain?"

"I did," Reinders replied. "Five years ago when she sailed on my ship from Liverpool to New York."

"And many times since, I'm sure," Wakefield conceded graciously.

"Hundreds." Reinders could not resist the urge to have the last word, though it made him feel childish. "Thousands." He felt his face grow warm. "We'd better be on our way."

Wakefield nodded. "Enjoy the performance. I hear it's delightful. And don't worry about tomorrow—I'll take her to the Mulhoneys at first light and, from there, to Chinatown."

"*I'll* take her." Reinders overrode him. "I know my way around those alleys better than most people."

"Certainly. I only wanted to see the place myself in case some of the family heirlooms were still there."

"We can all go," Grace interjected. "Doctor Wakefield and I could meet you at the Mulhoneys, Peter, and leave from there."

"Fine," Reinders agreed curtly. "Most pawnshops open around ten. We'll meet at nine."

"Nine it is. The excitement never ceases, eh, Missus Donnelly?" Wakefield smiled wryly.

"I would've thought you'd've had enough excitement around here to last a lifetime." Peter proffered his arm to Grace. "Shall we go, then?"

"Peter!" she admonished quietly as he escorted her to the door.

Wakefield followed them. "You're quite right, Captain. I don't mean to make light of my sister's terrible distress. And I'm grateful for your discretion, by the way. Missus Donnelly has commented upon your compassion many times."

Reinders felt instantly ashamed and turned to face the doctor. "She's too kind," he said and put out his hand. "Good night, Wakefield. Thanks for the drink, and I'll see you in the morning."

Reinders was glad he'd tempered his mood when Grace rewarded him with a quick kiss in the hallway, just before they went into the kitchen to say good night to the children, who were being left in Enid's care. They had been outside, playing with the dogs, when Grace had made her discovery of the missing box, so she'd decided to say nothing to them about it until the matter had been resolved. They were sitting happily around the kitchen table, attempting to teach Enid and George a new card game Liam had showed them. Mary Kate rose from her seat immediately and kissed both her mother and the captain warmly, promising to be a good girl; Jack kissed his mother and dutifully shook the captain's hand, promising to try his best. Enid and George both wished them a lovely evening out and, with that, Grace and Peter left the warm, cheery kitchen and stepped out into a cool, breezy March evening.

Reinders handed Grace up into the covered buggy, then climbed in himself and turned the horses around, driving carefully down the hills, then across town toward the plaza. Not wanting to press Grace, who seemed unusually quiet, Peter kept up a light commentary on the weather, the new buildings going up, and tonight's performance, for which he'd gotten them box seats. For her part, Grace could only nod; her mind was full of what she'd lost, of the sickening thought that her most treasured possessions might have been tossed into the mucky banks of the harbor once Hopkins realized there was nothing there of monetary value. She clung to the hope that tomorrow they would find the right pawnshop and that perhaps the box had been abandoned there, or at least Morgan's ring and the earrings, which might have fetched a small price. It was upsetting that the picture of Dugan and Mary Kate's ring from Aislinn might be gone forever, but the worst thing, that of which she could hardly bear to think, was the loss of the letter that meant so much to her, far more—though she hated to admit it—than the beautiful emerald ring Peter had given her. She turned slightly toward him now, intent upon giving him her full attention, upon keeping her word that this evening would not be ruined.

At last, he drew up the carriage in front of a French restaurant that had opened to glowing reports, jokingly reassuring her that she would not have to eat snails or frog legs. She laughed politely, reminding herself that he had never experienced true hunger, let alone starvation; people ate what was available to them, what they had to eat in order to stay alive. Jokes like this weren't funny to her, but she needn't make an issue of it, especially not tonight when clearly her nerves were raw. Peter was a kind and sensitive man, she told herself, and she needed to keep her focus on the many things they had in common rather than on those things that made them different. She shook her head, determined to clear it of gloom, to fill it with the pleasure of this evening and of this man whom she loved.

"Look at the crowd!" She made her voice lively as he helped her down. "Are they all waiting to get in?"

"It's a popular place," he confided, proud of his decision to come here. "But I reserved our table in advance."

Reinders took her arm and led her through the crowd, which parted reluctantly until the people realized that this was quality coming out to dine. All eyes took in the lovely auburn-haired woman in the green dress escorted by the tall, commanding gentleman in top hat and evening clothes. Once inside, they were greeted by a harried, yet elegant-looking maître d'hôtel who led them to an intimate table on the far side of the room. He seated them both, then proceeded to announce in his heavily accented English that oysters were the specialty of the evening, presented in several different dishes, which he described at length, much to Grace's delight. She stopped him several times to ask about the ingredients in certain sauces and to beg an explanation of the process of soufflé, giving him in exchange her grandmother's secret for delicate sorrel sauce over salmon and buttermilk potatoes. The two got on so well that the maître d' pulled up a chair and joined them, calling for a bottle of champagne, his gift to a fellow gourmand. Only the increasing grumbles of waiting patrons interrupted their conversation, and it was with clear reluctance that the fellow left at last, promising to return before the end of their meal.

"Another admirer to add to your collection," Reinders teased. "And this one comes with champagne! I don't know how you do it. Even old Wakefield is smitten."

"He's not so old," Grace replied, fingers touching the stem of her wineglass. "And he's certainly not smitten. Grateful, perhaps, for my seeing to Abigail and the house, but nothing more than that."

"Grace." Reinders waited for her to look up. "Believe me, the man's smitten. He can't take his eyes off you for a minute, and his posturing . . . well, it's proprietary, at best."

"Do you mean he acts as if he owns me?" Grace frowned.

"Not own, no," Reinders clarified. "But clearly he considers there to be a bond between you that is equal to, or maybe even greater than, the bond between you and me."

Grace shook her head. "You're wrong, Peter. He'd no one else to talk with about Abigail and the child, for privacy's sake, you know. But now

Doctor Fairfax is back, the two of them will take it all over and leave me to my kitchen."

"You don't know men like I do. Wakefield has no intention of leaving you to your kitchen."

"What are you saying? That the doctor plans on seducing me away from you? Is that what it is?" Grace asked angrily. "Because if so, then you're giving me no credit a'tall for being my own person."

"I'm just saying he's a man." Reinders leaned back defensively. "No different from any other man."

"And you're all just dogs, is that it? Only interested in what the other one's chewing on, looking to take it away?" Grace sighed and her anger fell away as quickly as it had come up. "I don't want to argue with you, Peter. Doctor Wakefield's never been less than a gentleman with me, but if my working for him bothers you—and I'm thinking it does—then I say let's be done with the whole thing."

"What?" Reinders blanched.

"That's right. I'll quit the place straight off and come to you. We can be married next week, if you like."

"Next week? But what about the May wedding—church, flowers, dress, all that?"

Grace shrugged wearily. "They're only things. And things don't matter next to people." She leaned forward. "I know how much you wanted Lars and Detra to be at the wedding, how disappointed you were when you found out they wouldn't be."

"Disappointed with Lars," Reinders pointed out. "Not with you. Lars is the one who decided he had to be in Europe for the summer season and booked an earlier steamer without consulting anyone. I never expected you to change the wedding date because of that."

"But aren't they your closest friends, your business partners all these years? Didn't you say how you wished he could stand up with you?"

"Well, sure." Reinders slipped a finger inside his collar to loosen it. "But listen, Mack'll do it. And Liam's here, too. The important thing is that we've set a date and we're moving forward on that. The house won't be ready until then anyway, and I'm sure the children won't want to leave Wakefield's just yet."

Grace dismissed those reasons with a wave of her hand. "And why would they not? You've said Jack and Mary Kate can bring their dogs along, and won't Mister Hewitt be happy to teach them wherever they live? As for the house, your housekeeper and I can take care of it ourselves."

Reinders was floored; for all his badgering, Grace had never once wavered in her resolve that theirs would be a May wedding, and he realized now that he hadn't expected her to. The thought of marrying next week, of bringing Grace and the children—especially Jack, whom he had yet to win over—into the house, into his daily life, gave him serious pause, and he found himself stalling.

"What about Abigail? You said before that you wanted to be there when she meets her child, help her with all that. And you'll need more than a week to find a new cook for them unless Enid takes over. But then you'll have to hire a new housekeeper . . ." Reinders' voice trailed off as he felt the pressure of her hand on top of his.

"Did we not have this very conversation at Christmastime? Only I believe 'twas I making all the excuses." Grace smiled ruefully. "I'm tired, Peter. I don't mind admitting it. I was tired before I left Kansas and now I'm all done in, weary to my very soul. I can't take another step."

Silenced by the honesty of her confession, the captain picked up her hand instead and pressed it to his lips.

"I came here to marry you, Peter; really I did. Mary Kate and Jack, they've been through so much, and I wanted a peaceful life for us all, a life with you. But instead, I got us all caught up in the lives of others." Grace's eyes filled with tears. "I should've married you in New York. But maybe Jack wouldn't've found me. Maybe Mary Kate would've died in the cholera." She shook her head. "I just don't know. I don't know anything anymore. I didn't marry you then, and I'm sorry. And I hope you can forgive me, and that you still want me after all I've been such an eejit, wasting so much time and all."

"I do," he said quietly. "I do want you. More than you know."

They looked at one another through the flickering candlelight, and then the waiter arrived, setting before them each a beautifully arranged plate and another bottle of wine, which he opened with a flourish.

"Are you all right?" Reinders asked when they were alone again.

She nodded, but her hand shook as she lifted the glass to her lips and drank.

"You're overwrought. I can see that. It *has* been too much for you, and, sick as I've been, I've only added to your burden." He leaned forward. "But you'll feel better in the morning, Grace, and I think you'd regret rushing our wedding when everything has been arranged for May."

Grace nodded again and tried to smile, lips trembling tearfully as she fought to suppress the sadness now flooding her heart. Something had slipped away from them in that moment, she knew it even as she tried not to. Something had been lost, and no matter what happened now, they would have to go on without it.

"We *will* be married," Reinders promised fervently. "I only want you to be happy, Grace. Whatever that means, whatever it is, I want you to have it. And you *will* have it. Just wait a little longer; that's all."

"Aye," she agreed quietly. "You're right. 'Tis best to wait."

"That's my girl." He patted her hand, then picked up his fork. "Watch out; here comes your new admirer to see how you like your dinner. Better try a bite."

Grace dutifully lifted a forkful of baked oysters in butter and cream and breadcrumbs to her mouth and felt it melt there, though she tasted nothing at all.

"How does madame like?" The maître d'hôtel waited anxiously for her reply. "Too much pepper, maybe, for you?"

" 'Tis delicious," Grace pronounced, smiling up at him. "The finest oysters I ever ate in all my life. The sauce is perfect."

"I am so very happy." The maître d' beamed. "And after your last course, you will have my famous *gâteau chocolat*. It is compliments of your friend Doctor Rowen Wakefield, as a gift for you on this special evening."

Grace bit her lip and looked at Reinders, who burst out laughing.

"Maybe I'd better marry you next week after all," the captain chuckled.

"But of course." The maître d' shrugged his shoulders as if it were obvious. "Only a fool would not."

Customers of the the House of Good Fortune usually appeared surreptitiously and one at a time, two at the most, so the arrival of three together—two men and a woman—put Mei Ling on her guard.

"Good morning," she greeted them in her careful English. "Ah, how may I help?"

"Good morning, madam." Wakefield took off his hat and approached the counter. "Who is the owner of this establishment?"

Mei Ling considered Chang-Li's extended absence. "Mister Sung come later. Mei Ling can serve."

Wakefield suspected Mister Sung was at this very moment asleep in the room behind that curtain; though the shop had been aired, his trained nose caught a hint of stale opium smoke.

"Mister Sung?" he called firmly. "Come out at once!"

Mei Ling followed Wakefield's eyes to the curtain and then she turned back to him, frowning.

Clearly Wakefield was going to have to deal with this young woman. "We are looking for particular things," he explained. "Things which have been stolen from us."

Mei Ling shook her head. "We buy only, sell only."

"Of course." Now Wakefield spoke slowly, as if to a child, and raised his voice, as if the child were hard of hearing. "A woman—a servant . . . servant"—he repeated, pointing to Mei Ling—"stole from us. Jewelry." He looked at Grace, but she was wearing none, so he mimed earrings, bracelets, a necklace. "Jewelry," he repeated. "Understand?"

Mei Ling nodded once, her face impassive.

"Brought it here," he continued. "To the House of Good Fortune. We want it back. We *buy* it back," he corrected, and when she appeared puzzled, he began all over again. "A woman—my housekeeper—*stole* from us—"

Exasperated, Captain Reinders stepped forward.

"Excuse me, Wakefield." He moved the doctor out of the way and then, to everyone's amazement, he spoke to the girl in her own language, though haltingly and with much correction. Mei Ling listened more intently now, head tipped to one side, and then replied.

"Could've saved me the trouble." Wakefield's tone carried a hint of irritation. "Why didn't you say you knew Chinese?"

"I don't. Just enough to bark at dockworkers and order dumplings in a noodle house, but clearly you weren't getting anywhere, so . . ." Reinders shrugged. "I tried to tell her about the stolen box and the things inside, and to describe your housekeeper. I don't know if she understood me or not, but she did say 'no' twice."

Mei Ling watched them talk, only her eyes shifting in a neutral face; she understood them perfectly well—Missus Smith of the injured-husband-and-many-children story had been a servant of these people and had stolen from them, had taken away from them the wooden box. Mei Ling could not fully ascertain who the two men were, but the woman with eyes the color of a troubled sea was familiar. Mei Ling studied this woman out of the corner of her own eye and then it came to her—the portrait that hung in the window of the William Shew Gallery. There were several images currently displayed there, but Mei Ling had found herself drawn to that of the mother and children, to their quiet dignity and the way the children looked upon the mother with such love. Mei Ling had wished for the courage to go inside the gallery and see the others, but simply walking the streets as an independent person took all of her inner fortitude, and so she had been content to simply stand on the sidewalk and gaze at the mother from there. The mother. Mei Ling held herself very still.

"We'll look around, madam. Miss." Wakefield's voice boomed in the small shop, breaking Mei Ling's reverie. "Tell her, Captain."

Reinders glanced at Mei Ling, who nodded politely and gestured to the glass-topped counter under which lay displays of jewelry, coins, timepieces, guns, knives, and a selection of table silver. Grace came forward and joined Wakefield, bending over the case and shading her eyes to see more clearly through the glass. Slowly, they inched their way along, until suddenly Wakefield stood straight and tapped the glass excitedly.

"Aha!" the doctor exclaimed. "This bracelet belonged to Abigail! She wore it at Christmas! See here, Missus Donnelly—does it look familiar to you?"

Grace moved in closer. "Aye," she agreed. "I think you're right."

"Madam! Miss!" Wakefield waved Mei Ling over and showed her what he was interested in. "This belonged to my sister. How much to buy it back from you? How . . . much?"

Mei Ling opened the back of the case and removed the bracelet, then checked the little tag that hung from it. "Thirty dollar." She kept her eyes lowered.

Wakefield looked as if he were about to protest for a moment, but then he closed his mouth and got out his wallet. Mei Ling reached under the counter for paper in which to wrap his purchase. Grace continued to look through the things, hoping to see Morgan's ring or gold hoops, but it was Captain Reinders who exclaimed next.

"Those are my cuff links, by God!" The captain put both hands on the case and peered even more closely. "And that's"—he looked up at Grace incredulously, and then back down—"that's Darmstadt's pocket watch!"

"Arnott," Grace said, voicing her suspicion.

"The bastard. I'll have him strung up by the ballocks for this. Damn his eyes!"

"Captain." Wakefield glanced pointedly at Grace and the young Chinese woman.

"Pardon me, ladies," Reinders apologized between clenched teeth, but then continued his muttering. "Lot of nerve . . . top dollar and time off, beside. I'll give him time off, all right." He turned to Mei Ling. "Wrap these up."

Again Mei Ling opened the case and removed the objects, checked their tags, and announced their price. Reinders paid, threatening to take it out of Arnott's hide, while Grace continued to look the length of the case, eyes straining to see into every corner. And finally she spied something familiar.

"Peter! Your ring!"

He came over immediately, then squeezed her shoulders when he saw what she'd found.

"Here!" He called over his shoulder. "We'll take this one, too."

"Hopkins *must've* brought the box in," Grace speculated hopefully. "The ring was in the box. It *must* be here!"

"I'll ask again, but . . ." Reinders hesitated. "Hopkins might've taken the ring out, Grace. She might've thrown the box away before she ever got to this shop. Just don't get your hopes up."

Grace nodded and turned to Mei Ling, watching the girl's face with excruciating focus as Reinders attempted again to communicate. When he described the box, gesturing with both hands, Grace was sure she saw a flicker of something on the girl's face— recognition, perhaps, she hoped, and her heart soared—but then Mei Ling lowered her eyes and shook her head, saying only a few quiet words.

"Either she doesn't know what I'm talking about, or she doesn't have the box. She says the woman who brought in the bracelet also brought in the emerald. That's all. I'm sorry."

"At least we got your ring back." Grace tried to smile. "That's something, then."

"*Your* ring." Reinders handed it to her. "And it's not much. Considering what you wanted to find."

Grace's eyes filled with tears and she turned away, hoping he wouldn't notice, but suddenly she was sobbing, unable to control herself. She covered her face with her hands, mortified and desperately trying to regain her composure.

"My dear!" Wakefield hurried to her side and started to put an arm around her, but then patted her shoulder instead. "Please, Missus Donnelly, please. Calm yourself now. All's not lost. I promise we won't leave any stone unturned."

"What else do you suggest?" Reinders asked, irritated with the doctor for what he thought was nothing more than the prolonging of Grace's misery. "What other stone is there?"

Mei Ling slipped around to the front of the counter and withdrew a clean handkerchief from the sleeve of her tunic, silently handing it to the weeping woman. Grace looked at her then, eyes red and swollen and infinitely sad, and accepted the cloth with grateful stoicism despite the trembling of her chin. Mei Ling watched as the woman dried her eyes, then smoothed her hair, took a deep breath and—collecting herself—replaced the sorrow in her eyes with calm acceptance before she turned around to face the men.

"There is no other stone," Grace acknowledged, her voice low. " 'Twas our only hope, this. And now I'll let it go."

"Very brave of you, Missus Donnelly," Wakefield commended softly.

"Ah no, doctor." Grace shook her head, thinking of the old people on the ship from Ireland, the young families in their wagons on the trail. "Bravery is something else altogether. I'm only being reasonable. 'Tis only things I've lost. Things are nothing next to people."

"Well, I know, but . . ." Wakefield wished he had something more to say, something to take away the pain of this woman he admired so greatly, to offer her comfort, to apologize for having unwittingly involved her in something that turned out to have such great personal cost.

"I think we've done all we can this morning. Shall we go, then?" Reinders put his hand on Grace's elbow, ready to escort her.

Grace looked through him as if she had not heard, then turned back to Mei Ling, quietly studying the girl, seeing now the bits of light—not much larger than motes—that hovered around her. She took Mei Ling's hand and held it for a moment, peering deeply into the young woman's eyes until the room around them dissolved.

"I'm sorry for you, Mei Ling," Grace told her softly. "You've lost children. But God will bless you with others." She pressed the young woman's hand gently. "Do you understand me?"

Mei Ling repeated the words in her head, and then suddenly they were as clear as if spoken in her own tongue. Mei Ling, who had not shed tears since the loss of her first unborn child, felt one now as it ran down her cheek, and in her heart she felt the shifting of the stone that had blocked its entrance for so very long.

"Come," Mei Ling whispered, leading Grace by the hand across the room and behind the counter, hesitating for a moment, ashamed of not having returned such treasure the moment its owner had been revealed, though determined to do so now. She knelt on the floor, reaching far back on the lowest shelf, to the furthest corner, until her fingers brushed the worn wood of the box, which she withdrew and offered humbly to Grace. "*Maa maa,*" she said, her head bowed.

"By God!" Wakefield exclaimed, coming to look. "Is that the box?"

Grace held it tightly to her chest with one hand, helping Mei Ling to her feet with the other. "Thank you." She kissed the young woman tenderly on the cheek. "Thank you, Mei Ling."

"Look inside," Reinders urged.

Grace set the box on the counter and carefully lifted the lid. She saw immediately that Dugan's picture was still there and, beneath it, the envelope that held Morgan's letter. On top were Mary Kate's ring, the earrings, and Lord Evans' signet ring.

"Everything there?" Reinders asked.

Grace nodded, then tipped the box to show its contents.

"Well, this is wonderful!" Wakefield rubbed his hands together in delight. "How on earth did you get her to understand you?"

Grace looked at Mei Ling, whose fingertips were tracing the letters on the lid one last time. "We are both mothers," she said quietly. "Doctor, do you have a calling card?"

Wakefield felt in his pocket for the case, then pulled out a card and handed it to her. Grace turned it over on the counter, took the pen from its well, and wrote her name and the house number on the back.

"I'm Grace Donnelly." She handed the card to Mei Ling. "And this is where I live. If you should ever need anything."

"And this is *my* card." Reinders slipped his on top of Wakefield's. "For when she's my wife."

As Mei Ling examined both cards, she heard the faint creak of the cot in the back room and knew that Mister Sung had come in. She looked up at Grace and thought how similar they were—the woman and Mister Sung—though perhaps it was only in the way they held themselves, the way in which they spoke, or perhaps it was the way in which they both held her attention.

"Come drink tea," Mei Ling decided, bravely issuing her first personal invitation. "Mei Ling prepare for honored guest."

"Thank you." Grace touched the young woman's shoulder. "I will. And I'll bring my children to meet you. Good-bye for now, Mei Ling."

Mei Ling escorted them to the door and held it open, bowing as they left the shop, watching as the woman was helped into a waiting carriage and driven away, though not before she had turned around one last time to lift her hand in farewell, to show Mei Ling her eyes. Happy, Mei Ling came back into the shop and closed the door, the sound of which drew Sean from the back room.

"Did I actually hear you inviting someone to tea, Mei Ling?" He grinned, though his voice was hoarse and his face ashy from the long night before. "Soon you'll be the toast of San Francisco's finest. Who's your new friend, then?"

Mei Ling smiled shyly and offered the calling cards to him, unsure of her ability to pronounce the names properly.

"Doctor Rowen Wakefield," Sean read out loud. "Captain Peter Reinders." He looked up, even more pale than before. "I know Captain Reinders. What did he want here?"

Haltingly, Mei Ling related the information that these were the employers of the woman she and Mister Sung knew as Missus Smith, and that they had come to retrieve what had been stolen from them. The men had paid for their things, she assured Mister Sung, but since no money had been loaned for the box in the first place, Mei Ling had simply returned it to the woman.

"What box?" Sean demanded, more harshly than he'd intended. "What woman?"

A box of personal things, Mei Ling told him, with no monetary value. Then she turned over Doctor Wakefield's card so he could read the name on the back. "Belong this woman. Mei Ling new friend."

Sean stared at the name on the card, and his knees began to give way. Mei Ling moved quickly to support him and, his arm over her shoulder, helped him to a chair in the corner of the shop, where he sat, dazed, until she brought him a cup of water.

"Mei Ling." He looked up at her when he'd finished. "What did she look like? Did she have hair this color?" He put his hand on the dark red wood of the counter. "And eyes like that?" He pointed to a bottle of green glass.

Mei Ling nodded, brightening at once. "Same talk Mister Sung!"

"Oh my God." Sean's face was a mixture of joy and anguish. "It's my sister, Mei Ling—the one I thought died in the fire! *Meimei.*" He hoped it was the right word. "*Meimei* is Grace Donnelly."

This woman of today was Mister Sung's dead sister? Mei Ling sank to her knees beside Sean's chair, baffled. Mister Sung had said once that he and Mei Ling were alike, alone in the world with no family; he had unfolded the worn piece of newspaper he carried in his wallet and read to her about the fire and the people who died in it. How could it be that he had not known his sister had survived? Mei Ling wondered. How could he have simply accepted what was written by men who wanted only to sell papers? Didn't he look for himself?

"Go now!" Mei Ling ordered in a tone that was foreign even to her. "See *meimei* now!"

Startled, Sean turned to her at once, but remained seated.

"Go!" Mei Ling got to her feet and pointed at the door.

Sean struggled to his feet now, too, but then all the color drained from his face again and he sank back into the chair.

"Why didn't she ever answer my letters, if she's been alive all this time?" he asked. "Why didn't she come looking for me? Maybe she gave up on me, Mei Ling—I abandoned her, after all. Maybe she doesn't care whether I'm alive or not! And why is she living with this Wakefield? Why isn't she married to Captain Reinders? It doesn't make any sense."

It was Mister Sung who was not making any sense, and Mei Ling waved away his questions like so many irritating flies.

"No say to Mei Ling, 'why.' Say to *meimei.*"

"Oh my God!" Sean sat upright and wondered aloud. "Is Mary Kate alive, then? Her daughter?"

Mei Ling nodded enthusiastically and told him about the portrait that hung in the gallery, about Grace with her son and daughter.

Sean frowned. "No boy," he corrected. "Only girl. Can't be boy if she's not married to Reinders," he speculated quietly. "Maybe it's not Grace after all."

Mei Ling felt her face go red with exasperation. "Mei Ling show Mister Sung. Go now." She didn't wait for a reply but got the key from the hook and locked up the front door, then pulled him to his feet and led him out to the alley, leaving him leaning against the wall while she hailed a jinriksha; it wasn't so very far, and Mei Ling could have easily walked the distance, but Mister Sung was clearly not well.

She got him into the jinriksha and directed the runner to the gallery. They stopped once for Sean to vomit over the side—whether from poison in his body or turmoil in his head, Mei Ling did not know—but finally pulled up in front of William Shew's. Mei Ling ordered the driver to wait, then helped Sean out of the cart and up to the window, pointing out the portrait of the mother and children. His body went rigid as he looked first at the face of his sister, and then at the face of his beloved niece, but when he looked at the face of the little boy, his limbs turned to rubber. "Morgan," he gasped, and then he passed out.

Thirty-five

Morgan and Quinn had been glad to get off the steamer—glad to leave behind the cramped accommodations, be-weeviled pilot bread and navy biscuit, dried beef and salt pork, greasy dandy funk, and bad water. It would have been much worse had they been forced to sail around South America, however; salt pork and biscuit, they'd been told, gradually became a nasty hash called "lobscouse," and foul drinking water, diluted with liberal quantities of molasses and vinegar in order to make it potable, became "switchel". Seasickness would have been rampant and the endless days at sea—in light of the men's urgency—would've been unbearable. And so they'd been glad to get off the steamer, glad to leave the discomfort behind, but had felt no need to voice their complaints, as others in the party had done, as they began making arrangements for the next leg of the journey.

They had disembarked on the Caribbean side, at the mouth of the Chagres River, a fever-plagued region of swamps with but one slight elevation, upon which stood the ruined fortress of San Lorenzo, where three hundred men had been killed in an attack nearly two hundred years before by the dread pirate Morgan. Quinn, brightening for the first time since they'd left New York, had nudged Morgan and commented that it was probably no coincidence that both he and Grace had pirates in their pasts. Morgan arranged for the two of them to join a party of four young men from their steamer; Powell, Jeffers, Merriman, and Downey had already hired a bungo and the native boatmen necessary to pole the dugout across to the Cruces. Ortiz and Pascal appeared to be men of mixed Spanish and Indian descent, while Juan was almost certainly of African descent; they were also young men, though far stronger and clearly better natured than the four East Coasters, whose sense of adventure seemed to wither by the hour.

For four days, their party had worked its way along the sharply curving Chagres, avoiding treacherous rocks upon which hung the wreckage of less fortunate canoes, and hoping to avoid the malaria-carrying mosquitoes that hung thick above the stream and the jungle on either side. Morgan and Quinn had bought bottles of local rum and brandy to dole out to the boatsmen but drank little themselves, though the other men in their party were usually drunk by midafternoon. Merriman and Powell were wealthy dandies from the Northeast, and Jeffers and Downey were from the wealthy South; they'd met at Harvard University and had made a pact to seek adventure and pleasure in the West before assuming careers in banking, law, politics, and real estate. Soon enough they would be wed to social calendars and proper wives, but for now they fancied themselves daring young men, their waistbands bristling with too many pistols and brand-new bowie knives. They were loud and boisterous, amusing themselves by drinking copious amounts of brandy and shooting off their guns at the alligators, iguanas, parrots, and anything else that moved upon the crumbling red banks. Quinn was wary of them and said little in their company; Morgan followed suit, though he spoke up when two of them fired randomly toward a small group of thatched huts, scattering Indian women and children into the jungle. The dandies had not appreciated Morgan's interference, but the boatmen showed their approval in small ways—at night, Morgan and Quinn were shown to bamboo huts with wooden floors and given larger portions of the monkey or iguana meat that Pascal had roasted. When the brandy was passed around, Juan offered Morgan and Quinn cocoa shells with which to dip up a chaser of river water.

As the days passed and the heat became paralyzing, the dandies grew more and more irritated by the boatsmen's habit of overcoming fatigue with frequent siestas, or by simply disappearing into the jungle for hours, after which they'd return ebullient with rum and singing passé American songs such as "Old Susanna" and "Yankee Doodle Dandy." Again Morgan and Quinn came to the defense of their guides, pointing out that they were in the middle of a country none of them knew anything about, and there was nothing to be gained by bullying the natives, who could simply decide not to return to their bungo charges — ever. They were almost to Cruces, Morgan reasoned. Why rock the boat now?

"We would have been there yesterday," Merriman declared from where he stood in the bow, "if they didn't like their drink so much. No thanks to you."

" 'Tis custom." Morgan eyed him warily. "You were told, as well as us."

"Never met an Irishman didn't like his drink, either," Powell snorted.

Beside him on the box, Morgan felt Quinn tense. "You're Irish, then, are you, Mister Powell?" He glanced at the bottle Powell had been swigging from all morning.

"One hundred percent American!" Powell raised his bottle good-naturedly. "All the way back to the Mayflower."

"Mayflower's a pub, then, is it?" Morgan asked with seeming innocence.

Jeffers and Downing were sitting up now, watching the drama unfold from beneath the brims of matching straw hats.

"If you're looking for trouble"—Merriman pulled his bowie knife out of its sheath—"look over here."

"Oh, I say. Good show, Merriman!" Downing applauded.

"You swing that knife round plenty enough." Morgan stood up. "But I've yet to see you use it."

"Take a notch out of him," Powell urged drunkenly. "Show him he's no match for a trained gentleman."

"Trained, are you?" Morgan took a step closer. "In notch taking, no less."

Behind him, Quinn rose to his full height and moved forward; the boat, pulled only halfway up on the bank, rocked slightly in the murky water. An alligator slid off the bank on the far side, its splash launching a cloud of screaming parrots from the tree canopy above.

Merriman stood his ground, but the sweat on his forehead had begun to drip down along his sideburns and was heavy on his upper lip; he touched the tip of his tongue to it, nervously.

"You don't want to fight me," Morgan said evenly, not taking his eyes off the man. "Nor I, you. Put the knife down, and we'll forget it."

Unsure, Merriman glanced at Powell, and in that second, Morgan moved quickly forward and slapped the knife out of the young man's hand, then picked it up and threw it overboard. Merriman lurched to the side as if to go after it, but Morgan grabbed his arm.

"Don't." He pointed out the alligator. " 'Tis over and done with. Forget it."

Angrily, Merriman jerked his arm away and returned to the bow of the canoe, where he turned his back on the Irishmen and awaited the return of their guides, his bottle by his side, his pistol now tucked awkwardly down the front of his trousers.

"Loaded, do you think?" Quinn asked quietly from the shade in the back of the boat.

"Oh, aye. He's just the sort shoots himself in the ballocks." Morgan grinned wryly. "Best stay clear of him 'til Cruces. One more day is all. How you holding up?"

"I'm enjoying the change," Quinn replied dryly. "Nice to see close up how the better half lives."

Morgan laughed quietly and handed him a piece of chewy white meat.

"Fish of some kind, is it, then?" Quinn turned it over to examine the other side.

"Didn't ask. Must be nourishing, though, if it stays down."

"True enough." Quinn took a bite and chewed contentedly beside his friend.

The guides returned—rested, fed, and well oiled—and they made a few more miles before settling in for the night, though Morgan did not sleep, aware of the heightened tension in the little boat. The four dandies were not awake when Juan and Ortiz pushed off again at dawn, and so they did not realize how many hours had passed when the boatsmen decided to stop again for a rest.

"Oh, for God's sake!" Powell complained bitterly, his hand to his aching head, dried spittle in the corners of his mouth. "Not again! Absolutely not. I won't stand for it."

"Quite right!" Jeffers joined in. "Don't let them off." He stood up and blocked the front of the boat, as did Downey.

Pascal put down his pole, shrugged good-naturedly, and dove overboard, swimming a few strokes around the boat to the beach. Ortiz and

Juan laughed and were about to follow suit when Merriman grabbed
Juan by the arm and shoved the pistol up against his temple.

"No!" he shouted at the boatsman, shaking his head for added em-
phasis. "Stay on board! Keep going!"

"Get back here, you!" Powell brandished his own pistol at the man
on shore.

"Well done!" Downey stood up and patted the weapon in his belt.

Jeffers went a step further and fired a shot over the top of Pascal's
head. "Now!" he commanded, but Pascal did not return; instead, the
boatman drew a long boning knife out of its case.

Juan's face was neutral as his eyes flicked between Pascal and Ortiz,
though clearly he was communicating something; Ortiz bent down
slowly, despite Powell's demand to stop, and picked up a wooden
fishing spear with a metal tip. Morgan, his own pistol within reach,
and Quinn, who held his knife behind his back, stood silently, each
measuring the distance between aggressors, hostage, defenders, and
themselves.

"Let him go and they might not kill you," Morgan said quietly. "Pull
the trigger and you'll have to shoot them all. Then where will you be?"

"Shut up, shut up!" Merriman screamed, his face red. He pressed the
muzzle even more firmly into Juan's flesh. "Drop your weapons! Not
you!" he cried as Powell's gun hit the deck and skittered away.

Before he could retrieve it, Quinn had scooped it up.

"Definitely not Irish," the big man said, pointing the pistol at Powell. "He shoots Pascal. I shoot you. Start talking."

"No!" Powell turned to his friend. "Put it down, Merriman! For
God's sakes—these people are crazy! Do as he says."

"They'll kill us anyway." Merriman's eyes darted frantically. "They
will. Or they'll leave us out here to die."

"Or they may be better men than you, and let you live," Morgan
said calmly. "You don't have any choice, Merriman. Throw your gun
overboard. Now."

Furious, and fighting against desperation, Merriman began to release Pascal, lowering the pistol by degrees. Suddenly, Pascal wrenched
free and Merriman turned the gun on Morgan; Quinn whipped his
knife out from behind his back and threw it at Merriman, hitting the

man in the arm at the moment he fired. Morgan went down. Quinn dropped to his knees, while Pascal and his friends began to make short work of the others.

"No." Morgan opened his eyes. "No killing."

"Stop!" Quinn yelled. "God in Heaven, I'll rip every last one of you limb from limb, if you don't stop right now and get this man to a doctor."

Juan knocked Merriman cold and dragged him to the center of the boat, and Pascal herded the other three to the same place, shoving them down so that they were back to back, then roping their hands together. Ortiz pushed off with his long pole and began moving the boat along as quickly as possible, Pascal helping him. Juan brought a pail of water and one of the gentlemen's shirts, which he proceeded to tear into strips for Quinn to tie around Morgan's upper arm to stop the bleeding.

"Are you hurt?" Morgan asked weakly.

"Not a scratch on me," Quinn replied. "And isn't it just like old times—you getting us into trouble, me getting us out?"

Morgan looked him in the eye. "Guess I was right about needing you to come along."

"Aren't you always, then?" Quinn put his hand on the top of Morgan's head. "Close your eyes now and rest. We'll be there soon."

They reached the village of Cruces late in the afternoon, and Quinn saw right away that they'd get no medical help there. The next leg of the journey was twenty-one miles of steep hill country, traveled on the back of a mule; Morgan couldn't make that with a bullet in him. They would have to stop and take it out; even then it could well go septic in this climate and kill him. There was no other choice, Quinn told himself; he knew what had to be done and he would do it.

The boatmen threw Merriman, his friends, and their luggage out on the muddy shore, then paddled to the other end of the small village, where they carried Morgan ashore, Quinn behind with their packs. He followed them to a crude hotel, the size of six or seven bamboo huts put together, then listened while they negotiated with the man who appeared to run the place.

"We put him there." Pascal pointed to the far corner of the hotel, which had a long wooden table. "Bring fire, water. You cut. Must be."

Quinn nodded. "Must be, is right." He followed them over to the table, where they set Morgan gently, then left, only to return moments later with two rusty lanterns, a rush torch, a wooden bucket of river water, and a jug of potent local rum.

"Thank you, Pascal," Quinn said, rolling up his sleeves. "Thanks, Juan, Ortiz. What'll happen now to those dandies?"

The boatmen looked at one another and shrugged their shoulders. "Maybe trunk gone." Ortiz smiled ever so slightly, and Quinn suddenly remembered the extra one still on board. "Maybe no one sell to them mules, but for much money. Maybe they stuck here." Again he shrugged. "But not you and him. You go soon."

"Right." Quinn nodded. "As soon as I get this bullet out of his shoulder and he rests a little, we'll be on our way."

"He good man," Juan said quietly.

"That's God's truth, brother," Quinn told him. "Now, if you're going to stick around and watch, hold that light up, will you?"

They stayed in Cruces two days before setting out on what Quinn decided must be one of the roughest roads in the world; the few women travelers put on pants and boots for the ride, their children carried in slings or on the backs of native guides. Snakes and wild animals were everywhere, and the party was constantly bogged down by the mud. Quinn prayed every step of the way that Morgan, weak as he was, would not fall prey to the yellow fever or malaria that affected so many along the way; bad enough, he suffered from dysentery, further weakening his already fragile health. Finally and with great sighs of relief, they arrived in Panama City. Once the magnificent, legendary seat of Spanish power in the New World, Panama City was now a decrepit town of tumbledown shacks and ruined buildings, grass-choked streets and crumbling plazas, where fate met so many Argonauts in the form of cholera. Gamblers, prostitutes, opportunists of every sort, wandered in and out of questionable hotels looking for their next mark, and Quinn was determined to get himself and Morgan out of this place as quickly as he could. He found a small, relatively clean hotel near the ticket agents and left Morgan to rest while he booked their passage on the next steamer to San Francisco. It would be another two days, and then a month up the coast; he was fortunate, the old ticket agent told him, back in the days before steamers, a ship might have to reach far out into the Pacific, as far as Hawaii, before a favorable wind could be harnessed for the run back to San Francisco—it could take twice as long as steamers did now. *Fortunate,* Quinn thought on his way back to the hotel—*aye, I'll call myself that and please God help me get him there alive; please God let us find her.*

Thirty-six

Sean lay beneath a single sheet, drenched in his own sweat, feverish and moaning. Mei Ling had been to the apothecary, but as Sean grew only worse, she found the courage to go to the great Chinese doctor Li Po Tai, whose office faced the square. Here she waited three hours, only to be told that the doctor was not in town and not expected for some time; his clerk had mercy upon her, however, and listened to her description of Mister Sung's symptoms. It was not cholera, he assured her, nor was it yellow fever; it could be the ague, or, he suggested carefully, it could be opium poisoning. When she did not reply, he gave her milk thistle for Mister Sung's liver, as well as several herbs purported to cleanse his organs, and recommended plenty of fluids—water, teas, and broths.

Mei Ling rushed home again, terrified that she would find Mister Sung dead upon her arrival, but he was not. She prepared the milk thistle and brewed his tea, then carried the tray up to his room. It was stuffy and close, the smell bad, but she was afraid to open the window—would she be letting bad spirits out or allowing them to come in? Would the fresh air help Mister Sung's breathing or would he worsen with the chills? She sat down on the bed next to him, cradling his head and shoulders against her chest while, with the other hand, she encouraged him to sip his tea. He tried and spluttered, tried again, moaned, and closed his eyes.

It was all her fault; Mei Ling knew it in her heart and could hardly bear the thought. Something had sprung out of that portrait of Mister Sung's sister and children, possessing his body and causing him pain.

Mei Ling had prayed to every god she knew, and tonight she had added the American God of the stable, kneeling before the figures still in place since Christmas and Chang-Li's departure. She had begged the American God to save the life of Mister Sung because he was a worthy man and because—Mei Ling could admit it now that she was so close to losing him—she had love for him. She reminded the American God that He was all-powerful and could do anything, so she had faith He would honor her request. She did not know what was traditional in the way of offering, so she simply offered her love for Him and her trust in Him, and hoped it was enough. And then she ran back up the stairs and stood in the doorway to Mister Sung's room, listening as his ragged breath began to calm.

Mei Ling opened the curtains to the last of the evening sun, then opened the window a little, too, so that Mister Sung might hear the confident good-night call of the robins. The sheet that covered him was wet and so she pulled it off, then sat him up and removed the rest of his clothes. Mei Ling wiped him down with the cooled tea, paying tender attention to the crippled arm he kept hidden away from her—it was a beautiful arm and she kissed it reverently; wiping down the leg that was bent slightly and shorter than the other—it was a beautiful leg and she laid her cheek against his thigh for a moment. Then she wrapped one of Chang-Li's silk robes around him and covered him with a clean sheet, sitting down beside him afterward, smoothing the hair back from his forehead. Without his spectacles and with his eyes closed, Mister Sung looked vulnerable and wounded—she pressed her lips to his forehead. He groaned in his sleep and turned onto his side, away from her, his hand brushing against her leg; she slid down behind him on the bed and aligned her body with his, put an arm under his, letting it fall across his chest.

"Mister Sung," Mei Ling whispered. "Mister Sung, Mister Sung . . ." And she held him securely, rocking him gently until they both slept.

Mei Ling opened her eyes at dawn, when the birds outside were just beginning their morning assertions, and found that Mister Sung was also awake, though neither of them moved.

"I cannot go to see my sister," he whispered, his back to her, his hand gripping hers. "I am afraid."

"Yes," Mei Ling agreed softly. "Mister Sung have shame."

"I am not Mister Sung. My name is Sean. Sean O'Malley."

"Sean," Mei Ling tried, then repeated it several times until it began to sound the way he'd said it. "Yes, Mei Ling know Sean now."

He held her hand tightly to his chest then, and began to weep, his body shaking against hers.

Mei Ling listened as he whispered to her about growing up with his beloved sister, the best and most loyal friend he'd ever had. He told her of coming to America, of Grace's coming to America, of all their hopes; how Grace had earned the love and respect of everyone she met, while he—her superior-minded brother—had thrown it all over for something that in the end was worth nothing. He had abandoned her with the children, leaving her to fend for herself, believing she would come around to his way of thinking eventually. But then she had died—or he had believed she had died—and something in him had died, as well. Mei Ling felt him shudder. He'd given up on God, turned his back on everything he knew of decency, and let himself sink into the abyss, hoping for a swift end. But God had not let him go so quickly, had let the world tease him with her treasures—wealth, which excited and then left him jaded; sex, which thrilled and then left him corrupted; drugs and drink, which enhanced pleasure and then left him numb. It had been his intention, Sean confessed to her now, to put a bullet in his head this past Christmas, the very day that Chang-Li had tried to give him Mei Ling. Sean had convinced himself that he would do one honorable thing before he left the earth; that he would see Mei Ling safely into a life of freedom, but then he found that he could not bring himself to abandon her after all. Now it was Mei Ling who pressed herself more tightly against Sean. He had begun to think that maybe life was worth living just a little longer, but the shock of finding out that Grace was alive and that, somehow, miraculously, Morgan's son was alive—for clearly it was Morgan's son; the boy looked just like his father, and this was perhaps the greatest shock of all—had made him realize how far from that life he'd fallen, how far away he was from any kind of redemption.

"I'm a criminal, Mei Ling," Sean confessed. "A gambler, a drinker, a whoremonger, an opium addict. I am the lowest of the low."

"Yes," Mei Ling said simply. "But kind."

"Not even that. I would only bring shame to her and the children, to Mary Kate and Morgan's boy." Sean's voice cracked. "Better to leave things as they are. At least, for now."

And so, Mei Ling said to herself, *you would leave your fate again to chance; you would risk the loss of your only family rather than humble yourself in going as you are.* She thought about this, about what she might do for this very brilliant, very stupid man, and then she knew.

It was a week before Sean's strength returned and he came back into the shop. He still needed to lie down on the cot in the back once or twice each day, but he no longer picked up his pipe; he simply lay on his back with his hands folded beneath his head, staring up at the dark ceiling. Mei Ling prepared tea for him and small meals of rice and fish, noodles and clear soup, which she saw that he ate, and slowly he became less of a shadow and more of a man, though he still said nothing of his sister. Mei Ling did not trouble him with it but made two extra trips to the apothecary, who it was said could make the English letters. She had him write out a note for her, then paid the young son of the apothecary to deliver the note to the address she showed him on the small white card. And then it was out of her hands, so she simply waited and watched.

It was a spectacular morning, the clouds high and white over the harbor, great flocks of seagulls sailing over the wharves, smaller flocks of little brown sparrows swooping over the city, looking for places to alight and rest. The air was good, the spring warm and comfortable, yet not so hot as to bake the manure in the streets, the outdoor privies, the garbage piled in side yards. Mei Ling loved springtime the best; it was a sweet season, full of energy and expectation. There were fresh chickens at the Chinese market this morning, and Mei Ling thought she might purchase one for their dinner tonight; if she went home early, she could rub it with oil and herbs, then roast it over the fire. The scent alone was sure to whet Sean's appetite even further. Yes, she decided, she would make the chicken, and she would also see what fresh vegetables were in the market, look to see if the new rice had come in.

"Mei Ling prepare chicken tonight," she called over her shoulder.

"That would be lovely. Thank you, Mei Ling," Sean answered from the small room behind the curtain.

Mei Ling nodded, happy with herself, happy with her life despite the small knot of anxiety in her belly. And then the door to the shop opened and the knot tightened, though Mei Ling was determined to ignore it.

"Welcome to House of Good Fortune." She greeted her guests warmly in the doorway.

"Mei Ling." Grace held a child's hand in each of her own. "These are my children—Jack and Mary Kate. Children, this is Mei Ling."

Mei Ling bowed politely to the little girl with dark curling hair like her mother's and great sober eyes that betokened an old and wise spirit; Mary Kate bowed in return. Then Mei Ling turned and bowed to the little boy, whose spirit bristled with a glowing energy and whose spectacles reminded her of Sean; Jack followed his sister's example and bowed to Mei Ling.

"Is this a shop?" the little boy asked. "Are you a Chinawoman?"

"Yes." Mei Ling smiled. "And yes."

"Thank you for inviting us to tea." Grace kissed Mei Ling on the cheek. "I'm very happy to see you again. Will we come in, or are we going somewhere else?"

"Come in." Mei Ling stood aside so they could enter, and then she placed a finger to her lips for silence. "Please to wait," she instructed, her heart beating wildly. "Mei Ling have gift for family."

Grace tipped her head to one side, puzzled, but she nodded and stood quite still in the middle of the room, a hand on the shoulder of each child, though Jack was breaking his neck trying to get a look at everything in the room.

Mei Ling went to the curtained door in the very back. "Mister Sung? Please to come out."

Since she'd called him by his business name, Sean assumed there were customers who needed more attention than Mei Ling could give, and so he came out at once, buttoning his vest and straightening his cuffs as he looked first at her and then at the people in the shop. He froze.

"Please to meet *meimei*," Mei Ling introduced quietly, sliding behind the counter.

"How do you do?" Grace came forward with her hand out, prepared to greet Mei Ling's boss, an odd looking man, she thought as she approached, not Chinese after all, but European, though his hair was . . . And now she, too, stopped in her tracks. "Sean?" she whispered.

He stared at her and then began to nod, eyes misting behind the glass of his spectacles.

"Sean!" Grace threw her arms around him. "Oh, Sean!" She took another look at his face and then began to cry in earnest, her mouth trembling against his cheek as she kissed him. "Oh, Sean," she wept. "Thank God, thank God."

Sean's arms went around tentatively at first, and then his embrace tightened and he, too, wept. "I'm sorry, Gracelin," he whispered, kissing her hair. "I'm so very sorry. Please forgive me. Please."

The children watched wide-eyed, and then Mary Kate dropped her brother's hand and stepped forward.

"Uncle Sean?"

Grace and Sean separated, both wiping their eyes as they turned toward the little girl. Sean nodded and got down on one knee.

"Aye." He reached out a hand toward her. "Will you come and kiss your uncle, then, Mary Kathleen?"

Mary Kate rushed into his arms, practically knocking him over, and he stood and held her, rocking her in a fierce embrace.

"Oh, my darling girl," he murmured in her ear. "I've missed you more than you'll ever know."

Mary Kate pulled away and looked into his eyes. "We've been looking for you everywhere, Uncle Sean," she informed him matter-of-factly.

"Have you, now?" Sean replied, voice breaking. "Well, you found me at last." He kissed her again and set her down, though he kept ahold of her hand. "And who is this fine young man?" he asked, looking at Jack.

The little boy came closer but stood next to his mother, pushing himself into her skirts.

"This"—Grace swallowed hard and put a hand on his head—"this is John Paul Morgan McDonagh. But we call him Jack."

A sob escaped Sean's lips, but he controlled himself enough to ask Grace, "How in Heaven's name . . . ?"

"Julia Martin had him all along. Cared for him, then brought him to me in Boston."

Sean shook his head in wonder, then looked down at the little boy, who watched him cautiously. "Will you shake my hand, young Jack? I'm your uncle Sean, and I knew your da."

Jack stepped away from his mother and put out a small hand, which Sean took in both of his.

"Aren't you just like him, then? Like when we were boys." Sean's eyes met Grace's. " 'Tis a miracle, this."

"Aye." She nodded tearfully. "All of it."

"Mei Ling." Sean looked at her, standing quietly behind the counter, hands in her sleeves, head bowed. "Did you do this?"

The room was still as all eyes turned to the young woman, who raised her head, looked at Sean, and nodded. "Family," Mei Ling pronounced with quiet dignity, "is all."

"Aye." Sean went to her and put his arms around her. "Family is all. Thank you, Mei Ling. Thank you."

There was a great deal to explain; Sean closed and locked the shop and took everyone back to his house, where Mei Ling made them tea, surprised that they remained in the kitchen with her, surprised when they pulled chairs around the table, including one for her. She sat in their midst, hands warming around the thin cup she held, listening to the talk of all they'd done these past years, the places they'd seen, the many people they knew. Mei Ling listened as they laughed, then wept again, then laughed again. She watched their faces closely, wondering at the love that shone from their eyes, the way they touched one another so freely with such affection and tenderness it brought tears to her own eyes; and she bowed her head over the little cup to hide them.

Sean saw and covered Mei Ling's hand with his own. "This woman has set me free," he told his sister, but the words were for Mei Ling. "I love her," he announced to everyone, and Mei Ling looked up into his eyes to see if it was true. "I love you," he said directly to her, and she realized that it was.

"Is Uncle Sean a Chinaman?" Jack asked then, and they all laughed.

"Irish, like your mam," Sean told him. "American, as well. But if I'm lucky, I might have China children in the mix."

Mei Ling stared at him, hardly daring to believe, and then at his sister, who had told her such a thing might one day be true.

"Can't wait to meet them," Grace said quietly, meeting Mei Ling's gaze. "Welcome to the family, sister. Mei Ling O'Malley." She grinned. "Now there's a modern American name if I ever heard one."

Thirty-seven

There were two letters from America in the packet Abban picked up when he and Gavin Donohue went into the city for supplies: the first, he noted with relief, was from Grace, who appeared to be in a place called San Francisco, California; the second was from New York City, and that gave him pause as they had no family there any longer. With time left before Gavin came for him, Abban sat down on the bench outside the postmaster's and had a closer look at the writing, which was vaguely familiar. He set the other parcels aside and opened the letter carefully, taking out two sheets of paper, and then he began to read.

> *Dear Abban and Barbara,*
> *I have only just now learned that you survived and joined yourselves in marriage, and my heart is full of joy for you both. I wanted you to know by my own hand that I have survived, as well, though it may be hard for you to believe that your old friend and brother, Morgan McDonagh, is really alive. . . .*

Abban's hand fell into his lap and he raised his eyes to the sky, giving thanks to God with every beat of his heart. Morgan was alive. He shook his head, hardly able to believe that this was not one of those dreams he had on occasion where he walked into the kitchen of his house and found Morgan sitting there, laughing up a storm with Barbara, young and confident and full of life. He picked up the letter again and read it through, then wiped his eyes and read it again.

"Bad news, then, Abban?" Gavin had pulled the cart up and gotten down, and Abban hadn't so much as lifted his head.

"No, son," he said now. "The best news there is, as a matter of fact. Barbara and Aislinn's brother is alive and living in America."

Gavin looked puzzled. "They've no brother but one, and we all know he was killed."

Abban shook his head and held out the letter as proof. "But he wasn't. It's all here. He's been living in the great forests of Canada, sick and broken, but now he's gone to New York looking for Grace. He says Dugan helped him, and now he and Quinn Sheehan are going west to find her." He paused, swallowing the lump in his throat. "I didn't know Quinn was in America. Fine lad, Quinn Sheehan. 'Tis a wonder they're together."

"Aye, 'tis the best of news. Aislinn'll be so happy now." Gavin grinned. "And Barbara, of course. C'mon, then, let's get home!"

They loaded the wagon, and Abban climbed on, letting Gavin take them home while he absorbed the incredible news. God was gracious, he acknowledged, to have worked such good out of such misfortune.

When they pulled up in the yard of the little asylum, Abban could barely greet the children, who abandoned their games with Peigi O'Reardon to clamor around him; not even his beloved twins could attract his full attention, though he scooped up Nally and carried him into the house, Declan close behind. Barbara turned from the stove to greet him, the smile dying on her lips when she saw his face.

"What's happened, then?" she asked, wiping her hands on her apron.

Abban set the mail packet on the table, then handed her the letter from New York. " 'Tis wonderful news," he told her. "Read for yourself, Aislinn!" he called up the stair. "Come down! We've letters from America."

The young woman came down the old stairs with a clatter, pausing to smile at Gavin, who stood in the doorway, hat in hand.

"What's the news?" Aislinn's face was flushed from her work and the heat of the day, her hair escaping its bun.

"He's alive." Barbara had sunk into a kitchen chair, dazed. "Our Morgan's alive." She handed the letter to Aislinn, who tore through it in minutes, then shrieked.

"Oh, Barbara!" She swooped down and embraced her sister, then flung her arms around Abban. "He's alive!" Aislinn hesitated only a moment, and then grabbed Gavin by the hands and danced him round the room, singing the good news, much to the delight of the twins, who laughed and clapped their hands.

"I can hardly believe 'tis true," Barbara said as Abban sat down across from her. "Does Grace know he's coming, then? He doesn't say."

Abban's eyes went wide. "There's a letter from her, as well." He found it in the packet and handed it to his wife.

While Barbara opened it and read, Aislinn and Gavin sat down at the table to wait.

"Well." Barbara looked round at them all. "Mary Kate's been ill, but now she's well. They're in San Francisco now. Living in the house of a doctor, no less, Grace doing the work of cook." She paused and bit her lip, her eyes seeking those of her husband. "She's doesn't know he's coming, Abban. She and Captain Reinders are set to marry the end of May."

"But he'll get there in time," Aislinn insisted.

" 'Tis anyone's guess," Abban offered weakly, "though he says he's traveling by steamer, then overland, then another steamer, which is the fastest way, so perhaps he's almost there now."

"Please God," Barbara added.

They sat in silence, and the older children, sensing something out of the ordinary had occurred, began to file into the room.

"He'll make it." Aislinn pounded the table with his fist. "And even if he doesn't"—she got up and looked around the room—"even if he doesn't, she's still his wife."

"Aye," Barbara agreed. "But it'll be hard on all of them. Years have passed, you know. People change, and she may well love this other man the way she once did our Morgan. And there are the children to consider." She got up and headed for the stair.

"Where are you going, Barbara?" Abban watched her retreat with concern.

"Where do you think? Upstairs to pray, and don't look for me anytime soon."

Aislinn and Abban exchanged glances, and then Abban shrugged.

"Well, if He's going to listen to anyone, you know 'tis her." He rose from the table now, too. "Best get on with my work, then, seeing as how Barbara's got the divine miracle end covered."

"Will we write to Julia?" Aislinn asked. " 'Twill be a shock for her, as well."

"She's coming up with the doctor and wee Aiden next week. Best she reads the letters for herself then. C'mon, children." Abban herded the little flock toward the door. "Back outside now, to enjoy this happy day. Will you see to finishing up the supper, Aislinn?"

Aislinn nodded absentmindedly but turned toward the stove, seemingly unaware that Gavin still sat at the table. The young man got up quietly and came to stand beside her.

"I've been thinking I might go to America someday myself," he announced. "To see the place, and all."

Aislinn put down the stirring spoon and looked at him, hands on her hips. "And what would you travel on, Gavin Donohue—you who won't take so much as a penny in pay?"

Gavin shrugged sheepishly. "I didn't say I was going right off, did I? In the future, I'm thinking. And only if this place is squared away. But then, aye. My back is strong and I don't mind hard work. I'm a young man, still." He reached out a tentative finger and touched a strand of her hair. "And you're a young woman, you know."

"The life I led before makes a person old in more ways than years," Aislinn told him. "I'm no man's blushing bride."

"I know all about you, Aislinn McDonagh, and it matters not a whit to me. America's the place to be free from all that, to start again. That's where your brother's gone, after all." Gavin paused. "I'd like to meet him one of these days, you know. He's a great man. I'd like to tell him how much I love his sister."

Aislinn didn't look at him, but she blushed and her fingers curled into his hand.

"We've our whole lives ahead of us," Gavin pressed, encouraged by her touch. "A chance to do more than just survive. I think we ought to see for ourselves what the world has to offer, but if you want to stay in Ireland, Aislinn, then we will."

"You're presuming a lot of things, Mister Donohue," she said quietly.

"I lost my heart to you, girl, the minute you stepped out of that carriage, though I could see you'd been hurt and needed time among your people." Gavin put his finger under her chin and gently tipped it up so he could see into her eyes. "I know you've come to care for me, Aislinn, but tell me I'm wrong and I'll never say another word."

"You're not wrong," she whispered.

The young man nodded soberly, though inside his heart flooded with joy. "Then whenever you hear me talking about the future, know 'tis *ours* I'm referring to, and give me your opinion. I want to know what you think, Aislinn. I care about what you think."

"I think you should give me more time," she said and saw that he did not flinch. In another moment, she added, "And then perhaps we'll go to America."

Gavin's face lit up, and he kissed her with such passion that her feet came off the floor.

"You won't be sorry, Aislinn—ever," he promised. "I'll work hard to make a good life for us, for the children we'll have."

Her smile faltered just a little, and he put his arms around her again, held her close and whispered in her ear, "I know. I know about him, and I'll remember him with you no matter how many others we have. He's a part of you forever, and I love you, Aislinn."

She felt the roughness of his shirt against her cheek, listened to the steady beat of his heart, felt the strength of those arms around her. "I love you, as well, Gavin Donohue," she whispered then, and hung on as he swept her off her feet.

Thirty-eight

Quinn and Morgan presented themselves to the customs officers at the end of the long wharf, then left the building and started up the hill.

"Give me your pack," Quinn ordered. "You don't want it rubbing against that scar."

"Which, by the way, is the ugliest thing I've ever seen," Morgan commented, shifting the pack to his other shoulder. "What were you doing in there, anyway? Digging for gold?"

Quinn laughed. "Never had a chance to finish medical school," he quipped. "Now hand it over."

"I'm fine, Quinn. Only a bit stiff, but otherwise good. You did well by me, friend. You don't have to worry."

"I'm not worrying. Only I wanted to save your strength for when we find your wife." He laughed again. "Do you know where he lives, then, this Captain Reinders?"

"No idea," Morgan confessed and stopped. "What do you think?"

Quinn looked his partner over, took in the shaggy, matted hair and heavy beard, the stained and oily clothes, sniffed the air, and knew they were bad off if he could smell this over the stench of the waterfront. "I think we look like criminals and smell like their dogs."

Morgan glanced down at himself, then back at Quinn, then frowned. "Can't show up on Reinders' doorstep looking less the men than we are," he decided. "So here's what we're going to do—we have enough money left to buy us new clothes, a bath, and a shave, and still get our tickets for Oregon Territory."

"Enough for a decent meal, besides, do you think?" Quinn asked hopefully, his stomach rumbling.

"Aye. You deserve as much, though we might be sleeping on the ground tonight. C'mon."

Quinn followed Morgan as he shouldered his way through the throngs of people waiting for the mail packet to be off-loaded, waiting for friends and family to come ashore, waiting for foreign cargo, or simply waiting for the action that always occurred when people grew hot and irritable and tired of waiting.

From directions given by a helpful pedestrian, Morgan and Quinn walked up Clay Street until they came to the City Hotel, across from Portsmouth Square; from there, they entered the square—marveling at the industry and architecture—and stopped at the first men's clothing shop they came to. No need to worry about the state of their current dress, Morgan saw at once, as the place had plenty of rough-and-tumble men, most of them miners come to town for fresh kit. After too much help from an overeager clerk, Morgan and Quinn each walked out with a paper-wrapped bundle that contained undergarments, a shirt and trousers, and a vest.

"Expensive town," Quinn mentioned. "Maybe we'll give dinner a miss, buy something off a stand."

"Aye. Suppose they'll want an arm and a leg for the bath, as well."

"Got to have it, though. No point laying new clothes over old dirt."

They headed toward Chinatown, where public baths were said to be had, and suddenly they were in a different world. This must be like China itself, Morgan thought, his senses overwhelmed by the sound of the language, the sight of the people so similarly dressed, the smell of exotic foods, the signs written in foreign characters below their English translations.

"Look over there." Quinn jabbed him in the ribs. "Maybe we ought to go in, buy a little of that?"

" 'House of Good Fortune,' " Morgan read aloud. Below the sign, a Chinawoman opened the door and began to sweep out the entry, pausing for a moment to speak to a small, braid-bearded man in spectacles whose hand lay upon her arm; the tender gesture pricked his heart, and he turned away. "Down there." He pointed. " 'Hot Water Long Bath Good Shave.' That's us, then."

It felt good to peel off the clothes in which they'd been living for months, and the moment he sunk his grimy body into the steaming water, Morgan vowed never to put them on again; they were nothing but rags now, anyway, not even fit to wash. He tipped his head back against the lip of the tub and let the heat penetrate his bones. From the tub next to his, Quinn let out a long groan of satisfaction.

"Happy, darling?" Morgan asked, and Quinn flipped water at him, though his eyes remained determinedly closed.

They stayed in the tubs a good hour, the man coming in regularly to remove tepid gray water with one bucket, then add fresh steaming water with another. After the grime had loosened, Morgan and Quinn gave their heads and bodies a good scrub with the brushes provided, then stood up and let the bath man pour warm water over them to rinse the soap away. They got out, weak with the heat and more relaxed than either could ever remember, dried themselves off, and dressed in their new, clean clothes, directing the attendant to throw the old ones away.

From the bathing rooms, Morgan and Quinn were led upstairs to a barbershop, where two men showed them to chairs, draped large pieces of cloth around each of their necks, and then began to cut off their beards. It was slow going, and the two barbers made disconcerting noises as they hacked through the growth, a necessary step before applying the straight razor. Quinn and Morgan exchanged one last look, grinning through the lather on their faces.

"Hope you're not as ugly as I remember," Quinn said.

"You must be thinking of the only girl you ever kissed," Morgan replied, and both men laughed.

When it was over and they were again out on the street—two handsome Irishmen with glistening hair and fresh, bold faces—heads turned toward them instead of away, and the women they passed eyed them flirtatiously from beneath the brims of their fancy bonnets.

"Couple of lady-killers we turned out to be, eh, boy?" Quinn draped his long arm around the shoulders of his friend. "They don't know there's but one lady for us. Now let's go see that captain."

Reinders was pacing the house. With Lars and Detra gone, and only himself and Liam in quarters, it was simply too big. Too many servants were required to run the place, in his opinion, though the new man,

Jameson, was a far better butler than Arnott had ever been. Arnott had smugly denied any pilfering until Reinders put a pistol to his head and threatened to have him shanghaied, and then he came clean, turning over a personal trunk filled with items that had gone missing over the years. Reinders had had him shanghaied anyway, and it gave him a sense of justice to think of the arrogant little man swabbing decks and heating tar on a rough ship headed for the Sandwich Islands. If he survived in one piece, he might find that he preferred the tropics, with their native delights. Not much to steal down there, but the people could be friendly.

Anyway, the house was too big, he told himself, returning to his original line of thought. Even with Grace and the children, it would seem cavernous; he'd never really grown accustomed to this style of living, much preferring the tidy organization of his cabin on the ship. But he was about to become a married man, so somewhere between ship's cabin and Nob Hill mansion, a compromise must be reached.

The problem, he admitted to himself, was really that San Francisco had become too crowded for him, too busy and self-important. The problem, if he were to be completely honest, was that he wanted to build a house in New Whatcom . . . and Grace did not—especially not now she'd found her brother. Sean was a far cry from the vibrant, brilliant man Reinders had met in New York, his potential wasted away to nothing, like the body that was now no more than skin and bones. He was a broken man, a man who would never rise again but only exist, though Reinders did not say this to Grace. She was so very happy these days and saw her brother as often as she could in the house he shared with his China mistress, when she was not tending to the needs of the woman with the illegitimate child. Reinders shook his head, disgusted with himself. When had he become so judgmental of others? he wondered. When had the concern of what others might think replaced his confidence in his own opinions? He shook his head again—it was this town, he told himself. San Francisco loved its high society and had adopted the very social code Reinders had hoped to leave behind forever. And yet, here he was—wondering what his friends thought about his marrying an Irish housekeeper, wondering why he cared, longing to go north, where the town was small and respect was earned through hard work and diligence, where more and more he felt his true friends were. Even Mackley talked of settling there when he married at the end of the summer.

Reinders stopped pacing now and stood instead in front of the window, watching absentmindedly as two men, packs slung over their shoulders, started up the hill. In many ways, he thought, life was easier when everything you owned fit in a pack, when you could pick up and go on a moment's notice. He sat down in his chair, legs sprawled out before him. It was only wedding jitters, he told himself, and the restlessness that came over a seaman when he'd been too long off the ship. That's what he needed, he realized then—a long voyage. He and Liam were off for Hawaii in August, but before that he could take Grace and the children up the coast to New Whatcom. Astrid and Teresa would make her feel welcome, and perhaps she'd come to love it the way he did. Maybe he'd even dangle the carrot of agreeing to attend church services with her, though he wouldn't say anything about that yet. First, he'd have to get Jack on board the ship, and the boy simply refused to set foot on the *Eliza J,* much to Reinders' great irritation. He could swear that child set out to thwart him on purpose sometimes, though again he'd never say this to Grace. The list of things he couldn't say to Grace seemed to be growing, and he missed the days when he felt he could tell her anything. They seemed only to find things about which they disagreed these days; only last night they had quarreled over which rooms the children would occupy when they moved into the house! It was ridiculous, he thought; why had he argued with her over something he cared nothing about?

"Oh, God, I've got to stop this." Reinders rubbed a hand wearily over his face and stood up. "Grace and I are going to be married, and nothing is going to get in the way of that. Nothing." His voice rang out in the empty room, and then the door opened and Jameson came in.

"Excuse me, Captain Reinders. Gentlemen here to see you, sir."

"Which gentlemen?"

"They preferred not to give their names, sir. Friends of Missus Donnelly, they say."

"Show them in," Reinders ordered. "And bring in the bar. Might have to offer them a drink."

"Very good, sir." Jameson closed the door, but he was back a moment later. "This way, gentlemen."

Two dark-haired men entered the room, the taller one hanging back while the other came forward.

"Captain Reinders?"

"Yes." Reinders looked him up and down, taking in the new clothes and fresh grooming, the offered hand. "And you are . . . ?"

"Morgan McDonagh, sir." There was a long pause as the captain stood, dumbfounded. "I've come about my wife."

Quinn never said a word the entire time the two men talked, just sipped his drink and watched as Morgan and the captain came to a mutual understanding and even respect for each other; and why shouldn't they, Quinn asked himself, for were they not the two men Grace loved most in the world? Reinders was a good man, Quinn determined, though a bit rigid and stubborn, as any man might be in the face of such an unbelievable revelation. The captain resisted at first the fact that Morgan was who he claimed to be, but Morgan persisted, telling his story from the days with Grace in Ireland up to the very moment they arrived in San Francisco, and finally Reinders accepted what, of course, was the truth: McDonagh was alive, and he was Grace's husband. She was not in Oregon, he told the Irishmen, but living here in San Francisco; he would take them to her right away.

"Do you know her brother is here, too?" The captain stood and set his glass aside, his demeanor one of gracious defeat.

"Sean's in San Francisco?" Morgan looked at Quinn. "We heard he'd gone off with the Mormons, never to be seen again."

"Partly true. I don't know exactly when he got to the city, but he and Grace have only just found each other. He's not in a good way, I'm afraid."

"Sick, then?"

Reinders considered. "Defeated," he replied. "Broken."

"Best he sees people who know him, then," Quinn said quietly. "People who know about that. If you tell me where he is, Captain, I'll go to him while you take Morgan to Grace."

Reinders nodded and wrote down the address in Chinatown, along with directions, then called for his buggy, climbing into the driver's seat with Morgan beside him. It was a silent ride down the hill and across town, then up the long hill to the Wakefields'. As they drew closer to the house, Reinders' heart began to pound and sweat broke out on his forehead as the realization that Grace was lost to him forever smashed into his being with full force. His hands shook and his vision suddenly blurred.

"I'll drive," Morgan offered, gently taking the reins. "Or do you want to let me out here?"

Reinders shook his head and took a deep breath to clear the ocean in his ears. "No." His voice cracked. "No," he repeated. "Best to do it together. I don't want her joy to be—" He stopped to collect himself. "I don't want her to worry about me."

Morgan returned the reins. "I'm sorry, Captain."

"Don't be. She's your wife. She's always been your wife. And always would've been, I think."

They pulled around to the side of the house and agreed that the captain should go first, to ease the shock. Reinders could see through the window that they were all gathered around the table for supper and, for a moment, he stood and cherished the look of the woman who would've been his wife. Grace laughed then at something Mary Kate said, and the sound of it caught in his chest; why was it, Reinders asked himself, that too often we let love be overshadowed by things that simply don't matter? *Too late*—the words soared through his head—*too late, too late, too late*. He pulled himself together then, and knocked on the door, then stood back, snatching off his hat at the last minute.

"Peter!" Grace was delighted to see him and contrite in the same moment. "Oh, Peter," she said, stepping into the yard. "I'm so sorry about last night. I never meant to argue with you over nothing. Whatever you want is fine with me. Really, I only want us to be—"

Reinders laid a finger across her lips to silence her. "Grace." His eyes swept over her face and he tried to smile, though it faltered.

"What is it, Peter? Are you all right? Is it Liam?"

He shook his head. "Good news," he managed. "It's good news, Grace. Unbelievable news, really." He took her hand, wondering how to say it, but then it just came out. "Your husband is alive."

Grace's mouth fell open, her eyes searching his for some sign of what this was all about. "No," she whispered. "What are you saying to me, Peter?"

"Yes." Reinders took her other hand now, too. "Morgan McDonagh is alive. You better come with me."

In a state of disbelief, Grace let herself be led around the corner of the house to where Reinders' carriage stood, a man waiting expectantly beside it.

"There he is," Reinders said softly. "Your husband."

Grace's eyes locked onto Morgan's face—for surely it was Morgan's, though older now, fully a man instead of a lad, but still there were the freckles that ran down beneath one eye, the eyes so blue . . . she felt the ground beneath her feet give way and gripped Peter's arm.

"Steady, now. It really is him. Your wife needs you, McDonagh," Reinders called to the man, then gently moved out of Grace's grasp, walking rapidly away from her to the garden behind the house.

Morgan stood before her, the man she'd always loved and the man she knew not at all anymore, for he was someone the same and very different, and she shook her head, trying to clear it of the dream, praying it was not a dream, not knowing what to believe.

"Will you come here to me, Gracelin O'Malley?" Morgan asked, and then she knew it was real.

She stepped forward and into arms that wrapped around her, crushing her to the body she'd longed for, listening to the voice she'd heard only in her dreams as it repeated her name over and over and over until she wept. Dazed, she pulled away and looked at him again, both their faces damp now, eyes spilling over with tears.

"Where in God's name have you been?" she demanded incredulously.

"Canada," Morgan replied, then laughed at how simple it sounded. "Canada and then New York City. Panama. Now here. Oh, Grace." His smile trembled with heartache. "Can you forgive me, Grace, for not being with you all these years, for not finding you sooner? Will you still have me, Grace?"

"I thought you were dead." Grace felt sick to her stomach, and her voice was muffled by the ringing in her ears. "I tried to let go of you. I tried, but I couldn't. I'm engaged to be married!" She looked at him, stunned. "To Peter—and I love Peter!" She buried her face in Morgan's shirt and clung to him. "Oh God, dear God . . . 'tis really you?"

Morgan clung to her as well, his eyes closed. " 'Tis, Grace, 'tis. I never let go of you either, Grace. Every day I thought of you. Every night I prayed for you. I never gave up hope. I want you to know that. Never once. I love you, Gracelin. Never have I loved anyone but you." Now he lifted her chin so that he could see her eyes. "I know about our son, Grace. Dugan told me. I know about him."

"He's called Jack," she whispered.

"Aye." Morgan smiled through his tears. " 'Tis a fine name his sister gave him. How is Mary Kate?"

Grace stepped back and wiped her face with her apron. "They're inside." Her chin trembled and her head felt thick. "They'll never believe it. Never believe 'tis you." She paused and looked over her shoulder. "Where is Peter?"

"In the garden." Morgan pointed.

"I must speak to him," she said gravely, fresh tears coming into her eyes.

"Aye." Morgan took her hand. "He's a good man. He loves you."

They walked slowly around the corner to the back of the house, and suddenly the kitchen door burst open and Jack tumbled out, followed by Mary Kate. The children pulled up short when they saw their mother holding hands with an unfamiliar man.

"Children." Grace's voice quivered slightly. "Come here to me. I want you to . . . there's someone you should—" She stopped, lightheaded, her throat thick with emotion.

Mary Kate came over immediately and stood before the man, studying him intently.

"You don't remember me, Mary Kathleen, but I knew you in Ireland." Morgan bent down so they were face-to-face. "You were a wee thing then, but you've grown into a fine young woman."

"I know you." Mary Kate held his gaze. "But we thought you were dead."

"Only lost," Morgan replied soberly. "For a long time, and I'm sorry about that."

Mary Kate reached behind her and pulled her brother forward. "This is Jack. You'll want to meet him."

Morgan squatted even lower, eyes roaming hungrily over the little boy's face. "Hallo, Jack."

Jack eyed him suspiciously. "Who're you, then?"

Grace put a hand on her son's shoulder. " 'Tis your da, Jack," she said as gently as she could. "Morgan McDonagh."

The boy's eyes widened in astonishment, and then he grinned. "Well, I knew you'd come," he announced confidently. "I knew you would."

"Sorry it took me so long," Morgan apologized. "But I'm glad you didn't give up on me."

"I'm five now."

Morgan nodded, eyes glistening. "A big boy, then."

"And I have a dog," Jack boasted. "You can see it if you like."

Morgan stood, then looked down in wonder at the little hand that had slipped into his own. As Jack towed him toward the stable, Morgan offered his other hand to Mary Kate. "Will you come with us?" he urged, and the girl nodded, shyly taking his other hand, glancing at him with the beginnings of a smile.

"That's going to be a nice family, once they all get used to one another."

Grace turned at the sound of his voice, her face twisted with anguish. "Oh, Peter, I'm sorry . . ."

"McDonagh said the same thing." Reinders smiled wryly. "He's a lot like you, you know. We had a long talk before I brought him up here, and I was struck by how alike the two of you are, though I'd be hard pressed to say why, exactly."

"I love you, Peter."

"I know you do." The captain took her hand. "And I know we would've been very happy together. But"—he shrugged his shoulders— "I told you once that I only wanted you to be happy—whatever that meant, whatever that was, I wanted you to have it. Do you remember?"

Grace nodded.

"Your true happiness lies with that man over there—with that man and his son and your daughter."

"What about you?" she asked him quietly.

"I have Liam," Reinders reminded her. "And he is everything in the world to me. I can truly say that I am happiest when the *Eliza J* is ripping up the sea and my boy stands beside me, calling orders. I love you very much, Grace, and we will always be friends," he promised. "Always."

"Thank you, Peter." She moved into his arms one last time. "Thank you for everything."

"It has been my honor, Missus McDonagh." Reinders kissed the top of her head. "Good-bye, my dear."

He did not turn around once, but disappeared behind the house; Grace heard the sound of the horse pulling the buggy down the drive and resisted the urge to run after him, for what was there left to say?

Morgan spoke to the children, then left them with their dogs and returned to Grace, taking her in his arms.

"Have you a kiss for me, Pirate? Or perhaps 'tis too soon."

"Aye," she whispered, answering both questions, but he kissed her anyway, tentatively at first, and then with the passion she'd never been able to forget.

"Marry me, Grace?" Morgan fell to his knees, imploring her. "Marry me again—not in secret, in the middle of the night, but in front of God and the whole world, in the bright morning light. Say you will, Grace. Say it."

She looked at him, thinking, *Any minute I'll wake up from this and he'll be gone away.* "I'll marry you," she said quickly before the dream ended. "Only you're never to leave my sight ever again, Morgan McDonagh, do you hear me now? Not ever."

The children, having crept up close to see the kiss, now cheered, then shrieked with joy as Morgan tossed into the air first Mary Kate, then Jack, settling the boy on his shoulders, his hand on the head of the girl.

"Do you live with us now?" Jack bent over to ask.

"If you'll have me," Morgan said.

"Aye, but where will you sleep, then?"

Morgan lowered him down to the ground, then took Grace in his arms once again.

"Next to my wife, of course." He kissed her cheek tenderly, breathing in the warm scent of her. "God willing, I'll lie beside your mother every single night for the rest of my life. I promise you that," he whispered in her ear. "And now let's go inside, young Jack and dear Mary Kate, for we've things to talk about."

"Like what?" Jack asked.

"Like a wedding," Morgan told him. "Aye, my love?" He looked down into Grace's eyes. "And all the days beyond?"

Oh, aye." She touched his cheek.

"All the days beyond," Mary Kate echoed, looking from her mother's face to Morgan's, then to her brother's. "C'mon, Jack." She grabbed his hand. "I'll race you to the door."

Epilogue—1862

The day of the wedding dawned warm and clear, the air fragrant with the scent of blossoms carried on a sea breeze; it was as beautiful as any day Grace could ever remember, and she reached for the hand of the man beside her, who put his arm around her instead and pulled her close as he always did.

"Aren't they grand?" Morgan whispered to his wife from where they sat on a shady bench in the churchyard garden.

Grace looked into his deep blue eyes, surprised as always by the intensity of her love for him, surprised as always that he was truly the man by her side, even though he'd never left it in the ten years they'd been together. Morgan returned her gaze, reading her mind as always, then pressed his lips gently to hers, caressing her cheek with his hand.

"Ah, go on," Sean chided them good-naturedly. "You'd think it was your wedding day instead of Mary Kate's and Liam's."

"Every wedding's good reason to kiss your bride, you daft eejit." Morgan grinned. "And where's Mei Ling and the boys? She's the only reason we invited you, don't you know."

"Nursing the baby." Sean ignored the slight good-naturedly. "But most likely she'll be back any minute, carrying the wee thing on a golden pillow, warning everyone to be quiet if she's sleeping."

"You're not fooling us, Sean O'Malley." Grace laughed. "We all know 'tis you can barely set that girl down for two minutes together."

"She *is* the most beautiful baby God ever made, isn't she?" Sean said proudly, then glanced over his shoulder and saw Mei Ling coming around the corner, the baby in her arms. "Be right back. Set up the throne, will you?"

Morgan and Grace laughed again as they watched him rush to the side of his wife, pull back the baby's blanket, and coo into the little face. Mei Ling smiled contentedly; the two little boys had come one after the other, but then nothing for years, and Mei Ling had put aside her wish for a daughter, only to be surprised with the gift of this one six months ago.

"Mei Ling says he brings the baby down to the newspaper all the time, and that it's a good thing he's editor with his own private office so no one can hear the silly noises he makes." Grace shook her head. "He was always soft for the babies."

"Daughters are grand. Look at your one over there. Isn't she beautiful?"

"Oh, aye. But she's *our* daughter."

"Oh, I know. I know she is," Morgan agreed. "We love each other madly, 'tis true, but you were mam and da both to her all those years, and 'tis you she loves the most."

"Not anymore." Grace's eyes filled with tears as she looked upon her amazing child. "But that's as it should be now."

Mary Kate stood beside her husband, graciously greeting her many admiring guests. She was the loveliest of brides, Grace thought proudly, dressed as she was in cream linen and the Irish lace Barbara and Abban had sent in a wedding package. Her shining auburn hair lay softly curled atop her head, interwoven with a strand of tiny pearls that had come as a gift from Captain Reinders. Around her neck, she wore a locket from Doctor Wakefield, who considered her his protégée and who had written the letters that got her accepted to college in the East. Mary Kate stood taller than her mother and was more sober in her countenance, but her eyes burned intelligently and her smile radiated a quiet confidence. With money she'd received from the sale of Donnelly House in Ireland, she'd started a school for girls here in the city, and this she ran with a firm, attentive hand. Well educated herself and knowing that her love of learning would be lifelong, she had decided upon this course for her future, stating to all who would listen that the man who wanted her for a wife would have to be different from most other men; he would have to be patient and understanding, exceptional in his compassion, or she would simply never marry him.

Mary Kate had grown into a young woman of uncommon substance and singular determination, and Liam would never have dreamed of asking her to be a traditional wife—he'd always known she would want more and he had always been enthusiastic about her life, even when she went away to college; he made the pursuit of her goals his own challenge, and strove to be her partner in every way possible.

Look at them now, these two young people who met on a famine ship from Ireland sixteen years ago—the girl had always understood the heart of the boy and loved him purely; the boy had never even considered anyone besides the girl, so much did he admire her, though neither had admitted their true feelings to the other until they'd both grown up and understood what their love for each other really meant.

The future was bright for them, this first generation of Irish survivors raised in America. The future was theirs; they owned it in a way their parents could not, having passed childhoods in other lands. San Francisco was their home and would continue to be so, with Mary Kate overseeing the day-to-day operations of her popular school while Liam sailed the Pacific Rim on the *Siobahn*. They will be very happy together, these two, and whenever opportunity allows, Mary Kate will travel with her exuberant husband—it will be a trip to the stunningly lush Hawaiian Islands in several years' time that brings her home again with a child on the way, their first, a little boy whom they will call Peter, much to the delight of all those who will consider themselves grandparents to the child.

Although this child was years from being born, his spirit was present on this happy day, and Grace could see a hint of him in the glow of light that pulsed between Mary Kate and Liam. She leaned past Morgan and looked around the garden for Peter, who had come down from New Whatcom in order to be here. He stood by the drinks table, talking to Dugan, his hand on the shoulder of his wife, who sat in a chair beside him, sipping her cold cider. Astrid's first husband had died over ten years ago and, after a proper period of mourning, Peter had asked her to marry him. Grace had been delighted; Astrid was a kind, strong woman who gave Peter the happiness he so deserved. They'd built a fine house up there, on a bluff overlooking the bay, and Astrid sailed with Peter everywhere he went. Though they had no children, Liam was every inch their son and honored them as his parents, just as he honored Grace. She had seen less and less of Peter over the years, though they kept up with each other through Liam; he looked well today, she thought, his hair was silver now, which was handsome atop the tan, weathered face. He looked over at her, smiled, and gave her a quick wink.

"I saw that," Morgan said out of the corner of his mouth. "Always knew you were keeping him on the side. Too good-looking, that one."

Grace elbowed him in the ribs.

"And here comes your other admirer. 'Tis the tallishness attracts you— is that it?" Morgan sat up a little straighter, pulled back his shoulders.

Doctor Wakefield made a beeline for the bride and groom, Doctor Fairfax close behind. The two men had remained devoted friends over the years, their bond strengthened by a mutual commitment to the advancement of medicine and the compassionate treatment of any man, woman, or child needing care, particularly in the emigrant communities. They both adored Mary Kathleen and had followed her scholastic achievements with unbridled glee. At least once a month, they took her to dinner, often in the company of Doctor Wakefield's niece, another delightful young woman whose education they intended to sponsor.

Eden Wakefield and Abigail Hewitt had played a beautiful piano duet for the wedding and now sat at one of the linen-draped tables with Senora Calderon, whom Eden called "*Mamacita*" and still saw regularly. There would always be those who would snub the Wakefield-Hewitt family, none of whom cared a whit for the type of people who remained mired in the past. As far as this family was concerned, the future was a bright and shining star, and her name was Eden Wakefield; they would not tolerate anyone's attempts to make less of this young woman simply because of her color, and they had become active in bringing abolitionist educators to town, in establishing financial support for escaped slaves, and in donating goods and land to former slaves who arrived with nothing. Rowen and Abigail had cut their ties with their family in the East and lived on Doctor Wakefield's income from the hospitals and from investments in land, as well as Hewitt's modest income as headmaster of a boy's school. None of this would ever make up for the grave mistakes of Abigail's or Rowen's pasts, nor did they ever make excuses; rather, they accepted humbly any forgiveness offered them, especially from the Negro community, and were grateful for the blessing of the girl they all thought of as their daughter.

"Mam! Da!" Jack hurried over with Caolon Ogue in tow. "Can we go down to the square later, on our own, like?"

"No," Morgan said firmly, then eased his tone. " 'Tis your sister's wedding day, Jack! Tomorrow," he promised, unable to disappoint the boy. "I'll take you round the sights myself; then you two can go off while Dugan and I have a cold one with Sean and Quinn."

"Fine by me." Caolon shrugged his big shoulders, looking just like his father. "Me da won't like me going off without him anyway."

"We want to hear the debates, is all," Jack tried once more.

"Sorry, son. We're not turning our minds to war on such a happy day as this. Go on, now. There must be ten girls standing in the corner of the yard over there, just dying to make the acquaintance of handsome Irishmen such as yourselves."

The two boys hung back, eyeing the girls with wary interest, until Morgan gave them a good shove in that direction.

"Dugan says they heard President Lincoln speak about freeing the slaves and holding the country together, and 'tis all he can do to keep Caolon from joining now the fight's heating up," Grace confided. "Tara hopes it'll all be over soon."

"Won't, though." Morgan's tone was grim. "And 'tis as much about land and money as freedom—but 'tis freedom pulls the young men in."

"Our Jack wants to fight, you know," Grace remarked quietly. "For his country, he says."

Morgan looked at his son and remembered another young man with the same kind of stubborn determination; he wondered for a moment, as he often did, whether Nacoute still lived, whether his mother and sister were still with their people, or whether they'd been wiped out, as was happening to so many tribes.

"I told him no. This family stays together. We've paid for our freedom, and I'll not send him off to be cannon fodder."

"He wants to be a hero like his da."

"I'm no hero, Grace, only a man did the best he could in terrible times." Morgan looked to where his son was standing. "When Jack's a man, he can decide for himself with a man's wisdom and I'll stand behind him. I told him that. But he's still a lad, and lad's are too easily swayed by the call to war. Fighting's in their blood, but they've no idea how easily that blood is spilled. 'Tis men who start wars, and should be men as does the fighting. Not boys."

Grace picked up his hand and held it. "Will he go, anyway, do you think?"

"I made him promise before God, and he did. Reluctantly, and with great noise, of course, but he did. No gloom today, now." Morgan squeezed her hand, then let go and got to his feet. "I'll go tell Ogue what's brewing, bring you back a glass of punch."

"Tell him thanks from me," Grace requested. "Good of him to help George serve up the drinks."

"Well, you know, he says he can't hardly talk unless he's working a bar." Morgan grinned, then left her to join Dugan and George Litton, who were filling glasses and greeted him with great shouts.

Grace's eyes shifted to a smaller table that held the wedding cake she'd made; from behind this table, Enid Litton grinned and waggled her fingers at Grace, her two smallest children tumbling at her feet. George and Enid raised prize chickens on their farm, and Grace and Morgan rode out often to visit with them. Enid's brother had died shortly after her marriage to George, but Mister Hopkins lived with them and helped with his grandchildren; Enid reported the odd letter from her mother but did not fear a visit as Missus Hopkins was quite content to run a small boardinghouse in Cornwall with her sister.

"There you are!" Aislinn plunked herself down on the bench beside Grace. "Hide me," she begged. "The children are seeking and I'm out of places."

Grace laughed. "Your children? Or all the children together?"

"Seems like *hordes*," Aislinn gasped. "I'm sure mine are in there somewhere. I'll have to send Gavin to ferret them out."

"He looked worse for wear," Grace sympathized. "Quinn says they fought the hotel fire 'til dawn. Good of them to come anyway, after a night like that."

"They wouldn't've missed it for the world," Aislinn replied. "You know Quinn can't go a day without seeing Morgan, and now my Gavin's as bad, the three of them always palling around at one place or the other." She glanced around, then leaned in close and whispered, "Quinn's Margaret is having *a baby*!"

Grace shoved her off. "Go on!" She grinned. "Well, what do you know about that? Here he's raised those five Mulhoneys, and now's he set to have one of his own. I think it's grand."

"So does he!" Aislinn laughed. "The man's gone soft over it. Can't do enough for Margaret, as if he didn't always treat her like a queen."

"And wasn't Rose a beautiful maid of honor?" Grace sighed. "And Davey always so handsome, showing people to their seats? 'Tis a fine family Quinn and Margaret have, and I'm happy for them seeing another baby into the world."

"You and Gavin," Aislinn scoffed lightly. "Sunshine and laughter, bread and wine, birdsong and roses . . . makes a body ill sometimes."

"Ah, you know you're as soft as the rest of us." Grace gave her a quick hug. "Better run," she warned her. "Here come the children."

Aislinn, always the gayest person at a party, made a great show of dashing off while the gaggle of children shrieked and chased after her.

Grace sat for a moment, enjoying herself while around her the air filled with the laughter and provincial talk that Aislinn pretended was so annoying, though Grace knew she was happier than she'd ever been in her life. The men had gathered in a knot over by the drinks, the young married couples by Liam and Mary Kate, teenaged boys including Jack and Caolon mixed with the pretty misses, while older women like herself presided over the state of things from chairs and benches set in the shade of canopy trees. Mary Kate caught her mother's eye, and Grace watched as her daughter crossed the yard, skirts held up daintily by gloved fingertips.

"What a day!" Mary Kate sat down in a great swoop of linen, much the same way her auntie Aislinn had just done.

"Mind that skirt. You'll . . ." Grace stopped herself; Mary Kate was no longer her child, but a married woman. "You look so beautiful, Mary Kathleen. You've become such a fine young lady. And now a wife."

Mary Kate got out her handkerchief and blotted her mother's tears. "You've been crying all day, Mam," she scolded gently. "I hardly know if I'm wed or dead!"

Grace laughed and caught her daughter's hand to her lips, closed her eyes, and kissed the fingers that had once been so small.

"I'm not going anywhere, Mam," Mary Kate promised. "You know I'd never leave you."

"You're my own dear girl. I don't know why I'm all over myself like this."

Mary Kate kissed her mother's cheek and leaned back beside her, Grace's hand in her own. "It's because we're here," she announced readily. "In this place. Together. I was reading through my journals last night, reading about our lives, about all the things you told me and all the things I remembered myself—and you know, Mam, it's a miracle that we're all gathered here together today."

Grace nodded, the truth of those words flooding her eyes with fresh emotion.

"I don't know if I could do what you did," Mary Kate continued. "Bury husbands and babies, come alone with a small child to a strange country, cross that country in a wagon with two little children, one of them Jack." She laughed but then became earnest again. "I remember all that, you know, but I don't ever remember being afraid. Because I was with you. I thought that's just what women did—they take care of things, of people—but now that *I'm* a woman, I realize it was what *you* did. And, Mam—I'd like to know your secret."

Grace considered the request. " 'Tis no secret. Only faith. In God and in the love you have for your children. You can move mountains for your children." And then she began to weep in earnest, and reached out blindly for Mary Kate's handkerchief again, disgusted with herself.

"Oh, Mam." Mary Kate put her arms around her mother. "It's all right. It's all right now. We're all here. That's what I mean by a miracle. Just look"—her arm swept out in front of her—"Jack and Da, and Uncle Sean, and Quinn. There's Auntie Aislinn and Uncle Gavin. My Liam. All of us. All of us here. And all of the children!" she added in amazement. "Just look at all the children we've brought into the world!"

Grace nodded against her daughter's solid shoulder, soothed by the hand on her back, the scent of the girl she'd loved forever. "I know," she whispered. "I'm done with tears for today." She made a show of pretending to wring out the handkerchief before returning it.

Mary Kate laughed and tenderly pushed a strand of her mother's hair back into place. "And, Mam, I want you to know that Jack's not going anywhere. I know he's full of war talk, but he'd never leave you and Da. Ever. He told me that himself. He wants to go, but he says he loves the two of you too much to ever risk breaking your hearts."

"Better give that back." Grace reached for the sodden cloth in her daughter's hand and Mary Kate kissed her again.

"What's all this, then?" Morgan stood above them, holding two glasses of punch. "Tears of joy, or Jack?"

"Only a mother's foolishness on her daughter's wedding day." Grace smiled affectionately at Mary Kate.

"Well, that's all right, then." Morgan sat down. "You're a beautiful bride, our Mary Kate. I've shed a few tears myself today."

"Thanks, Da." She leaned across her mother and kissed him on the cheek. "Thank you for everything."

"Sure and 'tis my pleasure, darling girl. Don't I wish I could throw you a wedding every day of your life?" He looked to where the musicians were tuning their instruments, and at Liam crossing the green. "Hallo, young man," Morgan greeted him. "Come to claim your bride for a dance, have you?"

"Begging your pardon, Missus Kelley." Liam winked at Mary Kate. "But I believe it's traditional to dance with me mam first." He held out his hand to Grace.

"Go on, then," the bride laughed. "But don't wear her out—she's a line waiting already." Mary Kate nudged Morgan, who saw that Hewitt, Wakefield, Fairfax, Quinn, Dugan, and a few others were looking their way now the music had picked up.

"Mind you bring her straight on back to me, son," Morgan warned agreeably. "Or we'll have a good old-fashioned Irish brawl on our hands."

They all laughed, and Grace and Liam started off the dancing, and then Liam danced with his bride, who blushed and looked so elegant in his arms. Doctor Wakefield did indeed get his dance with Grace, as did Captain Reinders, while Morgan danced with Astrid. Dugan and Tara took a turn in the square, as did George and Enid, Aislinn and Gavin, Quinn and his glowing Margaret; Abigail danced with Doctor Fairfax and then with her dear husband. Jack danced with Eden and Rose, who then found partners in Sean and Gavin; George danced with each of his little girls, and Morgan took Senora Calderon out for a twirl, but was cut out by Quinn, who made a deep bow, and then by Dugan, who tried out his elementary Spanish on the poor woman. Then Captain Reinders danced with Mei Ling, while Sean held the baby up to watch, the boys by his side. Dugan and Grace had a dance together and laughed as they swung past Jack and Caolon, both with young silly maids who blushed and giggled.

As the sun began to set in the fiery bay and the swallows swooped and called as they headed for home, flirting began in earnest among the youth, while the older couples found one another for a last slow go-round. Morgan gathered up his own beloved bride in his arms, and Grace rested her head upon his shoulder.

"Look at them," pronounced an old woman to her cronies as they sat in the last bit of sun by the stone wall. "Those two out there." She pointed her cane at Morgan, who had stopped dancing in the middle of the square and was kissing Grace with all the passion of a man who'd found his true love at last. "Just look at them! Married all this time and they carry on like that. Bah!"

The women's heads bobbed up and down, up and down, and they cackled like chickens, though privately some were moved by the sight of this man and his wife.

"Are you talking about those two?" Dugan had come round with a cold pitcher of punch. "Have you never heard the story of them, then?"

The old women looked up at the big man with the smashed nose and they shook their heads in unison.

"Well, now." Dugan pulled up a chair and settled in among them. "Let me fill your glasses, ladies, and we'll start at the beginning."

Ann Moore was born in England and raised in the Pacific Northwest. She lives in Bellingham, Washington, with her husband and two teenage children.

ANN MOORE

'Til Morning Light

This Conversation Guide is intended to enrich the
individual reading experience, as well as encourage us
to explore these topics together—because books,
and life, are meant for sharing.

In 1848, Yerba Beuna was a small fishing village. By 1852, despite having burned down several times, it was the magnificent city of San Francisco in the brand-new state of California. The Mexican War had ended and many of those soldiers had drifted west; the gold was petering out, but many of the miners, wealthy now and attached to the west, remained; gamblers and entrepreneurs flourished in the climate of prosperity, as did merchants and entertainers. The city was awash with immigrants from China, South America, Great Britain, Russia, France, and with the Irish, many of whom had escaped the penal colonies of Australia. I knew it spoke of Gracelin's character—her yearning for the sea, for a place where she could create a new life that would advance the future of her children, the place where her beloved friend Peter Reinders had made his home. When I began to write the first chapter, the scene unfolded immediately and I knew that while I would reference her life in Kansas Territory, the action of this book would take place in San Francisco.

Q. *Slavery was an issue in* Leaving Ireland, *and even more so in* 'Til Morning Light. *Was that a conscious decision?*

A. Absolutely. I would think it nearly impossible to write about our country during this time and not include that then-polarizing subject. As new states were created, they declared themselves slave state or free. California was free, but placed heavy restrictions on African-Americans there, forbidding them—among other things—the right to vote, attend public school, ride public transportation. African-Americans accepted this because they had the greater freedom of governing their own lives, and of course, they hoped that future freedoms would eventually be won. This cause was advanced after the Civil War, but it took another one hundred years after that before they were able to claim their civil rights, and even longer before they began to gain the recognition

A CONVERSATION WIT
ANN MOORE

Q. In this final book about Gracelin O'Malley's extraordi
you bring her all the way across the country to California.
you to write about San Francisco in 1852?

A. During this time, the United States was a fascinating pl
sheer number of immigrants in bigger cities was forcing a p
alogue, conducted primarily in the newspapers, about cha
adaptation, the need for adequate housing and the mea
which to educate the masses, the potential for growth and
sion that arose from the suddenly much larger labor for
gious leaders were not the only ones raising moral qu
politicians weighed in, aware of the impact of new voters, a
were groups such as the abolitionists who were determine
slavery for the good of all, and who were active politically a
religiously, despite protestations from the South that clai
region could not survive without a slave labor force. We w
experiencing the expansion into the West, which was basic
long steady wagon train feeding thousands upon thousands
ilies into new territories. These territories, such as Kansas,
political hotbeds as those who wanted them to remain fre
battled those who wanted them to be admitted into the U
slave states. I had, at first, considered opening Gracelin's
Kansas Territory, but decided to move it forward a few ye
take her to California, where Captain Reinders awaited.

and respect they deserved for their vast contributions to the development of this country.

And as I wrote about physical slavery, I became aware of emotional and psychological slavery, the ways in which we enslave *ourselves* and the damage this does to our lives. Sean and Abigail are both slaves to their guilt, and it drags them toward self-destruction through drug and alcohol addictions, and self-mutilation. Agnes Hopkins is a slave to her grief; her life is twisted with bitterness and her distorted outlook nearly destroys the lives of those around her. Quinn Sheehan becomes a slave to despair and loses his ability to function in any but the most restrictive environment. And Mei Ling, while not legally a slave, is enslaved by her own inability to imagine a free life for herself where no would dictate the hours of her day.

Q. There are so many stereotypes attached to the Irish. Do you find yourself working to counter those in your writing?

A. I sought to portray my Irish characters—and all characters, be they African-American, American Indian, Chinese, British, Italian—as the complex people they may well have been in real life, particularly because I'm writing about the nineteenth century, a time rife with open prejudice. Like so many groups, the Irish were victims of racial, social, and religious prejudice; they were considered subhuman—caricatured as monkeylike and ignorant, people who bedded down next to their livestock, who bore children to keep themselves warm at night, superstitious Papists with an immoral bent for drink. They were unable to escape this perception even by crossing three thousand miles of ocean; the attitude in America toward the Irish was every bit as cruel as that in Europe. Were some Irish mean, ignorant drunkards who lived like animals? Yes. Were some God-fearing, kind, hardworking people who sacrificed their lives for their children? Yes, again. As in every immigrant group that arrived on the shores of America, there were individual human beings with all the varying degrees of strength and weakness that exist within us today. What I enjoyed most about portraying the Irish of this time was their enormous faith in God and a quick, dry sense of humor, even in the face of terrible adversity, as well as their great affection for children and family events, the love of society that brought them together on any and every occasion. They are a remarkable people who affected the growth of the United States in every conceivable way.

Q. The true love of Grace's life, Morgan McDonagh, reappears in this book. Had you planned this at the beginning of the trilogy?

A. No! To be quite honest, I had not planned on another book beyond *Gracelin O'Malley*. Even as I wrote that first book, I didn't know until the very end that Morgan would not live; after a certain point in the writing, characters really do dictate their own destinies and it does the author little good to impose her will upon them. I loved Morgan with all my heart and was very sad when I finished writing that book, but I also knew that its outcome was far more true to what so many experienced during those terrible famine years, and so I accepted it. At book events, some readers were quite adamant—despite my protestations— that Morgan still lived; after all, they pointed out, I had not written his *actual* death. My own husband was in this last camp, so I considered it as I began *Leaving Ireland*; I listened for Morgan's voice, hoping that he was still alive, but he remained silent, and by the close of that second book, I was sure he would never reappear. Feeling that there was one last tale in Gracelin's saga, I began *'Til Morning Light* intending to bring her to Captain Reinders in San Francisco. But sometimes the writing takes on a life of its own, and my fingers can barely keep up with what is spilling out; these are the most wonderful moments in writing, worth all of the others put together, and this is what happened when I began the chapter where Morgan is washing his bloody hands in the creek. I stopped only long enough to ask the same question of him that everyone else does later in the book, "Where on earth have you been?" Needless to say, I was overjoyed at his reappearance, and the story changed radically from that point on.

Q. Writers today spend a great deal of their time speaking at literary events and to book groups. Is there a particularly memorable event that stands out in your mind?

A. I've met so many interesting people since *Gracelin O'Malley* first came out, and I appreciate the gift these books have given me—the opportunity to meet and speak with readers of all ages. I've had many encounters that moved me, but the most special are those with older people whose grandparents or great-grandparents were Irish immigrants and who never really understood the full story of why they came because of the curtain of shame that hung over this event. Those ancestors carried a sense of failure with them, a feeling that somehow the famine was their own fault and they were ashamed for having been so poor and living so low. When they got to America, all they wanted was to put it behind them and forget it—they wanted to raise children who were American and proud of it. That's why there are several generations who never knew how terrible the famine really was or what part the British government played in it, how very courageous their ancestors were to get on a ship with nothing but the clothes on their backs and come to a new land. Five thousand ships crossed the Atlantic during the famine years, bringing to New York City alone an average of three hundred immigrants a day. Daily living was brutal, yet the Irish grabbed on to the bottom rung of the ladder and didn't let go—economically and socially, they rose dramatically in just a single generation and continued to climb until their sons and daughters were on stable ground. So when one of these older readers comes up quietly to shake my hand and tell me how much it meant to them to finally have a clear picture of what it was like for their ancestors, to understand completely what happened in Ireland all those years ago, and to have rediscovered a pride in their heritage—those are the moments that mean the most to me.

QUESTIONS FOR DISCUSSION

1. *Gracelin O'Malley, Leaving Ireland,* and *'Til Morning Light* explore the themes of loss, mourning, and redemption. What is the meaning of redemption in relation to the characters of the final book? From what are they redeemed and how or by whom?

2. Although slavery is illegal in the United States and in most countries, it exists and even flourishes elsewhere. How does the existence of slavery in the world affect our lives today? How do we contribute to it? How can we be more active in ending it?

3. Discuss the two most frequent emotions in literature by and about the Irish— humor and melancholy. What do they say about the Irish and their view of the world? What are examples of humor and melancholy from this book?

4. What did you think about the reappearance of Morgan McDonagh? In your own personal experience, have you ever come across a love as deep as that between Morgan and Grace? Do you think such love exists?

5. In the epilogue, Mary Kate speaks of her deep appreciation for her mother, for the woman Gracelin really was and for what she did for her children. As you matured, did you come to a deeper understanding of the woman your mother is/was? What is your relationship with her now?